Anonymous

Memoirs of the Prince de Talleyrand

Anonymous

Memoirs of the Prince de Talleyrand

ISBN/EAN: 9783337167899

Printed in Europe, USA, Canada, Australia, Japan

Cover: Foto ©Raphael Reischuk / pixelio.de

More available books at **www.hansebooks.com**

MEMOIRS

OF THE

PRINCE DE TALLEYRAND

EDITED, WITH A PREFACE AND NOTES, BY

THE DUC DE BROGLIE

Of the French Academy

TRANSLATED BY

MRS. ANGUS HALL

VOLUME IV

WITH A PORTRAIT

GRIFFITH FARRAN AND CO., LIMITED
NEWBERY HOUSE, CHARING CROSS ROAD, LONDON
AND SYDNEY
1891

CONTENTS.

MEMOIRS

OF THE

PRINCE DE TALLEYRAND

PART X.—*Continued.*

PART X.—*Continued.*

THE REVOLUTION OF 1830.—APPENDIX.

1830—1832.

The choice of a sovereign for Belgium still undecided—Talleyrand by a bold stroke obtains the recognition of the neutrality of that kingdom by the Powers—This measure is strongly supported by Lord Palmerston —The Prince of Orange very unpopular in Belgium—A violent scene in the Congress when M. Maclagan brings his name forward for the throne—Talleyrand never wavers in his preference for Prince Leopold of Saxe-Coburg—He considers separation of Belgium from Holland of greater importance than the choice of a sovereign—The Duc de Nemours is proclaimed King of Belgium—Suggestion to nominate the Prince of Orange King of Poland—Talleyrand's reply—M. de Krüdener and Lord Ponsonby accused of intriguing in favour of the Prince of Orange—M. Bresson for the Duc de Leuchtenberg—France asks that Lord Ponsonby should be recalled as well as M. Bresson—The English government refuses—Louis Philippe refuses the Belgian crown for the Duc de Nemours—A fierce onslaught on Talleyrand in the *Courrier Français*—Great alarm everywhere at the generally unsettled state of the Continent—Riots in Paris on the anniversary of the Duc de Berry's death—Disturbances in Lisbon—Insurrectionary movement in favour of Donna Maria—M. Casimir Périer succeeds M. Lafitte as head of the French Cabinet—The Reform Bill presented in the House of Commons by Lord John Russell—Belgian Deputies arrive in London to offer the crown to Prince Leopold of Saxe-Coburg—His conditional acceptance—He is elected king by a large majority—Talleyrand tries to arouse interest in favour of the Poles—Their brilliant victories in Lithuania excite great sympathy in France—Lord Grey, influenced by Princess Lieven, refuses any assistance—Private letter of Lord Palmerston respecting Poland—Revolution in Brazil—Dom Pedro and his family take refuge on board an English man-of-war and come to England—The Dutch troops, despite the armistice, invade Belgium—King Leopold appeals to France for aid—Animated scene in Parliament between Lord Aberdeen and Lord Grey respecting the King of France—The King of Holland is commanded to withdraw his troops—Louis Philippe wishes half the French forces to remain in Belgium for a time—Private letter of Lord Palmerston to Lord Granville on this subject—Comte Latour-Maubourg is sent to Brussels

to obtain an undertaking from King Leopold that he will destroy
the frontier fortresses—The " H. B." political caricatures, Lord Palmerston resents that entitled "The lame leading the blind " (Talleyrand and himself)—Serious disturbances in Paris on hearing that
the Poles have been defeated—Violent discussions in the Chambers
—Lord Londonderry attacks Talleyrand hotly in the House of
Lords—The Duke of Wellington, Lord Holland, and others on both
sides of the House warmly defend the prince—Extract from the
Times—The Reform Bill is thrown out of the Lords—The French
Peerage Law is passed by the Chamber of Deputies—Serious riots at
Lyons—An army of 32,000 men under Marshal Soult and the Duc
d'Orléans is sent to put them down—M. Latour-Maubourg's mission to
Brussels objected to by the Opposition in Parliament—Explanation
of this step by Lord Grey and Lord Palmerston—Illness of General
Sebastiani—The Chamber of Peers confirms the vote of the Chamber of
Deputies on the peerage question—The plot of the *Rue des Prouvaires*
—The Emperor of Russia sends Comte Orloff to the Hague—
The French expedition to Ancona complicates matters in London
—Comte Orloff arrives in England—Casimir Périer is attacked by
cholera in Paris—The Pope finally consents to the liberal concessions
demanded by France—The French troops to remain at Ancona until
the Austrians have evacuated Papal territory—The ratification of
Russia arrives at last—Madame Adelaide and others sound Talleyrand
as to whether he would take General Sebastiani's place—Talleyrand's
reply to Baron Louis—Comte Orloff returns to Russia—Talleyrand
asks for four months' leave to recruit his health—He requests that
M. Durant de Mareuil should replace him in London during his absence
—Death of M. Casimir Périer—Account of the meeting at Compiègne
between the French Royal Family and King Leopold—The marriage
is arranged between him and the king's eldest daughter—The rising in
La Vendée is put down—A serious outbreak takes place in Paris after
the funeral of General Lamarque—Graphic account by Madame Adelaide
of the outbreak in Paris—Talleyrand leaves London on the 20th of
June—Arrives in Paris on the 22nd—Appendix, containing some further
private correspondence.

IN summing up the various points of Belgian affairs, at the
beginning of January, 1831, we were brought to a standstill,
first at the *Hague* by the King of the Netherlands, who had
ended by acquiescing in the independence of Belgium, but
accompanied his consent with impossible conditions as to
frontiers and the division of the debt; then at *Brussels* by
the Congress, which still advocated the reunion of Belgium with
France, in other words—a European war, or calling the Duc de
Nemours to the throne, thereby securing the protection of

France, and the annexation of Luxemburg, which would equally entail war; again at *Paris* by the fear lest the choice of Prince Leopold of Saxe-Coburg might appear in the light of a humiliating concession to England; and finally in *London* by the Russian plenipotentiaries, who, while authorised by their Sovereign to sign the Act which gave Belgium her independence, were expressly forbidden to consent to any other selection as sovereign of that country than a prince of the house of Nassau.

It was necessary to meet these complications by a prompt and bold stroke. I therefore decided to propose to the other three Powers of the Conference not to wait for Russia's refusal respecting the choice of the sovereign, as it was not necessary that the recognition should be simultaneous; and Belgium would become a kingdom as soon as four of the great Powers had recognised her as such. I also insisted that no notice should be taken of the objections made by the Dutch and Belgians, and wrote to Paris[1] as follows:

"The question now is no longer one of such and such a boundary, or whether the share of the debt is to be large or small; it no longer rests with the house of Nassau or that of Bavaria—it is solely a question of a martial or a pacific system. The former will inevitably have whatever it wants, either the re-union of Belgium with France, or the acceptance of the choice of M. le Duc de Nemours. The latter will be satisfied with the selection of the Prince of Naples, which the Conference is also inclined to adopt. But it is very important that the French Government, when coming to a decision, should ascertain the inclinations of Belgium on this point. If M. de Celles is favorable to this view, he might be very useful in furthering arrangements. Then again, our Ministry must be prepared to contend with the Mauguin and Lamarque party as to the Neapolitan scheme; they are certain to raise some objections either in Brussels or Paris. If, in order to embarrass us, the intriguers in Paris cause M. le Duc de Nemours to be proclaimed, a formal refusal on the part of the king puts us perfectly straight with respect to the Powers. The dilatory answer mentioned in the despatch of the 2nd, which I have just received, will I fear deal a very serious blow to the confidence of the cabinets.

---

[1] Prince de Talleyrand to Madame Adelaide, January 3rd, 1831.

Russia, ever ready to take umbrage at the policy of England, will profit by this circumstance to push social hostilities (which here exercise an immense influence) to extremes. If therefore the king, as I think, believes himself strong enough to preserve peace, he must give an absolute refusal respecting the Duc de Nemours. It seems to me that there is a very erroneous opinion abroad in France, viz.: that we could keep peace with England, while making war with the rest of the Continent ; it is certain that enormous sacrifices, quite incompatible with our dignity, would be required, and would even then probably be insufficient to make her impartial. M. de Flahaut, who did not believe this on his arrival here, is now convinced of its truth.[1] It now remains to be seen, whether France is in a position to make war with the Continent : I believe she is, but is she able to make war with the Continent and with England ? I do not think so. When I read our newspapers and our parliamentary discussions, I am dismayed at the marvellous ignorance, prejudice, and blind presumption which pervade them. It is noticed here that the tone of our discussions changes ; we are blamed for this, our effervescence causes uneasiness, but they do not fear us.

" I feel it is my duty not to conceal all this. I could add a great deal more as to the difficulty of a position, in which one is, when in charge of the affairs of a kingdom in a state of ferment and amongst people who are still in the old groove. My devotion; however, gives me courage to contend against the old English jealousy, ever ready to crop up, without any hope of pleasing my own country.

" But the Duc de Nemours once set aside, if Belgium persists in her choice of him or of the Duc de Leuchtenberg, it will be necessary to recall the English and French Commissioners, who are in Brussels, and only receive jointly whatever communications the Belgians may wish to make. If they go to war with Holland, or Holland with them, as no one wants war at his own door, it will be necessary to blockade the ports of whichever country attacks the other. That done, we can rest quietly, and leave it to time to bring about some reasonable combination. . . . ."

I believed these observations had produced some effect in Paris, on receiving the following reply from General Sebastiani,. dated January 5th :—

---

[1] It will be remembered that the Comte de Flahaut had been sent to London by General Sebastiani to propose a scheme for the division of Belgium to M. de Talleyrand. (See vol. iii. p. 284.)

MON PRINCE,

We have never wavered as to the side we should take respecting Belgium. We should unhesitatingly refuse, both her re-union with France, and the offer of the crown to M. le Duc de Nemours. It is true, we did think that some arrangement other than her independence, would more certainly secure the peace of Europe, but we must wait till the Great Powers are convinced of this, especially England. However far removed that period may be, we are prepared to await it.

The King of the French will set an example of disinterested-ness and political loyalty, that will serve as a model. This he is firmly resolved upon, mon Prince, and he desires me to tell you so. You can therefore make positive engagements on this head with the Powers, without fear that anything will shake his resolution. Let peace, mon Prince, be the object of your labours, and after this declaration there is nothing I think that ought to compromise its preservation. Our language towards the Belgians has always been clear and positive. I trust there-fore that they will not commit any follies.

The king's confidence in your sagacity and devotion to his service is so great, that he trusts to you to take whatever course is most conducive to the dignity of his crown and the interests of your country.

Feeling assured by the declarations contained in this letter, that I might count on the king's support (in which I was wrong, as will be seen), I was less disturbed by the flights of fancy in which General Sebastiani and the other Ministers indulged, and still less, I must confess, by the views of the Bel-gians, which one of the Commissioners at the Conference in Brussels, M. Bresson, certainly did not depict in very favourable colours to me. I did not therefore at all expect the surprise they had prepared for us in that quarter.

A new candidate for the Belgian throne had suddenly arisen in Brussels, in the person of Prince Otto of Bavaria, aged four-teen. General Sebastiani, who had been informed of this by M. Bresson, had at once replied that the French Government would have no objection to the selection of Prince Otto, provided it was quite understood that he would marry a daughter of the King of the French. M. Bresson had submitted General Sebas-tiani's letter to the principal members of the Congress, who hastened to publish, print and placard it, in the streets of Brussels. Such a communication assumed a character of great importance, when made by an agent who represented at once, the Conference and the French Government.[1]

As soon as I knew that there was a question of Prince Otto, I wrote to Paris on the 6th January that he would not be assented to by any one :—[2]

" This prince," I said, "can only come to the throne sur-rounded by counsellors, who, by their number and their connec-tions, inspire the Cabinets of Europe with no confidence whatever.[3] We have not yet received news of the decision which has been come to, but when the last courier left, it was considered prob-able that the choice would fall on him,[4] and as he is only fourteen years old, M. de Mérode will be the one who will be placed beside him, to act as Regent.

" This great step has been taken with a degree of thought-lessness that appears extraordinary to every one. In the first place, it is by no means certain that the King of Bavaria will consent to it ; secondly, it is unwise [5] to place a new kingdom in the hands of a child ; thirdly, a new dynasty which begins with a regency is very liable to be surrounded by intrigues, and fourthly, M. de Mérode has relations in France who would pro-bably create dissension among several of the powers."

Three days later, on the 9th January, when the details of what had taken place in Brussels became known to the Con-

---

[1] In addition to this publication, M. le Comte d'Arschot had read to the Congress on January 8th, two letters from Messrs. Gendebien and Rogier, in which the Belgian envoys at Paris said that M. Sebastiani had given them a formal promise to recognize Prince Otto, who would marry Princess Marie d'Orleans (see the debates of January 11th). This candidature of Prince Otto had no results. The party which supported him very soon substituted the Duc de Leuchtenberg in his place.

[2] *Prince Talleyrand to Comte Sebastiani.*—This letter is dated January 7th in the text of the archives. We shall continue as heretofore to indicate the variation in the two texts. It will be seen that M. de Talleyrand has generally only inserted portions of his correspondence with M. Sebastiani. He did not adopt our method of repro-ducing in a note the actual text of the dispatches, and we have kept to the existing variations in the passages noted. The breaks will indicate the omissions.

[3] Var.: . . . . *à Bruxelles ; on s'occupe de faire un roi qui vraisemblablement n'aura l'assentiment de personne, s'il ne doit* monter sur le trône, qu'entouré des conseillers, qui par *leurs* noms, etc. = *in Brussels ; they occupy themselves in making a king who probably will not have the sanction of any one, if he only* mounts the throne surrounded by Counsellors, who by *their names*—&c.

[4] Var. : Sur le jeune prince Othon de Bavière qui déjà était destiné au trône de la Grèce. = *on the young Prince Otto of Bavaria who was already destined for the throne of Greece.*

[5] Var. : pas très vraisemblable = not very likely.

ference, I renewed, in my despatches to Paris, the disapprobation
expressed in London at the manner in which this affair had been
carried on. I did not stop there, but wrote to Madame Adelaide,
the king's sister, what I wished her to communicate to his
majesty :—

"I have not troubled Mademoiselle lately with all my
worries. To say the truth, I have been all the more pained by
seeing the very grave injury that is being done to the progress
of affairs, distrust increases visibly, and it requires great efforts,
and will require all the confidence which everyone here is disposed to show me, to preserve unchanged the position of the
French Ambassador. My own feelings are of little consequence ;
but I am keenly alive to anything that may injure the king's
service. I will give Mademoiselle an example. It was through the
corps diplomatique that I heard of the letter *placarded* at Brussels.
I was greatly embarrassed at so positive a fact, and one which
takes from my words the credit so essential to them. Any one
else in a similar position would undoubtedly have quitted his
post, and the members of the Conference, who dread my leaving,
have several times declared to me that my departure would be
the signal for a rupture. I have therefore remained, actuated by
the desire not to allow any personal consideration to interfere
with the course of affairs, and feeling also that being Mademoiselle's ambassador she would be pained if I thus left the
place where she wished me to be. But I could not be of service
here, unless means are found to give all necessary weight to my
words, and to satisfy the Powers here assembled. It appears
from the papers, for the despatches from Paris do not mention it,
that M. Bresson has, without authority, caused General Sebastiani's letter to be placarded. I therefore ask that the imprudent
zeal of M. Bresson should be censured, that he should be sent
back to his post in London, and that I may be authorized to declare that the French Cabinet has no intention of separating
itself in the Belgian question from the course adopted by the
Great Powers. I should also like my despatches to be more
carefully read, so that simple propositions are not mistaken for
absolute decisions. This would obviate my being written to,
that the protocol, *which never existed, is coloured with partiality.*
It is necessary that the Belgian question should be entrusted entirely to the Conference, otherwise we shall always be accused of
playing a double game. The king will thereby be the gainer, as
he will no longer be importuned by the intrigues of the Belgians,
who are much too active in Paris. . . ."

The members of the Conference, reassured by the very distinct declarations I was bound to give them, on the subject of
Prince Otto of Bavaria, signed at my request protocol No. 9.
In this (setting aside the question of the prince as if it did not
exist as far as we were concerned) we, in the firmest manner
possible, invited the King of the Netherlands, on the one hand, to
raise the blockade of the port of Antwerp, which was a chief
cause of irritation to the Belgians, and on the other, requested
the Belgians to cease the hostilities they were keeping up in the
environs of Maëstricht.

I also insisted at Paris, that Lord Ponsonby should be allowed
to make all possible attempts at Brussels in favour of the Princes
of Nassau, being convinced that the failure of these attempts
would induce the English Government to still further espouse
the cause of the Prince of Saxe-Coburg, who in my estimation
still remained the candidate most to be preferred.   The *comité
diplomatique* of the Brussels Congress, had deputed several of their
members to proceed to Paris and London to arrange with us as
to which prince would be most agreeable to us.   I counted on
this deputation to aid us in making a reasonable choice, and was
not deceived in that expectation.   From that moment the most
able man of the deputation, M. van de Weyer, entered into correspondence with the Prince of Coburg, and ably supported him
in Brussels, in spite of all the incidents which obstructed the
prince's candidature.

I tried to alleviate the anxieties that were apparent every
day from Paris, by writing to Mademoiselle on the 12th
January :—

"I have not written for the last few days to Mademoiselle,
because I wished to answer when fully cognizant of the matter.
Mademoiselle has had the goodness to ask my advice ; it is impossible for me to reply categorically respecting a state of affairs
which is not merely very complicated, but which changes from
hour to hour. The dilatoriness of the English, the vacillation of the
Belgians, the obstinacy of the Dutch, and the necessity of having
to treat with people who only acquiesce unwillingly in concessions
opposed to their inclinations, and often to their interests, makes
everything difficult. It is often necessary to begin again the
next morning that which had been definitely decided upon the

evening before ; fresh arguments have to be brought forward to efface the effect of a letter from Lord Ponsonby, who does not always take the same views as M. Bresson. The presence and influence of the Prince of Orange, and the countenance given to him by Madame de Lieven, Lord Grey's particular friend : such are the obstacles that constantly arise, and which would discourage a zeal and affection less sincere and ardent than I possess. I do not see that there is any practical advice that I can give at this moment. The king's conduct has been admirable throughout ; I ask that this cautious attitude may be continued for a few days longer. I believe that during this short delay, the English Government will be further undeceived as to the Prince of Orange's chances in Belgium, and then we shall be in a position to support with advantage and authority, either the Prince of Bavaria or the Prince of Naples, but especially the latter."

On January 13th I again wrote to her :—

" I can well understand that the dilatoriness of the London Conference is displeasing to Mademoiselle ; I venture to say that I am no less vexed thereat, although I am not beset, like the king, with all the importunities and agitations of political wire-pullers, so active with us, and so obstructive to our Ministers. The English Cabinet never hurries itself about anything for it has no impatient demands to satisfy. In Paris we only think of pushing on the Government; here they only think of holding it back. What also greatly retard our progress and take up a great deal of time in explanations of all kinds, are the communications made and published by the Belgians.[1] It is necessary to explain more or less fully all the utterances which they make in public, and repair, as far as possible, the faults these political *débutants* commit every day. The English Cabinet wishes the Belgian question settled before the 3rd of April. The king will have seen by protocol No. 9, that, despite obstacles, we are arriving at some results, and that all parties are following suit. There is no Conference to-day, I am therefore going down to Brighton to pay my respects to the king, and get a breath of fresh air. . . ."

On my return from Brighton I had a long interview with Lord Grey ; I sent the account of it to Paris on the 17th of January [2] :—

---

[1] An allusion to various facts that had occurred in Brussels, (see page 8, also page 19) the Sebastiani-Rogier incident.

[2] *Prince Talleyrand to General Sebastiani.* Official despatch already published.

". . . I have had a long conversation this morning with Lord Grey. I was able to be very explicit with him, being authorised to do so by the letter you did me the honour to write on the 14th of this month, and in consequence of information I have obtained here, which has shown me that the affairs of the Prince of Orange were less settled than the English Government is pleased to imagine. I told Lord Grey that the delays had changed public opinion ; that the Prince of Orange's party was less strong than they fancied ; that the Catholics did not want and would never have him ; that those who desired the re-union with France were against him ; that to follow the direction now taken would inevitably end in civil war ; that a civil war in Belgium affected France too closely not to complicate all other questions ; that it was absolutely necessary to come to some decision as to a sovereign ; that this sovereign must be a Catholic, and that the choice rested between Prince John of Saxony, Prince Otto of Bavaria, and Prince Ferdinand of Naples.[1]

" Lord Grey then replied that they had thought it expedient to let the Prince of Orange have every possible chance, so that having once failed, Russia would no longer have him to oppose to us, and would agree to side with us ; that as to the Prince of Bavaria, he could not understand why we did not prefer the king's brother, Prince Charles. ' Because,' I replied, ' he was strongly opposed to the last revolution in France, and we do not want to have a prince near us who is inclined to take part in everything that anti-French politics might concoct.' ' But Prince Otto of Bavaria is too young,' objected Lord Grey ; ' the Government would have to be administered by a Regency, and who would be the Regents ? Some of those agitators of whom we have so much cause to complain ! ' ' Why not then choose the Prince of Naples ? ' I replied, ' he has not this drawback, as he is eighteen.' ' He is only seventeen,'[2] he answered, ' and besides, he is too nearly allied to us not to complicate matters with Parliament.' I then remarked to Lord Grey that this was no real difficulty, for a similar objection might have been made when there was a question of Prince Leopold of Saxe Coburg, and that I had deemed it no obstacle. Moreover, it was our desire to act in concert with England, but it was absolutely necessary for us to break through the dangerous position in which Belgium, had placed Europe,[3] and especially France ; that whatever choice was made by them and by us would certainly be adopted,

---

[1] Charles Ferdinand, Prince of Capua. He is generally known under the name of Prince Charles.

[2] Prince Charles of Naples was born October 10th, 1811.

[3] Var. : l'Europe en général = Europe in general.

but that to accomplish this, mutual concessions were necessary.
'The reasons you give for refusing the Princes of Naples and
Bavaria,' I said in conclusion, 'do not appear to me sufficient,
and if Europe is troubled by such motives it will not reproach
us.'
   " The impression I received from this long conversation was,
that, the chances of the Prince of Orange once gone, the choice
would be limited to the three houses I have named above. My
efforts will be centred on the Prince of Naples ; but in order to
keep my position with regard to the members of the Conference,
I must allow the combination in favour of the Prince of Orange
to exhaust itself."

   At the same time, or rather I should say on the top of this
very complicated question of the selection of a future sovereign
for Belgium, there was another even more immediately threatening, namely, the renewal of hostilities between the Dutch and
the Belgians, which would inevitably involve a general European
war. The King of Holland, who, as has been already stated,
desired war above all things, hoping that it might lead to the
restoration of his government in Belgium, worked with untiring
obstinacy to bring it about. By blockading the Scheldt, and
the port of Antwerp, he put a stop to all commerce in Belgium,
and thus caused extreme irritation among the Belgians, who as
an act of reprisal besieged the town of Maëstricht which was
only occupied by a weak Dutch garrison. Both these acts were
in direct contravention to the armistice made under the auspices
of the Conference. We had therefore notified to the King of
Holland, by a protocol, that he must raise the blockade of the
Scheldt not later than January 20th, and to the Belgians that
they must cease hostilities round Maëstricht.[1]   So far neither
one side nor the other had obeyed. The King of Holland had
ordered his troops to march on Maëstricht, and Prussia seemed
quite ready to aid him in this enterprise. The Bonapartist and
republican party in Brussels (who had taken advantage of the
irritation caused by the blockade of the Scheldt to provoke
hostilities at Maëstricht) only waited for the commencement of
the struggle in order to claim the aid of France, cherishing the
hope, equally with the King of Holland, though with another

[1] Protocol of January 9th, 1831.

aim, that a general war would bring about the overthrow of the French Government and the reunion of Belgium and France under a republic.

It was imperative to provide against such dangers. The Conference renewed the formal notification to the King of Holland to raise the blockade of the Scheldt, and threatened the Belgians with a blockade of all their ports by an Anglo-French squadron, if they did not cease their attempts on Maëstricht. It had been proposed by some members of the Conference to employ the Prussian army to prevent the march of the Belgians on Maëstricht ; this I peremptorily opposed, and so obtained the adoption of the threat to blockade the Belgian ports. Here I found the advantage of my having already proposed this as regards the Dutch ports, when it was a question of forcing King William to raise the blockade of Antwerp, and it was my intention to turn it to account again, if by the 20th January, our protocol of the 9th had not been carried out.

But all these measures were only temporary remedies to secure us from permanent dangers. For several days I had thought over a counter-stroke which I considered would be decisive, inasmuch as it would put an end to the hopes of the revolutionary party in Belgium and France, as well as to the reactionary attempts of the King of Holland : this was, a declaration by the Powers of the neutrality of Belgium. I submitted it to the Conference at the sitting of the 20th of January, and had the satisfaction of obtaining its adoption, and insertion in the protocol of that day.[1] The account of this sitting, which I sent to

---

[1] The protocol of January 20th contained two series of decisions. It fixed the limits of Belgium and Holland on the basis of the *statu quo* of 1790 ; it then proclaimed the neutrality of the new state in the following terms :

" The plenipotentiaries . . . are unanimously agreed that the five Powers deem it due to their own interests, to their union, to the tranquillity of Europe, and to the accomplishment of the views recorded in their protocol of December 20th, to make a solemn manifestation and striking proof of their firm determination not to seek (in any of the arrangements respecting Belgium, or under any circumstances that may still arise) any increase of territory, any exclusive influence, or any isolated advantage, and to give to that country itself, as well as to the states which surround it, the strongest guarantees for peace and security. In consequence of these resolutions, and after careful consideration, the plenipotentiaries have decided to add the following to the preceding articles :

" Art. 5th.—Belgium, within the limits arranged and defined according to the

Paris on the 21st January, will show the importance of the results I had obtained.

THE PRINCE DE TALLEYRAND TO GENERAL SEBASTIANI.

M. LE COMTE,

I have the honour to transmit herewith the protocol of our Conference yesterday. By it you will see that, following up the idea I expressed to you in my despatch No. 70 of the 10th of this month, we have succeeded in procuring the recognition in principle of the neutrality of Belgium by the plenipotentiaries. I was strongly supported in this by Lord Palmerston, whom I always find very straightforward, and of a really pacific disposition.

I need hardly tell you that the struggle has been long and difficult. The importance of this decision was fully felt by all the members of the Conference, and in consequence, our sitting lasted eight hours and a half.

The recognition of the neutrality of Belgium places that country in the same position as Switzerland, and consequently upsets the political system adopted by the Powers in 1815, out of hatred to France. The thirteen fortresses of Belgium, by means of which our northern frontier was perpetually threatened, will fall, so to speak, in consequence of this resolution, and we shall henceforth be free from troublesome obstructions. The humiliating conditions proposed in 1815 caused me to retire at that time from public affairs, and I confess that it is gratifying to me now to have been able to assist in retrieving the position of France in this respect.

You will agree with me, M. le Comte, as to the *immense*[1] advantage that this resolution will afford to the maintenance of peace. The Belgians, finding themselves isolated, and at liberty to choose a form of government in accordance with their traditions and customs, will cease troubling Europe, and will without doubt become easier to manage when they know that their follies can only recoil on themselves. As to France, I have reason to hope that she will in this find a brilliant satisfaction for the past, and a pledge of security for the future.

basis laid down in Articles 1, 2, and 4 of the present protocol, will form a neutral state in perpetuity. The five Powers guarantee her this perpetual neutrality, as well as the integrity and inviolability of her territory within the above-mentioned limits

"Art. 6th.—Belgium will be reciprocally bound to observe the same neutrality towards all the other states, and not to make any attempt to disturb their interior or exterior tranquillity."

[1] Suppressed in the text of the Archives.

The difficulties I experienced during the discussion were more especially with reference to the latter part of the protocol, in which I had inserted that other countries would be at liberty to join in the recognized neutrality of Belgium. I thought that this would, later on, furnish the best possible solution of the thorny question of the duchy of Luxemburg. The Prussian minister foreseeing the same result, resisted for a long time; but, in the end I carried my point, and the paragraph was inserted, though in a rather more vague form than I desired.[1]

However, the question of the duchy of Luxemburg, being under the jurisdiction of the Germanic Confederation, cannot be dealt with here, where difficulties would only be raised by persons interested, without the powers of solving them.

It has been arranged with Lord Palmerston that the protocol is not to be sent to Brussels for some days; we deemed it better first to settle some of the points therein laid down. . .

This great victory, for even now I consider it as such, came just in time to enable me to allay the anxieties, and disquietudes, constantly reported from Paris and Brussels, and which are fairly summarised in the following letters of General Sebastiani and M. de Bresson.

GENERAL SEBASTIANI TO THE PRINCE DE TALLEYRAND.

MON PRINCE,

I pray you to read the account of yesterday's sitting with the most serious attention (the sitting of the French Chamber of Deputies of January 15th). A petition from a Belgian furnished General Lamarque with an opportunity for a speech, in which he reviewed the foreign policy of the

---

[1] Var. . . . *à peu près* comme je le désirais = almost as I wished. The same day, January 21st, Lord Palmerston wrote to Lord Granville :

MY DEAR GRANVILLE,
    The protocol which I send you is the result of two long days of work . . . Talleyrand wished that Luxemburg should be included in the neutrality, but objections were raised to this on the ground that that duchy belonged to an independent sovereign, and to a confederation of which he is a member ; that the Conference has not the right to negotiate concerning either war or peace as regards Luxemburg, as this right belongs only to the sovereign of the country and to the Confederation. . . . Talleyrand fought like a lion over this ; he declared that he would not consent to the neutrality of Belgium, would have nothing to do with this neutrality, and ended by saying, that he wanted Philippeville and Marienburg in exchange . . . Finally, we got him to come to an arrangement, in the way that juries are made unanimous, namely, by starvation. Between nine and ten o'clock, he agreed to our proposals, quite satisfied at heart I feel sure, in seeing the neutrality of Belgium secured . . .
    (*Private Correspondence of Lord Palmerston*, translated into French by Aug. Craven.)

government since the revolution of July. The affairs of Belgium were evidently the subject he proposed to handle. His attacks were violent, and his object was to lead us into war. I, however, refused to take up the gauntlet, and the whole Chamber approved my discretion. But the Orleanist party, who had intended broaching these questions, declared themselves offended, and M. Guizot occupied the floor for a long time. M. Mauguin answered him with great vehemence and heat, and, it must be admitted, thoroughly roused the national feeling which is so strong in the country. M. Dupin was not happy in his reply, and General La Fayette did not show his usual tact, so noticeable in all party questions. The effect of this sitting on the nation will be to impose a still greater degree of caution, if possible, on the actions of the government. We must avoid not only injuring the interests and the dignity of France, but we must also humour her pride, and, it must be admitted, her earnest desires.

The attempt the English ministry is just now making in Belgium, compromises, it cannot be denied, the peace of Europe. The Prince of Orange heads a party, but it is weak, timid and vanquished, though less by force of arms than by national hatred. We have for a long time supported the cause of this prince, we have tried to make it a success either in his own person or in that of his children, but our efforts have been fruitless. The sincere wish for peace, on which our policy is founded, has guided and will continue to guide our conduct with regard to Belgium. The Prince of Orange is about to renew his efforts, supported by the influence of England. We shall hold aloof from this movement ; but we foresee with pain, that we shall not be able to do so from the consequences that may follow. If the Prince of Orange is called to the throne by the free and earnest wish of the Belgians, we shall respect this choice, for we shall always honour the independence of Belgium. But you have seen, mon Prince, what has been the success of the proposition made to the Congress by M. Maclagan.[1]

Does the English Cabinet thoroughly understand the differ-

---

[1] M. Maclagan was at that time deputy for Ostend. At the sitting of January 12th, he presented a motion in favour of the Prince of Orange, which provoked a violent uproar. This is the official account given of the incident :

M. Maclagan does not approve of either of the names presented (the Duc de Leuchtenberg and Prince Otto). The Powers reserve to themselves the making of our laws ; we are not independent. The Prince of Orange will bring Limburg, Luxemburg, and the left bank of the Scheldt back to us, and the Powers . . . (at the word " Prince of Orange," cries of " order ! " " Down with him ! " were heard from all sides. The greatest excitement prevailed in the assembly).

M. le Président.—I beg to remind M. Maclagan, that he has no doubt forgotten that the Congress has for ever excluded the whole House of Orange. (Cries of Bravo ! bravo !" In the midst of the tumult, the voice of M. A. de Rodenbach was heard

ence between the position of Belgium before the exclusion of Nassau, and her present position ?   Then everything was possible and permissible ; but now an armistice has been concluded, and placed under the guarantee of the Great Powers, subsequent to the exclusion of the House of Nassau, the separation of Holland and Belgium has been pronounced, and the independence of Belgium has been recognized.   How, for example, could the Prince of Orange have recourse to the Dutch forces, without damaging the object of the armistice—the separation and independence of Belgium ?   Does the Prince of Orange desire to undertake the conquest of Belgium, with the aid of his Belgian partisans ?   He would then find himself struggling with the provisional government and the Congress, and would embark on a civil war, which France could hardly regard with indifference when at her very doors.   Besides, who could tell what such a civil war might not bring about ?   You must admit, mon Prince, such an attempt would be altogether too hazardous for me to recognize therein the long-sighted and wise policy of such a government as that of England.   But the prudence of Lord Grey and Lord Palmerston reassures me.   Deceived by false accounts of the lively hopes and restlessness of the Prince of Orange, what has just taken place in the Congress will have enlightened them, and I have no doubt but that they have cancelled the instructions they gave to Lord Ponsonby.   Our attitude will be calm, our conduct loyal, but our anxiety can easily be imagined.   Both your position, mon Prince, and that of the Conference, under such very grave circumstances, is extremely difficult.   I can quite understand that you are greatly fatigued with all this, though no one has ever shown a nobler nature or greater ability than you have done.   Never let them lose sight of the fact in London that the Belgian cannon will find an echo in France, and that in this world it does not do for a country to look to its own interests alone.   .   .   .

M. de Bresson, on his part, wrote to me from Brussels as follows, on January 17th :

MON PRINCE,

I have to inform you that Lord Ponsonby has this evening written to Lord Palmerston : *that he has received inform-*

exclaiming : "He is English, M. Maclagan, he is English ! he is not Belgian ! Order !")
 M. le Président.—I know my duty, I call M. Maclagan to order . . .
 M. Maclagan declares that the Congress must reconsider its sentence of exclusion, in order to give complete liberty to its commissioners. (The outcry begins again, until M. Maclagan definitely quits the tribune).

ation from a reliable source, that advice has been sent from the War Department of France to the Belgian Government to provision and prepare for siege the fortresses of Namur, Liége, and Huy. I do not know whether this fact has any foundation, and if it is true, how Lord Ponsonby has arrived at its knowledge. But as it is possible that explanations may be demanded from you, I thought it prudent to let you know it beforehand.

I have read in the papers M. Sebastiani's letter to M. Rogier[1] with unspeakable pleasure. The Congress and the Belgian government needed a lesson of this kind.[2]

The French party, thoroughly dissatisfied, (M. Stassart,[3] at its head,) proposes in order to revenge itself on us, to endeavour to take the Congress by surprise, and obtain the election of M. le Duc de Leuchtenberg, under the pretext that the Belgians had only this means left of asserting their independence. I trust they will fail ; I will, at least, do my utmost to bring it about.

The Prince of Orange's party has now also begun to stir. The crisis is approaching, and I am far from feeling easy. It is

---

[1] Firmin Rogier, Belgian diplomat, born in 1791, was first, professor at the French university. After 1815, he took up journalism and opposed the government of King William. In 1830, he was made Secretary to the Embassy in Paris, and for some time acted as *chargé d'affaires*. Later on he was made Minister Plenipotentiary and did not retire till 1864.

[2] A somewhat irregular incident had just at this time caused some bitterness between the French Cabinet and the Belgian government. M. de Celles had read aloud from the tribune, letters from M. Firmin Rogier and M. Bresson, relative to the candidature of the Duc de Leuchtenberg. Count Sebastiani had every reason to be dissatisfied with the way in which the Belgian government had thus made public most important secret documents, and that words he had spoken in familiar conversation had been officially reported. He complained bitterly of this to M. Rogier, and wrote him the following letter.

PARIS, *January* 14*th*.

MONSIEUR,

You told me a few days ago, that the papers had given a very incorrect version of the letters you had written to the provisional government ; but they now ascribe a fresh despatch to you, in which it is imposible for me to recognize what was said at our last interview.

As a minister, I have never had occasion to interview the king as to any arrangements connected with his family. The king has therefore been made either to refuse or concede what has never been demanded of him. I may further add that neither as a man, nor as the interpreter of the royal thoughts, should I ever have expressed myself with such levity concerning a prince, whose memory is highly esteemed by the king, and under whose orders I had myself, for a long time, the honour of fighting for the glory and independence of France. I console myself in thinking that the letter in question was not written by you ; were it otherwise, I should feel obliged never to have any other relations with you except in writing.

I have the honour to be, &c.,

HORACE SEBASTIANI.

[3] M. de Stassart, governor of the province of Namur, was at that time Vice-President of the Congress.

C 2

very important that I should know your views as to the Prince of Orange and Prince Leopold. We have to do with a strong and well-supported party in Paris. For the last three days there has been a rumour that Generals Excelmans,[1] Fabvier,[2] and Lallemand [3] were at Brussels incognito. It is now said that they have gone to Namur and Liége, and it is in that quarter that the French movement will break out, if the Orange movement takes place here and at Ghent.

We shall have great trouble in arriving at a satisfactory solution here. It is knowledge rather than good will which is wanting at the Congress, but it is ungovernable. . . .

All this greatly complicated matters, and it became necessary, in order to get out of this labyrinth of intrigues, to adopt a decided line of conduct, and not allow oneself to be turned aside from one's aim by passing incidents. According to my view, there seemed no other course for us but to remain firmly united to England. Our union meant the union of the other three powers, and assured general peace. I was perfectly convinced, that dislike to the House of Nassau was too strong in Belgium for the Prince of Orange even to hope to re-establish himself there. I therefore saw no risk in letting England make the attempt. I knew that the Cabinet must show Parliament that the claim had been allowed, tried, and found impracticable ; that a certain feeling of shamefacedness obliged them to give this token of condescension to Holland, whose colonies, which she gave up in exchange for the Belgian provinces,[4] England

---

[1] General Count Excelmans (1775–1852) was one of the most brilliant cavalry generals of the Empire. He was at that time a peer of France. In 1849 he became Grand Chancellor of the Legion of Honour, Marshal of France and a Senator.

[2] General Baron Fabvier was born in 1782, entered the army in 1804, was entrusted under the Empire with various missions to Turkey, and later on to Persia. In 1814 he was obliged to sign the Capitulation of Paris. Placed on the unattached list under the Restoration, he went to Greece in 1823, and served in the War of Independence. In 1830, he was made Major-General, then Governor of Paris, Lieutenant-General in 1839, a peer of France in 1845. In 1848, he was elected deputy and went as Ambassador to Constantinople, and then to Copenhagen. He died in 1855.

[3] General Charles Lallemand, born in 1774, entered the service in 1798, and was made Brigadier-General in 1815. Condemned to death as defaulter, at the second Restoration, he went to America, returned to France in 1830, became member of the Chamber of Peers, and died in 1839.

[4] By a convention dated August 13th and 14th, 1814, England undertook to restore to the King of the Netherlands the colonies she had taken possession of during the war, with the exception of Cape Colony, and various other possessions on the coasts of Guiana and Malabar.

had retained ; and finally I felt convinced, that the English
Cabinet would later on give me credit for the good faith we
showed in not openly opposing the election of the Prince of
Orange. Strengthened by these considerations, I determined
not to occupy myself so much with the choice of a sovereign for
Belgium, as with the care of widening and confirming the separation of that kingdom from Holland.

The protocol of January 20th had established the first basis
of this separation, by declaring the neutrality of Belgium. It
now remained to develop this, and obtain its acceptance by the
King of Holland. This sovereign had already submitted, with a
very bad grace it is true, to the protocol, by which we had insisted
on his raising the blockade of the Scheldt : this was a perpetual
source of irritation to the Belgians, whose commerce was thus
completely shut out.

I believed that I had chosen the best course, and was following it up actively, when M. de Flahaut again appeared in London,
the bearer of a letter from General Sebastiani, and charged to
reopen the famous project of the partition of Belgium, which I
believed had been buried in oblivion. *En route*, M. de Flahaut
had passed the courier, who carried the declaration of neutrality
to Paris ; consequently, he was not aware of it. General Sebastiani's letter of January 21st was the theme, by means of
which it was hoped that I would be induced to participate in
the dismay, which the possibility of the election of the Duc de
Leuchtenberg had caused in Paris ; it was on this point that M.
de Flahaut was to enlarge.

Here is the letter :—

MON PRINCE,

You will have heard, almost as soon as we did, of the
position of Belgium. The Congress is to elect a sovereign on the
28th, and there is every fear that its choice will fall on the Duc
de Leuchtenberg. M. Bresson has received orders to declare
officially, that his election will not be recognized by France.
He must renew the refusal to consent to the election of M. le
Duc de Nemours, and also the re-union of Belgium with France.
What the Belgians want, what the French wish, is nevertheless
this very re-union, and soon perhaps we shall not be in a

position to prevent it. We will continue to do our best, but we are beginning to lose hopes of success. Our strength is exhausted in this ungrateful struggle. The earnest desire of France is to-day expressed by the lips of men whose prudence you most appreciate, and whose character you most admire. Our situation is such, that the King and the Council believe it cannot have been truly represented to you in the despatches, and the king's government has decided to send to you M. le Comte de Flahaut, who will be able to make you acquainted with all the facts, and place them before his Britannic Majesty. That is his mission; it remains for you to make the most of it both for the service of the King and of France. It is needless to write you a long letter. M. de Flahaut will tell you everything that it is important you should know. Time presses; let us make the best use we can of the days and hours, and let us preserve that peace which can alone save social order in Europe.

P.S.—We have been so taken unawares by the fatally short date of the 28th, that we are unable to consult you before deciding to send to London.

It was after I had read this letter, that M. de Flahaut tried to prove to me that there was no other safety for France and Europe, but the partition of Belgium. I spoke in the strongest possible manner against this view, which, according to my ideas, was both impolitic and impracticable, and then wrote as follows to M. Sebastiani :[1]

MONSIEUR LE COMTE,

M. le Comte de Flahaut arrived here the night before last, and handed me the letter with which you had entrusted him. I thank you for having chosen him to bring it to me.

The raising of the blockade of Antwerp, and the irritation of the King of Holland, show that the Conference has been, as it was intended, sufficiently peremptory towards both parties, in order to obtain the results aimed at.

The conversation of M. de Flahaut has given me very valuable information, as to the intentions of the king's government respecting the affairs I am charged with here, and popular opinion in France. Nevertheless, I regret exceedingly, that he should have quitted Paris before the arrival of my despatch of the 21st. The news it contained, of the resolution adopted by the Conference, must necessarily have some influence on the views of the King

---

[1] Official despatch already published.

and of his Council, and also on the conduct to be pursued with
regard to Belgium. I continue to congratulate myself on the
declaration of neutrality, which up to the present has been
received with immense approbation by the statesmen of those
countries who have been told of it. All, no matter to what
party they belong, look upon it as a great act of policy, an
honour to modern civilization, and calculated to insure the maintenance of peace·by the facility it offers for conciliating, if not all
the demands, at least all the most important interests. I must
add, that, in agreeing to it, they all without exception believe
that this act is entirely to the advantage of France.

I can understand, that at the point at which affairs have
arrived in Belgium, and in the difficulties in which it seems likely
to involve France and Europe, men's minds have been ready to
adopt the most opposite schemes. But, neutrality once acknowledged, the greater part of these schemes are rendered
impossible, and I am enabled to bring forward again advantageously the question of the Prince of Naples, to which hitherto,
so much opposition has been raised. I believe indeed that we
shall arrive at a completely successful issue *on this point,*[1] by
turning Antwerp into a free port, or rather by making it a
Hanseatic town, and it has not *yet*[2] been proved to me that this
cannot be accomplished without Antwerp ceasing to belong, as
a free port, to Belgium. This is the line I have taken ever
since the protocol has been signed, and which I will continue to
hold unless you send me orders to the contrary.

This combination has the advantage of showing how far it
would be useless to make concessions to England on the Continent. I may even say that it is with the view of putting such
an idea quite out of the question, that I hold to the course I am
now pursuing. I should never wish to see the king's name and
yours attached to a clause, which, according to my view, would
have placed our government on the same level as those who give
no thought to the judgment of future ages.

History has testified to the great difficulty which the occupation[3] of Calais by the English entailed on us. It has also shown
the great popularity gained by the Guises, when they freed
France from this terrible disgrace. These lessons must not be lost
on us; the same faults might produce the same results, and
tarnish the brilliancy of that flower of independence which has
marked all the acts of the king's government. I feel assured that
his noble mind would not allow him to retain for any length of

[1] Suppressed in the text of the Archives.
[2] Suppressed in the text of the Archives.
[3] Var. : prolongée = prolonged.

time views which, without directly affecting our country, would not remove the reproaches that would be cast on our foreign policy.

No one would dream of denying that the re-union of Belgium with France offers great advantages to the latter, though an extension of the Rhenish frontier would better suit my views of French policy. I also admit that this re-union would, for some time, make the government which had achieved it very popular, notwithstanding the inconvenience [1] to French industry accruing therefrom.   But believe me, M. le Comte, such popularity would be very fleeting, if it had to be purchased at the price proposed.   There is not a reputation that would not be shaken by such an act, there is not an individual who does not blame the peace of Teschen for having brought the Russians into Europe ; what severe condemnation would not be passed then on those who should introduce the English on to the Continent ? One should never come into collision with those whom one cannot attack at home.

I am convinced, M. le Comte, that if you were plenipotentiary here, you would never sign your name to an act which not even the longest and most unfortunate war could justify. . . .

I do not know whether this despatch convinced those to whom it was addressed, but at least the effect was, that I heard no further mention of the intended project of dividing Belgium.

It is perhaps fair to say, that there was nothing very startling in this idea, as the atmosphere of Paris at that time disturbed even the best disposed people: This is evinced in some passages of the following letter, which the Duc de Dalberg wrote to me on the 22nd January :

THE DUC DE DALBERG TO THE PRINCE DE TALLEYRAND.

MON CHER PRINCE,

Here, nothing ever recovers itself or becomes consolidated.   The Belgian affairs compromise everybody, beginning with your chief, if there is a chief.   Lafitte's proceedings have brought him into such disrepute, as President of the Council, that they greatly prejudice the powers that be.   M. Thiers is pointed at on account of his baseness.

I had a talk with Pasquier and Sémonville yesterday.   We

---

[1] Var. : réels = real.

asked each other how all this could possibly go on ? Sémonville said : " I see the time of the Directory coming again. Soult alone is doing his work, and organizing four hundred thousand men at the expense of the Treasury. When they are enrolled, can they be kept together without a war ? If we go to war, will a system of pillage and requisition be renewed ? " These are questions one cannot solve. Disorder and anarchy are behind the scenes, because there is no authority anywhere. People's minds have been so strangely excited, that there is no talk of anything but the injuries received by France in 1814 and 1815, and how they must be revenged by retaking the Rhine frontier. One is as much out of it as a Chinaman, if one maintains that all these follies will end in upsetting the country.

The Congress in Brussels is a curious comment on your Conference in London ; it is time all this is put a stop to. How is it that no military commander has been found to march on Brussels and put an end to this Congress ?

Poland also greatly occupies us, but she does not exhaust our purses. The Polish Committee have up to now only collected sixty thousand francs, of which twenty thousand come from M. de la Fayette.

Poor M. de Mortemart [1] is playing the part of M. de Caulaincourt [2] but with less wisdom and talent.

What is your idea, mon Prince, as to the best ruler for Greece ? Prince Paul of Wurtemburg [3] worries everyone by his anxiety to be called to that throne. But no one listens to him here ; the minority of the Prince of Bavaria seems favourable to the claims of Capo d'Istria, who ought to be left at his post there.

The appointment of M. de Bouillé to Carlsruhe and of M. Alleyne to Frankfort has caused much dissatisfaction. It is thought that the latter has been appointed with a view to his doing all in his power to bring about a rupture in the Confederation. I believe he will produce the opposite effect. No one can explain the King's fancy in making such a choice. . . .

[1] Casimir Louis Victorien de Rochechouart, Duc de Mortemart, born in 1787, emigrated in 1791, returned to France under the Consulate, and became orderly officer to the emperor. At the Restoration, he was made peer of France (1814), then Brigadier-General and Ambassador to Russia. On the July 29th, 1830, Charles X. desired him to form a Cabinet, but his efforts failed, and he joined Louis Philippe. He was sent on a special mission to St. Petersburg and definitely accredited to this post in 1831. He became senator in 1852, and died in 1876.

[2] M. de Caulaincourt had been ambassador under the Empire, where he had to undertake the delicate task of gaining over Russian opinion to the policy of France at that period.—(Note by M. de Bacourt.)

[3] Paul, Prince of Wurtemburg, born in 1785, married in 1805 to the Princess Catherine, daughter of the Duke of Saxe-Altenburg, died in 1851. He was the brother of the King of Wurtemburg.

It required a certain amount of perseverance not to become discouraged between these echoes from Paris, the follies of the Belgians, and the obstinate resistance of the King of the Netherlands. Nevertheless, I was not much disturbed, and firmly and quietly pursued the line I had marked out for myself without concerning myself with the imprudent velleities in Paris, or even the Duc de Leuchtenberg, whom they wished to nominate in Brussels. I felt assured he would never be recognized by the Powers, and urged the Conference to complete the separation of Belgium from Holland. In our sitting of the 27th January, we touched upon the financial and commercial questions which had reference to this separation, and we placed them upon such an equitable basis as would, later on, reconcile the true interests of both parties. In sending the protocol of this sitting to Paris on January 29th,[1] I wrote as follows :

THE PRINCE DE TALLEYRAND TO GENERAL SEBASTIANI.

M. LE COMTE,

I send you the protocol of our Conference of the 27th ; it treats of various financial and commercial questions connected with the separation of Holland and Belgium. This piece of work has been drawn up by M. le Baron de Wessenberg and M. le Comte Matusiewicz, who considered they ought to subject the measures they proposed to take for the separation to the same principles which had formed the union. These two plenipotentiaries, especially M. de Wessenberg, possessed information on this matter of which everyone else, particularly myself, was ignorant. Nevertheless, in sending it to our commissioners in Brussels, we have added instructions, by which we have left it to them to choose the most opportune moment to present it to the Belgian Government. As it is possible that this protocol may raise fresh difficulties in Brussels, I beg you to retard its publication until you know what our commissioners have done in Brussels, after having sounded the opinion of those persons with whom they come most in contact.[2]

---

[1] Official despatch already published.

[2] This protocol of January 27th did not contain any *decisions*, but simply the propositions of the Conference, which had no executive powers. It proposed a project for the division of the debts between the two countries, and gave Belgium the right to participate in the colonial commerce of Spain.

This point must be kept in view, as M. de Talleyrand refers to it later on.

There will probably be a good deal of discussion on several questions dealt with by this protocol, but we believe that it will to a great extent satisfy the needs of the two countries. The King of Holland is sufficiently well treated, so that the relations between him and Belgium need not occasion perpetual difficulties which would end in becoming insurmountable. On the other hand, the Belgians, being great manufacturers and producers, will have markets which will remove the necessity for constant smuggling with France. The opinion of all those best acquainted with such matters in England, is that, if we insisted on less favourable terms for Holland, that country could not exist, owing to the enormous burden with which she would be weighted. It is for you, with your knowledge, to decide this point ; you will no doubt find that it touches many important political interests. . . . .

I quite foresaw that neither these measures nor the declaration of the neutrality of Belgium were of a nature to at once satisfy the impatient spirits in Paris, or the requirements of Brussels and the Hague ; but the essential point was to maintain the good relations between ourselves and England, and by this means to impose on the other Cabinets resolutions as reasonable and fair as we should have done between ourselves. All else was but secondary, as far as I was concerned. I sought the true interests of France, where I hoped really to find them, and not in wild dreams that could only lead to her destruction.

In fact, a general war, even if only against the three northern Powers, must have been fatal to us, for it would immediately have developed a revolutionary character, which would have separated England from us. It was therefore necessary, above all things, to avoid such a dangerous state of affairs ; and yet it was equally important to do so by means which were not dishonourable to France, but might even turn to her advantage. All I had hitherto done entirely followed out this view. Thus, instead of having the kingdom of the Netherlands, with a population of seven millions, and a line of formidable fortresses opposed to us, we had already obtained the separation of that country into two, and on our frontier a neutral Belgium, reduced to four million inhabitants. This neutrality, which was at first ridiculed as an impossibility, is nevertheless pretty solid, and will, I hope, be more durable than people fancy, as long as France does not attempt general and revolutionary wars against the whole of Europe, which is what no sound policy could ever admit into its calculations. If France went to war with England, we should have an equal interest with Germany in preserving the neutrality of Belgium ; if, on the other hand, France goes to war with Germany without the participation of England, the latter will defend the neutrality of Belgium. In any case, therefore, this neutrality is secured, provided always, that we are the first to respect it. The assured neutrality of Belgium will give us the same protection from Dunkirk to Luxemburg, as we now experience from Basle to Chambéry by the neutrality of Switzerland. This neutrality having been agreed to in London by the Conference of the Great Powers, I confess that the choice of the sovereign to reign over Belgium, had lost much of its importance as far as I was concerned, for I felt sure from the first, that the chief interest of that sovereign, whoever he was, would be to make friends with France, and live in kindly relations with her. It was most important that the separation of Belgium and Holland should be effected on such an equitable basis, that the two countries might prosper individually, and that, after a certain lapse of time (to allow all ill-feeling to subside), friendly intercourse might be resumed between them. Towards this end I used all my endeavours during my mission in London, and I do not think that I have failed.

After this digression, which does not appear to me out of place, we will return to the course of events which were still to retard, for a long time, the accomplishment of my views, and to begin with, we will cite a letter from M. Bresson, dated Brussels, January 30th :

M. BRESSON TO THE PRINCE DE TALLEYRAND.

MON PRINCE,

Matters here grow worse from day to day—general excitement has reached the last stage of exasperation. I quite foresaw that at any moment we might expect a disastrous combination, when I supported that which chose the Prince of Bavaria, though in itself neutral and inoffensive. I told you then that we were surrounded by dangers; now we have to face them. Unfortunately, the disapproval has come too quickly, un- certainty has succeeded certainty, the field has been thrown open to evil-doers and intrigues, and they have not lost their chance.

Had the Prince of Naples, or any other candidate, been brought forward in time (it is now six weeks since I urgently requested that everything should be subordinated to the election of a head for the State), he would have had the very best possible chance. But for this, the co-operation and assistance of England were required. This co-operation, this assistance, we did not receive *even against the Duc de Leuchtenberg;* he was allowed to gain ground ; no attempt was made to crush the idea *that he might be acceptable to the Powers, just because he was hostile to France ;* and even now promises are given and steps taken in his favour. The result, as might be expected, is that the friends of France, of their own accord, and despite our previous declarations, have brought M. le Duc de Nemours for- ward in opposition, as the only candidate likely to be successful. We are therefore now placed between a choice hostile to France, or hostile to the Powers, a cruel alternative, which cannot be decided either one way or the other, without terrible mis- fortunes.

People were greatly mistaken from the very first, as to the chances of the Prince of Orange, and they persevered in their efforts, because they only came in contact with people of the same views. No doubt (as I thought myself, and wrote to you), if the Prince of Orange was unanimously recalled, it would settle the whole difficulty. But, mon Prince, it is no longer a case of anti- pathy, it is downright hatred. I have heard the most atrocious things said, and miserable wretches come forward openly, offering to give him his death-blow if he returns. The Prince of Orange is impossible without a civil war. This people listens to neither reason nor interest, it only obeys its passions. The Prince's life, in the midst of these demoniacs, would not have been safe. Nevertheless, in the hope of bringing him back all the reasonable measures we have offered have been sacri- ficed ; now there is nothing but an abyss before us. What will happen ? They are inclined to blame others for the faults they have themselves committed. Irritation is rife everywhere, and people forget their own words. But good care is taken not to return to moderation.

Matters appeared so grave, mon Prince, that I deemed it necessary to go to Paris, to explain them in person to the king and the minister. My journey only occupied sixty-six hours. During my absence the protocol of the 20th (that respecting the neutrality) reached Lord Ponsonby, and was communicated by him. You will hardly credit me. The scheme contains a grand idea, and ought to excite both admiration and gratitude; alas! it has only provoked anger. You may judge of these men by this one act. The newspaper I send herewith will give you full details. To-morrow or the day after, the protest will be discussed at the Congress. [1] . . . .

I have quoted this letter, as much to show the actual state of affairs in Brussels, as to point out the danger brought about by the despatches of a too excitable agent. M. Bresson was undoubtedly a capable and intelligent man, but he wished to justify the fault he had committed, in supporting the candidature of the Prince of Bavaria without the authority of the Conference, whose commissioner he was. He was therefore anxious to throw the blame on his colleague, Lord Ponsonby, and depicted in fiery language and with evident exaggeration the disposition of the people in Brussels. He had made a journey to Paris, where entire credence was given to his words, and I quickly felt the consequences in London. Fortunately, I did not allow myself to be worried, or permit my plans to be upset by the intemperate warmth of others. My idea as to the choice of a sovereign for Belgium had never wavered. My candidate was and would always be, Prince Leopold of Saxe-Coburg, and I was in no way disturbed by the noise and excitement which existed everywhere upon this question. I had hopes; first, that King Louis Philippe would certainly refuse the crown for his son, the Duc de Nemours; secondly, that the Powers would reject the Duc de Leuchtenberg; and thirdly, that the Belgians would

---

[1] The Congress had been greatly irritated by the evident intention of the Conference to settle by itself the questions relating to Belgium. The following phrase of the protocol of January 20th, "Holland and Belgium each possessing enclosed lands in their respective territories, the five Powers will make such exchanges and arrangements between the two countries, as will ensure to them the reciprocal advantages of an entire contiguous possession, &c.," had specially startled the susceptibilities of the Assembly. Finally, the question of Luxemburg had roused the patriotism of the deputies. Thus the reading of the protocol at the sitting of January 20th brought forth violent protestations. "The national sovereignty," cried one deputy, M. Nothcomb, "has been transferred from Brussels to the Foreign Office." On the 30th the protest was carried by 163 votes against 9.

never agree to recall the Prince of Orange. Therefore, without troubling myself on this matter, I wished steadily to pursue what, in my eyes, was the really important question, namely, the separation of Belgium from Holland. But, if I was at ease on this point, there was no lack of trouble from other quarters, and the whole of February was passed in anxiety as to the course of home events in France, and the indecision of the French Government. This requires some explanation.

I have already said that the Conference, by its protocol of January 27th, had drawn up a division of the debts between Holland and Belgium, as well as some other mercantile measures, essentially only provisional, and with the exception of the question of the frontier limits fixed according to the position of the two countries in 1790—the only fair and admissible one—the rest of this protocol was open to discussion, and could be modified according to the wishes brought forward on either side. It was in this sense that I had written to Paris, but there the Belgian side was warmly and exclusively adopted. The arrangements proposed in the protocol were therefore found fault with, as not being favourable enough to Belgium, and I myself was blamed for having signed the protocol.

A few days after the signature of this protocol, several members of the Conference, alarmed at the news received from Brussels, which represented France as perpetually intriguing in favour of the election of the Duc de Nemours, proposed on the 1st February to draw up a protocol, in which the five Powers would formally undertake (in imitation of what had been done when choosing a sovereign for Greece) that, in no case, should the sovereign of Belgium be chosen from among the princes of the reigning families of the five Courts represented at the Conference in London. I persistently refused to sign this protocol, which seemed to me to show distrust of France, to whom alone, at this time, it could possibly apply.

Having given these explanations to make plain what follows, I will now confine myself to inserting in chronological order the extracts from my despatches, and the letters written and received during the month of February. The progress of events will be easily followed in them.

THE PRINCE DE TALLEYRAND TO GENERAL SEBASTIANI.

LONDON, *Feb.* 1*st*, 1831.

MONSIEUR LE COMTE,

I have just left the Conference, which lasted until half-past eight this evening. The courier, by whom I am sending this, is hurried on account of the tide ; I have, therefore, not much time to write to you. Nevertheless, on reading the protocol I have the honour to send you, you will see that I have refused to sign it. I am bound to give you some explanation of this refusal.

When the English plenipotentiary elicited the opinion which prevailed at the Conference, and which is found embodied in the protocol, I opposed it at once, stating that I could only see in this resolution a direct hit at France ; that it did not seem to me favourable to the maintenance of friendly relations between the Powers ; and that besides, the very terms of protocols 11 and 12, on which such stress was laid, sufficiently expressed the views of the five Powers. Here are the terms of these protocols :

"*Protocol No.* 11.—The plenipotentiaries are unanimously agreed that the five Powers owe it to their own interests, to their union, to the tranquillity of Europe, and to the accomplishment of the views embodied in the protocol of December 20th, to make a solemn manifestation and give a striking proof of their firm determination not to seek any augmentation of territory, any exclusive influence, any isolated advantage in the arrangements relating to Belgium, or in any other circumstances that may present themselves.

"*Protocol No.* 12.—The sovereign of Belgium must, by his individual position, necessarily guarantee the security of the neighbouring States."

I thought, M. le Comte, that after such very decided stipulations, it would be useless to give any fresh explanations ; for this reason, I have asked that the matter be referred to the government of the king, and also for instructions, which I trust you will not delay in sending me.

The article in the protocol having reference to Greece, to which Lord Palmerston alluded, is drawn up as follows, and is under date of March 22nd, 1829 : " In no case shall the ruler be chosen from among the princes of the families who reign at the Courts of the signatory Powers. . . .

M. BRESSON TO THE PRINCE DE TALLEYRAND.

BRUSSELS, *Feb.* 3*rd*, 1831.

MON PRINCE,

H.R.H. the Duc de Nemours was nominated and proclaimed King of the Belgians at twenty-five minutes past four precisely this afternoon.

At the first ballot 191 voted ; M. le Duc de Nemours had 89 votes, the Duc de Leuchtenberg 67, and the Archduke Charles of Austria 35. It was necessary to have 101 votes.

At the second ballot, 192 voted. The absolute majority required was 97. M. le Duc de Nemours obtained this exactly ; M. le Duc de Leuchtenberg had 47 votes, and the Archduke 21.

The President of the Congress then proclaimed the Duc de Nemours, King of the Belgians, subject to the condition of his accepting the constitution decreed by the Congress.

The greatest enthusiasm, and the most perfect tranquillity, reign in the town . . .

THE PRINCE DE TALLEYRAND TO GENERAL SEBASTIANI.

LONDON, *February* 4*th*, 1831.

MONSIEUR LE COMTE,

Yesterday evening, I received your letter of January 31st, and this morning, that of February 1st, which I hasten to answer. You will see first of all by the schedule annexed to protocol No. 12 (which I could not send you sooner, because it was only issued yesterday evening from the Chancellor's office), that some of the objections raised in your despatches have been solved by the principles contained in this schedule. Thus you will observe, that in order not to deviate too much from the system that has been adopted, the second paragraph relating to financial and commercial affairs is entitled : *Proposed Arrangements*, which allows all parties both time and means to furnish fresh explanations. This title gives positive indication, that we do not wish to settle on our own authority all the questions which are enumerated in the protocol ; and this is so evident, that, in the instructions given to our commissioners at Brussels, we recommend them to sound all the persons of influence, whom they come across, as to the probable effect of this protocol. At the same time, we leave the selection of their opportunity for so doing to their discretion. I wrote to you to this effect on January 29th.

Your opinion, as to the small importance to Belgium of the

commerce which she would gain from the Dutch colonies, is opposed to that of the chief merchants of the city of London. They all think, and the most able have been consulted, that it is to this commerce that Belgium owes the development of her industries for the last fifteen years ; the petitions from North and South Flanders confirm this opinion. The difficulty which you foresee with regard to Holland in the execution of this condition, would, I fancy, be easily removed at the time of the definite treaty : guarantees could then be imposed from which it would be impossible for Holland to escape.

We have not proceeded any further, as you seem to think, with the question of the Grand Duchy of Luxembourg ; it has been referred to those who have the right and the power to do so. The observations on this subject, contained in my despatch No. 274, cannot have escaped you.

As to the fixture of the territory and frontiers of Belgium, it seems to me that it was impossible to adjust them otherwise than we have done. We wished to recognize the independence of Belgium ; to this end, we had first to learn what was Belgium, and then to determine the frontiers of the country whose independence we were initiating. Could we, without injustice, have laid down any others than those which existed in 1790, when Holland and Belgium formed two separate States ? The Conference, too, formally declared in its protocol of January 20th, that both parties would regulate, under its mediation, the limits or assignments, and thus facilitate definite arrangements. That, you see, comes within the bounds which you assign to the Conference.

You announce, M. le Comte, that the government of the king has not adhered to the protocol of January 27th. I do not, I confess, understand in what way it could adhere or not adhere to a provisionary act which contains nothing but contingent stipulations, as may be seen by the schedule I send you to-day.

In replying to the portion of your letter of February 1st, relating to the future sovereign of Belgium, I ought not to conceal from you the uneasiness, which the resolution you seem to have arrived at, should the Congress designate M. le Duc de Nemours, causes me. I do not think it would be at all pru- dent to delay in expressing your refusal. A dilatory answer, in such a case, would excite in England the utmost discontent ; she would see in it the confirmation of those intrigues with which she reproaches the French government ; and Russia will not fail to profit by this circumstance to accuse you of keeping something in the background. This, M. le Comte, is my opinion, formed from my relations with the English Cabinet.

As to the Prince of Naples, I do not believe it is necessary to suspend your decision, in order to render his chances more favourable. It is for you to judge what action it is best to take at Brussels, respecting this choice. You can see by my correspondence, that I have prepared the way here for him with the English Ministers and the members of the Conference, and I do not think I am taking too much on myself in declaring to you, that when this question comes forward, we shall not find any opposition on the part of the English government, which is sure of the assent of Austria and Prussia; the time necessary for instructions will retard that of Russia. This happy situation would be changed by irresolute measures, which would compromise, without doubt, the maintenance of peace with England, this is at present assured to us, and should be our sole aim. . . .[1]

MADAME ADELAIDE TO THE PRINCE DE TALLEYRAND.[2]

PARIS, *February 5th*, 1831.

The King charges me, mon cher Prince, to acquaint you with the view he takes with regard to the last protocol which you have so rightly refused to sign, and of which I am sure you will feel the justice. It is that even the Powers cannot compare it with that which had been arranged for Greece, as the circumstances are entirely different. In the case of Greece, it was the three Powers who chose and nominated the sovereign ; here it is the Belgian Congress and Belgium (the independence of which has been recognized by the five Powers), who must choose their sovereign without restraint.

Here we have Nemours elected, in spite of the persistent refusal of the King and his government. A fresh despatch reiterating and persisting in this refusal, was sent yesterday to M. Bresson, at Brussels, four hours before the news of the election of Nemours reached us by telegraphic despatch. We are consequently open and loyal, mon cher Prince. You will make good and clever use of this, and I have firm confidence that we shall come out of it with honour and glory ; we only want, we only wish for, and that sincerely, the real welfare of all, without any personal interest. Truth will triumph

---

[1] Suppressed in the text of the Archives.
[2] It may be useful to notice, that by following the chronological order in which the letters are written, M. de Talleyrand could not place the answers exactly following the letters themselves, and that it took, at that time, from two to three days, according to the state of the sea, for the transmission of a letter to Brussels or Paris, and *vice versâ*.—(Note of M. de Bacourt.)

over stratagem and intrigue ; and you will have the glory and
satisfaction of contributing powerfully to it, by your talent and
ability.

I long, more than I can tell you, for your news, but you
must now take the high hand in London, mon cher Prince.
They play with us, they leave us in a condition which is neither
peace nor war ; and Belgium is on the brink of frightful anarchy.
This cannot be endured ; we must understand one another, and
come frankly to some arrangement, some combination which
suits them and gives them security, and then all will go well.
But for them, for us, and for everyone, this is more imperative
than I can tell you. Experience (if it is any use to some
people) must prove to them that too much time has already
been lost over a miserable, foolish hope in the Prince of Orange,
which, they ought to see clearly now, cannot be entertained and
must be absolutely rejected. . . .

I am sure that Madame Adelaide, in writing this letter, and
the King, in dictating it, were perfectly sincere in their
declarations; but what could I think on receiving from
Brussels, the same day and under the same date, the following
letter ?

M. BRESSON TO THE PRINCE DE TALLEYRAND.

BRUSSELS, *February 5th*, 1831.

MON PRINCE,

Forced to change our position, and to engage in a
contest which we wished to avoid, we could only do one thing :
it was necessary to gain the day, and we have gained it. Now
we have to think of the consequences of this success, which is
not yet established. An idea occurs to me, which, if it finds
favour with you, may bear fruit. The Prince of Orange may, in a
way, consider himself deprived of his possessions by us. If we
procure him some compensations, which will at the same time
conduce to the peace and equilibrium of Europe ; if he receives
them through our influence and friendly intervention, we shall
be doing at once an act of goodwill and good policy ; we shall
facilitate the solution of all the complicated questions which
will be the outcome of M. le Duc de Nemours' election, and we
shall allay more than one irritation which it will produce. The
Prince of Orange is the Emperor of Russia's brother-in-law ; [1]

---

[1] It will be remembered that the Prince of Orange had married the Grand-Duchess
Anne, sister of the Emperor Nicholas.

he is acceptable to England; he is good-tempered; his manners are charming; he possesses a chivalrous nature, and his frivolities and indiscretions, which, in this rigidly Catholic country, have got him into great trouble, may be looked upon elsewhere with a more indulgent eye. Poland asks for a king; she seems determined upon a long and bloody resistance. If the Emperor of Russia can, before the rupture, be brought to an agreement, he will yield in favour of the Prince of Orange more readily than of any other; and if, at our initiative and our insistence, such a termination is given to the Polish revolution, we shall have served at once the cause of a generous nation, drawn towards us all hostile or disquieted minds, recomposed the European system destroyed by the division of Poland, and strengthened the throne of M. le Duc de Nemours. With you, mon Prince, it would be idle to enter into the working out of this idea. I confine myself to placing it before you. But I send you this letter by express; it may prove a sedative best applied at the beginning.

I am already exerting myself, and shall continue to do so, to prevent the chiefs of the insurrection at Ghent from being put to death.[1]

The reign of our young and amiable prince would begin well with an act of clemency; we must keep it in reserve.

I cannot portray to you too strongly, the effect that a refusal, or only a conditional acceptance from his Majesty, would produce on the country. It would mean the instantaneous upsetting of everything; civil war, the French cockade, the Orange cockade, disorder, murder, and anarchy in all their fury. We cannot look back any more, mon Prince. A retrograde movement would be a thousand times more dangerous, than a firm decisive attitude.

The protest of our government against the protocol of January 27th, deprived me in a way, of my functions as commissioner of the Conference. I had communicated it to M. Van de Weyer, because I knew that it would procure us the dissentient voices of Limburg and Luxemburg; he showed it, and then allowed it to be taken from him, and it was read from the Tribune and printed.

There is a very delicate point, which, if the king accepts for M. le Duc de Nemours, entails another protest against the protocol of January 20th. Of our ninety-seven votes, twenty

---

[1] On the 2nd February, an Orangist movement had broken out at Bruges and at Ghent. Lieut.-Col Gregoire incited his regiment encamped at Bruges to revolt. At its head, he penetrated into Ghent and forced the Governor to proclaim the Prince of Orange. But he was at once attacked in the town, defeated, and arrested. The movement was not followed up.

belong to Luxemburg ; so if we recognize Luxemburg as Dutch, we invalidate the election. A tacit understanding goes further than one would think. But the Prince of Orange, *proposed* by *us alone* for Poland, would effectively settle many things. . . .

I do not know if the grand scheme of policy shown in this letter, originated solely in M. Bresson's brain, but the assurance with which he insists upon it, makes me suppose that he is supported in some quarter. Be that as it may, I did not even take the trouble to answer such absurdities. But let us continue the extracts from despatches.

THE PRINCE DE TALLEYRAND TO GENERAL SEBASTIANI.

LONDON, *February 6th*, 1831.

M. LE COMTE,

The English Cabinet Council is at this moment deliberating over a despatch which has just arrived from Lord Ponsonby, in which he announces that M. Bresson has caused a sort of declaration from the French government to be circulated in Brussels. This declaration, of which I am quite ignorant, contains, it is said, a positive assurance, that it will not acknowledge the last protocols of the London Conference.[1]

[1] It is necessary to show here the singularly delicate situation of M. Bresson at Brussels, at once a dependent of the Conference and of General Sebastiani, it was often very difficult for him to obey both the orders from London and from Paris. Thus, the French Cabinet had at first refused to recognize the protocols of 20th and 27th January, and the 7th February : the first, fixing the limits of Holland and Belgium ; the second, regulating certain commercial and financial questions resulting from the separation ; the third, confirming the resolution of King Louis Philippe already announced, to refuse the crown offered to the Duc de Nemours. M. de Talleyrand had signed these protocols, and had sent them to M. Bresson to be communicated to the Belgian government. But almost the same day, General Sebastiani, who had instituted a line of policy at Paris opposed to that of M. de Talleyrand, wrote to M. Bresson :

" PARIS, *February 1st.*
" SIR,
" If, as I hope, you have not yet communicated to the Belgian government the protocol of January 27th, you will object to this communication, because the government of the king has not adhered to its resolutions. In the question of liabilities, as in that of fixing the extent and limits of the Belgian and Dutch territories, we have always understood that the co-operation and free consent of both States was necessary. The London Conference is a mediator, and the intention of the government of the king, is, that it should not lose that character in any way.

" Receive, &c.
" HORACE SEBASTIANI."

M. Bresson communicated this letter to M. Van de Weyer, President of the Diplomatic Committee, who read it to the Congress on February 3rd. It is to this incident, which greatly astonished him, that M. de Talleyrand alludes in his letter of February 6th.

It has produced a most unfortunate effect here, as may be easily understood. In charging their plenipotentiaries in London, to provide for the difficulties brought about by the rising in Belgium, the five Powers have had in view the prevention of complications which would disturb the peace of Europe.

In accordance with the treaties between the Powers, Belgium was re-united to Holland in 1814; from the moment that this union was rendered impossible by the Belgian revolution, these same Powers were under the obligation of seeking the combinations most favourable to the maintenance of harmony between them, and which would offer the strongest guarantees for the interests of each. This has been the principle which directed the London Conference. A declaration, such as that which was said to have been made at Brussels, in the name of the French government, would necessarily attack that principle, and would prove that France was not one with the other Powers. We should consequently find ourselves separated from the policy of the rest of Europe.

People are astonished, and rightly so it seems to me, that the French Cabinet, if it wished to express its disapprobation of the last protocol of the Conference, did not address itself solely to this Conference, instead of to the Belgians, to whom the last protocol was not to be communicated. Such a proceeding, M. le Comte, I will not conceal from you, has excited most bitter complaints here, and has rendered my position extremely difficult. You must lose no time in preventing the calamitous consequences which may ensue therefrom, if you do not wish the unfavourable dispositions of several Powers respecting us, to develop.

My last despatch must have shown you, that there was never any question of adhesion or non-adhesion on your part, to a protocol containing only proposals. It will thus be easy to retrace this useless, or at least imprudent step.

I learnt this morning by a courier from M. Bresson, the result of the deliberations of the Congress at Brussels; I am convinced that the king will refuse, without any hesitation, the crown which is offered to M. le Duc de Nemours. You must clearly understand that all measures which lead to consultations with the Powers, will be regarded as dilatory, and that a decided and spontaneous refusal will alone secure England, whose alliance we are on the point of losing. Your despatches have authorised me to declare that there will be a refusal; I have done so, and I continue to hope that the assurances I have given, will be supported by the king and by you.

England will reject M. le Duc de Leuchtenburg, and will accept, without doubt, the choice of the Prince of Naples; but I repeat, it will be at the price of a prompt and decisive refusal on your part, to grant M. le Duc de Nemours to the Belgians.

You see, M. le Comte, it is a question of peace or immediate war. I frankly avow, that I do not consider Belgium sufficiently important, for us now to sacrifice peace for her.

I beg you to write me a letter, as promptly as possible, which I can show to the members of the Conference, and in which you can authorise me to declare, that the intention of the government of the king is not in any way to isolate itself from the other Powers. . . .

THE PRINCE DE TALLEYRAND TO GENERAL SEBASTIANI.

LONDON, *February 7th*, 1831.

M. LE COMTE,

The Cabinet Council, of which I had the honour to acquaint you yesterday, lasted more than three hours, and was occupied exclusively with the question of the Duc de Nemours' election. All the ministers agreed as to the necessity of immediate war, should this election be recognized by France. If I am properly informed, they have even resolved to carry out the war with great energy.

Such were the resolutions adopted by the English Cabinet, M. le Comte, when I received your despatch of the 4th at seven o'clock yesterday evening. Warned as I had been of the decisions of the Council, I lost no time in communicating to Lord Grey and Lord Palmerston, the assurances which your despatch contained; they were received with the most lively satisfaction by the ministers, as well as by those members of the diplomatic body to whom I have made them known. I tried to see as many people as possible during the evening, in order to destroy the effect of the morning's council. The loyalty which directed the actions of the French government has been generally recognized, and it is looked upon as the principal guarantee of the maintenance of peace.

It is my duty, however, to inform you of the effect produced by the election of the Duc de Nemours, and above all, the declaration which was to have been made in the name of France to Brussels, of her refusal to recognize our last protocol. These two facts have been considered, not only in the city and among mercantile men, but in the upper classes of society, as an imminent cause of war. All the ambassadors of the Great Powers have declared, that the decision of the English Cabinet on this point would serve to regulate the conduct to be pursued by their governments. To-day this language has totally changed, and the rumours of war have given way to protestations of peace and friendship.

I am able to judge from this event, M. le Comte, of the importance that our government has regained in Europe ; on it, evidently, peace or war henceforth depend, for Belgium counts for little. She commits too many foolish acts to inspire great interest. You will desire to retain the advantageous position which we now occupy, and I do not hesitate to repeat, that this can only be done by founding our policy on a close union with England. This union will guarantee us against any hostile dispositions that the other Powers may cherish ; it will give us time and means to strengthen our government, whereas by separating ourselves from her, we shall inevitably bring on a general war, the danger of which it is easy to comprehend. Even supposing we have great successes on the Continent, would they compensate for the ruin of our commerce and industries ? Will they prevent factions from disturbing the interior of France ?

The powerful armaments which England is in a position to bring forward, and of which I have already told you, will give you an idea of the results that a maritime war would have for us.

I am convinced, and I declare to you on my own responsibility, that we can obtain the union of which I have just spoken, by adopting a line of conduct, at once firm and prudent, such as would befit the dignity of the King of France. But it must be borne in mind, that the English Cabinet is never guided but by its own interests, and that it is only by treating these with respect (without, however, displaying a compliance that would compromise our own), that we can hope on our side for an intimate union. I have remarked, and with great pleasure, the passage in your last despatch, where you express the intention of not isolating our policy from that of the other Powers of Europe. I believe that this resolution will have the most happy results for us. We must ever remember, that there can be no Holy Alliance when France is a member of the Conference. That will answer any parliamentary questions.

I send you the protocol of our conference to-day, which the king, I hope, will peruse with pleasure.[1]

---

[1] This protocol declared, that the Powers would not, on any condition, recognize the Duc de Leuchtenburg as King of the Belgians.

THE PRINCE DE TALLEYRAND TO GENERAL SEBASTIANI.

LONDON, *February 8th*, 1831.

M. LE COMTE,

I had the honour to receive yesterday evening, a few minutes after the departure of M. le Comte de Flahaut, your despatch of the 5th instant. I judge from the contents, that your disquietude is renewed on the subject of Belgium. I am not surprised at it. The position in which the government is placed, must necessarily create fresh embarrassments each day. There is, I believe, an easy method of getting rid of these, but it must be employed in a prompt and firm manner.

The refusal in Paris of the crown of Belgium for M. le Duc de Nemours, and the assurance given in London that the Duc de Leuchtenburg would not be recognized by the Powers, places the king's government in a position to declare that, as it is in accord with the Conference on the necessity of regulating the affairs of Belgium in such a way as to reconcile the interests of all the Powers, it henceforth relegates to the Conference the task of arranging them.

In making such a declaration, you rid yourself of a question, of which it is beyond your power to make an end, without the joint action of the other Powers. If you attempt it, you will turn them against you, and you will bring about fresh difficulties. In my opinion, it is impossible for any one Power to take upon itself the sole charge of directing Belgium ; whereas the authority vested in the hands of the Conference gives some hope of success. This Conference may meander on the confines of intervention or non-intervention, without getting into difficulties thereby, and it will believe it has religiously fulfilled its duties, if it preserves the independence of Belgium, prevents her from troubling her neighbours, and, in addition, preserves the peace of Europe.

It seems to me, M. le Comte, that the king cannot[1] find any serious inconvenience in the step that I now advise ; it accords entirely with his dignity and his interests.

However, I must repeat that if this step is not taken, my presence here would be useless, both to the king and to the affairs of France. I have had to bear the brunt (most disagreeable for me) of the announcement made by M. Bresson at Brussels, because I was sure that, if I retired from the Conference, the other four plenipotentiaries would withdraw at once, and I did not wish to be the cause of an event which would

---

[1] Var. : *ne doit* = ought not.

have had such unfortunate results. But pray understand, that in future, it will be impossible for me to play any other *rôle* here, than that which belongs to the ambassador of the king.

THE PRINCE DE TALLEYRAND TO GENERAL SEBASTIANI.

LONDON, *February 9th*, 1831.

MONSIEUR LE COMTE,

I have the honour to send you herewith, a copy of the protocol of our yesterday's conference. We were obliged, as you will see on reading it, to ask for the fulfilment of the armistice, which continues to be violated by the Belgian troops round Maëstricht. The King of Holland having raised the blockade of the Scheldt, leaves the provisional government no pretext whatever for the evident violation of an undertaking given to the Powers. The terms of this undertaking are very positive. "The privilege will be accorded to both parties, of communicating freely by land and sea with the territories, fortresses, and positions respectively occupied by the troops outside the limits which separated Belgium from the United Provinces of the Netherlands, before the treaty of Paris, May 30th, 1814."

When there was a question of transmitting the instructions (of which you will find a copy herewith) to the commissioners at Brussels, M. Bresson was again taken into consideration as commissioner of the Conference ; it is partly out of regard for me that they have here shut their eyes to what has occurred at Brussels, but such a situation cannot continue. I request you, therefore, to send M. Bresson back here, where I can in a short time, let him take up the work he did before.

Our conferences will not be so continuous just now ; it will be well to suspend them, in order to give men's minds time to calm down. When the Belgians find only coolness both in Paris and London, it will perhaps be possible that the language of reason may make itself heard, and then will be the time for clever agents to put the choice of Prince Charles of Naples— whom you wish, and whom England will not oppose—into their heads. I think this time of relaxation will be useful in the interests of peace, which are, and will continue to be, my one aim here. . . .

LONDON, *February 10th*, 1831.

MONSIEUR LE COMTE,

You have requested me to express to the English government, the disquietude that may be caused by the measures

Lord Ponsonby continues to take at Brussels in favour of the Prince of Orange. I have had an interview on the subject with Lord Palmerston, to whom I stated our reasons for desiring to prevent efforts which could only result in civil war. Lord Palmerston quite understood me, and told me that orders would be sent to Lord Ponsonby, to discontinue in future from mixing himself up in the affairs of the Prince of Orange. . . .

I have this morning received your despatch of the 8th, in which you inform me, that his Majesty, with a view to prevent the vexatious scenes of trouble and disorder at Brussels, has decided to defer the official announcement of his refusal to the Belgian deputation, which has come to Paris to offer the crown of Belgium[1] to M. le Duc de Nemours. As this determination is entirely opposed to the declaration made by M. de Flahaut and myself to the English ministers, in order to obtain the exclusion of the Duc de Leuchtenberg, I have decided not to mention your despatch of this morning to Lord Palmerston. Whatever the reasons may be which have influenced the king's decision, any delay in the refusal will only give occasion here for suspicion, and I think we ought to avoid that above everything. Since the arrival of the Paris papers, I have received three letters this morning from members of the English Cabinet best disposed towards us, all evincing the desire that a firm and clear refusal by the French government should furnish a fresh proof of its loyalty, and put an end to all this uncertainty. . . .

THE PRINCE DE TALLEYRAND TO GENERAL SEBASTIANI.

LONDON, *February 12th*, 1831.

MONSIEUR LE COMTE,

I must thank you for your despatch of the 9th; it contains assurances from you and the king, which will contribute powerfully in restoring the confidence, which recent circumstances have withdrawn from us.

There is one point in your letter, however, which will not quite satisfy them here, and respecting which, I have need of precise explanation. You tell me, with regard to the imprudent (to say the very least) measures of M. Bresson at Brussels: " that it is possible the news of the protocol of January 27th

---

[1] This deputation was composed of ten members, Messrs. Surlet de Chokier, Felix de Mérode, d'Arschot, Gendebien, Lehon, de Brouckère, Marlet, the Abbé Bouqueau, Barthélemy, and de Rodes. The Deputies arrived at Paris February 6th. It was only the 17th that they were received officially, and that the king notified his refusal to them. (See the *Débats* of February 19th.)

may have got spread abroad in Brussels ; that it had produced a very bad effect, and that M. Bresson, in order to calm the suspicion and irritation, had been led to publish the non-adhesion of the French government to the stipulations of this protocol."

I understand, and perhaps I may succeed in making them understand here, the reasons that determined the course adopted by M. Bresson ; but it is absolutely necessary that you should declare to me in a letter for public use, that this step was only taken to get over a momentary difficulty, which has been successfully overcome by this means, and that you have never ceased to be, in all points, at one with the Conference. Some such declaration can alone reassure the English Cabinet and the members of the Conference ; it will also, besides, be in harmony with all that M. de Flahaut and I have said, and without laying stress on the personal interest that I have in it, I must tell you, that it is expected here [1] as a guarantee of their pledges. . . .

LONDON, *February* 13*th*, 1831.

MONSIEUR LE COMTE,

Yesterday evening, after the departure of the courier I sent to you, I received intelligence from Lord Palmerston of a letter written by Lord Ponsonby, in which he states that M. Bresson has refused to present protocol No. 15, of our conference of February 17th,[2] to the Diplomatic Committee of the Congress.

This new departure of M. Bresson's, places me in the greatest embarrassment. I have endeavoured to justify the publication of your letter at Brussels, up to a certain point, by considering it in the light of a measure of urgency ; but this excuse will not avail for refusing to present the protocol of the 29th February.

M. Bresson left London, entrusted with powers by the Conference ; it is in this capacity, that he has corresponded with us for the last two months, when all at once, without giving any warning to this Conference, he ceases his correspondence with it, and acts in direct opposition to its instructions. Such conduct must appear inexplicable even to the most unprejudiced mind.

---

[1] Var. : *par nos amis* = by our friends.

[2] This protocol contained a fresh affirmation on the part of M. de Talleyrand, made in the name of his government, that the king would not accept the crown offered to the Duc de Nemours. He added, with regard to the candidature of the Duc de Leuchtenberg, that this prince would not be recognized by any of the five Powers. By acting as he was doing, M. Bresson only obeyed the orders he had received from Paris.

Everyone here therefore declares, that it is quite evident M. Bresson could not, of his own accord, first protest against the protocol of January 27th, and then refuse to present that of February 7th. His conduct is attributed to orders received from the French government, and as such orders must be in direct opposition to the communications that you have instructed me to make here, distrust in the policy of our Cabinet is spread abroad; this, a new government ought above all to avoid.

The ignorance in which you have left me, as to the motives which have guided M. Bresson lately, has rendered my position here extremely difficult, for I seem to be either unaware of the intentions of the government of the king, or else in agreement with Paris or Brussels to mislead the Conference here. What I have just said, M. le Comte, does not result from personal susceptibility, but I have found positive disadvantage resulting therefrom to the French government, of which it was my duty to make you aware, and which you will doubtless be able to appreciate.

I require, I repeat, a frank and clear explanation of all that has passed between Paris and Brussels: it is only by having this explanation that I can regain with the English Cabinet, and the Conference, a position useful to the service of the king. You must also show, that no confusion is made between what is settled and what is proposed; as for instance, the protocol of January 20th and the protocol of the 27th.

That of the 20th, is based on the ancient division of Holland and Belgium, and map in hand, it cannot be contested. That of the 27th is open to discussion, but it was necessary to propose some basis, since having requested that the Belgian commissioners sent here, should be given power to act, they, on being asked, declared they had none. The matter would otherwise become interminable.

You cannot send M. Bresson back here too soon, for his prolonged residence at Brussels will only increase the uneasiness of all the Cabinets. . . .

M. BRESSON TO THE PRINCE DE TALLEYRAND.

BRUSSELS, *February 11th,* 1831.

MON PRINCE,

I received, the day before yesterday, and to-day, the letters which you did me the honour to write, dated the

7th and 9th inst., together with the documents that accompanied them.

You are so considerate, mon Prince, that you only permit the expression of your dissatisfaction to reach me in the form of an enigma. I cannot but be touched by conduct so replete with goodwill, and could I believe myself guilty, my regret would be increased a thousandfold.

But I confess that I never for a moment imagined that you in London, were not informed by the Foreign Office, as I was in Brussels, of the determination come to by the Ministry, not to adhere to the protocol of January 27th. In my haste to despatch to you the news of the election of M. le Duc de Nemours, I forgot to send you what was not a placard, posted up in the streets, but a document printed by the Congress.[1]

As for the communications and publications usual in such cases, it would be too much to make a diplomatic agent here responsible for them. The Belgian government has taken no measures at all with respect to the matter.

It would be most imprudent to confide to paper, details of all that pertains to the choice of a Head for the State. I will give them all to you verbally, when I have the honour of seeing you again ; and perhaps then (when above all, you know those connected with my journey to Paris) you will be more inclined to pity than to blame me.

How I regret that the protocol of the 7th inst. (that which rejected the Duc de Leuchtenberg) was not drawn up a month ago ! The crisis which is coming, and which I believe will be terrible, would probably then have been avoided.

This protocol, mon Prince, arrived the day before yesterday. Lord Ponsonby made it known, without even consulting me. M. Van de Weyer sent it back to him yesterday, under the pretext, that the Congress, having elected M. le Duc de Nemours, could receive no communication with regard to this election, except through the deputation now in Paris. In the newspaper sent herewith, you will find the debates in the Congress, to which this incident gave rise. I have just been assured that Lord Ponsonby will himself to-day, make the communication direct to the President of the Assembly. Seeing the extreme state of agitation in the country, I would, had I been consulted by him, most certainly have begged him to withhold this communication for

---

[1] That is to say, that the letter of General Sebastiani to M. Bresson of February 4th had not been placarded in the streets, as M. de Talleyrand had believed after the rumours which reached London, but had only been read to the Congress, and naturally printed in the account given of the sitting.

a few days, especially, as it arrived too greatly shorn of its most favourable points. The king, alone, can soften the effect of the refusal, and calm down the susceptibilities which it will arouse.

But, mon Prince, I was not given the choice. Here is a paragraph from Lord Ponsonby's notification : " I was given to understand, that the Conference had not deemed it advisable to engage you to co-operate with me in communicating this protocol ; it awaits the explanation or disavowal of the letter of February 1st, that is to say, the one from Count Sebastiani, which you communicated to the Congress."

From that moment, I considered myself suspended from my functions as commissioner of the Conference, until further explanation, and it is this explanation, mon Prince, that I to-day beg you will give me. Yesterday the instructions, dated February 8th, arrived safely, addressed to both Lord Ponsonby and myself. But I begged him to execute them by himself, until I had referred to the Conference that paragraph of his letter, which indicates a distinction made between him and me, and a species of interruption of confidence. Have the goodness to tell me, if it still considers me as invested with the same position and powers as Lord Ponsonby.

Your letter of the 9th, mon Prince, restores me to hope. To return to you, has been my sole ambition since I left you. Here, for having faithfully fulfilled the instructions of the Conference and of the king's government, I am openly made the subject of abuse by party men ; for three weeks past, a set of villains has publicly insulted me ; my life is menaced every day, by anonymous letters in the cafés and smoking-rooms. Sadness fills my heart ; my health is undermined. I have passed through most cruel trials, and shall probably only reap reproaches. It is so easy to sacrifice a poor devil !

The *poor devil* had not, however, so much to complain of as he feared. They would not send him back to me, lest he should give me too clear an explanation of what had passed between him and Paris ; but a few weeks later they gave him the post of Minister-plenipotentiary to Hanover, and a few months later he was sent to Berlin. I was very glad of this, as also of having been the author of this good fortune, by sending him from London to Brussels. I was besides informed, that the truth would in the end come to light at Paris ; the Duc de Dalberg wrote to me as follows :

THE DUC DE DALBERG TO THE PRINCE DE TALLEYRAND.

PARIS, *February* 12*th*, 1831.

MON PRINCE,

Your letter of the 8th, points out two truths with which my mind has been impressed for some time : one, that the five Powers alone when agreed, must dictate to the Belgians, swayed as they are by the turbulent passions of our Paris Jacobins ; the other, that these miserable intrigues are cropping up, because those who rule us, are disunited and incapable.

You have done well to put up with the indignities which have been heaped upon the London Conference and its proceedings. You will gain favour by it, because France does not want war, either to bring about the reunion of Belgium or, still less, the election of the Duc de Nemours.

If the combination in favour of the Prince of Naples succeeds, so much the better ; but I doubt it. The Belgian deputies do not relish it. What I gather from the utterances of the most capable of them is : 1st, that three-fourths of the country does not trouble itself about reunion with France ; 2nd, that with the exception of those who were inculpated in the revolution, all desire complete separation from Holland, though admitting the sovereignty of the House of Nassau, in order to resume the relations of commerce and industry, established between the two countries.

The Prince of Naples does not please them, because they say he does not remove any of the difficulties under which they labour, owing to the Custom duties which restrict and smother them.

Two days later, the Duc de Dalberg wrote to me again, directly after the scandalous events which took place at Paris : the pillage and burning of the archbishop's palace.[1] His letter is characteristic :

THE DUC DE DALBERG TO THE PRINCE DE TALLEYRAND.

PARIS, *February* 14*th*, 1831.

MON CHER PRINCE,

Our situation gets worse and worse. The scenes of yesterday, which the authorities ought to have foreseen and

[1] A riot had broken out in Paris, February 14th, on the occasion of the anniversary of the death of the Duc de Berry when a service had been held at Saint Germain l'Auxerrois. The populace went to the church and devastated it. The archiepiscopal palace shared the same fate.

prevented, were very serious. The Churches of St. Etienne-du-Mont and of St. Germain l'Auxerrois have been pillaged. The archbishop's palace is entirely stripped. The seminary of St. Sulpice was likewise attacked. Authority is ignored everywhere. The idiotic intrigues with respect to Belgium, have brought upon the king and his ministers discredit such as cannot be expressed. One risks being mixed up in the business even, to explain things, or to excuse them, on the plea of a father wishing to gain advantages for his country and his family. But public opinion, which has more sagacity than calmness, is profoundly irritated, and has only been momentarily duped by all this.

The War party in its frenzy, would compass its end at any price. As it sees that Belgium does not bring it about, Italy has been put in motion, and *Fayettisme* has laid hold of Modena and Bologna, where all was ready, and where the hot-bed of Italian societies[1] is to be found

My opinion is that the Austrians will interfere, and that it will be of no use stupidly to adhere to the principle of *non-intervention ;* we must bring the ordering of Italian affairs before a new Conference.

Above all, the five Great Powers must not be embroiled, so that war would result between them. I am not sure that it is possible to preserve the present state of things in Europe ; but if there is any salvation, it is decidedly only in what may result from a deliberate understanding between the great Cabinets.

If M. Sebastiani had believed me, he would not now be the laughing-stock of the diplomatic body and the Chambers ; he would have opposed with spirit the intrigues of the Palais Royal. He has acted in the Belgian business, as he did in that of Greece. Under such direction one does not know what will happen. The Belgians here, do not seem disposed to receive the Prince of Naples. They say that they do not want a prince who can only bring them macaroni and Capuchin monks. The intrigues of M. de Celles, from what I can hear, incline them rather to wait and see what will *turn up.* Hasten, then the decisions in London, and let them prove themselves to be more than mere words.

M. Sebastiani told a person from whom I have it :—" These conferences in London are conversations, nothing more." I am sure that he said it, and yet I am also sure that he does not

---

[1] The revolution broke out at Modena on February 3rd, the Duke was forced to fly, and a provisional government was established with a dictator and three consuls. On February 4th, the insurrection triumphed equally at Bologna ; the pontifical prolegate had to retire, and a provisional government was forthwith installed.

think it. But as Rigny[1] truly says, " He puts his finger in every pie." He sees both Chatelain[2] and Bertin de Vaux[3] every morning. All this is pitiable. Meanwhile the country is going to ruin. Lafitte declared to me, that he could not find a loan of ten millions at long date for the Treasury, and yet they talk of making war. Peace, mon cher Prince, or everything will go to the devil !

Pozzo said to me yesterday : " I warned Sebastiani, that England knew nothing of the intrigues at Brussels, and that Flahaut would weigh but one ounce in the scales of a negotiation. M. de Talleyrand, I will do him this justice, has been the only one who has looked at things as they ought to be looked at."

It seems that M. Sebastiani was not convinced by M. Pozzo's arguments, or was irritated at being found out in his own intrigues. He wrote to me, to complain of the manner in which the Conference was proceeding, and to forbid me to accept henceforth, any protocol except *ad referendum.*

THE PRINCE DE TALLEYRAND TO GENERAL SEBASTIANI.

LONDON, *February* 15*th*, 1831.

M. LE COMTE,

I this morning received your despatch of the 12th. I cannot too promptly reply to its contents.

It is easy to judge from your letter, that the direction followed by the Conference has not had the approbation of the

[1] Henry Gautier Comte de Rigny, born in 1782, entered the navy in 1798. He was a captain in 1816, rear-admiral in 1825, and vice-admiral after the battle of Navarino, where he commanded the French fleet. On the 13th of March, 1831, he was appointed Minister of Marine. In 1834 he took up foreign affairs. He quitted this post the next year, but kept the title of Cabinet Minister till his death (1835).

[2] Proprietor of the *Courrier Français*, the paper holding the most violent opinions in revolutionary opposition. (Note of M. de Bacourt.) René Théophile Chatelain, born in 1790, had served in the armies of the empire. He left the service in 1830, and became a journalist, was on the staff of the *Courrier Français* and the *National* for a long time, and died in 1838.

[3] Proprietor of the *Journal des Débats*, which supported the government. (Note of M. de Bacourt.)
Louis François Bertin de Vaux, born in 1766 ; began as far back as 1793, to oppose, in connection with journalism, the revolutionary parties in the *Journal Français, l'Éclair*, and the *Courrier Universel.* After the 18th brumaire, he founded he *Journal des Débats*, which was devoted at first exclusively to art and literature. Implicated in a royalist conspiracy, Bertin passed eight months at the Temple, and was then sent to Elba. Returning to Paris, after some time, he resumed the direction of his paper, but the government was not long in appropriating this public organ. A new manager, Fiévée, was imposed upon it and its name changed to *Journal de*

king's government, and that *under such circumstances*[1] I should
have done wrong to adopt its views.   I must therefore give you
some explanation on this subject.

When I left Paris in the month of September last, I was
given, a quarter of an hour before my departure, some general
instructions on questions which have not been applicable since
I have been here; they promised to send me detailed instructions
shortly; since that time however, I have begged in vain for them,
and have had to be guided, by the only injunction contained in
nearly all the despatches you did me the honour to send me,
namely, to maintain peace, consistent with preserving intact the
dignity of France.   It is from this point, M. le Comte, that I
have based all my intercourse with the Conference, and I believe
I have succeeded, though with some difficulty, in securing the
end the king had in view.   You do not share this opinion, and
you wish me henceforth only to act upon special instructions.
I shall submit to your orders, but I think I should fail in my
duty, if I did not bring to your notice, the serious inconveniences
which this method of conducting business will entail.   It will
deprive the Conference of a portion of the weight which it had
on public opinion, by placing each of its members in a state of
dependence, which will arrest all negotiation, and of this I can
give you an example : the protocol of the neutrality of Belgium
was signed after a conference which lasted ten and a half hours,
two days later, the Prussian plenipotentiary would probably
not have signed it.

This leads me to tell you, that in the question of boundaries,
there has been no more intervention, than there has been in that
of the recognition[2] of Belgium, which resulted in the determination of her boundaries.

The boundaries are a fact, and this fact is an old one—the
Conference had only to declare it.   Geography tells us what
was Belgium and what was Holland, before their union.   Nothing
has been changed as to the territory of the two countries ; even
the question of the enclosed lands has not been decided.   All
the members of the Conference say, that it would only be with
the idea of taking away some of its own territory from one of

---

l'Empire.   In spite of this, the *Journal de l'Empire* was seized in 1811, and the
copyright confiscated, by the State.   M. Bertin only recovered it in 1814.   In 1815,
he followed the king to Ghent, where he edited the *Moniteur de Gand.*   Under the
Restoration, Bertin joined the moderate opposition.   In 1830, he energetically adopted
the new monarchy.   The *Journal des Débats* was at this period the first organ of the
Monarchical party, and it remained so during the continuance of the government of
July.   Bertin died in 1841.

[1] Suppressed in the text of the Archives.
[2] Var. : *De l'indépendance* = of the independence.

the two countries, that the basis which has been adopted could be objected to,[1] and that such a change would be a real intervention. It is therefore plain, that in the protocol of January 20th, the Conference has not deviated in any way, and has not wished to deviate, from the principle of non-intervention.[2]

I am very glad to be able to show you once more, that the Conference has not departed from the principle of non-intervention, with regard to the two points which seem to have chiefly attracted your attention.

The English government, which ever since Canning's time is very susceptible on this score, established the same doctrine, and would not have consented, any more than ourselves, to deviate from it. Lord Palmerston supports it now in the English Parliament, in the same words I use to you.

Besides, I ought to tell you, that if, in my own opinion, war became imminent, by the refusal of my signature to a protocol proposed by the members of the Conference and one which would not affect the *individual*[3] interests of France, I feel it would be my duty, according to my original general instructions, to sign it. To-morrow, I will answer what you have written to me, relative to Lord Ponsonby and M. de Krüdener. . . .[4]

LONDON, *February* 16*th*, 1831.

MONSIEUR LE COMTE,

I have, according to the orders of the government, spoken to Lord Palmerston about the recall of Lord Ponsonby. I believe it would have been easy to obtain it before the publication of your letter by M. Bresson, and the refusal of the latter to execute the orders of the Conference ; but now it would put Lord Ponsonby and M. Bresson on the same level with regard to the Conference, and the English Cabinet is not disposed to consent to it.

---

[1] Var. : *attaquerait* = would attack.
[2] Var. : quant à la question des dettes on a fait seulement des propositions d'après lesquelles on demande à être conduit dans une route juste et équitable = as to the question of the debts, only a proposal has been made, according to which it is desired to act in a fair and equitable manner.
[3] Suppressed in the text of the Archives.
[4] General Sebastiani had announced to M. de Talleyrand, that M. de Krüdener, sent by the Prince de Lieven, had openly proposed the Prince of Orange at Brussels, and that Lord Ponsonby supported him energetically. M. de Krüdener was an old Russian diplomat. He was at Brussels without any official mission, and was the active agent of the Prince of Orange, whose interests were supported by Russia. He proposed to have him excepted from the exclusion pronounced upon his family. M. de Krüdener was expelled by order of the Congress. (See Juste : Congress of Brussels.)

I have already written to you, that Lord Palmerston has transmitted orders to Lord Ponsonby, to continue to watch the tendency of opinions without meddling in any way with the interests of the Prince of Orange. Lord Palmerston has, besides, never disguised that the combination that would place this prince on the Belgian throne, had always seemed to his government, the one most suited to the prompt termination of the affairs of Belgium, of which England, equally with us, desires to see the settlement ; but he no longer believes in his success.

I also spoke to the Prince de Lieven, both yesterday and this morning, on the subject of the intrigues that are attributed to M. de Krüdener at Brussels. He replied that M. de Krüdener was in London on leave ; that he had a great wish to learn from him the state of things in Belgium and that he had desired him to give him an account of it. He assured me positively, that he had given him no order relative to the affairs of the Prince of Orange, and that he ought to limit himself to instructing his Court, as to what he could gather respecting the chances that the prince would have in the country. The active party of the intrigue, favourable to the Prince of Orange, is headed by the inhabitants of the two Flanders, of whom several are to be found at this moment in London, working in his interests. M. de Krüdener would be little suited to fulfil a mission entirely of intrigue, for you know he is almost completely deaf. You will remember, that by protocol No. 15, which I beg you to reperuse, the provisional government was invited to stop the troops then approaching Maëstricht, and to retire them, as had been arranged, within the limits of the armistice. The answer is so long in coming, and the Dutch are so disquieted at the state of provisions in Maëstricht, that if it does not arrive to-morrow, we shall be obliged, in common justice, to allow the King of Holland to re-establish communications with that town. He had previously, on receipt of the protocol, stopped the march of his troops. We shall meet to-morrow with this object.

I send you the _Times_ of to-day ; you will there find Lord Palmerston's first speech since he has been Minister of Foreign Affairs ; you should read it attentively, because it is remarkable for the assurance with which he answered the different questions which were put to him.[1]

You will also find in the same paper an article which contains the opinion of the whole of England, as to the limits within which the members of Parliament who question the

[1] Sitting of the House of Commons, February 15th. Vivian put a question to Lord Palmerston on Belgian affairs, and complained particularly of the concentration of French troops in the _Département du Nord._

ministers, and the ministers who answer them, must keep. This article seems to me worth studying. . . .

My memory recalls the fact, that M. Sebastiani never answered these two last despatches. I continue to give mine, which follow.

LONDON, *February* 17*th*, 1831.

MONSIEUR LE COMTE,

I am able to acquaint you with the views of the English Cabinet and the members of the Conference, on the choice of the Prince of Naples as sovereign of Belgium. The English ministers, in spite of their predilection for the Prince of Orange, which they have never concealed from me, will not offer any obstacle to the choice of the Prince of Naples, but we must not count on their concurrence to facilitate it.

The Austrian plenipotentiary has expressed to me, his desire to see this arrangement succeed ; when I asked him if there was an Austrian agent at Brussels, he added that there was not, but if there was one, he would certainly not make any difficulty in seconding the interests of the Prince of Naples.

The Prussian minister has no instructions on this point ; but I have received from him an assurance, that his sovereign would only look with pleasure on anything that would tend to re-establish order in Belgium, and put an end to difficulties, the consequences of which he dreads for the neighbouring countries.

As for Prince Lieven, although we are on the best of terms, he is not obliged to communicate his opinion upon a choice which does not enter into the views of his court. But Prince Esterhazy told me, that if we were all agreed about the Prince of Naples, he was convinced that Russia would later on, be brought to recognize him, and in this I agree with him.

You can judge from this, the state of opinion on this question. It remains for the king's government to decide what it will do, and to employ all its efforts at Brussels to secure success. If it does not find support from all the Powers, it will at least meet with no opposition on their part ; of this I am sure.

I ought to tell you that in all the conversations which I have had on this subject, nothing but pacific intentions have been expressed. The English ministers and all the plenipotentiaries have assured me, that the earnest desire of their governments is to maintain peace, and that only some aggression on the part of France would furnish ground for war.

I have just come from a conference at which the protocol, which I announced to you yesterday,[1] has been drawn up. One would lose oneself in a crowd of difficulties, if one did not adhere to the previous arrangements agreed to between the Conference, Belgium, and Holland. This protocol is only addressed to Lord Ponsonby, because M. Bresson refused to present the last one, and the Conference no longer looks upon him as its representative in Belgium. From the tendency of opinion, I advise you strongly, if your intention was to send him back here, to delay his return. . . .

LONDON, *February 19th*, 1831.

MONSIEUR LE COMTE,[2]

I have the honour to transmit to you, protocol No. 18 of our conference yesterday. You will find in it, the adherence of the King of Holland to the protocols of January 20th and 27th. This adherence is complete and entire, but it was only obtained with difficulty ; the resolutions, with which he was menaced by the Conference, decided him to yield.

An English schooner, unloading at Poole, brings the news that when she left Lisbon they were fighting in the streets ; the insurrection was very formidable, and the prisons had been broken open.

Dom Miguel had placed himself at the head of the troops. . . .[3]

THE DUC DE DALBERG TO THE PRINCE DE TALLEYRAND.

PARIS, *February 21st*, 1831.

MON CHER PRINCE,

If you are asked where France will have got to six months hence, say boldly that you cannot possibly tell. The king sides with the minority as Bonaparte did, as also did Louis XVIII. and Charles X., and it seems to me, that M. Lafitte is a M. de Polignac with the Jacobins, as M. de Polignac was the blind instrument of the *émigrés.*

All parties are working to bring about the dissolution of the present session, and it can no longer be averted. It was said

---

[1] Var. : Et que je vous envoie = and which I send you.

[2] This letter is not found in M. Pallain's collection.

[3] On February 7th, the government of Dom Miguel had given orders to expedite the trial of the political prisoners. A decree of February 9th created military commissions to this end, furnished with extraordinary powers. This conduct provoked an insurrectionary movement in favour of Donna Maria. Its suppression was prompt and sanguinary. Two Frenchmen were arrested and sent to Africa.

yesterday that the quarrel between the Minister Montalivet [1] and the Prefect of the Seine, M. Odilon Barrot, [2] would end in the retirement of the former. M. d'Argout was to replace him, and Rigny was destined for the navy. With the men who govern us at present, one could amuse oneself by repeating a thousand such combinations without hitting the right one. Facts alone tell. All minds are gloomy with various apprehensions. If we are lucky enough to preserve peace, we may perhaps extricate ourselves from this home crisis, and find ourselves in smooth water once more; but all that is in great uncertainty. . . .

PRINCE DE TALLEYRAND TO GENERAL SEBASTIANI.

LONDON, *February 23rd*, 1831.

MONSIEUR LE COMTE,

The events which took place in Paris last week, caused a disquietude in London difficult to describe. The total absence of news from France during the 19th, 20th, and 21st, was a splendid opportunity for the speculators, who spread the most alarming reports, and attained their ends by producing a considerable depreciation in the public funds. Since the revolution of the month of July there has not been such agitation " On 'Change," and among all classes of society ; the idea of war is believed in to such an extent, as to raise insurance policies to a very high premium. I think I have used the most suitable language under the circumstances, but the ignorance in which I remain, as to what is taking place in Paris, makes my position here extremely difficult. My house is never free from people coming for news.

I yesterday received your despatch of the 19th, and I regret

---

[1] Comte Bachasson de Montalivet, born 1801, entered (1823, by heredity) the Chamber of Peers. In 1830, he became Minister of the Interior (November 2nd), then Minister of Education and Religion (March 13th, 1831), and again Minister of the Interior after the death of Casimir Perrier in 1832. He retired October 10th, 1832, became Intendant-General of the Civil List, and was twice again Minister of the Interior in 1836 and 1837. He retired into private life in 1848. In 1879 he was made a permanent Senator, and died the following year.

[2] Odilon Barrot, born in 1791, son of the member of the National Convention of that name, was, during the Restoration, an advocate in the Court of Appeal. In 1830, he was Secretary to the Municipal Commission, and was, as such, one of the commissioners charged to escort Charles X. He then became Deputy and Prefect of the Seine, after the riot of February 14th, against which he could not, or would not, act in any way. He was publicly censured by M. de Montalivet, then Minister of the Interior, and dismissed a few days after. He kept his seat in the Chamber till 1852. In February 1848, he was charged by the king to form a Cabinet with M. Thiers, but he did not succeed in it. In the month of December, he entered the first Cabinet of the Prince-President. He withdrew from public life in 1852. In 1872, he became Vice-President of the Council of State, and died the next year.

not to have had it sooner. According to the orders that it contains, I should not perhaps have admitted, excepting *ad referendum*, the protocol which I have the honour to send you to-day,
and the rough draft of which I agreed to on the 19th. If,
conformably to your letter of the 19th, which I only received
on the 22nd, I had refused to sign it, I should have put myself in
opposition to what you have written to me several times, viz.,
that you wished to be in accord with the Conference. Besides
you will certainly notice on reading it, that the Conference only
wanted to make clear the motives which have guided it since it
has assembled ; the spirit of justice and the moderation which
have directed all its deliberations, are again referred to, so as to
show that it has never passed the limits which were imposed on
it, both by the law of nations and by respect for treaties. The
protocol really contains nothing, which was not in the preceding
protocols.[1]

I do not think that there will be any need for the Conference
to reassemble here for some time ; but whatever may be the aim
in future of its meetings, or the result of its resolutions, I will
not affix my signature to a single essential act, before receiving
the king's authority, as you enjoin upon me in your despatch
of the 19th.

I have acquainted the Conference, and particularly the
English ministers, with your desire to see Lord Ponsonby
recalled from Brussels at the same time as M. Bresson, as they
are no longer placed on the same footing. I was told that a
parallel could not be established between these two agents ;
that Lord Ponsonby, as commissioner of the Conference, had
never refused to execute the orders which he had received,

---

[1] The protocol of February 19th, is only a lengthy declaration of the principles on
which the Conference determined to intervene in Belgium. It declares that treaties do
not lose their power, whatever changes may supervene in the interior organization of
nations ; that the spirit of the treaty of 1814 had in particular, survived the dislocation
of the kingdom of the Netherlands, and that it pertained to the Powers to take into
consideration the re-establishment of equilibrium in Europe ; that the tranquillity
and serenity of the European community limited the rights of each State ; that the
Powers have the right, and that it is their duty, to prevent all source of conflict
which could degenerate into an actual war. In consequence of these principles the
Conference decides : —

    1. That the arrangements agreed to in the protocol of January 20th, were funda-
mental and irrevocable :

    2. That the independence of Belgium will only be recognized according to the
conditions of the said protocol ;

    3. That the principle of the neutrality of Belgium was obligatory on the five
Powers ;

    4. That the five Powers assure to themselves the full right of declaring, that the
sovereign of Belgium must be answerable, by his personal position, for the existence
of Belgium, must give assurance of safety to the other States, accept the protocol of
the 20th January, and be able to secure free enjoyment of it to the Belgians.

while M. Bresson, also one of the commissioners of the Conference, has refused to present the protocols he was charged to communicate. I have several times tried to show how perfectly useless, nay, even injurious, Lord Ponsonby's presence was in Brussels, but his family connections and his position here, render the success of my efforts very difficult ;[1] all the more so, because Lord Palmerston, holding a despatch of Lord Granville's[2] in his hand, said to me, " The French government is beginning to do justice to Lord Ponsonby, and no longer imagines that all his measures are taken in opposition to whatever France desires."

However,[3] no one here has any belief in the chances of the Prince of Orange. . . . .

THE PRINCE DE TALLEYRAND TO MADAME ADELAIDE.

LONDON, *February* 23*rd*, 1831.

. . . . Mademoiselle will not find a single fresh resolution in the protocol I am sending to Paris to-day ; it only contains the *résumé* of what has been done up to now, and the announcement of the conservative and fundamental principles for which we have striven. I flatter myself, that the king will be satisfied with the spirit that directed our work. I feel assured that it is only by keeping strictly to the principles which have guided the members of the Conference, that we shall be able not only to settle Belgian affairs, but also to prevent ancient Europe from crumbling to ruins, and engulfing thrones, kings, institutions, and liberties in its fall.

I will not weary Mademoiselle with the sad thoughts that have for the last few days preoccupied me. I do not intend to give way to any discouragement, and in whatever colours the state of France may be painted to the outside world, I have full confidence that the king's wisdom will enable the sacred cause of liberty to triumph, freed from all the blots with which others seek to sully it.

I believe that the king, by keeping allied as I hear he wishes to do, with the four Powers, may be quite at ease about Belgian

---

[1] Lord Ponsonby was Lord Grey's brother-in-law.

[2] Thomas Leveson Gower, Earl Granville, born in 1773, entered the House of Commons at the age of 22, became a Lord of the Treasury in 1800, Chancellor of the Exchequer in 1802, and Ambassador at St. Petersburg in 1804. In 1815, he took his seat in the House of Lords. He was nominated Minister at the Hague, and went thence to Paris, which he did not quit until 1828. He was sent there again in 1831 until 1834, and also from 1835 to 1841. He died in 1846.

[3] Var. : *en général* = generally speaking.

matters, with which it is best to meddle as little as possible ; if anything unpleasant has to be dealt with, it must be referred to the Conference.

THE PRINCE DE TALLEYRAND TO GENERAL SEBASTIANI.

LONDON, *February 24th,* 1831.

MONSIEUR LE COMTE,

I must tell you of the effect produced here, by the king's speech in reply to the Belgian deputation. It has made a most favourable impression, and this morning, at the grand reception at Court, in honour of the Queen's birthday, several persons spoke to me about it, all loud in its praises.

But people at this reception were also much concerned by the news from Paris, which had caused extraordinary anxiety. I do not exaggerate when I tell you, that had I kept aloof from the four Powers[1] and refused to sign the protocol of the 19th, people here would have believed a war imminent, the funds would at once have fallen three or four per cent.,[2] and, those in Paris would have also been strongly affected in like manner.

You will have noticed, that in the protocol of the 19th, only the treaty of 1814 is mentioned, which treaty had been as fortunate, as circumstances permitted, for our country ; for our enemies cleared out of French territory at the end of six weeks ; ancient France had become greatly enlarged, her borders were altered to her own advantage, and by the possession of a large part of Savoy, Lyons was not as it is now, almost a frontier fortress ; the *Musée Napoléon* remained intact, and the archives of France were enriched by those of Venice and Rome. No reference has been made to the treaty of 1815, with which I had nothing to do, for I sent in my resignation to escape signing it, though I must nevertheless admit, that it was followed by fifteen years of peace.

In your letters to me of the 9th and 17th of this month, you said that we must go with the Powers ; this is more necessary than ever now. I do not know what may be the outcome of the present European crisis, but it is essential for us to be in accord, as long as possible, with the four Powers. Such a union is fruitful in resources, and there ought to be no difficulty in gaining support for it in the Chambers. . . .

I was not quite correct when I wrote, that every one had approved the speech made by King Louis Philippe to the

---

[1] Var. : Cinq = Five.
[2] Var. : Quatre à cinq pour cent = 4 to 5 per cent.

Belgian deputation, when refusing the crown for the Duc de
Nemours, which they had come to offer him. I have found a
note written to me by Lord Grey (the Prime Minister) on the
occasion of this speech, which, when read between the lines
exhibits a distrust that only the facts themselves disproved
later on :—

LORD GREY TO THE PRINCE DE TALLEYRAND.

DOWNING STREET, *February* 19*th*, 1831.

DEAR PRINCE TALLEYRAND,

Accept my best thanks for sending me the answer of
your king to the Belgian deputies. I think it will probably be
criticized, as indicating, under the expression of regret, too
much desire for the crown which is refused ; but, looking at the
substance, I am quite satisfied with it.

I will only add my sincere and earnest wish, that nothing
may arise to disappoint our endeavours to procure peace.

I am, . . .
GREY.

THE PRINCE DE TALLEYRAND TO GENERAL SEBASTIANI.

LONDON, *February* 25*th*, 1831.

MONSIEUR LE COMTE,

The birthday of H.M. the Queen was celebrated yesterday in London by all classes of the nation, with the greatest
possible enthusiasm. Fêtes, brilliant illuminations, the joyous
shouts of the populace, all testified to the attachment felt for
the sovereign, and refute the slanderous publications of some of
the journalists.

The sittings of Parliament become more interesting each
day. The Ministry have met with some opposition, in the
discussion on the budget. The hesitation they have shown in
some of their measures, has emboldened the Opposition and
discouraged their own party.

In a few days the Parliamentary Reform Bill will be brought
in ; it ought to strengthen the government, but as it probably
will not satisfy all the demands of the Reform party, it will
offer as good a pretext for opposition to those who want complete reform, as to those who do not want any. It is just
possible, that when it comes to voting, these two parties may

coalesce, and if so, the position of the English Cabinet must suffer.

The state of the Continent is alarming every one ; the troubles in Paris, the attacks on the clergy, the revolution in Italy,[1] the disturbances in Germany, all give grave cause for reflection. They have had an immense influence on all commercial transactions, which are almost completely suspended just now.[2]

All those who take part in public affairs, believe that it is only by maintaining the alliance of the Great Powers, that the rapid progress of disorder everywhere can be arrested. I will cite Sir James Mackintosh's opinion,[3] which is quite above suspicion in this question. This distinguished man, whose career has been in complete opposition to the various Continental governments, is of opinion, that only the solid union of the five Great Powers can restore tranquillity to Europe. It is only thus, he says, that we can hope to overcome the dangers of despotism, of anarchy, and, later on, of martial governments, which a war of principles would inevitably bring upon the world. . . .

LONDON, *February 25th*, 1831.

MONSIEUR LE COMTE,

This morning I was summoned to the Foreign Office, together with the other members of the Conference, to hear a despatch from Lord Ponsonby, which states that the siege of Maëstrich continues, and that all communication with that place, as well as Northern Brabant and Aix-la-Chapelle, has been completely interrupted.

After reading this despatch, it was suggested to draw up a protocol, announcing the intention of at once taking rigorous measures against the Belgians, in accordance with protocol No. 10 of the 18th January, in order to put down this fresh breach of the armistice. In accordance with the orders I had received from you, I said that I must first refer to my Court before signing anything on so serious a matter. It was then decided that Lord Palmerston should send off a courier to Lord Granville, and that the latter should be directed to make known to you the views of

---

[1] The insurrections in Modena, Parma, and Romagna.

[2] Var. : Les polices d'assurances augmentent chaque jour = the insurance policies increase every day.

[3] Sir James Mackintosh, born in 1765, was an orator and a political writer. He entered the House of Commons in 1802, and was appointed Judge at Bombay. On his return to England, he re-entered Parliament, and became one of the most influential orators of the Whig party. In 1803, he formed part of the Whig Cabinet as commissioner for India. He died in 1832. Sir James was an eminent lawyer, and his name was equally well known in literature and philosophy.

the plenipotentiaries, and to ask what course you would suggest, to procure the fulfilment of an act which had been agreed to by the Belgian Government itself. Lord Granville must remind you, that you approved[1] of the cessation of hostilities between the Dutch and the Belgians, and the conditions thereby guaranteed, and that now the aim of the Conference is to insist on the strict execution of a Convention, agreed to by all parties.

The communication that will be made to you on this subject will, I feel sure, be done with all the deference you could possibly desire, for great stress is laid on acting in accord with you in all things, for the sake of the tranquillity of Europe, which is trembling in the balance. . . .

LONDON, *February* 27*th*, 1831.

MONSIEUR LE COMTE,

You wished me to have an explanation with M. le Prince de Lieven as to M. de Krüdener's journey to Brussels, and the steps he may have taken to favour the cause of the Prince of Orange in that city. I have had this explanation, as I have already had the honour of informing you, and the result is that the Prince de Lieven has recalled M. de Krüdener, who is now in London. I may further add, that as far as this matter is concerned, all attempts or even hopes here, regarding the Prince of Orange, have been completely given up.

A report has got abroad, that M. le Duc de Mortemart's mission to St. Petersburg has been unsuccessful.[2] This piece of news has arrived here by letter from Frankfort, and I am glad to think that no more credence need be given to this, than to the report which will probably reach you, that they say in Russia, the Russian plenipotentiaries in London only agreed to the last protocols *ad referendum*. You will have had no difficulty in discrediting this report, which is utterly without foundation : the signatures to all the protocols by Prince de Lieven and Count Matusiewicz, have been perfectly regular and complete, and, I think, most useful to us.

The nomination of Baron Surlet de Chokier as Regent of Belgium, was made known here yesterday morning.[3] If, as is

[1] Var. : admis = allowed.
[2] It will be remembered, that the Duc de Mortemart had been sent as Ambassador extraordinary, with a view to negotiate closer relations between the two countries.
[3] After the vote of the Belgian constitution and the refusal of the crown by the Duc de Nemours, the Congress decreed that a Regency should be established to govern the kingdom, until the nation had come to an understanding with the five Powers as to the choice of a sovereign (February 1823). The following day M. Surlet de Chokier was elected Regent by the Congress, by 108 votes, against 43 for M. Mérode and 5 for M. Gerlache.

reported, the king has accredited General Belliard[1] to Brussels, it seems to me that there is nothing further to prevent M. Bresson's, return to London after a few weeks' stay in Paris. I will undertake to give him his old place here, and I think that his remaining in England may further his career.

I regret you did not receive protocol No. 19, soon enough to enable you to make use of some of the facts and arguments it contains; it would have shown how far the attacks to which you had to reply in the sitting of. . . . were without foundation. . . .[2]

THE DUC DE DALBERG TO THE PRINCE DE TALLEYRAND.

PARIS, *February 27th*, 1831.

MON CHER PRINCE,

The position of matters grows worse each day. No payment can be got anywhere. France has never witnessed such a state of affairs since the time of the Directorate. There is no authority anywhere, and intrigue flourishes everywhere.

You are perfectly right in saying, that the London Conference is the only power in Europe that has any strength, and that it must be maintained at any price. But how can it influence our position at home? The Ministry, by its complete incapacity and its inclination to lean on the extreme Left, has placed itself in such a position with the Chamber, that I do not see any possibility of patching up a peace between the two parties. And how can the government escape getting into difficulties, when for three months it has been without the support of the Chambers?

The late events[3] clearly prove that there was an attempt at a Carlist conspiracy, got up by the Buonapartist-Republican party.

---

[1] General Comte Belliard, born in 1769, entered the army in 1792, took part in all the campaigns of the Revolution and the Empire. Made a General in 1791, he became General Commandant of the Cavalry of the Guard in 1814. Louis XVIII. made him a Peer of France and a Major-General. He took service during the Hundred Days, and lived in retirement during the second Restoration. In 1831, he was sent as Minister Plenipotentiary to Brussels. He died soon after on the 28th January, 1832.

[2] At the sitting of 23rd February, General Sebastiani had made a communication on foreign policy to the Chamber, and explained the king's motive for refusing the crown to the Duc de Nemours. General Lamarque and M. Mauguin had risen, and expressed themselves with great vehemence against the conduct of the Cabinet in this matter. "I cannot but grieve," the former had concluded, "at the refusal of the Belgian throne. I can but mourn at the undecided measures, the hesitations, the contradictions, which, when brought to the light of day, have shown our diplomacy in a state of nudity it has no reason to be proud of."

[3] The riots at Paris on the 14th and 15th of February.

This latter possesses all the energy, and will certainly gain the day, if the king does not think and act in such a way as to regain the people's confidence and respect. What is happening in Belgium, only helps to strengthen this party, and if to-morrow La Fayette wished to become President of a Regency for France, he would be summoned at once, and dismissed twenty-four hours after.

Your correspondence with the king and the Ministry, must have made you aware of what is needed. As for me and my friends, we constantly ask ourselves, whence will come the thunder-clap which shall overthrow the miserable edifice we have in front of us?—A sovereign who cannot make himself obeyed; a Chamber of Peers without any foundation, even in law; a Chamber of Deputies which is perpetually insulted, and which one would like to get rid of; a National guard becoming more and more disgusted, and which is not allowed to strike when needed; and a regular army which does not know whom it is to obey. That is our position at present. Try to find and point out some remedy for such a state of anarchy.

As for foreign affairs, we see nothing but underhand dealings to stir up the nations, and no unanimity, no force to stop them, or to re-establish order. After the treaty of Westphalia, an executive army was constituted to see that the decisions come to were respected. We shall have to resort to that yet, but first of all it must be understood, upon what footing the nations will be allowed to establish themselves.

It seems to me that we shall be obliged to return to military law, after a long series of anarchist agitations.

My family left Geneva on the 18th of this month. At that time everything was still quiet; but although here we knew that a body of insurgents had been formed at Lyons for the purpose of invading Savoy, no measures were taken to stop them, until after they had started.[1] And then people are surprised that Europe should seek security, by arming herself and contending against revolution! . . .

Your supposed chief Sebastiani, according to Rigny and Rayneval,[2] puts his finger in every pie. The editor Chatelain

---

[1] In consequence of the disturbances that had broken out in Savoy, the Sardinian refugees, who were in great numbers on the French frontier, tried, by a *coup-de-main*, to re-enter their country armed. Five or six hundred of them, accompanied by a certain number of the National Guard of Lyons, attempted to put this project into execution. They were dispersed by a squadron of cavalry on the 25th of February, and the incident had no further results.

[2] François Maximilien Gerard, Comte de Rayneval, born in 1778, was successively secretary to the Embassies of Stockholm, St. Petersburg, and Lisbon. Then again to St. Petersburg, and secretary to the French Legation at the Congress of Chatillon, Consul-General in London, 1814; Privy Seal to the Ministry, 1816; and

and Bertin de Vaux, breakfast with him every morning. The former has to-day made a regular onslaught on you.[1] The fact is we cannot do what we want. . . .

Were we to go to war, as good old Jourdan[2] says, it would only be by the aid of a Convention. Let the king look to this !

Accept my congratulations, that you are not living in the turmoil by which I am surrounded. . . .

Such a state of affairs as is here described by the Duc de Dalberg, could not continue long, and the king who had not been sorry I think, to let the men and the principles of which M. Lafitte was the representative, exhaust themselves, found himself obliged to consider the best means of escape from this state of anarchy. The Ministry had to be dismissed, or at least some of its members, and an energetic man, who fortunately was ready at hand, chosen from among the Conservative party in the Chamber of Deputies : this was M. Casimir Périer.[3]

Under-Secretary of State in 1821. He was then sent as Minister to Berlin, to Berne, and to Vienna, 1829. Recalled in 1830, he lived in retirement in Paris, until Casimir Périer, on M. de Talleyrand's recommendation, sent him to Madrid. He died there soon after in October 1832.

[1] See the *Courrier Français*, 28th February. We will give some extracts from this article, showing the opinion of the Republican opposition, against which the French Cabinet and M. de Talleyrand had to contend. " A letter of the 24th from London, which we saw yesterday, spoke of a protocol which had just been signed, and which will completely upset all the principles which have hitherto apparently directed our policy. It can hardly be conceived that a diplomatic body, whose acts will be known to the whole of Europe, should dare to state, that the treaties of 1815 were made between nation and nation, at the very time that these nations, penned, quartered, split up, and treated like brute beasts, rose up, over half Europe, against from a situation repugnant alike to their feelings and their interests. But M. de Talleyrand is there, and his presence renders it probable, that everything will be done to uphold the treaties in which he took part. It is certain that the policy of Europe and the policy of France, is decided in London, contrary to our interests, since it is M. de Talleyrand who there presides. If anything like what the *Temps* announces has been signed in London, the Ministry has nothing further to do than to recall its ambassador, and exercise the liberty still permitted us, at the cost of a general war. We shall then, at any rate, have the advantage of no longer being represented by M. de Talleyrand ; and also of regaining our independence. Diplomacy seems too much inclined to forget what France is ; that what she has done, she can do again, and that she can whenever she likes, again influence the destinies of Europe. It only needs one word for her to remember the past. If upheavals are desired, so be it ; the signal need only be given, and before a year is over it will be seen who remains standing."

[2] Marshal Jourdan, then sixty-nine years of age, had during the first days of the Monarchy in July, temporarily acted as Minister of Foreign Affairs. However, he retired on the 11th August, when he was made Governor of the "Invalides." He died November 23rd, 1833.

Casimir Périer, born at Grenoble in 1777, was at first an officer of engineers. After quitting the service, he, conjointly with his brother, founded a large banking

Some difficulties arose between him and Marshal Soult, as to the presidency of the Council ; these however were easily overcome. But it was a different matter with the conditions made by M. Périer on taking office, and which did not at all please the king. He was, however, obliged to yield in the end, in the face of a danger which threatened to carry away everything, and on the 13th March a Ministry was formed, which took its name from its chief M. Périer.[1] The king succeeded in keeping General Sebastiani as Minister of Foreign Affairs.

While these arrangements were being made in Paris, the Conference in London had some little respite, in consequence of the first discussions over the Reform Bill, which then occupied the English Cabinet. This Bill had been presented in the House of Commons on the 1st March by Lord John Russell,[2] who was

establishment, which rose rapidly to great importance. In 1817, he entered the Chamber of Deputies and sided with the opposition till 1830. After the July days he became President of the Chamber and Minister without a portfolio in the Cabinet of the 11th August. Head of the Cabinet on the 13th of March, he only remained in power one year, and died of cholera on 16th May, 1832.

[1] The Cabinet of May 13th was composed as follows : M. Casimir Périer, President of the Council and Minister of the Interior ; M. Barthe, Keeper of the Seals ; General Sebastiani, Minister of Foreign Affairs ; Baron Louis, Minister of Finance ; Marshal Soult, War Minister ; Admiral Rigny, Minister of Marine ; the Comte de Montalivet, Minister of Public Instruction and Religion ; and the Comte D'Argout, Minister of Trade and Public Works.

It is not without interest to see the effect produced in England by the advent of the new Cabinet. Lord Palmerston wrote to Lord Granville as follows :

("*Private.*")

FOREIGN OFFICE, *March* 15*th*, 1831.

MY DEAR GRANVILLE,

We are delighted with the nomination of Casimir Périer ; this event is, we hope, of a nature to give peace to France and to Europe. Please cultivate the new minister, and make him understand, I beg of you, that the English government has great confidence in him, and looks upon his nomination as a pledge of peace.

(*Confidential Correspondence of Lord Palmerston.*)

[2] Lord John Russell, third son of the Duke of Bedford, born in 1792, entered the House of Commons at twenty-one years of age under the Whig party. In 1830, he was made Paymaster-General, and although he had no seat in the Cabinet, was appointed, together with three other members of the Ministry, to prepare the draft of the Electoral Reform Bill, respecting which he had recently (simply as a member) brought in a motion.

The Bill was presented to the Commons on the 1st March, 1831, carried at the first reading by one vote, and thrown out at the second reading. After the dissolution of Parliament, and on the assembly of the new one, it was passed by 345 votes against 236 (September 21st). Taken into the House of Lords, on the 22nd of September it was thrown out. Presented again in December with a few slight modifications, the House put off the reading for three months. At last, on June 4th, 1832, it passed the Lords. This result was due in great part to the exertions of Lord John Russell.

In 1835, he was made Home Secretary, and in 1839 Colonial Secretary. In

generally listened to in the House with great good humour. It would be useless for me here to enter into the details of this great measure, destined to exercise so powerful an influence on England's future. It became the subject of prolonged discussions in both Houses of Parliament ; I shall confine myself to mentioning the results thereof, as they presented themselves from time to time.

I, on my side, had to carry on a discussion of a different nature, in my correspondence regarding the Belgian affairs, which they persisted in not looking at from my point of view, in Paris. Thus they continued to insist that Lord Ponsonby should be recalled from Brussels at the same time as M. Bresson, and that the Conference should show itself more favourably disposed to Belgian interests, to which they wished to give exclusive support. They did not hesitate to accuse the Conference of favouring the King of Holland ; whereas he, and with much greater reason, made loud complaints to Europe against us because having been, as he said, called upon by him for aid, we had countenanced a revolution, which had deprived him of more than half his States.

The Lafitte Ministry, or more correctly General Sebastiani, would have been glad I fancy, to separate the policy of France from that of the other four Powers in the Belgian question, so completely was he the dupe, voluntarily or involuntarily, of the Buonapartist and Republican intriguers, who alternately flattered him with the hope of the reunion of Belgium with France, or threatened him with a revolutionary war. But present necessities always brought him back to the Powers, and the events which followed shortly afterwards in Italy and Spain, obliged him at any rate to claim the assistance of England.

The revolutionary party in Italy, encouraged by their friends

1846, he became First Lord of the Treasury, and remained at the head of affairs till 1852. In December of the same year, he was made Minister of Foreign Affairs, then successively minister, President of the Council, and Colonial Secretary (1855). He quitted office the same year, remaining leader of the Whig party in Parliament, signed the Treaty of Commerce with France in 1860, and in 1861 was created a peer of the realm. He succeeded Lord Palmerston as head of the Cabinet (1865), and died in 1878.

in Paris, had taken up arms in the Papal States ;[1] two members of the Buonaparte family had gone thither, and the French government, less afraid of the struggle that was going on there, than of Austrian intervention, asked me to concert with England in order to prevent (by a mutual understanding with the Powers, if such were possible) the separate action of Austria. It was also wished in Paris, that Spanish affairs should be treated jointly by France and England.

In answer to these overtures, I wrote to General Sebastiani on the 5th March, 1831, as follows :

MONSIEUR LE COMTE,

I have to-day (5th) received the two despatches you did me the honour of writing on the 1st of this month.[2] (One related to the affairs of the Grand Duchy of Luxemburg, the other to the affairs of Italy.)

I have carefully studied the instructions they contain, and will conform to them on every point. I regret that I am obliged to delay communicating the contents of these despatches to the English Cabinet ; but the lengthy discussions on Parliamentary Reform absorb the ministers so completely night and day, that it is impossible to get them to attend seriously to any other matter just now.[3]

A somewhat remarkable incident occurred yesterday in the Commons. Mr. Wynn, the War Minister, rose and declared that after having carefully considered the proposed Reform Bill, he found he could not assent to it, and therefore withdrew from the Ministry. . . .[4]

I have spoken to M. de Bülow and M. de Wessenberg with regard to Luxemburg.[5] They both told me that they found it very difficult to write to *Frankfort*,[6] when they knew that the

---

[1] Bologna had revolted on February 2nd, 1831, against the Papal government. The whole of Romagna had followed suit. The two sons of Louis Buonaparte, Prince Charles and Prince Louis, took part in the movement. The former died of some malady at Forli ; the latter, who subsequently became the Emperor Napoleon III., nearly perished at Ancona.

[2] Var. : ainsi que les pièces qui y etaient jointes = as well as the papers that accompanied them.

[3] Var. : On pense que les débats finiront dans la séance du 7. Je verrai aussitôt après Lord Palmerston = it is thought the debates will end on the 7th. I will see Lord Palmerston immediately afterwards.

[4] Mr. Wynn was succeeded by Sir Henry Parnell, who in the same session retired for the same reason.

[5] Var. : Dont vous me parlez dans votre lettre du 22 = about which you speak to me in your letter of 22nd.

[6] Suppressed in the text of the Archives.

engagements entered into with them were not kept, and that up to the 28th of February, the fortress of Maëstricht continued to be besieged by Belgian troops, despite the assurances given by the Belgian government, and the orders that General Mellinet had received.[1]

The non-fulfilment of orders issued by the government, renders any sort of negotiation difficult. I have assured them that the Regent had ordered General Mellinet, under pain of dismissal, to reoccupy the positions fixed by the armistice, and they have informed me that as soon as they are assured of the retreat of the Belgian troops, they will at once write to Frankfort to postpone all the movements proposed by the Germanic Diet. . . .[2]

LONDON, *May 8th*, 1831.

MONSIEUR LE COMTE,

I have read the information on the state of Italy, contained in the despatches you did me the honour to send on the 1st of this month, with great attention. I thoroughly concur with your views as to the relations of France with Piedmont. As to the measures you have adopted regarding the Papal States, I believe it would be very expedient and quite possible to carry them out. I have spoken to Prince Esterhazy and Baron Wessenberg, the two Austrian plenipotentiaries, on the subject; they did not seem opposed to the idea, and although they had no instructions from their Court on this point. I saw plainly that they were not indisposed to adopt your views, and that they would write to Vienna in that spirit.

This morning I had a long conversation with Lord Palmerston, during which I was enabled to speak to him on everything mentioned in your letter of the 1st. The impression left upon me by this conversation is, that it will be quite possible to come to an understanding on the principal points, and that the

---

[1] François Aimé Mellinet, born in 1769, son of the member of the National Convention of that name, became a Colonel in 1793. He acted as Sub-Inspector at the reviews of 1800, and was made Chief of the Staff of the "young Guard" during the Hundred Days. He lived in retirement until 1830, when he entered Belgium at the head of a body of volunteers, commanded the artillery at Brussels during the days of September, and was placed in command of the troops which besieged Maëstricht. The Regent having deprived him of his command, he settled in Brussels, where he became chief of the Republican party. In 1848, he incited a revolutionary movement, was arrested, condemned to imprisonment, and died in 1852.

[2] The Diet had just been influenced by King William, who, as Grand Duke of Luxemburg, had taken upon himself to ask for assistance from the Germanic Confederation. In the sittings of 18th March, the Diet decreed the formation of an army-corps of 80,000 men, to re-establish the authority of the King of the Netherlands in the Grand Duchy, at the same time issuing orders for provisioning and preparing the fortresses of the Confederation.

difficulties which you have raised respecting several of our
protocols, are of a nature capable of explanation.

Respecting Italian affairs, Lord Palmerston told me that he
would gladly co-operate with our Cabinet and that of Vienna,
with the view to obtain from the Papal Government such concessions, as would place some portion of the administration of
the country in the hands of the laity. He greatly praised our
conduct as regards Piedmont, and expressed much satisfaction
at the orders issued to the French authorities on the frontier, for
the disarmament of the Piedmontese refugees.

The complaints you make against Spain, have led us to
believe that it might doubtless be easy to obtain the withdrawal
of Spanish troops from the Pyrenean frontier, if you on your
side, would insist on the Spanish refugees returning to the
north of France.

I am induced to think, that you could arrange this question
very advantageously with the Spanish Ambassador in Paris.
However, everything that you may ask in the spirit I have just
expressed to you, will be supported by the English Ministry.

Immediately after my conversation with Lord Palmerston,
the Conference assembled, ostensibly to hear the despatch read
which I had received from you ; there also I found a decidedly
favourable impression, and I believe we shall end by coming to
a mutual understanding. We have had to put off our next
meeting till Friday, on account of the debates in parliament,
which do not leave Lord Palmerston a moment's liberty.
On Friday, therefore, we shall begin the discussion of the
various points dealt with in your letter. If it is proposed to draw
up a protocol, I will only accept it *ad referendum*, and will
await the king's instructions before signing anything. . . .

When sending these despatches, I also wrote to Madame
Adelaide :

Mademoiselle will find that we have arrived at the wished-
for point with all the Powers, for they now realize, that, in order
to secure tranquillity for themselves, it is necessary that the
king's peace should not be disturbed. So far therefore from
desiring anything that might embarrass his government, they are
rather uneasy when any movements in Paris, the Departments, or
the Chambers, indicate an inclination towards disorder. Not one
of the Powers now wishes to disturb peace. All are in favour
of its preservation, and if it is not preserved, it will be due only
to the restless and aggressive spirit displayed by France. This
short-sighted policy is ever ready to sacrifice the real needs of

the country, to dreams of glory and aggrandisement. French-men forget, or fail to recognise, that to call everything in question abroad, is to end by calling everything in question at home.

The throne of King Louis Philippe now dates back to the days of St. Louis. War will make it a matter of yesterday. You have directed me to use every effort to avoid a war. You have asked me to induce the different Courts to become amicably disposed towards us ; in this I have completely succeeded, and I hope that Mademoiselle, whose wishes I have ever kept in view, in all I have done, is satisfied.

I cannot refrain from observing, that I have not as yet received any reply to the protocol of the 19th, which contains all the principles so desirable in a new monarchy. The diplo-matic body in London, as well as Rothschild, have for more than forty hours been aware that this document has reached Paris. Our newspapers speak of it, they alter the spirit of it, they change its expresions ; its actual publication therefore, becomes more and more necessary. It is beneficial to the king's service, that the country should know at what point in this document our Court takes first rank, and that when I speak of a treaty, it is that of 1814 to which I refer.

By this treaty, France remained great and strong. It is false therefore, to cite that of 1815 as the point of departure. I had retired before the stain was cast upon our country by the treaty of 1815, and I think I may say that I have quite as much national pride as anyone. . . . . .

I also wrote to my friend the Princess de Vandémont, who was on terms of great intimacy with Mme. Adelaide :

It is possible, since they say so in Paris, that I take too high-flown a view of matters, but it is only from a high stand-point that one can form a proper opinion.

It is impossible to place any reliance on such foolish and turbulent people as the Belgians. Belgium may perhaps come to us ; but that will be later on ; at present this is only a secon-dary interest. The pressure of affairs leads her towards France, but France must be first thoroughly matured, and this she cannot be, except by joining with the great Powers, who now *seek her*. It is to this point I have brought matters in London. Let us not quit this vantage ground. It has cost me much trouble to arrive thereat ; but I was anxious to serve the king whom I love, and *Mademoiselle*. Let us put aside all trivial interests, and think only of the great ones. It is of more consequence to be in accord with the great Powers, to be on the same footing with them, and to be their ally in the established order of things, than to be the friend of M. Van de Weyer & Co.

You must acknowledge that our protocol, which Belgium has sent you, is reasonable. The objections raised in France are very trifling. They say that it exhibits partiality for Holland. This is perfectly false, for nothing has been decided as to the question of the debts. A *Basis* has been proposed, subject to alteration when the two parties are face to face. We are accused of favouring the Dutch ; Holland reproaches us with humouring the Belgians. The King of Holland abuses us regularly every day ; he is thoroughly dissatisfied. But things are not far wrong when all in turn complain. In France only one side is listened to, that of M. de Celles, and to say truth, that is the least respectable. . . . . .

THE PRINCE DE TALLEYRAND TO GENERAL SEBASTIANI.

LONDON, *March* 13*th*, 1831.

MONSIEUR LE COMTE,

The Conference we were to have had yesterday has again been adjourned, and we shall not meet until to-morrow at the Foreign Office. I will, immediately after, inform you of the result of my communication of your letter to the members of the Conference, and also of any resolutions proposed. I will accept *ad referendum* whatever is agreed to by the other members ; for the king's government, having made some reservations to the protocols of the 20th and 27th Jan., I must not sign without orders, any document which might result in discussions between my government and the Conference. I called yesterday on Lord Palmerston to discuss the different subjects treated of in your last despatches. I began by speaking of the events in Warsaw, and the dangerous consequences to the peace of Europe that might result therefrom, if the Emperor Nicholas did not act with moderation and generosity towards the Poles. Lord Palmerston entered completely into our views on this subject. The English Ambassador at St. Petersburg will be instructed to demand from the Russian Cabinet, the maintenance of the stipulations of 1814, in virtue of which the kingdom of Poland was joined to the Russian Empire : he will above all insist that Poland shall not cease to be a separate state, and that she cannot be annexed as a Russian province. Lord Palmerston appreciates, as fully as we do, the importance to

Europe of making the voice of reason heard at St. Petersburg, and I feel assured from his language, that the instructions sent to the English Ambassador in Russia, will fully accord with those you have given to M. le Duc de Mortemart.

I then informed Lord Palmerston of the observations contained in your letter of the 7th, relative to the affairs of Greece. He replied, that Prince de Lieven had just communicated to him a despatch from his Court, which explains the species of difficulty in which Russia finds herself, as regards the question of the enlargement of the Greek frontier.

As a portion of the loan made to the Greeks, will be employed to indemnify the Turkish Government for the territory[1] it will lose as a result of the new delimitation, Russia (to whom this money will ultimately revert, as it will be employed to pay off the contribution imposed by the Treaty of Adrianople) has thought it in better taste not to come prominently forward, when it is a question of claiming an increase of territory in favour of the Greeks. "That is the reason," said Lord Palmerston, "why the Cabinet of St. Petersburg has decided to let England and France take the initiative ; but it is quite willing to join them in supporting the demands in favour of Greece, whenever the opportune moment arrives." The Prince de Lieven has asked for an interview, as he wishes to make a communication to me. I have reason to believe that it will be the same he has made to Lord Palmerston, and of which I have just informed you.

As to the situation of Portugal, and the questions connected therewith, which formed the subject of your despatches of the 4th inst., Lord Palmerston, to whom I spoke about it, has given me the reasons why it would not do for England to act in concert with France, to obtain redress for the grievances which both Powers have against the Portuguese Government. England has special treaties with Portugal, which give her some advantages we do not enjoy, and oblige her to act separately in all transactions with that kingdom. Thus, for instance, when a difficulty arises in which an Englishman is specially concerned, the English Government has the right, if it thinks fit, to have the matter tried by such Portuguese magistrate as it may choose. But I can tell you that Don Miguel's recognition is further off than ever, and I can give you the assurance, that whatever ulterior projects England may have regarding Portugal, she will do nothing without acquainting us. . . .

The Reform Bill has made some progress lately ; petitions

---

[1] Var : *pays*, country.

in its favour have come in from all parts, and the Ministry think
they are sure of a large majority. . . .

As I have already said, during the interval of the negotiations
which I have just related, a new Cabinet, with M. Périer at its
head, had been formed in Paris on March 13th. The Duc
de Dalberg wrote to me about this Ministry :—

THE DUC DE DALBERG TO THE PRINCE DE TALLEYRAND.

PARIS, *March 25th*, 1831.

A NEW Administration has arisen, mon Prince. It replaces
one, at once the most foolish, the most incapable, and the most
despicable that has ever been intrusted with the interests of
France ; bankruptcy was approaching with giant strides ; general
indignation was so strong, that probably the Chambers would
have hesitated to intrust the provisional four-twelfths to M.
Thiers and M. Lafitte. It would be as well if the English papers
took no notice of this. The revolutionary party is so strong here,
that our papers have not the courage to judge of it as it deserves.
Meanwhile, M. Lafitte has *found himself compelled* to provide
for fifty or sixty of his relations and friends, and, at the time of
his dismissal, to put nine of his clerks into the best places under
the Government.

And, now, will the new Ministry be able to last, amid the
confusion of ideas and unbridled insubordination which breaks
up all organization ? Two things are needed for its support.
First, there must be no trifling with these street riots ; this has
been decided on ; 70,000 men are around Paris, and three regiments of cavalry have entered the town ; let us hope, that the
deeds will be equal to the intentions. Secondly, it is necessary
that in the new Chamber (and there must be one) the Ministry
should have a majority. I believe that the elections will result in
returning a large number for the Left Centre ; if so, the victory
will be assured. The South will return more Carlists, for the
domiciliary visits have irritated all parties. That is what has
been gained thereby.

As regards foreign matters, the retention of General Sebastiani
is a mistake. He is nothing more than an instrument of the
weakness and intrigue that prevail at the Palais Royal. General
Sebastiani does not want war, and yet he has not been able to
secure peace. This is a grave fault.

Casimir Périer wishes to maintain peace, but I fear matters

have gone too far. By assigning as a reason for having these
huge armaments, that Europe wishes to attack us, the people
have become so excited, that it is impossible to calm them.
The utterances of the men who surround the King, such as
Valont,[1] Runigny,[2] and Trévise, are pitiable. To listen to them,.
one would fancy that we could easily swallow Europe, and that
she is actually outside the Barrière St. Denis. . . .

On the 19th March I wrote to General Sebastiani :—

MONSIEUR LE COMTE,

Last night I received the despatches you did me the
honour to write on the 16th of this month. The Belgian
Regent's proclamation with regard to the Grand Duchy of
Luxemburg, produced a most unpleasant impression[3] here, and
the very lucid explanations concerning this matter contained in
your letter, make me regret all the more that the proclamation
did not appear fifteen days earlier. The instructions you have
given to General Belliard would have been most useful to me, in
allaying the irritation caused here by the fresh follies of the
Belgian Government.[4] I could, perhaps, have stopped the
departure of some English men-of-war for the Scheldt (which has
just been announced), and enabled the Prussian plenipotentiaries
to give some positive assurances to the Diet at Frankfort.

But, anyhow, M. le Comte, I will not neglect to make the
utmost I can of your despatch of the 16th. The firm determination expressed both in Brussels and London, to accord with the

[1] Jean Valont, born in 1792, second in the prefectorial administration under the
Empire. In 1822 he joined the Orleanist party, was elected a Deputy in 1831, and
sat in the Chamber till 1848. He was elected President of the Council on Municipal
Buildings, and he entered the Academy in 1848, and died in the same year.

[2] Marie Théodore de Gueulluy, Comte de Runigny, born in 1789, entered the
army in 1805, and became a colonel in 1814. He was aide-de-camp to the Duc
d'Orleans during the Restoration. In 1830 he had the command of a brigade, and was
intrusted with the pacification of Vendée and Brittany. He took part in the expedition to Antwerp, and was elected deputy in 1831. He accompanied Louis Philippe
into exile in 1848, and was placed in retirement by the Provisional Government. He
died in 1860.

[3] On the 5th March, the Governor-General, Duc Bernard de Saxe-Weimar, who
had been sent by the King of the Netherlands to Luxemburg, published a proclamation
from the king, which promised an amnesty to all the inhabitants of the Grand Duchy
who tendered their submission. In reply to this, the Belgian Regent, M. Surlet de
Chokier, issued a counter proclamation, in which he adjured the people of Luxemburg to remain true to Belgium, and reject the advances made by the king. He
concluded thus : "accept, in the name of Belgium, the assurance that your
brethren will never forsake you :" this defiance launched at the decisions of the
Conference, caused some stir in Europe, and irritated the plenipotentiaries in London
exceedingly.

[4] Var. : *des Belges*, of the Belgians.

Powers, will I hope, lead to happy results, which the long-continued delays have somewhat endangered. . . . .

I had taken care, the night before, to address the following letter to M. Casimir Périer, and which even now I read with great satisfaction, as being a true exposition of the political views that directed my conduct during my mission in London :—

THE PRINCE DE TALLEYRAND TO M. CASIMIR PÉRIER.

LONDON, *March* 28*th*, 1831.

MONSIEUR,

After fifteen days of anxiety, perplexity, and sorrowful anticipations as to the fate of our beautiful France, the horizon has cleared, and all hopes have revived and centred themselves in your name. It is with real pleasure that I have observed this in the *Moniteur*. It satisfies the right-thinking people in England, it is pleasing to all the enlightened foreigners, whom the great interests of Europe have assembled here, and I may also add, to the many true friends of France now in this country. I am almost asked to express their satisfaction to you.

I must now render an account to the President of the Council, of the motives which have guided the conduct of the French Ambassador at London.

His principal aim has been to preserve peace, which, according to his view, can alone consolidate our new dynasty, maintain France in the position she ought to occupy, and save the whole of ancient Europe from a seriously threatened dissolution. This peace I could not be prevailed upon to sacrifice, except for the independence of our country, and never at any period has it been less assailed. It is this that has led me, in opposition to our youthful enthusiasts, to estimate the Belgian question as being of less importance than it is considered in France. I have seen with regret, that the tendency with us has been, to lean for support on a mere handful of men who are anarchists at heart, and by too much complaisance, to endeavour to solve a question of which time and the course of events will, at a more favourable period, undoubtedly make us masters, but which, until then, would only cause us trouble. Authority is needed somewhere for the preservation of peace and good order, and the misfortune of the present time is, that it is hardly to be found anywhere I can only perceive it in one direction, that is in the alliance of the five Powers, which, as it now stands, has nothing in common with the Holy Alliance. Non-intervention, when applied to the internal affairs of countries which change or modify their government, destroys the basis on which the Holy Alliance rested, and then non-intervention stands stripped of everything chimerical. Enlightened by past experience, the Powers here united will know what necessary concessions to make, while offering to society those safeguards, without which it is impossible that it can exist ; this, according to my view, is the true *point d'appui* of our new government.

It was necessary to make Europe wish for our establishment and preservation, as the one thing most important to her ; this I have succeeded in doing. Soon our influence will be pre-eminent, but first we must reassure them abroad, as to those designs of war with which we are accredited, and also show ourselves more masters at home, than we have done for the last three months.

The principle of non-intervention, very convenient in itself, and very appropriate to a given circumstance, becomes very little better than an absurdity, when regarded as absolute and when it is desired to apply it under conditions widely different. This principle is a matter of judgment, when to set it aside, and when to apply it. It was thus understood by Mr. Canning, and as it is a matter of judgment, you will know better than any one how to handle this new instrument, which is more often an excuse for doing nothing, than a reason for action.

I earnestly hope you will find my policy analogous to that which you would wish to adopt. Nevertheless I am too old not to have experienced misgivings, and am quite willing to be enlightened by all the considerations you may wish to impress upon me, and to follow the course which may seem most expedient to you.

I have the honour. . . .

I have reason to believe that this letter made some impression on M. Casimir Périer, who was besides quite determined to follow a more sensible policy than that of the preceding Cabinet. The modification of M. Sebastiani's language, already noticeable in his despatch of the 16th March, was due to this determination. In order therefore to keep up this new feeling, I hastened to write to him on the 20th March.

MONSIEUR LE COMTE,

I have this morning seen Lord Palmerston, Prince Esterhazy, and Baron de Bülow with regard to your despatch of the 16th ; they are all three entirely satisfied with what I told them respecting it, and said they would be glad to see France rid herself at last, of the embarrassments caused by Belgian affairs. That country, they each told me separately, only wishes to involve France; it is urged on by a revolutionary party, whose object is very far from being favourable to the tranquillity of France, and who would like to compromise her, with the rest of Europe. "Belgium has proved," said M. de Bülow, "that the Conference judged her rightly, when it made use in protocol No. 7, of the word *future* independence."

I have given you the decided opinion of the four Powers, with whom it is important we should act, and who are ready to act with us. The three members of our Conference whom I saw this morning again, each one separately, reiterated the most positive assurance, that their governments wished the present state of affairs in France to become permanent, that peace should be maintained in Europe, and that France should take the place there that she ought naturally to occupy. All feel the need of this, and it is this, they say, which will always guide their views. Besides, the Prussian and Austrian Plenipotentiaries have promised me to write to Frankfort, and I hope their advice will put a stop to the enterprises, which we have reason to fear on the part of the Germanic Confederation. . . .

The Prince of Orange embarked from London for Holland this morning, after having indulged in all the pleasures of this capital; he pretty loudly expressed his regret at leaving. His manner of life here gained him but scant consideration. . . .

The promise given me by the Austrian and Prussian Ministers to write to Frankfort, was not superfluous. The proclamation of the Belgian Regent, in which he openly announced his intention to demand the restitution of Luxemburg to his country, had excited the dissatisfaction of the German Diet to the highest degree: it would probably take some rigorous measures; but thanks to the communications I was able to make to M. d'Esterhazy and M. de Bülow, they put a stop to the hostile preparations made at Frankfort, by insisting strongly on the confidence that might be placed in the new French Ministry.

I had received instructions from Paris to propose to the English Government, that an English agent should be sent to Italy, to countenance the steps taken by our government for quieting the disturbances that were taking place there, especially in the Papal States, and if possible, to prevent the intervention of the Austrians. I had to write a few lines on this matter to Lord Palmerston, who was detained in the House of Commons by the discussion on the Reform Bill. The House passed this bill on the night of the 22nd of March, by a majority of one,[1] and Lord Palmerston then wrote me the following note :

MY DEAR PRINCE,

I thank you for your congratulations. Our motto is : *un me suffit.*

Sir Brooke Taylor, an excellent diplomat, is now in Florence, having passed the winter in Rome for his health. He is just the man we want, and I will send him the necessary instructions without delay, so that he can co-operate with you and Austria.[2]

It appears according to the last accounts from Florence, that Bologna is not Warsaw, that the revolution is dying out before the wind which blows from Milan, and that Bianchetti,[3] and another, whose name I forget, had just arrived in Tuscany, wishing to embark at Livorna, and take refuge either in France or England. We shall not have much difficulty in effecting a reconciliation between the Pope and these insurgents.

Ever yours,

PALMERSTON.

Thus all the questions which then agitated Europe, were really definitely settled in London, and it was therefore necessary to make a careful study of these questions so as to be in a position to discuss them with the English Cabinet and work in concert with it. This Italian affair was a fresh and serious complication for the French Government, but before entering upon it, I must continue to cite several despatches, indicating the progress of other questions.

---

[1] The Reform Bill was not actually passed on the night of the 22nd of March ; this was only the first reading. The principle of the Bill was however admitted, but the ministerial project was destined to fall through after the second reading.

[2] It will be remembered that the French Cabinet had invited England to act in concert with her in Italy, and so prevent an Austrian intervention. (See pages 69 and 71.)

[3] Comte César Bianchetti, formerly Chamberlain of the Emperor Napoleon, was one of the chiefs of the insurrection in Romagna.

THE PRINCE DE TALLEYRAND TO GENERAL SEBASTIANI.

LONDON, *March 25th,* 1831.

MONSIEUR LE COMTE,

I have not neglected speaking to Lord Palmerston, at various times, respecting the affairs of Poland, as you have requested in several of your despatches. Judging from this Minister's language, I have every reason to believe that the English Cabinet attaches some importance to the Polish cause, and that instructions have been sent to Lord Haytesbury,[1] its Ambassador at St. Petersburg, desiring him to urge moderation.

It seems to me, that it would be well to direct M. le Duc de Mortemart to enter into communication on this matter with Lord Haytesbury, who, I believe, has received directions which will in no wise be contrary to the instructions you have given to M. de Mortemart—official action taken simultaneously by both these ambassadors, assuredly cannot fail to produce some effect. The reason given for this step must be, to demand from the Russian Cabinet the maintenance of the treaties of 1814, which secured to Poland an independent existence under the Emperor of Russia's rule. The manifesto issued by that sovereign leads to the supposition that, in case of non-submission on the part of the Poles, he would subdue them by force, and at once incorporate them with his Empire ; such a measure would annul a very important article of the treaty of 1814, the fulfilment of which the Powers have a right to demand. It appears to me that this point of departure will give weight to every thing that may be said in favour of the Poles.

I have this morning seen the new Belgian Envoy, M. le Comte d'Arschot ;[2] we did not in the course of our conversation enter very deeply into the affairs which have brought him to London, for the Regent's proclamation has caused all the Ministers who are in London, to show some coolness to the Belgian Deputy. Nevertheless, I was able to make good use of a passage in your letter of the 16th, which states that France will only give her

---

[1] William A'Court, Baron Haytesbury, born in 1779, entered the House of Commons in 1817, and was sent as Ambassador to Madrid in 1820, and subsequently to Lisbon (1824). On his return to London, he was created a Peer (1828), and was soon after accredited to St. Petersburg. He remained there till 1833. After living ten years in retirement, he was made Viceroy of Ireland (1844), but only held this post for two years.

[2] Comte d'Arschot Schoonhoven, born in 1781, was a member of the Council intrusted to revise the National Law (1815), member of the first Chamber of the States General from 1825 to 1830, and Grand Marshal of the Palace and a Senator under Leopold I. He died in 1846.

support to Belgium so long as she does not, without provocation, rush into paths calculated to disturb the peace of Europe. This passage, rich in possibilities, in all of which I showed great interest, enabled me to conclude the interview, by impressing him with the view which the Conference took of the position of his country. "The Belgium of to-day," I said to him, "is the Belgium of 1790, plus the bishopric of Liége [1]; her independence is on the point of being recognized, and her neutrality has been guaranteed by all the Powers. All these advantages have been secured to her, on the sole condition that she will not disturb the peace of other nations."

I am looking forward to hear from you, the result of the dispatches sent from London to the members of the German Diet, with the view to put a stop to the hostile measures which the Regent's proclamation had induced them to take. Your direct action will surely have produced the effect you expected. . . . . .

LONDON, *March* 28*th*, 1831.

MONSIEUR LE COMTE,[2]

. . . . I have again had to see each of the members of the Conference separately, in order to ascertain their opinion as to the choice of the future sovereign for Belgium, and I have made use of the arguments contained in your letter of the 24th. They, one and all, corroborated what I wrote to you yesterday, *i.e.*, that it is impossible to decide on a sovereign for Belgium, before determining the limits of the country over which that sovereign is to reign. To act differently, would only be exposing this prince to the difficulty in which the Regent now finds himself. He would be obliged, in accepting the sovereignty, to swear to a constitution which contains an article proclaiming the maintenance of the integrity of a territory, which it has pleased the Belgians to enlarge to suit themselves. It is easy to foresee, that such a pledge would at once raise more difficulties. The plenipotentiaries are therefore unanimously of opinion, that it is above all absolutely necessary to adopt the protocol pure and simple, which fixes the limits of the Belgian territory. At the same time they quite recognize that, later on, it will be necessary to enter into some arrangement, as to which of the enclosed lands should belong to Belgium and which to Holland. The question

---

[1] Liége was formerly a sovereign-bishopric. The bishop was a prince of the Empire. In 1801, this principality had been joined to France by the peace of Lunéville. In 1815, it had been ceded to the King of the Netherlands. In 1831, it was given to Belgium.

[2] Official despatch already published.

as to the Duchy of Bouillon,[1] can then be easily settled. You are in a better position than I am to judge of the advantages and disadvantages that would accrue to the king's government by the choice of the Prince of Naples. As to the Prince of Saxe-Coburg, I have not seen the slightest opposition to him, on the part of any of the members of the Congress to whom I have mentioned his name. The English Cabinet, which, as I have often stated, always considered the Prince of Orange as the most suitable person, has now given up this idea; they will consent, without much trouble, to the selection of the Prince of Saxe-Coburg.

I have not been able to discuss the subject of a selection with the Russian Ambassador, as his instructions do not admit of his interesting himself in any one but the Prince of Orange. That, however, does not delay Belgian affairs. What we sought was, that Russia should not oppose the independence of that country, and this has been obtained. The recognition of the sovereign will come later on.

The demolition of the fortresses, which you demand if the Prince of Saxe-Coburg be elected, has always seemed to me easy of attainment, for according to my view, it has lost its real interest since the declaration of neutrality.

I know that in France, less importance is attached to this declaration than it deserves; nevertheless I feel convinced, that this neutrality was the best means of putting an end to the vexed question of the fortresses, which, when I left Paris, seemed to the most enlightened minds, one involving the self-love of all parties, the loss of many millions, and quite incapable of solution. However, we are not called on to deal with it just at present, and I shall no doubt have to return to this matter.

My personal opinion respecting the choice of a prince (reducing it, as you have done in your despatch, to the Prince of Naples and the Prince of Saxe-Coburg) is, that it is best to declare for whichever has the best chance of being elected. In the position of affairs four months ago, the Prince of Saxe-Coburg seemed more feasible than any of the others. Since then, your instructions having been different, I have thought no more about it. . . .

LONDON, *April 5th*, 1831.

MONSIEUR LE COMTE,

In the last letters I have had the honour to write to you, I have often pressed you to answer the note addressed to

---

[1] The Duchy of Bouillon at that time formed part of the Grand Duchy of Luxemburg. In 1831 it was handed over to Belgium.

you by the plenipotentiaries of the four Courts, as the long delay in giving an assent or any explanations, sometimes causes wrong interpretations, and makes everything more difficult. They endeavour to connect the silence of our Cabinet with your adherence to the boundaries of Holland and Belgium, such as I understood and spoke of it, in accordance with your despatch of March 30th, and as was expressed in the letters received here, from the Ambassadors who are in France.

If in the meantime, you have any doubts about the question of the fortresses, why not express these doubts in your reply to the plenipotentiaries of the four Powers ? The feeling of the Cabinets is friendly. There is some little uneasiness, but I do not see any irritation ; nay, I may even say, that the explanations given by our Cabinet relative to Bologna, have been more re-assuring than alarming, and every one hopes that they will have the desired effect in Vienna.

I notice that the choice of the Prince of Orange as sovereign of Belgium is looked upon here with less favour every day ; no one is really interested in him, and not a single government (unless I except Russia) will make a move in his favour.

You will no doubt have noticed, that the Belgian cause is daily losing supporters in England ; it is thought that they are but ill prepared for independence. In a country like England, where good sense is a predominant feature, the deliberations of the Brussels Congress, do not find much favour.

The speech of the President of the Council (M. Casimer Périer) has made a great sensation here, and every one yesterday was quoting this phrase : *Les promesses de politique intérieure sont dans la constitution ; s'agit il des affaires du dehors il n'y a de promesses que les traités.*[1]

Accept. . . . . .

The same day I wrote to Madame Adelaide :

LONDON, *April 5th*, 1831.

" I venture to entreat Mademoiselle to have pity on her old servant, and to insist that either M. Bresson, or some one else in his place, should be sent here without delay. Since M. Bresson's departure for Brussels five months ago, I have had no first Secretary of Legation, and have only had M. de Bacourt here,

---

[1] " The fulfilment of promises in home politics, rests with the constitution ; when it is a question of foreign affairs, the only real promises are treaties." Speech made in the Chamber of Deputies, March 30th, 1831.

with whom indeed I have been perfectly satisfied, but who for the last ten days has been seriously ill through overwork. The whole bulk of the business therefore, conferences, meetings, and embassy details, now falls on my shoulders, and despite my earnest endeavours, and the incessant assiduity with which I devote myself to them, I cannot carry on matters as I should like.

" I do not wish to weary Mademoiselle with a long political dissertation, but I venture to tell her, that we have arrived at the point when prompt and assured peace is essential to us ; without it, we shall be dragged by the restless spirit of a small number of daring intriguers into a war, the risks of which make me tremble for the objects of my most tender devotion. Peace will be secured to us, by a frank declaration from France to the Belgians. The ancient boundaries of Belgium must be recognized, with the exception of a few exchanges and the demolition of the fortresses. It is essential that this declaration should be made officially both in Brussels and to the Conference, and this is the more necessary, as all the accounts received by the English Ministry state, that in Brussels they are almost prepared to yield to the decision of the Conference, as soon as they are convinced that France is in accord with the Powers respecting Belgium.

" I am staving off by all possible means an outburst from the Germanic Confederation, but it can only be a question of days, and the delays in Paris may cause serious danger. I pray Mademoiselle to turn all her attention to the importance of bringing Belgian affairs to a speedy termination. I ask this from a conviction, the result of my increasing occupation with them, and with the utmost devotion . . . ."

M. Casimir Périer's accession to power speedily exercised a beneficial influence on home affairs in France, and also fortunately, soon produced an equally good effect on our foreign relations, notably those affecting the Belgian question. The French Government at last decided, to accept the protocol of the Conference of the 20th January, which fixed the boundaries between Holland and Belgium. General Sebastiani informed me of this acceptance, by a despatch dated April 4th. It will be seen by what motives he was influenced. The following despatches and letters will suffice to show the various incidents that were mixed up in it. I will begin with M. Casimir Périer's letters.

M. Casimir Périer to the Prince de Talleyrand.

Mon cher Prince,

You will excuse my employing one of my sons as an amanuensis, but my handwriting is such that no Cabinet possesses the key to it.

I regret exceedingly, that unceasing occupation has prevented my sooner thanking you for all the kind things you say of me. I have in no way desired what has come to me. In the present state of affairs, power has no great attraction ; but since I have been called to accept it, I am happy to find that I meet with confidence and receive support from the experienced and enlightened party. I trust that your good opinion of me will not prove a mistake, and that my name may, indeed, secure a few more friends for my country.

If that is to be done anywhere, it is in England. According to my views, the two countries ought to be more and more closely united ; in the main, their cause is the same. Those who are prejudiced will not admit this, but experience will prove it.

I now tell the French ambasador that we are anxious for peace, but at the same time, we are inclined to think that others desire it quite as much as we do. Thus with every wish to be fair, we shall not sacrifice any of our rights. By maintaining peace, France renders Europe a service sufficiently important to merit consideration. I also believe, that by being moderate we are of more use to other nations, than if we went proselytising, sword in hand.

I have however stated the whole of my policy from the Tribune. I have but one. I shall therefore always tell you my ideas frankly, and if there is the slightest change in my views, I will write to you at once.

I know that just now you are occupied with the question of the Belgian throne. It is wished that one and the same Act should definitely fix the frontiers of the new State. It is greatly to be desired, that the foreign difficulties which are at the bottom of this business, will not retard its conclusion. In these days it is generally wise to have a prompt and decided policy. The shifts and evasions up to now, have, I know well, despite your efforts, greatly prejudiced the success of our affairs. They must not however be allowed to continue, for they might lead to grave difficulties. Your intimate and profound knowledge of men and things, mon Prince, will suggest the best means of giving effect to our views.

Please write to me frequently. I really must know everything, and I count fully on your frank and able co-operation. I have sent my son to you, and ask your kind interest for him. I wish him to become acquainted with society and politics. He could not be in better hands than yours.

Please to accept . . . .

M. CASIMIR PÉRIER TO THE PRINCE DE TALLEYRAND.

PARIS, *April 4th,* 1831.

I have not been able, mon Prince, to carry out at once my wish of establishing direct comunications with you, from which I promise myself the happiest possible results for the good of our country. When the king sent for me to form a Cabinet, and take a leading part in the government, home affairs claimed my first attention. Their position was well known and had for a long time occupied my thoughts, and I was able to act promptly and decisively, according to views and plans arranged beforehand.

Our foreign relations, though no less bristling with difficulties, have through their complications and the secrecy with which they are necessarily surrounded, been less cavilled at by those who take no part in the direction of affairs. These relations, however, have necessarily been the object of my most earnest study from the moment of my joining the Council. This study, which does not enter into my special department, is by no means completed ; I need special enlightenment on many points.

The despatch agreed to in Council, which you will receive together with this letter, furnishes me with the opportunity of asking you to give me the benefit of that assistance which an experience, without equal in Europe, and your position as the representative of France at these Conferences (which may exercise such a grave influence on her destiny) enables you to do.

I have approved the diplomatic Note in question. It seemed to me well adapted to the general position of Europe, the actual state of the negotiations, and the recent events which have arisen to complicate the question of peace or war. But my concurrence is due, to the confidence I have in the opinion of my colleagues (who almost all formed part of the last Cabinet), rather than to a conviction founded on actual approval of previous diplomatic proceedings, or the progress of negotiations to which I was a stranger.

I therefore trust, mon Prince, that you will kindly communi-

cate confidentially to me, by one of the next couriers if possible,
your views as to the expediency of the Note that has been sent
you.   I adhered to it the more fully, as I was assured that it
was in perfect harmony with the spirit that had directed the
negotiations relative to the fate of Belgium ; and that it would
aid the impetus, you deemed it advisable to give them.   I
should be glad to receive the assurance, mon Prince, that
the Note is indeed calculated to further the aim which the
government has in view.   If, on the contrary, it appears to you
insufficient or incomplete in any way whatever, it is of moment
to me to be sure of this, so that the future decisions of the
Cabinet may contribute more efficaciously to the happy solution
of a question, which is a serious difficulty in the relations of
France with the Great Powers, while at the same time it continues to furnish nourishment for the disturbances and agitations, that are stirred up at home.

Pray accept. . . .

M. Bresson, who had spent a few days in London in the end
of March, before definitely quitting his post, also wrote to me :

M. BRESSON TO THE PRINCE DE TALLEYRAND.

PARIS, April 5th, 1831.

MON PRINCE,

I have worked incessantly to carry out your instructions satisfactorily, and you will hear to-night that the Conference will have all it desires, with only a few exceptions, to
which I think it as well to yield quietly, and spare the *amour
propre* of those who find themselves compromised.   My
principal argument has been, that as long as the Belgians
consider themselves to be a stand-point outside the Conference,
they will be less inclined to submit to necessity and listen to
reason.   I have been stimulated by the wish to redeem my in-
voluntary errors, and to show my gratitude for your kind
indulgence, as well as that of the other members of the Conference, whom I had the honour of seeing during my last stay
in London.   Kindly make known to them, mon Prince, the
feelings which have guided me.

The Ministry frankly proceeds on the course it has marked
out for itself, and the impulse given by M. Périer is very strong.
I have not the slightest doubt, but that the dissolution of the
Chamber will give him a large majority, even in our eastern
departments, which are apt to be cautious.   As for you per-

sonally, mon Prince, all those whose opinion can be of any importance to you, look upon you as the hope and pledge of peace in London ; and peace is not only the almost universal desire, but it is a necessity. The concessions made to the turbulent party *are not binding, and do not go* as far as that party supposes. You will understand, mon Prince, that I allude to *what* M. Périer promised me he would mention to you, in his private letter.

The accounts from Belgium are unsatisfactory. The reunionist party, pure and simple, has been largely increased by the present difficulties and by what is called the parcelling out of the country, which, it is said, renders independence impossible. The Prince of Saxe-Coburg gains favour ; but I am told that his marriage with a French princess, would be a *sine quâ non*. However, the effect produced in France by his election, would decide this union. . . .

I cannot find the letter in which General Sebastiani requested me to consider, as not having been received, the directions he had imposed upon me, respecting the protocol of the 20th January, which fixed the boundaries of Belgium.

The despatch below will enable the reader to gather the sense of his letter.

THE PRINCE DE TALLEYRAND TO GENERAL SEBASTIANI.[1]

LONDON, *April 7th*, 1831.

MONSIEUR LE COMTE,

I have this morning received your despatch of the 4th April. I have no doubt that, on many points, it will satisfy the Conference, to which I shall communicate it either on Monday or Tuesday next. You will perhaps be surprised that I put off this communication to that date ; but it is unavoidable, as several members of the Conference are absent from London.

The great difficulty *that remains*[2] will be that which will supervene on the exchanges you demand, on account of the position of Maëstricht. I will do my best, and will make use of all your arguments, to obtain what you enjoin on me with regard to this, in your despatch of the 4th. Success would have been much easier two months ago. The Belgians would not

---

[1] Official despatch already published. It is dated April 6th in the text of the Archives.

[2] Suppressed in the text of the Archives.

have then, as they have since done, excited the universal distrust I now find everywhere.   I have generally noticed, and it is as well to draw attention thereto, that delays are against us ; they do not simplify anything, and only serve to raise fresh difficulties.

In one of your previous despatches, you spoke of the resolutions that would have to be taken respecting the fortresses ; my opinion on this point is, that you will obtain the demolitions you require, but I think the question should be left to stand over until after the selection of the king ;[1] self-importance might now be offended thereat.   This question, as a requirement on the part of the Conference, can be much more advantageously handled, when dealing with the king.

Lord Grey will be informed before any of the other ministers, of the communication you wish me to make to the Conference, for I am engaged to spend next Friday with him at his country seat, where he is now, and I shall have an opportunity of speaking to him concerning the reassembly[2] of the Conference, for which I shall ask.   I prefer speaking to writing, on subjects that are[3] under discussion.

I have this morning seen Baron de Bülow and M. le Prince Esterhazy.   They will write to Frankfort to-morrow as you wish.   Prince Esterhazy will himself write to M. de Münch,[4] to induce him to keep the Diet in a conciliatory mood, respecting the Grand Duchy of Luxemburg.   I have insisted strongly that their action should be prompt and decisive, for I feel how very important the subjects contained in your despatches are with regard to this. . . .

I thank you for having established the truth of the facts, which General Lamarque declared he could not remember, when he attacked me in the Chamber.[5]   I have not read what you said in reply thereto, as I have not yet received the French papers of the 5th, which are the only ones that give an account of this sitting ; but I feel sure, that I shall find proofs in them of our old friendship.   It is strange, that they will insist upon my having been a member of the Holy Alliance, whereas it was

[1] Var. : Belge = Belgian.
[2] Suppressed in the text of the Archives.
[3] Var. : Encore = still.
[4] Edouard Joachim, Comte de Münch-Bellinghausen, an Austrian diplomat, had taken up a municipal career, and been made Mayor of Prague.   In 1823 he went as plenipotentiary to the German Diet.   As Austria took precedence at this Diet, her plenipotentiary received great consideration.   M. de Münch became Minister of State in 1841.   He retired 1848, and died in the same year.
[5] In the sitting of the 4th April, General Lamarque had made a violent attack on the foreign policy of the Cabinet.   M. de Talleyrand was taken to task and accused of defending the Act of the Congress of Vienna.

at Aix-la-Chapelle,[1] two years after my ministry, that M. de Richelieu entered into this new contract.

It is in truth a very grave error, to say that the Conference, by its acts, recalls the Holy Alliance. To be convinced of this, it is only necessary to compare what has been done at Naples and in Spain,[2] with what is now being done in Belgium, the independence of which, the Conference proclaimed at the end of two months. . . .

General Sebastiani, who had shown much ill-humour when asked to send me another secretary in place of M. de Bacourt, who had fallen seriously ill, was forced to give in to M. Casimir Périer's imperious insistance. M. Sebastiani wished to palm off one of his creatures upon me, whereas I had asked him to send me M. Tellier, a clerk dismissed by him from the Foreign Office, and who had been recommended to me by M. Bourjot, his former chief. M. Tellier at last arrived in London, bringing me a letter from M. Casimir Périer. He was also charged by him to tell me, that the king's government was quite determined to master the Belgians, in the same way as they had succeeded in putting down the riots in Paris ; the time had now arrived for showing *courage and firmness*, but that, in order to facilitate the action of the government, and to popularize it, so as not to give its detractors any excuse, it was necessary to obtain the evacuation of those portions of the Papal States, which the Austrian troops had occupied. M. Périer was very anxious that some resolution should be promptly come to on this point. He himself wrote to me about it :

M. CASIMIR PÉRIER TO THE PRINCE DE TALLEYRAND.

PARIS, *April 8th*, 1831.

MON PRINCE,

I herewith confirm the last letter I had the honour to write to you, in which I mentioned the despatch relating

[1] The Congress of Aix-la-Chapelle (September and October 1818) put an end to the foreign occupation of France, by means of a pecuniary indemnity on her part. In addition, a formal treaty permitted France to join the Holy Alliance, from which she had been excluded 1815.

[2] The intervention of Austria in Naples in 1821, when General Frimont re-established the absolute power of King Ferdinand. The war in Spain (1823), when France went to the aid of King Ferdinand VII, and helped him to overcome the constitutionalists.

to Belgian affairs, which you would receive from the Minister
for Foreign Affairs. I asked you to point out to me, what modifications you would consider it advisable to suggest, respecting
the course we thought of adopting with regard to Belgium, and
which seemed to us to be in accordance with the protocol signed
by you in London. We have determined to speak out plainly
to that small body of individuals who have too long ruled our
foreign policy, as the mob-leaders have ruled our home policy.
We believe that, with your help, we shall easily attain this end.

Here matters are going very smoothly ; we are assured as to
home matters, and we can be certain of maintaining peace, if
Austria will give us satisfaction for her occupation of the Papal
States. There must be some means of arranging matters in an
honourable way for both countries. If England is sincere and
wishes to support us, she can effectually assist this very desirable
arrangement.

All the accounts we receive from Vienna and Russia are
most reassuring. M. de Mortemart's last despatch was very
satisfactory, although it was sent off, before the formation of the
new Ministry was known in Russia.

The Chamber will be prorogued in a few days, [1] and we hope
to carry all our measures by a large majority. To-day's sitting
was very satisfactory ; the Bill for the extraordinary credit of
100 millions, had only thirty-two black balls against it.

You stand so high, mon Prince, both at home and abroad,
that I attach the greatest possible value to your opinion with regard to the course we propose to follow ; I shall therefore be very
gratified if you will send me your views and ideas on this matter.
General Sebastiani's last speech in the Chamber will have satisfied you. He rendered you the justice that was your due ; it
was high time, and he did it with the best grace in the world.
M. Tellier is taking this letter. I have at last got General
Sebastiani to decide on sending him, in place of M. Bresson,
knowing that you would prefer this. . . .

M. Périer's letter and the accounts I received from Paris, all
showed, that we had at last got out of the vexatious groove in
which matters had remained so long, owing to the action of
intriguers.

I felt I could count on efficacious help from M. Périer, and
this was most important to the success of my mission in England.
M. Périer had not what is generally called *esprit*, but he

---

[1] The Chamber was prorogued to the 15th June, by order of 15th April.

possessed instead, in a high degree, that firmness and uprightness found in men who have carved their own fortunes. He saw what was wanted, made up his mind, and never swerved from it. He was even so fortunate, that his very faults became valuable, in the difficult position in which he was placed. He was self-willed, even somewhat obstinate, and at times passionate ; but all this gave the appearance of a firm and indomitable will, and produced the best possible effect at a time, when the weakness of some, and the intrigues and violence of others, needed a strong barrier opposed to them. For my part, my relations with him were very satisfactory, and I have much pleasure in acknowledging, that his presence at the head of affairs, contributed greatly to facilitate the solution of those which had been intrusted to me.

I gave an account to M. Sebastiani of the sitting of the Conference, at which I had communicated his despatch of April 4th.

THE PRINCE DE TALLEYRAND TO GENERAL SEBASTIANI.[1]

LONDON, *April* 13*th*, 1831.

M. LE COMTE,

The members of the Conference returned to town the night before last, and met yesterday evening. I communicated to them the despatch of the 4th inst., which you did me the honour to send. It has produced a very favourable impression ; they were very pleased to see that the views of the king's government are so closely allied to those of the Conference ; I also noticed, that the present position of France, the progress of public opinion, and the many victories of his Majesty's Government, were fully and justly appreciated by all the members. They asked me to allow a copy of this despatch to be made ; but I refused, as mention is made therein of M d'Appony [2], and we must avoid everything that would displease Austria. . . .

The next sitting will take place on Thursday or Friday. Parliamentary affairs do not allow of an earlier meeting. The Conference will send you a speedy reply, and, in my opinion, one that will thoroughly satisfy you.

---

[1] Official despatch already published.

[2] Antoine Rudolph, Comte d'Appony, was at that time Austrian Ambassador in Paris. Born in 1782 ; he had been accredited to Florence, Rome, and London. He remained over twenty years in Paris, which he did not leave till 1849. He died in 1852. Comte d'Appony was one of Prince Metternich's most intimate friends.

I deemed it advisable, M. le Comte, not to bring the subject of your despatch of the 8th before the Conference; but I have already mentioned it to each of the members separately, and their views, so far as I have seen, lead me to believe, that the greater and more important part of our demands will be acceded to.

I have pointed out to the Austrian Ambassador, as well as to the Prussian Minister, how very undesirable it is, that their Cabinets should procrastinate so much in discussing questions referred to them, and concerning which general interest requires a speedy solution. Besides, the despatches which Prince Esterhazy has communicated to me, and which area re ply to the demands I asked him to forward to the Court of Vienna, do not leave any doubt that M. de Metternich is quite disposed to second the wishes and hopes, made known to him by the king's government. These despatches also speak in the most flattering manner, of the feeling of security which the ability of the French Government has produced in the other European States.

The sentiments of England continue equally favourable towards us, and her Cabinet will support us in everything that M. de Sainte-Aulaire [1] has been directed to demand from *Rome*.[2]

The Reform Bill will come on again on Monday; an animated discussion is expected, as the Ministers have to bring forward some modifications, which will not lessen the number of their opponents, but will on the contrary, alienate many advocates of reform. . . .

Our affairs in Paris were going on more satisfactorily, at least those with which I had to deal. But complications of all sorts did not fail to arise, both at home and abroad; we only seemed to get out of one, to tumble into another. It could not be expected, that the sole presence of M. Périer at the head of the government, would quiet all discord and re-establish order. The Duc de Dalberg thus wrote to me :

[1] Louis-Claire de Beaupoil, Comte de Sainte-Aulaire, born in 1778, had been chamberlain to the emperor and *préfet* of the Meuse (1813). Under the first Restoration he was *préfet* of Haute-Garonne. He rejoined the emperor during the Hundred Days, entered the Chamber in 1815, was removed in 1816 by the age clause, fixed at forty, but was re-elected in 1818, and sided with the moderate Liberals. He failed in the election of 1823, but re-entered Parliament in 1827, became vice-president of the Chamber and Peer of France in 1829. In 1830, he took up diplomacy, was accredited to Rome in 1831, to Vienna in 1833, and to London 1841. He retired in 1847, and died in 1854. M. de Sainte-Aulaire, was a member of the Académie Française. His daughter married the Duc Decazes in 1818.

[2] Suppressed in the text of the Archives.

THE DUC DE DALBERG TO THE PRINCE DE TALLEYRAND.

PARIS, *April* 12*th*, 1831.

THEY will tell you, mon cher Prince, that matters are more settled here ; I do not believe a word of it. Society is gradually going to pieces. M. Périer has just made an incalculable mistake, by the decree which replaces the statue of Buonaparte on the column in the Place Vendôme.[1] The Buonapartist party, led by the Republicans and Monarchists, will gain fresh strength. They will insist on the return of the whole Buonaparte family, and this will serve as a pretext for intrigues, which the government will not be able to deal with. The Nuncio told me that in Italy, they wished to have nothing more to do with that family. If *non-intervention* in the affairs of Italy had not been resolved upon here, Prince Metternich would have been quite ready to make use of the Duc de Reichstadt, to add to the already existing dissensions in France. You may take that as certain. The affairs of Poland give a fresh aspect to the whole situation. The coalition abroad is just now less to be feared, than the increasing embarrassments of the Treasury. The loan of the 19th must be raised at all hazards, otherwise payment will be suspended,[2] and what shall we do then with our 450,000 men ? . . .

A fund of truth lay beneath M. de Dalberg's somewhat exaggerated humour, but nevertheless, it was necessary to keep straight to one's own path, and provide as well as one could, for the fresh difficulties that each day brought forth. The following despatches give an account of some that had arisen :

THE PRINCE DE TALLEYRAND TO GENERAL SEBASTIANI.[3]

LONDON, *April* 16*th*, 1831.

MONSIEUR LE COMTE,

I have received your despatch of the 12th, in which you point out the serious grounds for uneasiness, which the entry of the troops of the German Confederation into the Grand Duchy

[1] See Casimer Périer's announcement which preceded the king's proclamation, ordering the statue of Napoleon to be replaced (*Journal des Débats*, April 12th).
[2] The loan of 120 millions at 5 per cent., which was obtained on the 19th April. It was at first suggested to raise it by public subscription, but only twenty millions were thus procured. A company was then formed, composed of all the most celebrated financiers in Paris, which accepted the loan at the rate of 84 francs, and thus saved the situation.
[3] Official despatch already published.

of Luxemburg will cause France. You also, M. le Comte, express a fear that the Diet may be drawn into a war through the influence of its President, and you observe with reason, that the movement of the Federal troops must not be regulated solely at Frankfort, adding, that to the representatives of the five Powers assembled in London, is left the decision as to the time when this important step will have become necessary.

I believe I can give a very satisfactory reply to these different observations.

The king's government having, from the very commencement of the differences between Belgium and the Germanic Confederation, desired that the Diet should not take any hasty steps, but rather adopt a wise and deliberate policy, I have proceeded on these lines with those members of the Conference whose sovereigns are allied to the Germanic Confederation, and I feel assured that their advice has, in reality, had a powerful influence up to the present on the deliberations at Frankfort, for if a Federal corps has been decided on for some time, you will doubtless have noticed the dilatoriness that has marked its definite organization.

The Diet would probably have continued this system of temporizing, if the recent proclamation of the Belgian Regent relative to the Grand Duchy of Luxemburg, and the discussions of the Congress, had not given sufficiently grave dissatisfaction to the Germanic assembly, to determine the Diet to adopt stringent measures, in order to put themselves beyond the reach of censure.

Nevertheless, M. le Comte, after the orders you transmitted to me, I had an interview with Prince Esterhazy and Baron de Bülow, both of whom seem quite inclined to adopt conciliatory views, and I have obtained their promise to use their best endeavours with the President of the Diet, to induce him to suspend all the hostile resolutions which appear to have been adopted at Frankfort.

The daily communications I have had with these two members of the Conference, leave me in but little doubt as to the actual feelings of the Diet, and everything tends to assure me that they are not of a nature to make us uneasy. Its military measures do not point to any immediate action—they are only *preparative*. You will no doubt have noticed from what a distance they are bringing their troops : contingents from Holstein, Oldenburg, the Hanseatic towns, and Mecklenburg, have been ordered to march towards the Rhine, while close at hand they had other troops which they could have sent off at once. But they did not wish to do this, and they have also avoided an appeal to the Prussians, foreseeing that their intervention would entail other disagreeables.

It therefore seems perfectly plain to me, that the disposition of the Diet, as well as its military measures, are not of a character to make us fear any immediate act of aggression. As for the President of that assembly, whom private information has depicted to you as desirous for war with Belgium, I do not think his influence is stronger than the wishes of his government, and we know for certain, partly by the measures countenanced by Prince Esterhazy, and partly by the direct and indirect communications of his Court, that Austria has no desire to kindle war in any part of Europe.

In addition to which, the Diet is not in a position to pronounce alone on such a very serious matter. The Conference always retains the power of advising the Diet ; and I can assure you, M. le Comte, that no order to take the field will leave Frankfort, before the Conference has made known to them that no other means of settlement are available. .

The repeated and brilliant successes of the Poles have caused a very keen sensation here as well as in France.[1] If the rising that has broken out in Lithuania, near the borders of Courland, results in adding to the number of Russia's enemies, it must not be forgotten, that the insurrection in Warsaw will have produced much more serious consequences than were at first anticipated.[2] The friends of peace and order, M. le Comte, cannot but applaud the language you held at the last two sittings of the Chamber of Deputies. It is only thus, as you remark in the end of your despatch, *that we can put an end to the disturbances which agitate Belgium.*

There has been nothing remarkable in the Parliamentary discussions here during the last two days, but they will be highly interesting on Monday or Tuesday . . . .

LONDON, *April* 19*th*, 1831.

MONSIEUR LE COMTE,[3]

I have received a communication from Lord Palmerston, informing me, that in consequence of some of his Britannic

---

[1] The Poles had been victorious at Grochow (February 19th). After the drawn battle of Prague (February 25th), they had again an advantage at Waver, Dembe Wilkie (March 30 and 31), and at Inganie (April 10th). Warsaw had been relieved and the Russians thrown back beyond the Bug. Lithuania revolted at the same time, and a Polish army had gone to raise Volhynia.

[2] Var. : Qu'on avait pu d'abord entrevoir = than one could at first have foreseen.

[3] This letter is not in M. Pallain's collection.

Majesty's subjects having suffered outrage and insult in Portugal, which the Portuguese authorities have condoned rather than punished, the English government has at once despatched two men of war to demand reparation and indemnity. If these are not obtained, the commander of this force is authorized to declare, that he will take the law into his own hands, and will treat with severity any Portuguese vessels he may meet at sea.[1]

LONDON, *April 20th,* 1831.

MONSIEUR LE COMTE,[2]

I have received the despatch you did me the honour to write on the 16th instant, relative to the hostile treatment of Frenchmen in Portugal. The communication made to me by Lord Palmerston, of which I acquainted you in my letter of yesterday, will show you that the English do not hesitate to act independently and alone, in their dispute with Portugal. They demand reparation, the amount of which they will decide ; and if they do not obtain it, the capture of all Portuguese vessels met at sea, will follow the refusal of Dom Miguel's agents. But there is no doubt that the cowardice which always accompanies cruelty, will make them yield at once and offer all possible amends.

I inform you of the steps taken by the English government in this matter, as you may probably find that a similar course would be most advantageous for us. Lord Palmerston feels sure, that threats are all that are needed.

I have given very close attention, M. le Comte, to the details you did me the honour to transmit, relative to the inhabitants of Samos ;[3] but without losing sight of Greek matters, it has been impossible lately to give them much attention, partly on account of Belgian affairs, and partly owing to the heavy Parliamentary duties of the English ministers. I trust, however, that we shall soon have a Conference on this subject.

---

[1] For some months past, England had had cause of complaint against Portugal. In the autumn of 1830, an English-vessel had been seized by Portuguese ships. At Lisbon, the English residents were subjected to all kinds of annoyance. In April 1831, the English Cabinet decided to take action and send a squadron to the Tagus. The Portuguese government at once gave in (May 2nd). France followed this example, and demanded satisfaction for the disgraceful treatment of two French merchants at Lisbon. Upon the refusal of Portugal, all the ships of that country, then in French ports, were seized. In addition, a French squadron under Admiral Roussin was held in readiness to proceed to the mouth of the Tagus (9th July).

[2] Official despatch already published.

[3] The island of Samos had been given to Turkey in addition to Candia, but the Conference wished to impose upon the Porte, such conditions as were necessary to protect the liberty of the inhabitants of those islands.

The Ministry have just suffered a defeat on General Gascoigne's amendment to the Reform Bill.[1] They are now in consultation, as to the best means of getting out of the difficulty thereby created. You will read the debates with great interest ; they lasted till five in the morning. I shall not hear the decision of the Council to-day till after post-time, but I will have the honour of communicating it to you to-morrow . . . .

LONDON, *April* 21*st*, 1831.

MONSIEUR LE COMTE,[2]

In my letter of yesterday I had the honour to inform you, that the Ministry had been defeated, and that the Council was then assembled to consider the means of escaping from its difficulty. The position has become still more difficult since yesterday, because Lord Wharncliffe, a member of the House of Lords,[3] had given notice, that he would propose an address to the king, praying his Majesty not to consent to the dissolution of Parliament which his ministers might recommend to him.

This state of affairs—the uncertainty as to the king's intentions,—the possible influences which the members of his family, whose views are in opposition, might bring to bear on his Majesty—the gravity of the Reform measure itself—have all contributed to produce a considerable amount of tension and uncertainty everywhere, during the last twenty-four hours.

Nevertheless, yesterday morning, the Ministry had obtained a positive promise from the king, that he would dissolve Parliament, provided the Bill relating to the Queen's dowry is voted before the dissolution, which would cause a delay of one or two days. But the announcement of Lord Wharncliffe's proposal having shown the Cabinet that they would have fresh difficulties to contend with, which delay would only increase, his Majesty determined to prorogue Parliament at once, which, according to custom, is followed by dissolution twenty-four hours afterwards. For this purpose the king went to the House to day.

[1] This Bill was again introduced into the Commons on the 9th of April. General Gascoigne's amendment to retain the same number of representatives for England and Wales, that is, to keep the *rotten boroughs*, was hotly discussed. The Ministry opposed this amendment, which nevertheless was carried by 299 votes to 291.
[2] Official despatch already published. It is dated April 22nd in the text of the Archives.
[3] James Stuart, Lord Wharncliffe, born in 1776, first entered the army, but quitted the service in 1801, and became a member of the House of Commons on the Tory side. In 1826 he succeeded his father in the House of Lords, and was one of the opponents of the Reform Bill in 1831. In 1834 he became Lord Privy Seal in Mr. Peel's Cabinet. In 1841 he was again President of the Council. He died in 1845.

You are aware, M. le Comte, that forty days must now elapse before a new Parliament can be assembled. Each party will take advantage of this respite to secure votes, and the greatest efforts will be made that one or the other side should triumph. All the members of Parliament are already preparing to leave town, for the different places which they have to canvass for their elections.

Four Belgian Deputies, M. le Comte de Mérode, M. Villain XIV,[1] l'Abbé Foere [2] and M. de Brouckère [3] arrived in London yesterday.

As far as we can learn, they have come to offer the crown to Prince Leopold of Saxe-Coburg. In my next despatch, I shall have the honour to inform you of the actual object of their mission, how they propose to carry it out, and the reply given thereto *by the prince*.[4] It is probable that this answer will be couched in rather evasive terms, and that his Royal Highness will avoid expressing either an actual acceptance, or a positive refusal, until Belgium has agreed to the protocol of January 20th. *Such at least is the opinion of those who know the prince intimately. . . .*[5]

I send you, herewith, the king's speech to Parliament this morning.

LONDON, *April 25th,* 1831.

MONSIEUR LE COMTE,[6]

I have this morning received [7] the despatch you did me the honour to write on the 22nd of this month. I experienced great satisfaction on perceiving, that the king's government had agreed to protocols Nos. 21 [8] and 22, and that they had only

---

[1] Charles Hippolyte Villain XIV., a Belgian diplomatist, was born in 1796. He had been returned for the States of West Flanders, and in 1830 was elected to the Congress. Under King Leopold's reign, he was Minister at Florence (1840), then at Turin, and lastly at Naples (1855).

[2] Léon de Foere, born in 1787, was Vicar of Bruges. From 1815, he had taken part in politics, and started a review to awaken national enthusiasm, which subjected him to numerous prosecutions. In 1830, he was elected deputy for Bruges. In the Congress, he was one of the chiefs of the anti-French party. He was continuously re-elected until 1848, when he retired from public life, and died in 1851.

[3] Henry de Brouckère, born in 1801, became public prosecutor in 1830. He threw himself hotly into the Revolution, and was elected deputy. In 1840 he was made civil Governor of Antwerp. He was appointed Minister of State in 1847, and President of the Council in 1852. He retired in 1855. He re-entered the Chamber in 1857, but did not take up public affairs again. He was head of the Liberal party.

[4] Suppressed in the text of the Archives

[5] Suppressed in the text of the Archives.

[6] Official despatch already published.

[7] Var. : *Par M. Casimir Périer* = By M. Casimir Périer.

[8] Protocol No. 21 (April 17th) confirmed the official adhesion of France to the protocol of January 20th, and settled some points of detail relative to territorial

occasioned some slight remarks. I shall submit them to the Conference, supporting them by the arguments contained in your despatch.

I would make the communication to them at once, if Lord Palmerston had not gone to Cambridge concerning his re-election. He will not return till the middle of next week, but during the interval, I will take care to see each of the other members of the Conference separately.

The desire of the king's government, that the five Powers should act in concert to determine the number of troops that should be employed in Luxemburg, and to fix the date when they should move, seems to me very fair, and quite in conformity with prudent counsel ; I believe that the Conference will be quite disposed to admit this.

As to the evacuation of Venloo and the citadel of Antwerp, it does not seem possible that any difficulties could be raised on this point, since the Belgians will have distinctly adhered to the protocol of January 20th.

Respecting the exchanges to be effected between Holland and Belgium, you are aware, M. le Comte, that by protocol No. 21, the Conference had declared this question to be premature, and that it must be adjourned to the time, when some light will have been thrown on it by the labours of the boundary commissioners. I shall find it very difficult to change the views[1] here on this point ; it will no doubt, be objected, that the King of Holland, having already agreed to the boundary protocol, would only expose himself to many difficulties, if fresh modifications are now brought forward. Nevertheless, I will do my utmost to induce the plenipotentiaries to adopt the views you have expressed.

The delay that you wish to grant the Belgians to make up their minds definitely, seems to me, I must confess, too pro-longed, if extended to June 1st. I should have thought it would perhaps have been better for his Majesty's government, as well as for the English government, to come before the Chambers (which in both countries assemble at the same period), after having completed all the principal affairs of Belgium.

arrangements between Belgium and Holland. Protocol No. 22, signed the same day, laid down that the commissioner of the Conference at Brussels, should receive orders to communicate to the Belgian government the protocol of January 27th, which fixed the basis of separation of the two States, and should ask for formal adhesion to this act, by insisting that Belgium should give up all claim to Luxemburg. In the event of her refusal, the Commissioner was ordered to quit Brussels at once, and the Powers warned the Belgian government, that they reserved to themselves the right to compel the Belgian troops to evacuate Dutch territory by force of arms.

[1] Var. : . . . . de voir *des plénipotentiaires* sur ce point, qui *m'objecteront* = the views of *the plenipotentiaries* on this point, *who will object*.

Prince Leopold has told the Deputies of that country, who have come to offer him the crown, that he will accept it on the day that Belgium agrees to the boundary protocol issued by the five Powers, from whom he does not intend to separate himself. Some of these Deputies have already quitted London ; they did not call either upon me or upon any other members of the Conference.

England is at this moment a prey to the most violent agitation, such as she has not felt since the revolution of 1688. The question of Parliamentary reform occupies every one, has roused all interests, and divides the nation, as it were, into two hostile camps. No one remains neutral, and every person who belongs to a party, throws himself heart and soul into the conflict, even to the extent of his fortune.[1] Subscriptions have been opened in various districts ; they have already risen to some enormous sums, one undertaking alone amounting to a hundred thousand pounds sterling. . . .

The agitation in England has communicated itself to Ireland, and in addition to the usual state of excitement in that country, serious riots are now disturbing the southern provinces. It seems to me, that this state of affairs gives France the opportunity of finding, in tranquillity, all those advantages that England loses by agitation.

Sir Frederick Lamb is appointed Ambassador to the Court of Vienna.[2] The Duc de Broglie has just arrived here. . . .

LONDON, April 26th, 1831.

M. LE COMTE,

I had the honour of telling you yesterday, that some of the Belgian Deputies had left London. This information is not quite correct. Just when they were about to depart, Prince Leopold asked them to dinner. They went ; Lord Grey was also there, and Belgian affairs were freely entered upon ; the discussion which had taken place, was renewed, and Prince Leopold, while persisting in the reply which I made known to you yesterday, has given fresh reasons and new motives for his decision. . . .

It has been decided, that the Abbé de Foere shall start alone this evening, and that the four other Deputies shall remain here, to await the result of the efforts he will make in Brussels. This is the gist of what was said to those Deputies : " First of all, you must agree to the protocol of January 20th, and elect your sovereign ; these two points being settled, you can proceed to

---

[1] Var. : en lui livrant même = even to the extent of giving up his fortune to it.
[2] Sir Frederick Lamb was Lord Melbourne's brother.

negotiate the exchanges, and you may rest assured that you will find the Conference very well disposed, when it is called upon to settle any points upon which you cannot agree."

Lord Grey argues very favourably of the conversation he and Prince Leopold had with the Deputies, although he does not conceal that matters are still very far from being settled.

Lord Palmerston has not yet returned ; therefore the day for our Conference is not yet settled. I still maintain the opinions expressed in my letter of yesterday, and I believe that, on the whole, you will be satisfied with the replies that will be sent you. . . .

A great stir has been made here, about a Note from General Guilleminot to Reis Effendi, which, it is affirmed, contains three declarations. The first is intended to prove to the Ottoman Porte, that the principles of the French government, being diametrically opposed to those professed by Russia and Austria, a war with those two Powers is inevitable. The second declaration announces, that England will either remain neutral, or will become the ally of France. The object of the third is to point out to the Porte, that she must think of her independence, and the doubtful benefits she would derive from an alliance with the Powers opposed to France.

When spoken to about this note, I was obliged to say, that I knew nothing whatever about what they told me had taken place at Constantinople, and that the loyalty both of my sovereign and his government did not admit of my belief in it. . . .

General Guilleminot's proceedings at Constantinople, of which mention is made in this despatch, had in truth occasioned some rather serious complaints to me from the English Cabinet. During the absence of Lord Palmerston, who was busy with his election at Cambridge, the Prime Minister, Earl Grey, had expressed himself to me with much warmth, respecting the conduct of our Ambassador at Constantinople. Being in total ignorance of the facts, I could but declare my utter incredulity. Next day, in sending me the reports of the English Ambassador at Constantinople, which were very explicit, he wrote as follows :

LORD GREY TO PRINCE DE TALLEYRAND.

DOWNING STREET, *April 26th*, 1831.

MY DEAR PRINCE,

I send herewith, copies of the information which has reached this government, respecting the proceedings of the French minister at Constantinople.

I feel confident, that conduct so contrary to good faith, can never have been sanctioned by the King of the French, and the character of his first minister affords me an equal assurance, that it requires only to be known to him, to be disavowed in the most direct and effectual manner.

I therefore forbear to offer any remarks on the character of the accompanying papers, which I shall be obliged to you to return to me, after having read them.

I am, with the highest regard and consideration,

Dear Prince Talleyrand,

Yours most faithfully,

GREY.

The documents he sent me, did in fact, confirm the announcement made by General Guilleminot to the Porte, that France was about to declare war against Russia and Austria, and that England would remain neutral or join France. It is difficult to understand, how so experienced a man as General Guilleminot could have hazarded such declarations, without instructions from his government. Be that as it may, as soon as M. Périer became aware of what had occurred, he at once recalled General Guilleminot. The latter, on his return to Paris, complained loudly of being disowned and abandoned by General Sebastiani, and the truth as to which of the two was in the wrong, has never been cleared up. But it remains no less certain, that such an incident was not calculated to inspire confidence in our government. The dates fortunately proved, that the proceedings of General Guilleminot had taken place at Constantinople, before the change which had installed M. Casimir Périer as President of the Council, could have been known there.

To return to my despatches:

THE PRINCE DE TALLEYRAND TO GENERAL SEBASTIANI.[1]

MONSIEUR LE COMTE,

LONDON, *April* 28*th*, 1831.

The assembly of the new Parliament gave occasion yesterday for numerous illuminations, as well as a good many

[1] Official despatch already published.

disturbances in London ; the mob broke the windows of several members known to be opposed to the Reform Bill ; this tumult however was not of a serious character, nor had it any results. You are aware that the parishes have to bear the cost of these popular outbreaks, which are pretty frequent in London. The last occurred after the trial of Queen Caroline, and on the passing of the Catholic Emancipation Bill. The proof that the present movement is not a serious one is, that it has had no effect whatever on the public funds.[1] The elections for the City commence to-morrow. . . .

LONDON, *April 29th*, 1831.

MONSIEUR LE COMTE,[2]

I have just had a long interview with the Belgian Deputies who have remained in London, which I must relate to you.

I began by showing these gentlemen the great interest which France takes in the welfare of Belgium. I added, that this interest would never belie itself, and that being fully convinced of the intentions of my government, I should always be ready to uphold their rights, and to give them proofs, as far as it depended on myself, of the sincere and disinterested friendship of France.

M. de Mérode then informed me, that he and his compatriots looked upon it as a matter of conscience, not to abandon the inhabitants of the Grand Duchy of Luxemburg, who had so unreservedly joined their cause and shared the risk. I tried to reassure him on this point by telling him, that the Conference had taken the particular position in which Luxemburg would be placed, into serious consideration, and that the right of the inhabitants of that country to a national representation, seemed to me assured, not only by the last protocol, No. 21, but also by the fundamental acts of the Germanic Confederation, of which the Grand Duchy formed an integral part.

The Deputies having passed on to the question of the exchanges, I begged them to notice how carefully with regard to this, the protocol of the 20th January, had laid down the principle for these exchanges, and the contiguity which would have to be established, in order to constitute a claim to the possessions of each State. If, I added, the execution of this clause has been adjourned, it is solely for the purpose of

---

[1] Var : *Ils sont aujourd'hui à 79. Aujourd'hui tout est rentré dans l'ordre* = They are to-day at 79. Everything has now returned to its former state.
[2] Official despatch already published.

allowing the boundary commissioners sufficient time to collect such views on these questions of exchange, as would better enlighten the five Powers, when they are called on to decide those points, on which Belgium and Holland might not be able to agree.

I wound up this explanation by telling the Belgian Deputies, that when the Conference once commenced this important work, they might rest assured, that all their demands which were founded on reason and equity, would be fully taken into consideration. . . .

They then finally enlarged on the difficulties by which the present government of Belgium was surrounded, and *vehemently*[1] expressed the wish to have a sovereign at their head, who could stand up for their rights. I told them that they ought certainly to make the choice of a sovereign the object of their earnest desires, and that they must remember that probably the prince on whom their choice fell, would not consent to accept the crown, until Belgium had agreed to the protocol of the 20th January, for he would recognize that this adhesion would place him from the very commencement of his reign, on a proper footing with the Great Powers, and one beneficial to Belgium. All this was said with a good deal of circumlocution, and a repetition of all the arguments we have used for the past month. This, M. le Comte, is the substance of my interview with the Belgian Deputies. I believe they will have found in it, the frank expression of my desire, always to support the views of the king's government, while looking after their interests here. The impression I received from this interview is, without doubt, entirely favourable as to the honest intentions of these Deputies ; but I could not fail to see, that they were very new to the business. . . .

LONDON, *May 1st*, 1831.

MONSIEUR LE COMTE,[2]

The elections are progressing entirely in favour of reform. From this it must not, however, be inferred, that this measure will be the same as that brought before the last Parliament, but it may be assumed that the majority of the electors wish for some kind of reform, and that very certainly they will get it.

Lord Palmerston having gone back to Cambridge, where his return is not at all certain, and M. de Wessenberg being seriously indisposed, the Conference has not met for some days,

---

[1] Suppressed in the text of the Archives.
[2] This letter is not in the text of the Archives.

and will, not assemble again till next week. Meanwhile, I will try and make the best possible use of the observations contained in your despatch of 28th April, on the proceedings attributed to General Guilleminot.

The Belgian Deputies dined yesterday with me. I did not gain much thereby; they are awaiting replies from the Abbé de Foere. . . .

LONDON, *May* 3*rd*, 1831.

MONSIEUR LE COMTE,[1]

Prince Leopold came to see me this morning, and I had a long conversation with him.

The prince seems to have decided to accept the Belgian throne, but he is perfectly aware, that to obtain the admission of the country among the European States, it is necessary that it should be on friendly relations with the Great Powers, and that it must first be placed in a position analogous to that of the King of Holland—a position which can alone end the difficulties, which have existed for the last six months.

His Royal Highness has frequently seen the Deputies who are in London, and he always expresses himself to them in the sense I have just indicated. The prince reminded them of the difficulties that had taken place when Antwerp was blockaded; the care and the efforts that had been expended, to induce the King of Holland to remove them ; that, consequently, it was necessary to avoid giving that sovereign fresh causes for disagreement, as it was not possible to see where it would end, and that the way to prevent this was to agree, as he had done, to the protocol of the 20th of January. In addition, the prince told the Deputies, that as soon as they had established proper relations with the Powers, he would himself take the deepest interest in the exchanges, and the other arrangements which concerned them most. He pointed out to them, that the principle of these exchanges had been included in the protocol of January 20th, because the aim of one of the conditions was, to assure to the Belgians and the King of Holland the contiguity of their possessions. He told them he had reason to believe, that on these terms they would receive marks of goodwill on the part of the Powers ; and that finally, he would use all his influence, to work unceasingly for the happiness of Belgium, so that that beautiful country might take its proper place in Europe, and develop all the sources of prosperity it possessed.

As for the Grand Duchy of Luxemburg, perhaps it will not

[1] Official despatch already published.

be impossible, M. le Comte, that while leaving the fortress with the Germanic Confederation, some arrangement can be made with the King of Holland, respecting the territorial part. Seeing it is so far distant from his other possessions, it is probably not of great value to him, and he might be induced to give it up for a sum of money, always, of course, after the Belgians have agreed to the protocol of January 20th. . . .

LONDON, May 6th, 1831.

MONSIEUR LE COMTE,[1]

I have received the despatch you did me the honour to write on the third of this month, relative to the recall of General Guilleminot. The information contained in my letter of April 20th, leaves little doubt respecting the facts which I had the honour to mention to you, and which I attributed in part to the intrigues of the Dragomans ; the unpleasantness that this affair created in our relations here, has quite blown over.

The king will not go to the dinner to which the City of London has invited him. It is thought better to avoid everything that gives the mob an excuse to congregate. There is reason to believe that Lord Palmerston will not be elected at Cambridge ; the influence of the clergy is very strong at that university.[2] The Ministry will procure his election for some less prominent place, which they have at their disposal ; if any peers are made, he might also perhaps be among those selected by the king.[3] Lord Palmerston will probably be here to-morrow. I think we shall then be able to hold a Conference, and that M. de Wessenberg's health will permit him to attend. . . .

The Polish Deputies, who are in London, think that if the engagement, which seems likely to take place in a few days, between Russia and their compatriots, is favourable to the latter, Austria and Prussia will offer their mediation, and this they dread. If France and England would take part in this mediation, they would feel satisfied. It seems to me, that England could not refuse to take part in it with us.[4] . . .

[1] Official despatch already published.
[2] Lord Palmerston failed at Cambridge, but was elected for the borough of Bletchingley.
[3] Var. : ainsi que Lord Sefton, qui a une promesse ancienne = as well as Lord Sefton, who has a promise of long standing.
[4] The following letter, which Lord Palmerston wrote to Lord Granville, will be read with interest, as showing the policy he intended to pursue with regard to Poland.

Private.
" FOREIGN OFFICE,
" 29th March, 1831.

. . . . " The Poles are fighting gallantly, and the Russians have suffered greater losses than is generally supposed, but the emperor must win in the end. I

LONDON, *May 9th*, 1831.

MONSIEUR LE COMTE,[1]

Our Conference was resumed to-day. We discussed the position of Belgium with regard to France and the other Powers of Europe. Full justice has been done to the Deputies who are here, and who seem endowed with much more common sense, than those who have hitherto been sent to us ; but, like them, they have no powers, and therefore no progress can be made in the questions relating to their country, and which it is high time were settled.

It has been agreed, in accordance with the wish expressed in your despatch of April 22nd, that the Belgians should be allowed until June 1st, to reply definitely to the proposals contained in protocol No. 22. This delay will be announced in the first protocol drawn up by the Conference.

I have the honour to send you, in case you have not already received it, the detail of the troops of the Germanic Confederation, which are to be employed in the Grand Duchy of Luxemburg. They are under the command of General Hinüber. It appears, according to the accounts received here, that their progress is very slow.

I have seen Prince Leopold to-day ; he has not altered his resolve ; he will not accept Belgium as it was defined by the Congress, and in which countries not even occupied by Belgians were included ; but he will accept Belgium as defined by the five Powers, and independent of the question of the Grand Duchy of Luxemburg.

The prince has had frequent interviews with the Deputies, and is always perfectly frank and open with them. They, on their side, are gaining confidence in him, and take every opportunity of expressing their desire to see him placed at their head, as they believe that only thus will peace be restored to their country ; but Prince Leopold does not conceal from them, that he will not be induced to go amongst them, until matters are further advanced, and there is no longer any uncertainty as to the resolutions of the provisional government, respecting the protocol of January 20th. Matters, you see, are still progress-

have had some conversation with Wielopolski and Waleski, and I told them we must hold to our treaties, and that, as on the one hand, we should protest, if Russia tried to evade the treaty of Vienna, we cannot on the other do so ourselves, by assisting Poland to become entirely independent."

(Private correspondence of Lord Palmerston, I. 32.) Lord Palmerston was therefore very far from acceding to the demands of the Polish Deputies, who wished to procure the active intervention of England.

[1] Official despatch already published.

ing but slowly. *In general however, the members of the Conference are anxious to complete affairs, and all expressed this wish to-day.*[1] . . .

LONDON, *May* 10*th*, 1831.

MONSIEUR LE COMTE,[2]

I have the honour to transmit herewith, the protocol drawn up by the Conference this morning, and which you will find is in thorough accord with the preceding protocols.[3] This protocol—the well-known adhesion of France to the resolutions adopted in London—Prince Leopold's acceptance conditionally announced to the Belgian Deputies, provided they agreed to the boundaries determined by the protocol of January 20th—the date of June 1st, which is fixed for their decision—all lead one to hope that reason will at last make itself heard in Belgium.

Lest, however, the Belgians should push matters to extremes, it was deemed prudent that the two members of the Conference, who are in regular correspondence with the Diet at Frankfort, should write to the President of that assembly, sending him, word for word, what we hope to find in M. de Münch's reply. This is the paragraph which will be inserted in the President's letter :

"The Confederation will not send the troops into Luxemburg, except for the purpose of asserting the rights of the Royal Grand Duke, and the supremacy of the treaties. Acting in the known and assured interests of the neighbouring States, it will also respect the neutrality of Belgium, on condition that Belgium herself will respect these principles."

You will notice that these precautions are only applicable, in case the Confederation, after the 1st June (the limit of the period granted to the Belgians), sees itself obliged to expel by force, those who are occupying territory which belongs to it.

My belief is that the Confederation is very anxious not to be compelled to have recourse to severe measures, and, above all, not to send its various contingents, whose movements it finds very costly, across the Rhine.

---

[1] Suppressed in the text of the Archives.
[2] Official despatch already published.
[3] The protocol of the 10th May (No. 23) confirmed protocol No. 22 of 17th April, and in completing it, fixed the 1st June, as the limit of the delay granted to the Belgians for acceptance of the said protocol. This period once past, the Powers declared their intention to break off relations with Belgium and leave the Germanic Confederation to act as it pleased in Luxemburg ; the protocol added, that violation of the armistice with Holland by the Belgians, would be looked upon by the Powers as a *casus belli.*

LONDON, *May* 12*th*, 1831.

MONSIEUR LE COMTE,[1]

I have received the despatch you did me the honour to write on the 10th of this month ; it describes the state of Belgium as it is now, and as we know it to be, from the accounts received here. In my letter of the 9th, I informed you how anxious the members of the Conference were to wind up this matter, but desiring to comply with your expressed wishes, they extended the delay accorded to the Belgians till the 1st of June.

The Belgian Deputies have been increased by another, M. Devaux,[2] who is a member both of the Congress and the Ministerial Council, and has just arrived here ; but he has no more power than those who preceded him.

Prince Leopold has seen M. Devaux ; he told him, as well as his colleagues, that he was quite ready to accept their offer, but that he would not give his assent as long as the state of Belgium is vague and uncertain, and above all, as long as the Belgians are not in friendly relations with the principal Powers of Europe.

. . . . I think it would be very advantageous, if you made known to General Belliard how matters stand here at present, so that he may use his influence, in inducing the Belgians to adopt the conciliatory measures proposed to them. . . .

I have nothing further to add to these despatches, which show sufficiently the numerous obstacles we had to overcome in our complicated negotiations. I must, however, make known the impression they made in Paris, and the echoes that came back to me from there. These will be found in the following letters, which I received during that period, and which, as will be seen, came from persons of sufficiently opposite views and ideas. Thus M. Casimir Périer wrote to me :

PARIS, *April* 23*rd*, 1831.

It is with great satisfaction, mon Prince, that we have received your last despatches, and the two protocols you have sent. At a council we held yesterday on this subject, we suc-

---

1 Official despatch already published.

2 Paul-Isidore Devaux, born at Bruges in 1809, very quickly made a name for himself as a journalist on the Liberal side. He was made deputy of the Congress in 1830, and minister without a portfolio under the Regency of M. Surlet de Chokier. He went to London, in May 1831, as commissioner to the Conference, retired from his ministerial duties on his return, but remained in the Chamber of Representatives until 1863. At that period he was attacked with blindness, and obliged to retire from political life.

ceeded in procuring their approval. The Minister of Foreign
Affairs is sending you some proposals to-day ; we shall be very
glad, if you will take into consideration the one relating to the
exchanges of territory, and obtain the consent of the Confederation thereto. These arrangements will, we believe, facilitate the
negotiations on Belgian affairs ; and if we hear that they have
been favourably received, we shall see the happy commencement
of a definite solution of all our earnest wishes. General Belliard
is about to leave, bearing instructions in conformity with the
communications made to you by the Minister of Foreign
Affairs ; nevertheless, he is not to make use of them, until
after we have received your reply on this subject.

The progress of home affairs becomes more satisfactory, and
the government is advancing more successfully towards the aim
it has in view. Our position is, however, none the less serious,
and in the midst of all this perturbation, peace is a necessity,
not only for France, but for the stability of all the States. We
especially meet with obstacles in that spirit of disorder and in-
novation, which is no longer confined to France, but which our
example seems to have made European.

But with perseverance, and the maintenance of peace, in
which you so ably support us, we shall escape from the difficult
position in which we have been placed. This is our hope ; and
now more than ever do we feel, that there is a necessity and a
duty, in fulfilling the mission we have imposed on ourselves. . . .

Comte Alexis de Noailles,[1] whom I may cite as a representative of the Faubourg St. Germain, wrote thus to me on the
30th of April :

MON PRINCE,

. . . . I am just about to start for my department, to
be present at the session of my *conseil général* and the elections.
Opinions vary as to the result, but every one's ideas change from
day to day ; those who are most alarmed, return to the opinion
that the elections in general, will be for the moderate party. It
is even asserted that M. Demarçay,[2] M. Corcelles,[3] and M.

[1] Formerly plenipotentiary at the Congress of Vienna. M. de Noailles, a
member of the last Chamber of the Restoration, had, as deputy, taken the oath to the
new government, but he was not re-elected in 1831.
[2] Marc-Jean Demarçay, born in 1772, entered the service when very young, and
retired as Brigadier-General in 1810. Under the Restoration he was elected deputy
for Deux-Sevres, and became one of the most active members of the opposition. He
was not returned in 1824, but was elected for the Seine in 1827. He supported the
July government for a short time, but soon re-joined the opposition, with which he
remained till his death in 1839.
[3] Claude Tircuy de la Barre Corcelles, born in 1768, was an officer of Cavalry in

Salverte,[1] will not be re-elected for Paris. The latter, being by far the most talented of all the members of the Left, will, I have no doubt, be always re-elected.   As for the others, their election is in fact very doubtful.

What a fate is yours, mon Prince, and what a glorious political destiny yours has been ! Thrice, during the greatest events, amidst threats of the immediate dissolution of this country, you have stepped in, guiding the vessel almost alone, and have succeeded in bringing it into port.   This time your services have been even greater, for you have had to struggle and contend, against an almost universal opinion. You have swayed not only negotiations and events, but even opinions, in accordance with your views. War just now would be a death-blow to France. The government is doing its best in the interests of peace ; all parties have come round to this opinion, and no one would venture to offer another. . . .

Let us hear what the Duc de Dalberg says :

PARIS, *May 3rd*, 1831.

. . . . The old fox of Luxemburg (M. de Sémonville[2]) holds to his prophecy that this state of affairs cannot last, and supports it by so many reasons that it is difficult not to agree with him. He believes in the recall of the little *eaglet* (the Duc de Reichstadt), who he thinks does not care much about it, but will leave the field open to other combinations among the pretenders.

I am almost sure, that while we were threatening Austria with war in Italy, the Buonapartist party here, ever active and on the move, received promises of assistance. Now, quite another tone has been adopted towards that party.

1789. He emigrated in 1792 and returned to France ; lived in retirement till 1814. Appointed Colonel of the Rhone National Guards during the Hundred Days, he was put under arrest after the second Restoration, and although released, was obliged to quit France, not returning thither till 1818. In 1819, he was elected deputy for the Rhone, and offered a strong opposition in the Chamber to the government. He remained on this side after 1830, retired from public life in 1835, and died in 1843.

[1] Anne-Joseph-Eusèbe Baconière-Salverte, born in 1771, was an advocate at the Châtelet prior to 1789. He took no part in the Revolution. Compromised under the directory in the Royalist reaction, he was condemned to death for contumacy after the 13th Vendémiaire ; but he appeared before his judges and was acquitted. He lived in retirement during the Empire, occupying himself solely with philosophical and literary works. Under the Restoration, he made a name for himself as a polemist in the Liberal party, and was elected to the Chamber of Deputies in 1828, and sat among the extreme Left. Re-elected for Paris in 1831, and 1834, he maintained the same attitude towards the July government, and died in 1839.

[2] M. de Sémonville was at that time chief Referendary to the Court of Peers.

If the Austrians are forced to quit the Papal States, disturbances will break out in every quarter. The conduct of the people at Parma and Modena is ridiculous. [1]

Casimir Périer does his best, but he has more difficulty with those *above him* than those below him.

The recall of General Guilleminot has made some impression. Latour-Maubourg,[2] who is at Naples, ought to replace him ; but it is said that Sebastiani intends sending his brother there,[3] which will please no one but his own family. . . .

PARIS, *May 10th,* 1831.

. . . . The party spirit which reigns here, and which is fostered by the weakness of the government, although the latter does its best, renders a stay here more unpleasant every day.

Buonapartism is now completely in the ascendant. It is used as a means to work upon the army and the lower classes, who are led away by the success of those, who have risen to thrones and become the recipients of fortune's favours. The government is wrong not to express more clearly its opinion of Imperial rule. Everyone has become a Buonapartist, because the *Palais Royal* and its *camarilla*, have neither fear nor respect for any other party. The result is that the movement gains strength. Mauguin said the other day, to a man from whom I have it, " We ought to have a provisional government, and a regency in the Duc de Reichstadt's name, and we shall come to that."

You may rely upon it, that if war broke out in Italy, Austria would further these intrigues. On the other hand, how could you restrain the ardour of the army which has been assembled, and that of the French populace, which has been so foolishly excited, by rumours of the foreigners who are anxious to attack France ?

However, in the next session of the Chambers, they will

---

[1] The Duke of Modena and the Duchess of Parma (the ex-Empress Marie-Louise) had given in when the riots broke out, and had gone away.

[2] Just de Fay, Marquis de Latour-Maubourg, born in 1781, entered the diplomatic service under the consulate, became secretary to the Embassy at Copenhagen and then at Constantinople, where he continued as *chargé d'affaires* till 1812. He then went to Stuttgart as minister (1813). At the Restoration he was made minister at Hanover, then ambassador at Dresden (1819), and at Constantinople (1823). The July government accredited him to Naples (1830), and then to Rome, where he remained until his death. M. de Latour-Maubourg became a member of the Chamber of Peers by right of heredity in 1831.

[3] Jean-André Tiburce, Viscomte Sebastiani, born in 1780, entered the army in 1806, became Brigadier-General in 1823. He was put on the Reserve list and entered the Chamber of Deputies in 1828. He did not obtain the Embassy at Constantinople, but was made Lieutenant-General and a Peer of France in 1837. He retired to Corsica in 1848.

have to see how they can best exorcise all these elements of discord. . . .

I will wind up these extracts with a rather long letter from Madame Adelaide d'Orléans, dated May 11th, which, as will be seen, is the most important of all.

MADAME ADELAIDE D'ORLÉANS TO THE PRINCE DE TALLEYRAND.

ST. CLOUD, *May 11th,* 1831.

It is much to be regretted, my dear Prince, that I am so far behindhand in my correspondence with you, but we have been so busy lately with our dear king's fête, which went off as well as we could possibly have wished, and then, immediately afterwards, in settling down here, that it was impossible, much as I wished it, to find a spare moment to write to you. I had the pleasure of seeing Madame de Dino yesterday, and of hearing from her, that you are now quite well again, and always busily occupied with this unfortunate Belgian business, which I should much like to see concluded. I think from what the Prince de Coburg writes to me, that he is strongly tempted to consent, but that his experience of having been too hasty in the Greek affair, prevents his acceptance until all arrangements are made ; which I must admit I can quite understand.[1] What he tells me respecting the arrangements for Luxemburg, seems to me to be very reasonable. It would be extremely desirable for the peace of France, Germany, and Belgium, if the King of Holland could be induced to cede that country, either for or against an indemnity, and I should be well pleased if this could be effected by the intervention of France through you, if it is, or may still be possible. It seems to me that this would suit us in every way, but perhaps I am reasoning thus, being only an ignoramus in political matters. Forgive me, mon cher Prince, and tell me your opinion about it.

I was in hopes of being able to tell you, that we were perfectly quiet here, and so we were until yesterday. But a

[1] Prince Leopold had in fact been almost nominated King of Greece. Approved of by the Powers and accepted by Greece, he would not however agree to the conditions imposed by the Conference. This latter, in its protocol of February 3rd, 1830, had so settled the boundaries of Greece, that Etolia and Acanarnia still remained to the Porte, together with the islands of Candia and Samos. Prince Leopold protested against this to the Conference (letter of the 11th of February) ; the latter maintained its decision, and the prince definitely refused the crown.

I 2

banquet given the night before last, to the leaders of those who
objected to the cross of July,[1] was followed by songs, shouts,
crowds in the streets, and some disturbance. Yesterday the
crowds were dispersed several times, but towards evening, the
mob having assembled in greater numbers in the Place de
Vendôme, the Riot Act was read, and they were then completely
dispersed by a charge of cavalry. The national guard and the
whole population of Paris, are incensed at these attempts on
the part of a small number of the rabble to create disturbance.
There is no reason for uneasiness, though it is very annoying. I trust this attempt, which is generally discountenanced
and disapproved of, will be the last.

The king starts on Monday next for a tour in Normandy,
which has long been asked for and desired, and which is sure to
have a good effect. He intends going to Rouen and Havre,
returning *via* Eu. He expects to be back here on the 26th.
During that time, the queen and I will remain at St. Cloud,
with my nieces and my grand-nephews. We have very good
accounts of our dear little sailor (the Prince de Joinville), who
must be at Toulon just now, where he embarks on the 15th.
He will go first to Corsica, then to Livorno, Naples, Sicily,
Malta, and Algiers ; thence to Mahon, where he will perform
quarantine. It is a lovely trip, and will benefit him in every
way. He will be back in about three months.

I have become quite reconciled to my stay at St. Cloud, to
which before coming here, I was not quite inclined. It is a
lovely spot ; the *environs* are charming and the drives delightful ;
and then the recollections of past days are very dear. I think
we shall remain here about six weeks.

Adieu, mon cher Prince. . . .

P.S.—I have just read to my brother the political ideas expressed in my letter to you, and have not received the compliments thereon which I fully expected. He told me that he would
no longer meddle with, or give advice to, either one side or the
other, as he had handed over the matter to be fought out by
the Conference, being rather tired of the distrust so constantly

---

[1] The proclamation of the 13th April, in accordance with the law of December
13th preceding, had created a special decoration for the combatants of July. The
recipients were required to take the oath of fidelity to the king and obedience to the
charter. The cross bore the motto "Given by the King of the French." These two
provisions, the oath and the motto, were deemed unconstitutional by the citizens
selected for the decoration. They protested against them and refused to submit to
them. The matter was finally arranged, but not without much noise and some disturbances in the vicinity of the Vendôme Column. It was on this occasion, that the
Comte de Lobau dispersed the rioters, by turning upon them the hoses of the fire
engines.

shown, which he had flattered himself he was beyond. Also that he did not intend favouring Prince Leopold more than any one else, not from want of confidence or friendship for him, quite the contrary, but because he did not wish his advice to be again misconstrued, and because he feared that if he did, some other motive, rather than the true feelings which dictated his conduct in this matter, would be attributed to him, namely, his earnest desire, and even impatience, to see the affairs of Belgium brought to a conclusion by the election of a sovereign, who would both insure her independence, and organize a government capable of maintaining peace and good order.

He desires me to tell you, that you have quite surpassed his expectations, by the ability and boldness with which you have induced the Conference, to *break up* the kingdom of the Netherlands and detach Belgium from Holland, or rather to recognize their separate independence. But he thinks that since this great step has been effected, the antipathy which the Belgians have inspired, has perverted the principal point of this measure, and that in the difficulty of managing them, the necessity of prevailing upon them, above all, to choose a sovereign, has been lost sight of. And my brother tells me, that he has never ceased to think, to say, and to reiterate, that this choice once effected to the satisfaction of Europe, and particularly of France, there would be no more trouble with the Belgians, for their co-operation would be assured, or at any rate easy to obtain ; whereas by insisting that the Belgians should act by themselves, matters have been thrown into the labyrinth of governing assemblies. That it was running a great risk, either to obtain nothing from them, (as had happened) but spontaneous and unacceptable selections, or to see the present state of anarchy and want of government still further prolonged, thereby throwing them more and more into the arms of the propaganda, and wild dreams of war and of a republic.

My brother tells me he never hesitated one moment about the protocol of the 20th January, and that he has never ceased to tell the Belgians this himself ; but that he did not wish to retard the choice of a sovereign, a delay which the Republican party has always desired, as it thought that, if the sovereign was once chosen, the Republican party would be beaten, and that it ought to be a matter of perfect indifference to their sovereign, whether this acceptance of the protocol of the 20th January, was insisted on before, or after his election, for everyone would know it had been insisted on. . . .

But in allowing me thus to send you his personal views, my brother wishes me to say, that he is always ready to give you

this mark of his confidence, and that he knows he need not tell
you to keep them to yourself. He wishes you to look upon
this, as if it were a conversation he had had with you sitting
beside him on the *couch*, and not in any way as an official communication, of which he would never wish me to become the
medium. . . .

I must pause at this long postscript to Madame Adelaide's
letter, which had evidently been dictated by the king. This, while
re establishing the facts, will enable me briefly to recall the
point at which the Dutch affairs had arrived, and which threatened to bring us to a dead-lock.

The Belgian Congress had voted for a constitution in which
the territory comprising Belgium, such as the Belgians
wished it, was clearly defined.[1]   In this definition they had included territories to which they had no claim whatever, under
the pretext, that as the inhabitants of these countries had joined
them in their revolution, they were in honour bound to demand
their incorporation, and the sovereign to be elected by them,
when accepting the crown, was to promise to maintain a constitution drawn up in this sense.   In opposition to this constitution,
was the protocol of the Conference of January 20th, by which
the boundaries of Belgian territory had been fixed in accordance
with treaties and historic precedents.   The King of Holland
deprived of Belgium, had consented, although reluctantly, to the
boundaries fixed by the Conference.   This was the state of
affairs, when the Belgian Congress decided to offer the crown
to Prince Leopold.   The most ordinary prudence clearly demanded, that this prince should not accept the crown until after
the Belgians had renounced their ill-founded claims.   Any other
course would have placed him in a most false and dangerous
position.   In fact, if after having accepted the crown and the
constitution, he had then insisted upon the Belgians giving up
the territories which they could not be permitted to retain, he
would have put himself in opposition to the constitution ; or,

---

[1] The Belgian Constitution was passed on the 7th of February.   Article I.
enumerated the territories claimed by the Congress, namely, the provinces of
Antwerp, Brabant, East and West Flanders, Hainault, Liège, Namur, Limburg, and
Luxemburg, excepting as regards its relations with the Germanic Confederation.

even supposing the Belgians had given in to his urgency, he would then have begun his reign under the worst possible auspices, for he would have been reproached with not having obtained what was hoped for from his election. If, on the contrary, Prince Leopold, having once become king, supported and upheld the ill-founded claims of the Belgians, he would thereby put himself in direct opposition to the five Powers represented at the Conference in London, and also to the Germanic Confederation, which claims the Grand Duchy of Luxemburg. It was therefore quite natural, that King Leopold should refuse to accept so compromising a position. This answers the observations of King Louis Philippe, given in Madame Adelaide's letter cited above.

It may be useful to recall, once more, the facts concerning the Grand Duchy of Luxemburg. It must not be forgotten, that this Grand Duchy belonged to the King of Holland personally ; it had been ceded to him in 1814, in exchange for the territories which, as a prince of the House of Nassau, he had the right of claiming in Germany, and of which part had been given to Prussia. In ceding the Grand Duchy to him, it had been specially stipulated, that it should remain connected with the Germanic Confederation on account of the fortress of Luxemburg, which was situated in it, and had been declared a Federal fortress. The King of Holland, at that time King of the Netherlands, had, it is true, subsequently united this Grand Duchy to the Netherlands to facilitate its administration ; but this union had not been complete, because, as Grand Duke of Luxemburg, he still remained a member of the Germanic Confederation, and was in consequence obliged to furnish a military contingent (drawn from the Grand Duchy itself) to the Federal army.

France, whatever may have been said about it in Paris, had only a very secondary interest in all these questions. The immense advantages she had gained by the dissolution of the kingdom of the Netherlands, the declaration of the independence and the neutrality of Belgium, and likewise by the demolition of a certain number of Belgian fortresses, had all been obtained without a war. Could it possibly benefit her to risk war, in order to insure a more or less limited frontier to the

Belgians? Assuredly not. I therefore troubled myself but very little with the declarations that came from Brussels and Paris on this subject, and pursued my own line of attaining as equitable an arrangement of Belgian affairs by the Conference, as was possible. They began at last fortunately to realize in Paris, that Prince Leopold was, of all the aspirants, the one who offered the best guarantees, and this somewhat facilitated my task, which continued to be sufficiently burdensome for some months to come.

Before continuing my despatches, I must mention a matter of no great importance in itself, but which gave rise to the most absurd comments in certain newspapers, and with regard to which I am very glad to be able to state the truth, so far as concerns myself. It is well known that the Duchesse de Saint-Leu,[1] after the death of her eldest son in Florence, during the disturbances in the Papal States, in which he had taken part, had gone to Paris *incognito,* accompanied by her second son, Prince Louis Napoleon. She was obliged to make her presence in the capital, known to the king and M. Casimir Périer who tolerated her stay there until her son, who was said to be unwell, was able to continue his journey. From Paris she went to London, and the king's government informed me of her arrival, giving me the details of her sojourn in Paris. She expressed a desire to see me, but I deemed it more prudent to avoid an interview with her, and I begged my niece, Madame de Dino, to call on her, and ask in what way I could be of service to her. She wanted a passport, to proceed with her son through France into Switzerland, where she has a residence. I transmitted this request to Paris, where, after some hesitation, they decided to authorize me to grant her a passport, which I hastened to do. I should have felt no awkwardness in seeing her, if my so doing would have been of any service to her. I had several times met Lucien and Joseph Buonaparte, the Emperor Napoleon's two brothers, in London society, and I had the same regard for them that I always shall have for the members of that family.

If, as I did in 1814, I now think the Napoleonic policy

---

[1] This was the name adopted by Queen Hortense during her exile. It will be remembered that her eldest son, Prince Charles, died at Forli.

dangerous to my country, I cannot forget what I owe to Napoleon, which is a sufficient reason for always exhibiting an interest founded on gratitude, to the members of his family, but without permitting it to exercise any influence on my political views. Madame la Duchesse de Saint-Leu wrote to me as follows, with respect to the passport, which confirms all I have just said:

THE DUCHESSE DE SAINT-LEU TO THE PRINCE DE TALLEYRAND.

TUNBRIDGE WELLS, 1831.

PRINCE,

I am authorized to ask you for a passport for Madame la Comtesse d'Arenenberg (this was the name of her property in Switzerland) and her suite. If you think the names of the persons composing the suite should be designated, you can add: her son, Mademoiselle Masuyer, two servants, and a lady's maid. I want my passport made out simply for Switzerland, whither I expect to go towards the end of this month. I am very glad, Prince, to have this opportunity of thanking you for the kindness you have shown me in this matter. I am sorry not to have seen Madame de Dino before my departure. Kindly express my regret to her, and receive for yourself, as well as for her, the expression of my sentiments.

HORTENSE.

We will now continue the despatches.[1]

PRINCE DE TALLEYRAND TO GENERAL SEBASTIANI.

LONDON, *May* 16*th*, 1831.

MONSIEUR LE COMTE,

. . . . No greater importance than they deserve, was attached here to the late events in Paris ; on the contrary, the continued rise of the funds was quite noticeable. Nevertheless, it is very desirable that the attention of the foreign Powers should not be drawn to us by the recurrence of such scenes.

The English papers announce to-day, that Dom Miguel's government had acceded to all the demands of the commander of the British forces, and they add, that probably it will request the good offices of England to arrange their differences with us.

---

[1] All the subsequent despatches up to p. 165 are official and departmental despatches, and have already been published.

No communication, however, has as yet been made to me to justify this allegation.

Lord Ponsonby arrived in London yesterday. He brought me a letter from General Belliard, informing me, that they both found it almost impossible to carry out the resolutions of the Conference, seeing that the government in Brussels dared not bring forward any discussions on this subject. This state of affairs is becoming more and more critical; it requires strong measures, for it is quite evident that the longer the delay granted to the Belgians, the graver becomes their position. The Conference will take cognizance of the facts made known by Lord Ponsonby to his government. I, on my side, will communicate to it the information transmitted to me by General Belliard, and we will endeavour to arrive at such measures as are best applicable to the state of things.

The information received in London as to affairs in Brussels, states, that Frenchmen have taken a very active part in the late disturbances, that out of seventeen persons arrested, twelve belonged to France, and that on one of them was found a sum of twenty-two thousand francs. It is also added, that the combination in Paris is in active correspondence with that in Brussels, furnishing it with arms and money. I must draw your attention to these reports, which are circulated pretty widely.

I yesterday saw the three Belgian Deputies, who were still in London, some hours before their departure. I again urged them most strongly, to use all the influence they possessed in Brussels, to make the Belgians realize their position. I combated some objections they yet had, respecting consideration for national honour, which would not allow them to abandon Luxemburg, or renounce their claim to the possession of Maëstricht. I told them, that views of national honour were not applicable to territories which never formed part of their country ; that they must first of all enter the world of Europe, and then discuss the questions now occupying them, one by one, according to their degree of importance.

Finally, I did my utmost to give them a good impression, and instil some sensible ideas which they might transmit to Brussels, but I found them greatly discouraged, and very anxious as to the future fate of their country. . . .

LONDON, *May* 18*th*, 1831.

. . . . Yesterday we had a conference respecting the situation of Belgium and to hear Lord Ponsonby's statement.

Having received your despatch of the 15th, a few hours before, I went to this Conference greatly desirous to procure the adoption of the conciliatory views which Lord Ponsonby had to bring forward. You will see by my answer to General Belliard, to whom I have given full details as to the results of the Conference, that a promise has been made to the Belgians, to open negotiations with the King of Holland, relative to the cession of Luxemburg, but that at the same time they have been told, that any aggression on the territory of that sovereign, will be repelled by the means which the Powers have at their disposal.

We trust that language so well disposed, though determined, will produce a good effect in Brussels. The other members of the Conference have written in the same sense.

Lord Ponsonby will probably leave this evening, after having seen M. de Zuylen, who has just arrived here. He is charged by the Court at the Hague, to point out the necessity of inducing the Belgians to fulfil the conditions of the separation of their country from Holland. They are becoming uneasy at the Hague, at the delays which the Belgians have obtained. They would like to ascertain what measures will be adopted in case of refusal. The Dutch government likewise complains of some partial aggressions on the part of Antwerp, close to Luxemburg, &c. You will, no doubt, find full details in a despatch which M. de Marcuil[1] has sent you from the Hague, and which I have the honour to transmit herewith. . . .

The members of the Conference on the Affairs of Greece, have heard with much pleasure, that the king's government has taken steps to send 500 men of General Schnieder's[2] brigade to the assistance of Comte Capo d'Istria's government. They have requested me to express to you their gratitude for this arrangement. . . .

LONDON, *May* 19*th*, 1831.[3]

The arrival of M. de Zuylen, who appears to be much in the King of Holland's confidence with respect to the Belgian

---

[1] Baron Durand de Marcuil had been minister at the Hague since 1830 ; he had been previously accredited, once before to the Hague in 1821, then to Washington in 1823, to Rio in 1829, and finally became ambassador at Naples in 1832.

[2] Antoine Schneider, born in 1780, entered the Engineers in 1799. He became a colonel in 1815, and took part in the Spanish campaign in 1823 ; in 1828 he was sent to the Morea as general of brigade, and became commander-in-chief after the departure of Marshal Maison. On his return to France, he became lieutenant-general (1831), was elected Deputy in 1834, and sat in the Chamber until his death (1847). He was War Minister for a short time, from 1839-1840.

[3] This letter is dated May 20th in the Archives.

question, delays Lord Ponsonby's departure for two days. I will have the honour to acquaint you, by the first courier, of the result of the communications that will take place to-day and to-morrow.

LONDON, *May 20th*, 1831.

. . . . The account which Lord Ponsonby gave us of the situation in Belgium, of the weakness of its government, and the anarchy to which this country has been given up, need not be retailed to you, as you thoroughly estimated it when you informed me in the despatch of the 10th, which you did me the honour to write, that the voice of reason would not be listened to in Brussels. The king's government deemed that this state of affairs still demanded consideration on its part, and I have received instructions to endeavour to prevent the employment of force and the renewal of hostilities. This I did, and you have seen by my despatch No. 143,[1] that the Conference has made a decided concession to your views, by promising the Belgians to open up negotiations with the King of Holland, in order to bring about, if possible, some understanding respecting Luxemburg. Nevertheless, I ought not to conceal from you, that the members of the Conference think that such a concession, instead of lessening the difficulties, will only render them still greater, by furnishing the Belgians with fresh encouragement for their foolish hopes. But the Conference was anxious to give fresh proof of its deference to His Majesty's government, and its desire for conciliation.

If this concession is not properly appreciated by the Belgians, if it does not induce them to accede to the fair demands that have been made to them during the last five months, if, on the contrary, it induces them to persist still further in their course of resistance to the Powers, I must tell you candidly, that in that event, the Conference will consider it has exhausted all possible means of conciliation. The king's government will then have to send me fresh instructions. . . .

M. de Zuylen has no powers, which will permit him in any way to further the matters we have now in hand. He declares that his sovereign, having reason to fear aggressive measures on the part of the Belgians, has put himself in a position to repel them.

Lord Ponsonby is still in London; he goes down to Claremont, to-morrow, to have an interview with Prince Leopold. I have reason to believe that the English govern-

[1] See page 122, despatch May 18th.

ment intends to further the prince's acceptance of the Belgian crown ; but I do not think it will succeed, as Prince Leopold is not inclined to accept anything which is uncertain. . . .

LONDON, *May 22nd* 1831.

MONSIEUR LE COMTE,

My despatch, No. 143, will have informed you of the concession the Conference was disposed to make to the Belgians, respecting the Grand Duchy of Luxemburg. Since then, it has been busily occupied concerting measures to facilitate prince Leopold's acceptance of the Belgian throne. That prince has seen several of the members of the Conference, and has given them fresh proofs of his wish to accept it.

We met again yesterday, and have drawn up protocol No. 24, of which I have the honour to send you a copy herewith.[1] You will see, that Prince Leopold of Saxe-Coburg is mentioned in this protocol in such a manner, as to show the Belgians, that if, as there is reason to believe, their choice falls on this prince, the Powers will give their consent thereto. I also beg you to notice, that this protocol is signed by the two plenipotentiaries of the Russian government, which up to the present, owing to its strong affection for the House of Nassau, had raised objections to the choice of Prince Leopold ; and that, consequently, it has now given its consent to this choice.

It is imperative, that the government of the king should now use all the influence it possesses in Brussels, to induce the Belgians to accede to such friendly overtures.

You will also observe, that the action of the Germanic Confederation has been adjourned, and subordinated to the negotiations with Holland, which will be a source of tranquillity to all parties.

For some time it seemed, as if the Belgian question was never likely to come to an [2] issue ; now, however, there appears to me to be a prospect of this, which I hope will conduce[3] to

---

[1] This protocol, signed May 21st, following on Lord Ponsonby's report of the situation of Belgium, deals with two subjects :

1st. The acquisition of Luxemburg, on conditional terms, by Belgium.

2nd. The eventual acceptance of the crown by Prince Leopold.

With regard to the first, the Conference undertakes "to open negotiations with the King of the Netherlands with the object of assuring, if possible, the possession of Luxemburg to Belgium, by means of such fair compensation as would still preserve its present relations with the Germanic Confederation." It adds, "that its object in thus acting, is to clear up the difficulties which might prevent Prince Leopold's acceptance of the sovereignty of Belgium, if, as everything leads one to believe, this sovereignty should be offered to him."

[2] Var. : satisfaisante = satisfactory.

[3] Var. : aujourd'hui nous en avons créé une qui pourra, je l'espère, nous conduire = now we have created one which may, I hope, lead us.

the end we have in view. I am congratulating myself all the more, as I have seldom had to conduct any business that required greater care. I most earnestly hope that the negotiations in which I have taken part, may prove as successful as could be wished ; I, at any rate, have left nothing undone that could further the interests of France and the maintenance of peace.

Lord Ponsonby leaves for Brussels to-day. . . .

LONDON, *May 24th,* 1831.

. . . . You did me the honour to inform me, on the 21st of this month, that the king's government had learnt with satisfaction, that the Conference had decided to open up negotiations relative to the cession of Luxemburg to Belgium. You will have seen by protocol No. 24, attached to my despatch of the 22nd, what has been the sequence of this decision, which has become a means of advancing Belgian affairs, if they only know how to appreciate and take proper advantage of it.

It would not be quite true, M. le Comte, to attribute the adoption of the measure just decided upon, solely to Lord Ponsonby, and to the impression he has made on the Conference. The letter I had received from General Belliard, and which I communicated to the Conference, produced far more effect, than Lord Ponsonby's *exposé ;* the proof of this, is the marked attention with which it was listened to, and the request from Lord Palmerston, that I should read it to them a second time. Whatever additional circumstances there may have been to influence the minds of the plenipotentiaries, and whatever measures may have been employed, I think we have all the more reason to congratulate ourselves on the decision that has been taken, as I had but little hopes of obtaining it the evening before the Conference, or even a few hours before. I think, however, that weariness, as well as the desire to see it ended, probably contributed thereto.

I never understood, that the relations which might still subsist between the Grand Duchy of Luxemburg and the Germanic Confederation, were applicable to anything beyond the fortress ; for it would be impossible that Belgium, having become neutral, her neutrality should not extend to the Grand Duchy of Luxemburg, as well as to any other acquisitions she may in future receive.

I had the honour of seeing Prince Leopold this morning. He told me that Lord Ponsonby was about to leave, which I have since ascertained he has done. Thus Belgian affairs are tending towards a solution, which could easily be arrived, at if they would only have the sense in Brussels to appreciate the consideration which the Powers, (of which the Conference is the organ), have shown to the Belgians ; for it is impossible not to admit, that their government has now every reason to be satisfied, and possesses the means of replying to the unreasonable demands of the factionists, by whom it is surrounded. Lastly, the chief points of the difficulties have been removed, and it only now remains to arrange details. Nevertheless, Prince Leopold feels as I do, that the crisis is not yet over, and we quite expect that this uncertainty will continue until next Tuesday, May 31st, the day before that on which the respite granted to the Belgians to make known their decision expires.

The conversation I have had with Prince Leopold, has given me fresh proofs of his determination to accept the sovereignty of Belgium, a determination based, however, on the condition that the Belgians accept the terms fixed by the protocol of January 20th, otherwise the prince does not consider himself as pledged. . . .

LONDON, *May* 25*th*, 1831.

MONSIEUR LE COMTE,

There is no doubt that the King of Holland hoped, that the resistance of the Belgians having at length exhausted the patience of the Powers, chances of a war would present themselves, on which he would eagerly have seized.

I have the honour to inform you, that M. de Zuylen arrived here in order to submit to the English government and to the Conference, such considerations, as might decide them to have recourse to rigorous measures.

But conciliatory views having on the contrary prevailed, and protocol No. 24 having been adopted, the hopes of war, nourished by Holland, must have become considerably damped ; on the other hand, however, we have to fear that she will not, without great difficulty, agree to enter into negotiations for the cession of Luxemburg. It is with the view of prevailing upon her to assent to this transaction, and in order to lessen as much as possible the difficulties surrounding this affair, that I and several other members of the Conference, have, since the adoption of protocol No. 24, and the departure of Lord Ponsonby, more particularly sought out the Dutch ministers who are in London. We have shown them, that we are as anxious as they can be, to see the King of Holland freed from all foreign anxieties, and able to devote himself entirely to the administration of his kingdom. We also added, that the general interest, which cannot be separated from his own, seems to demand, that he should lend himself to the negotiations that will be opened up with him, when the Belgians have acquiesced in the proposals just made to them, and as soon as they have made their choice of a sovereign.

We shall also point out to them, that Luxemburg is a country far removed from the other Dutch States, and very unwilling to come under King William's rule ; that the fewer points of contact they have with the Belgians, the less likely are occasions for dispute to arise between them, and that a large capital, or a well-regulated revenue, presents great advantages to so enlightened a statesman as the King of Holland. In fact, we shall not neglect a single argument, good or bad, in order to procure their adoption of our views, as to the utility of a measure to which our governments attach the greatest importance, as it will be the means, and probably the only means, of settling Belgian affairs.

I have the honour to send you a copy of a note, which a Belgian agent, named Michiels,[1] residing at Frankfort where he has started in business, had remitted to the President of the Diet, who communicated it to the members of the Conference. It is known here, through Frankfort, that this agent is in correspondence with M. Lebeau,[2] Minister of Foreign Affairs in Brussels. You will see, on reading this letter, that we should be justified in believing that the Belgian government is desirous of being closely united to the Germanic Confederation, and that it places its connection with Germany, far above its relations with France. I think the king's government might find some useful hints in this document. . . .

LONDON, *May 26th,* 1831.

At a time when, no doubt, you are anxious to receive frequent information on all matters relating to Belgian affairs, which are approaching a settlement, I will not allow a single

---

[1] T. Michiels, who had resided at Frankfort since 1830, was not the official agent of the minister, and was not recognized by the Diet.

[2] Jean Louis Joseph Lebeau, a Belgian statesman, born in 1794, had been an advocate and journalist under King William's government, to whom he was violently opposed. In 1830, he was made Advocate-General at Liége, that city sending him at the same time to the Congress. There he opposed the reunion with France, and in order to prevent the election of the Duc de Nemours, he was among those who proposed the candidature of the Duc de Leuchtenburg. M. Lebeau became Minister of Foreign Affairs in 1831, and as such supported Prince Leopold. He formed one of the deputation sent to offer the crown to that prince. In 1832, he was re-elected as Deputy, made Minister of Justice, and then Governor of the Province of Namur (1834). In 1839, he was accredited to the Diet, and in 1840 became Minister for Foreign Affairs and President of the Council. He retired in 1841, but kept his seat in the Chamber, where he sat on the Liberal side.

day to pass without writing, even if I have not much to tell you. . . .

M. van Praet,[1] who formed part of the last Belgian deputation, and who remained here, has just been with me. The account he gave me of the condition of his country is most disquieting, and reduces itself to this : that the government has no power, no authority, and is master of nothing. He told me that a large number of Frenchmen were among the volunteers, and that they received money from a bank in Paris, which, it appears, has large funds at its disposal. This fact is corroborated by a letter received· by M. van Praet from his government, and which I have read. The banker's name is not mentioned, but General Belliard could easily procure information on this point. This is a serious matter, and deserves the attention of the king's government. . . .

LONDON, *May* 29*th*, 1831.

. . . . I have received several letters from General Belliard, relative to the position of Belgian affairs, of which he tells me he has had the honour of sending you copies. That which followed Lord Ponsonby's arrival in Brussels, created some cause for anxiety, as to how the proposals, contained in the protocol of May 20th, would be received. However, a letter of the 27th, which reached me this morning, gives better hopes of success. You will also have received a copy of this.

The Conference met to-day to discuss this information, and likewise a despatch from Lord Ponsonby, which also arrived this morning. We had to determine, whether, in order to accelerate the arrangement of Belgian affairs, it would be better to grant the Belgians some further concessions, which these reports seemed to indicate were necessary. These concessions would have been relative to territory which the Belgians never have possessed, and do not even now possess.

The Conference decided, that it could add nothing further to the conditions contained in the last protocol, and that if the Belgians did not agree to the basis of the protocol of January 20th, by the 1st June, Lord Ponsonby must quit Brussels, in conformity with the instructions he had received on this subject.

I hastened to acquaint General Belliard of the results of this Conference, by at once sending to him Colonel Repecaud, who arrived here yesterday with despatches.

---

[1] Jules van Praet was born in 1806 at Bruges, was secretary of the Legation in London in 1831. Soon afterwards he became secretary to the king's Cabinet, and, in 1840, master of the king's household, which post he retained until the reign of King Leopold II.

I have the honour to send you a copy of my letter, in order that you may estimate the considerations, which the Conference is desirous of turning to the best account at Brussels. You will observe, that I have requested General Belliard to refer again to the instructions given¯ him when he was still at Paris ; they would be applicable, in case the Belgians should refuse to accede to the basis of the protocol of January 20th.

LONDON, *May* 31*st*, 1831.

News has been received here from the Hague, but it arrived too late for me to send you particulars by yesterday's courier. The King of Holland, on learning the last resolutions of the Conference, and the proposed cession of the Grand Duchy of Luxemburg, in exchange for compensations, expressed great dissatisfaction and a very decided determination not to sub-scribe to it.

He declared, that as he had shown great deference to the decisions of the Powers by being the first to agree, several months ago, to the basis of the separation, the Belgians ought in this respect, to put themselves in a position similar to his. He therefore considers himself entitled to demand, that the protocols, having become obligatory upon him, should also be carried out by the Belgians, and that until they have retired within their own boundaries and have submitted to the con-ditions of the separation, the king does not think that he should be asked to sanction any exchange of territory, or any arrangement concerning Luxemburg ; nor does he see what means of compensation can be offered him for the Grand Duchy.

This intelligence is of a nature to make us think, that we shall meet with some obstacles at the Hague, but I do not doubt we shall surmount them, if the Belgians agree to the basis of the separation. It would be well, I think, that our Legation at the Hague, should endeavour to overcome the obstinacy of the King of Holland : a disposition which is further increased, under present circumstances, by the irritation he experiences at the loss of four millions of his subjects, the weakness of his stability in Europe, and also by the conviction he must have that, notwithstanding the losses he has sustained, he has agreed to the basis of the separation, while those who are reaping all the benefits, are continually making difficulties about accepting them.

We must[1] be all the more urgent in our dealings with the

Var. : Je crois = I think.

King of Holland, as there is no doubt that he is quite ready to go to war, if the Belgians only furnish him with sufficient reason for so doing, to prevent his being reproached with having been the aggressor.

You have data as to the military strength of Holland. The land forces amount to about 60,000 men, without including the militia,[1] and the navy is very formidable, for besides fourteen ships of war, which are cruising before Antwerp, there are in that neighbourhood about three hundred pieces of ordnance. The bravery and impetuosity of the Belgians is well known here, but it is thought that their military resources are far inferior to those of Holland.

As a fact, the state of the finances of this kingdom, would not admit of her maintaining a considerable force on a war footing for any length of time ; but this is all the greater reason, that the Dutch should desire to see themselves speedily engaged in hostilities. . . .

LONDON, *June* 3*rd*, 1831.

MONSIEUR LE COMTE,

I have received the despatch which you did me the honour to write on May 31st, relative to the letter[2] which Lord Ponsonby, on his arrival in Brussels, addressed to the Belgian Minister for Foreign Affairs.

You have had too much experience in business, Monsieur le Comte, for one moment to credit the Conference with that letter, and I cannot believe that you could seriously have expressed any doubt, as to the part I could have had in its production. That letter was not drawn up in London, and it certainly does not emanate from the Conference ; you have only to read it, to be assured of this. Besides, the Conference would

---

[1] Suppressed in the text of the Archives.

[2] Lord Ponsonby, immediately on his return from London, had written a private letter to M. Lebeau, in which he exaggerated and distorted the views of the Conference. This letter, which was read to the Congress on the 28th of May, by M. Lebeau, roused a very strong feeling in Belgium. Lord Ponsonby exhorted the Belgian government to submit to the question of limitations decided on by the Conference, and not to raise fresh difficulties, which might end in the total extinction of the Belgian name. He added that the acceptance by the Congress of the protocol of January 20th, would be rewarded by the abandonment of Luxemburg. "A week ago," he said, "the Conference considered the preservation of this duchy to the House of Nassau, if not actually necessary, at least extremely desirable, and now it is disposed to mediate, with the avowed intention of obtaining this duchy for the sovereign of Belgium."

This transaction had indeed been contemplated by the Conference, but Lord Ponsonby had never been authorized to hold such decisive language, nor to mention the proposed scheme to the Belgians. (See Lord Ponsonby's letter in the *Débats* of May 21st.)

K 2

not have stated what Lord Ponsonby wrote to M. Lebeau, respecting changes which, in the space of one week, have taken place in its ideas, relative to the Grand Duchy of Luxemburg. Moreover, Lord Ponsonby himself says that his letter had been written very hurriedly, which proves that it had not been given him before he left London.

In accordance with the usual routine, it ought to have been communicated to General Belliard, before it was sent to the Belgian government, and from the way in which Lord Ponsonby spoke of General Belliard, while here, there is no reason to suppose that such an omission could have taken place. Nevertheless, it might be explained up to a certain point, as this letter was a *private letter*.

We see by the information that has reached us here from Brussels, and which General Belliard renders more exact and interesting, by the letters he is good enough to send me, that Prince Leopold is about to be elected sovereign of Belgium, but that the Congress will attach the same conditions to his election, which it did to that of Monsieur le Duc de Nemours ; moreover, that if it gives any sort of adhesion to the basis of the separation, it will only be in a very cautious manner, and without mentioning the word protocol ; and finally, that the Congress does not renounce its claims to Venloo, Maëstricht, and Limburg.

It is to be feared, that in following this course, the Belgians may frustrate the end in view, and that they will find great difficulty in getting Prince Leopold to accept the crown they intend to offer him ; at least, that is the opinion one can form from the replies he gave the Deputies who came to London.

Besides this, Maëstricht and Venloo are the only serious difficulties, for if, as the Belgians declare, they were the possessors before 1790 of five-sixths of Limburg, and if only fifty-four communes scattered through that province belonged to Holland, these are facts which the Boundary Commissioners can easily verify. It seems to me that any rights, however well established they may appear to the eyes of the Belgians, ought not to prevent their adhesion to the basis of the separation, the more so, as the protocol of January 20th, lays down a principle of exchange, which will necessarily apply to the Dutch Communes, which form the enclosed lands.

As to the idea of a mixed or a foreign garrison in Maëstricht,[1] I do not think it would ever be adopted. The

---

[1] Maëstricht had formerly been bought by Charles V. It was thus it had come into the Spanish Netherlands, but in 1784, the Emperor Joseph II. had ceded it to

claim of Belgium to sovereignty over Maëstricht is quite new; that of Holland is very old, dating back to the treaty of Münster; and there would besides, be many serious difficulties in placing Hanoverian troops in that fortress, as General Belliard proposed.

Thus, Monsieur le Comte, the affairs of Belgium still present many difficulties. Nevertheless, the majority who have spoken in favour of Prince Leopold in the Congress, declare, that the necessity of putting an end to the painful state of affairs in that country, is strongly felt in Belgium. But the obstinacy of the Belgians in not openly adhering to the basis of the separation, and in not relinquishing any of their claims, may lead to very troublesome results, which we have for a long time tried to prevent. I am induced to believe, that the measures indicated in the end of your despatch, combined with Lord Ponsonby's departure, and the recall of General Belliard, may be the best means of escaping from a difficult position, and one opposed to the conciliatory and pacific views of the principal States of Europe.

This is the opinion expressed by those members of the Congress whom I have seen privately, during the absence of the ministers at Ascot. . . .

LONDON, *June* 4*th*, 1831.

I have received the despatch you did me the honour to write on the 2nd of this month; it shows the importance attached by the king's government, to the punctual observance of the provisions adopted by the Conference, relative to the affairs of Belgium. I will take great pains, to persuade them to look upon the prolongation of the delay accorded to the Belgians by General Belliard, as a decision which he has taken upon himself. I must suppose that he consulted Lord Ponsonby on this matter, as his instructions prescribed; nevertheless, I am somewhat anxious on this point, because General Belliard, when telling me that he had taken on himself to retard, until the 10th of this month, the delay which had been fixed for the 1st, added, " I believe that Lord Ponsonby will be of my opinion."

I am vexed at the delay there has been in carrying out the orders given by you and the Conference, because this will probably deprive us of the effect, which the departure of the French and English agents would have produced. The

Holland. Belgium, therefore, had no right whatever to it in 1830, and, indeed, it was finally annexed to Holland.

reflections which their recall would have caused the Belgians, might have contributed to make them revert to their true interests, whereas now, they will believe much less in our threats. . . .

We have just received news from Lisbon, dated May 26th. I transmit them to you herewith, as it is possible, that the steamer which brought them to Portsmouth may not have carried any despatches for your department, or that of the navy. The French squadron has taken three Portuguese vessels ; the commander has informed the merchantmen, through the medium of Mr. Hoppner, the English Consul, that he had no orders to blockade Lisbon, but that he would take reprisals on all the Portuguese vessels he should meet at sea. An embargo has been laid by Dom Miguel, on all the Portuguese ships that were in the port of Lisbon ; neutrals do not meet with any obstacles on leaving. This information does not come from the government, but from English commercial circles. . . .

I must, here again, interrupt the series of my despatches, to point out the nature and cause of the fresh embarrassments, which had arisen to interrupt the negotiations between the Conference and the Belgian Congress. Ponsonby, intrusted with the powers of the Conference (with the view, no doubt, of frightening the Belgians), had made the serious mistake of telling M. Lebeau, Minister of Foreign Affairs in Brussels, in a *private letter*, that should the Congress elect Prince Leopold, according to the conditions imposed by the Conference, the Grand Duchy of Luxemburg would be ceded to Belgium ; but if they did not do so, the Powers had decided to break up Belgium. I need hardly say, that there never had been a question in the Conference of such an alternative. General Belliard, for his part, influenced by the intrigues that came from Paris, had been weak enough to prevail upon his chief to grant the Belgians an extension of the time fixed by the Conference, and to endeavour, with the aid of the leaders of the Congress, to find means of evading the conditions of the Conference. It was thus that the strange proposals arose, of giving the town of Maëstricht to the Belgians, and placing a Hanoverian garrison in the fortress, which had belonged to Holland since the peace of Westphalia. My despatches have shown the effect produced on the Conference by these strange departures. Consequently, I did not confine myself to my despatches, but wrote direct to M. Casimir Périer, who replied to me *as follows* on this subject :

M. CASIMIR PÉRIER TO THE PRINCE DE TALLEYRAND.

PARIS, *June 2nd*, 1831.

MON PRINCE,

I have only time to say two words, in reply to the letter you did me the honour to write on May 30th, being anxious to add this to the despatches, which the Minister of Foreign Affairs is sending you by courier.

By those despatches, you will see, mon Prince, that the government has not in any way, modified its principles with regard to Belgian affairs, nor changed its views on the very serious questions, which form the subject of your letter ; and that the instructions which had been sent to General Belliard, are in every respect identical with the spirit, in which you concurred in the deliberations of the Conference.

General Belliard, as you had foreseen, did go beyond his instructions with regard to this subject, in his dealings with the Belgian government.[1] The Minister for Foreign Affairs justly blamed him for such great imprudence. This is another proof of the difficulty of founding a Power, when it is a question of small men or great.

I will reply to-morrow, to that portion of your letter relative to the measures for compelling the Belgian government to subscribe to the acts of the Conference—measures as to which you tell me you desire to know all my views. . . .

---

[1] "GENERAL SEBASTIANI TO GENERAL BELLIARD.

". . . . I have learnt with the greatest surprise, that you have taken upon yourself to extend by ten days, the delay granted by the Conference to the Belgians, in order to agree to its resolutions, which had been fixed for the 1st of this month. This step has appeared to me still more extraordinary, as your often repeated instructions direct you to support the measures of the representative of the Conference. My letter of May 31st, directs you to quit Brussels at the same time as Lord Ponsonby, if the refusal of the Belgians to agree to the decisions of the Conference, imposed that necessity on him. I hasten to repeat this order in the most positive manner, and if, when this despatch reaches you, the obstinacy of the Belgians has obliged Lord Ponsonby to leave, you must at once quit Brussels without addressing any species of written communication to the Belgian government."

General Belliard left Brussels the same day he received this despatch, that is to say, the 11th of June. In fact, the Belgian minister, instead of agreeing to the protocol of the Conference, had, by order of the Congress, opened up fresh negotiations.

PARIS, *June 5th*, 1831.

MON PRINCE,

The despatches the Minister for Foreign Affairs is sending you by the courier who takes this letter, give a most satisfactory and complete reply to the different questions respecting which, you wish instructions.

By them you will see, mon Prince, that the view which dominated our approval of protocol No. 22, is always and entirely the same; that our decision as to the necessity of adopting the measures therein specified, in order to induce the Belgian government to subscribe to the deliberations of the Conference contained in that protocol, have in no way changed; and finally, that the instructions given to General Belliard, according to which, in a certain event, he should withdraw at the same time as Lord Ponsonby, are all in the same sense and quite identical.

You will, however, feel that if, unfortunately, it becomes necessary to put into execution the final measures laid down by the protocol, that is to say, the entry of the troops of the Germanic Confederation into Luxemburg, we should look to your far-sighted prudence (as the despatches will inform you), seeing the effect such a measure would have on public opinion in France, to use your best endeavours in the decisions of the Conference, with respect to the employment of a military force in such a manner, as to enable us to judge, according to the circumstances, how best to attain the end which we desire in every way, for more reasons than one. This remark, mon Prince, does not in any way refer to the modifications to which our decisions may have been subjected, but its sole object is to forestall any difficulties which might prevent our more surely obtaining our aim.

We must not conceal from ourselves, that matters are very serious; but we may hope the election of the Prince of Saxe-Coburg, of which the despatches convey to you the intelligence, will help to ameliorate the embarrassing position in which we find ourselves placed. We cannot, however, as yet, say anything on this subject, since, having up to the present only received a telegraphic despatch, we are ignorant as to what conditions may have been imposed at the election of the prince.

The king, as you will have learnt from the papers, starts on a long tour to-morrow. This political tour will serve, as did the first, to draw closer the ties which unite France to the sovereign she has chosen; it places the government, however, in a more difficult position respecting foreign matters, as we are deprived, during his absence, of His Majesty's valuable support and enlightened judgment. This is another reason for the wish I have expressed above.

In my next letter I will take the liberty, mon Prince, of telling you about our position here, which seems to improve in many respects, but still allows those who are at the head of affairs, to foresee innumerable difficulties. For fifty years we have striven for liberty ; the problem to be solved to-day, is to find the means of founding a government, which can conciliate the requirements of those who wish for liberty, and who as yet understand it so little. . . .

These letters from M. Casimir Périer gave me the full assurance that I could count on his firm support, but unfortunately I had not to do with him alone ; I felt there was always a hot-bed of intrigue in Paris, whence, by means of wicked insinuations, attempts were perpetually made to impede my proceedings. Thus the *Courier Français*, a newspaper patronized by General Sebastiani, dared to assert, that it was I who had suggested Lord Ponsonby's awkward letter to M. Lebeau (whereas it was from Paris I first heard of it), and that it had been severely condemned by the Conference.

I do not know how far all this was authorized by General Sebastiani, and I am induced to believe that he was quite as much a dupe as a leader, of the Buonapartist intrigue, the representatives of which surrounded the king and his ministers. The Duc de Dalberg wrote to me about this period :

M. LE DUC DE DALBERG TO THE PRINCE DE TALLEYRAND.

PARIS, *June 5th*, 1831.

MON CHER PRINCE,

I know nothing about the *Congress* except what is stated in the papers. I myself think it will only lead to embroiling matters still further, and end in a war. The real *Congress* is in London. If it remains in accord, and if no fresh intrigues are started here, peace will be maintained ; otherwise——not.

The coalition is complete ; it is a great mistake for people here to believe, that the *mountebanks of the Empire* will bring back the victories of Buonaparte. The fancy that Louis Philippe has for those sort of people is inexplicable. The Duc de Rovigo says he has got his promise of appointment as Ambassador to Constantinople. I know that in the Council both Sebastiani and Soult support this, but that the other ministers object to it, as an insult offered to Europe. I thus spoke to one of them about it. Can the king possibly forget the catastrophe of the Duc d'Enghien, the Spanish negotiations, and many other facts ? If he is nominated to the Chamber of Peers, I ask myself—Can any man of honour remain in it ?

The question of hereditary peerages loses support every day. The rage for equality so engrosses people's minds, that there was all but a riot, because the management of museums issued tickets, available for different hours than those in which the crowd makes it impossible to remain in the galleries. Unfortunate country ! Remain in London, my friend. . . .

The Duc de Dalberg's last piece of advice was decidedly good, and I had not waited for it to make up my mind to remain in London, as long as I could possibly be of any use there, and secure the maintenance of peace—that peace which seemed ever to evade us just when we thought we had attained it. At this time, the Belgians, by their foolish demands, threatened to compromise all our efforts. This takes me back to the continuation of my despatches to Paris.[1]

THE PRINCE DE TALLEYRAND TO GENERAL SEBASTIANI.

LONDON, *June 6th*, 1831.

MONSIEUR LE COMTE,

An English courier from Brussels, has this evening brought a letter, in which General Belliard informs me, that at the sitting of the 4th inst, the Congress elected Prince Leopold of Saxe-Coburg, King of Belgium by a majority of 155 votes to 44, and that a deputation of ten members, headed by M. de Gerlache, was about to start for London, to convey the result of this sitting to the prince.

If, as I had the honour of informing you in my letter of the 4th, the French and English representatives had quitted Belgium on the 1st of June, according to the instructions from their governments and of the Conference, this determination would probably have had such a moral effect on the Belgians, that the employment of force might have been dispensed with ; now,

---

[1] The official despatches to the department already published.

however, we have entered upon another phase altogether, which will render it necessary to take up other questions.

The news received from Belgium during the last few days, and the arrival of the courier this evening, occasioned a meeting of the Conference. The conduct of Lord Ponsonby (whose good intentions however no one doubts) was unanimously condemned, as being totally opposed to his instructions, and his immediate recall has been decided on.[1]

I here add a copy of the letter, which is to be sent him by a courier who will leave in a few hours ; it does not point out the reasons of his recall, for the Conference thought that by leaving them vague, they would produce greater effect, and that each party could then put their own interpretation upon it.[2]

The views of France, which are so very similar to those of the other Powers, coupled with the instructions which only recently were sent to General Belliard, leave no room to doubt, that he will quit Brussels at the same time as Lord Ponsonby. As for M. Lehon,[3] who is probably in Paris just now, I think I ought to point out to you, that his government having given just cause for discontent to that of the king, it does not seem possible that he should remain in France after the departure of General Belliard. Moreover, I would also add, that the protocol No. 22, which seems almost to have foreseen some of the events which have now occurred, stipulated, that in the event of Lord Ponsonby being obliged to quit Brussels, through the conduct of the Belgians, their envoy, who is in London,[4] would be called upon to leave at once. Lord Palmerston made this request this morning.

The Conference then discussed the measures, which the position taken by the Powers with regard to Belgium, might oblige them to adopt ; but the plenipotentiaries thought it indispensable, that they should first ascertain the king's wishes on various points, to which I shall have the honour of drawing your attention, and to which I beg you will kindly send me replies with the least possible delay.

The first of these points, or rather the first question is, What

[1] Lord Ponsonby had refused to present to the Belgian government, the protocol of May 10th (No. 23), which fixed the 1st of June, as the limit accorded to the Belgians for accepting the boundaries laid down by the Conference. The strange letter he wrote to M. Lebeau will also be remembered.

[2] Var. : lui attribuer une cause particulière = attributed to it a particular reason.

[3] Charles, Comte Lehon, born in 1792, was originally an advocate at Liége, and then a Deputy for that town to the States-General of the Netherlands. In 1831, he formed one of the deputation sent to offer the crown to the Duc de Nemours, and soon after went to Paris as Ambassador. He held this post till 1852, then returned to Belgium, and was elected Deputy. He died in 1868.

[4] Var. : Paris.

coercive measures can the king's government take with regard to the Belgians, which would not put it to any serious inconvenience ?

Second question. Would such measures consist in sending troops beyond French territory, or merely in concentrating a force on the French frontier ?

With regard to this, I think I ought to say, that in my opinion, it would suffice merely to assemble a force on our frontier : first, because troops thus assembled can at any moment, if required, enter the neighbouring territory, and because, as a consequence, their presence may of itself produce the desired effect. I would add that these troops should be picked troops, and placed under the command of a cautious and decided chief.

Third question. Would a French squadron take part in blockading the coast and ports of Belgium ?

It seems to me that if the Powers decide on this blockade, it would be advisable for France to take part in it, and that her forces should act in concert with those of England. I think I can recall to your recollection, that you thought of thus concentrating the maritime powers of these two nations, when there was a question of relieving Antwerp, at the time blockaded by a Dutch squadron.

The replies to these various questions, which I hope you will have the kindness to send me, will put me in a position, to satisfy the demands which the Conference may address to me. All the Powers are in accord as to their views and dispositions, for they all wish to maintain their present position, and to fulfil any engagements they may have in common, and likewise because France, England, and Prussia, being more specially called on by their position to undertake these mutually obligatory engagements, are determined to carry out their decisions in perfect harmony.

An agent from Dom Miguel has arrived here, to ask the English government to interpose in the differences between him and France. He has been told that the government does not wish to interfere in this dispute, but that if it did give any advice to the Portuguese government, it would be to accede to the demands of France ; and there the matter rests. . . .

LONDON, *June 7th*, 1831.

The Dutch ministers in London have addressed two notes to Lord Palmerston ; one to ask what resolution the Belgians had come to, at the expiration of the delay granted them to give their decision on the bases of the separation ; the other, to complain of the letter addressed by Lord Ponsonby to M. Lebeau, the Minister for Foreign Affairs at Brussels. These two notes having been communicated to the Conference, it was decided to reply to them. I have the honour to send you copies of these various documents, to which is added one of protocol No. 25, relative to the recall of Lord Ponsonby.

You will see by the replies of the Conference to the notes of the Dutch ministers, that their object is to keep King William in that course of moderation from which he has not yet departed, to calm the irritation caused by the conduct and the pretensions of the Belgians, and to give him satisfactory explanations with regard to the cession of Luxemburg, on conditional terms.

We have reason to believe, that these notes will produce at the Hague the effect hoped for here, and that they will prevent all aggressive acts on the part of the Dutch.

It was at the same time decided, that the ministers of the five Powers should write a letter to the representatives of their Courts at the Hague, of which I have the honour to transmit you the substance, and which is intended to submit to the King of Holland, in a combined and uniform manner, the observations and reasons likely to reassure him, as to the intentions of the Powers, and the maintenance of his rights. I think the king's government will deem it best to send M. le Baron de Mareuil some instructions, deduced from these documents.

I have just received the despatch you did me the honour to write on the 5th. I have reason to believe that when this despatch was sent off, you were not fully cognizant of the particulars of the act which nominates Prince Leopold King of Belgium. As they wished to compel him, to swear to uphold the integrity of territories which have not yet been settled, and to which the Belgians have added towns they do not possess.[1] I have but little doubt as to Prince Leopold's decision, which I think will be in conformity with what he has always expressed to the Belgian Deputies, who came here to ascertain his views.

The Belgians ought to have known, that the first thing they had to do, was to accede to the basis of the separation from Holland, and I notice in the letter of the French Chargé d'Affaires at Berlin (*of which you sent me a copy*),[2] that my views

---

[1] Var. : d'un territoire, qui n'est pas encore *régulièrement* déterminé, *et qui dans les idées les Belges doit s'étendre à* des villes qu'ils ne possèdent *même* pas. . . . = to a territory which is not yet properly settled, and which, according to Belgian ideas, ought to extend to towns they do not even possess.

[2] Suppressed in the text of the Archives.

on this matter, are the same as those of the Prussian Cabinet; for M. de Bernstorff told him, that to attain the end the Powers had in view, they must first induce the Belgians to see the necessity of conforming to the protocol, which had fixed the boundaries of their territory. All the Cabinets take the same view of this question.

As for the arrangements respecting Limburg, they can follow, but they cannot precede, the recognition of the boundaries. The proposals communicated to you by General Belliard, and concerning which you also wrote to me, were presented here by the Belgians some time ago, but without success.

You will have seen by my letter of yesterday that the steps the king's government may take, must be subordinated to the convenience of home affairs. I feel sure that every facility will be offered it on this point.

You will see by the documents of which I have the honour to send you copies, that no one here doubts the recall of General Belliard, which you authorized me to announce as the consequence of that of Lord Ponsonby. . . .

LONDON, *June 9th*, 1831.

MONSIEUR LE COMTE,

You did me the honour to inform me, by your despatch of the 5th, that the king's government desires that the fortress of Luxemburg should be no longer a Federal fortress, but should be demolished, adding that the carrying out of this negotiation was intrusted to me.

I fully realize the importance of this matter, but I do not think it can be dealt with in London, as it affects the special interests of the Germanic Confederation, and it is outside the questions which the Conference has been called upon to decide. The Conference has, besides, no special powers from the Germanic Confederation; it is true, two of the members are in continuous correspondence with it, and exercise some influence on its decisions, but they have no powers.

I think this negotiation should be carried out either in Berlin or Paris; and I see by the letter of the French Chargé d'Affaires (a copy of which accompanied your despatch), that the Prussian Cabinet seems quite willing to give its assent to the request of His Majesty's government. That is one more reason for continuing to treat direct with M. de Bülow respecting it, to whom I have spoken privately on this subject, and who shares my opinion, in thinking this matter should be left to be negotiated at Berlin.

You will, no doubt, have noticed, in the documents I had the honour to transmit to you the day before yesterday, the manner in which the Conference refutes the allegations of some public papers, which tried to infer, that it was cognizant of Lord Ponsonby's letter to M. Lebeau. The note addressed to the Dutch Cabinet, completely removes any doubt on that matter, if any could have existed.

I have not made known to General Belliard, the decisions that are about to be taken, as explanations give occasion for argument, and besides, it is only from you that he should receive his orders.

The Belgian deputation, which is instructed to offer the crown to Prince Leopold, arrived in London yesterday.[1] Two com-missioners, M. Devaux and M. Nothomb,[2] arrived at the same time ; they have seen Prince Leopold, and have informed him that they were intrusted with powers, but did not specify their particular object. If these powers are elastic, they may facilitate the arrangement of Belgian affairs.

Prince Leopold's conduct is straightforward and quiet ; he will probably accept the offer of the Belgians, if the powers possessed by the two Belgian commissioners are of a nature likely to lead to satisfactory results. These powers have not been communicated to the members of the deputation.[3] In a conver-sation I had yesterday with Prince Leopold, he expressed the wish, that if matters were settled, General Belliard might be sent to him.

We have heard here, through a merchantman coming from Brazils, that the Emperor Dom Pedro, having been unable to quell the efforts of the so-called National party, found himself obliged to quit Rio de Janeiro, together with the empress and all his family. It is added, that he has abdicated in favour of his son, but it is not known to whom he has confided this. It appears that the emperor has embarked for England.

This revolution may have a great influence on the affairs

[1] It consisted of M. de Gerlache, president ; Messrs. F. de Mérode, Van de Weyer, the Abbé de Foere, d'Arschot, H. Vilain XIV., Osy, Destauvelles, Duval de Beaulieu, and Thorn.

[2] Jean-Baptiste Nothomb, born in 1805, began as an advocate at Luxemburg, and was the political editor of the *Courrier des Pays-Bas*. Became a member of the Constitution in 1830, and Deputy to the Congress, where he was one of the leaders of the French party. He became Chief Secretary to the Minister for Foreign Affairs (February, 1831), and went to London after King Leopold's election, and negotiated the Treaty of the Fifteen Articles. He remained in the Foreign Office till 1836, then became Minister of Public Works (1837–1840), Minister of Foreign Affairs and President of the Council in 1843. He retired in 1845, after which he was sent on various diplomatic missions to Germany.

[3] Var. : Les commissaires n'ont pas communiqué ces pouvoirs au = the com-missioners have not communicated these powers to.

of Portugal. It has caused some anxiety here as to English commerce, which has considerable dealings with Brazil, and the public funds have consequently fallen somewhat.

News from Portugal has been received in London up to May 29th. It announces that the commander of the French squadron had blockaded the port of Lisbon, but only as regards Portuguese ships. It seems that Dom Miguel's government, having given up all hope of English intervention in his differences with France, is now going to solicit the mediation of Spain.

There are some rather serious popular demonstrations in Yorkshire and Northumberland. The Ministry are taking steps to put them down.[1]

P.S.—Since writing this letter, I learn that the revolution at Rio de Janeiro broke out on April 7th, in consequence of the emperor's decided refusal to dismiss his Ministry. On the 8th he went on board the English frigate *Warspite*, where he signed an act of abdication in favour of his son, and nominated a Council of Regency. This act was proclaimed at Rio de Janeiro on the 9th, and on the same day Dom Pedro, accompanied by the empress, his daughter, and a few other persons, embarked in the English frigate *Volage* bound for Portsmouth. They say that it will not be possible for the Council of Regency to hold out, and that a Federal Union or a Republic will be proclaimed in a few days. . . .

LONDON, *June 12th*, 1831.

I have received the despatch you did me the honour to write on the 9th of this month, and have carefully made myself acquainted with the instructions contained therein.

Here nothing is as yet decided. Prince Leopold wisely takes his time, ere giving an answer, which must in truth require some serious consideration. The Belgian Deputies continue to be entirely satisfied with his attitude and his frankness, and place great hopes on their future sovereign ; but up to this, they have not made a single concession on those points which are the real difficulties.

In thinking over the general interests to which this event may give rise, does it not seem that it might be advisable for France and England, to guarantee the existence of Belgium (when she has been constituted, and placed within assured and recognized boundaries) by a special treaty ? I have gone into

[1] These were local riots, due to the excitement of the elections.

this question several times, and it appears to me, that in the reasons for this treaty, means could be found of extending its stipulations to much higher interests, which, by insuring tranquillity to Europe, would contribute to the glory of France. . . .

LONDON, *June* 13*th*, 1831.

I have this morning received your telegraphic despatch of the 11th, which confirms those you did me the honour to write on the 5th and 9th.

You think that the Conference has been too precipitate in carrying out the measures it has adopted, and has rather lost sight of the modifications which recent circumstances should exercise on its proceedings.

These remarks seem to me unfounded, and I think I can answer them, by asking you to take notice that the Conference, being specially charged with the maintenance of peace, has not been able to concentrate its attentions solely on Belgium Holland also has needed close supervision, especially when such an amount of irritation exists in that country, that the slightest. circumstance may give rise to the most serious consequences. It became necessary, therefore, to endeavour to allay both the Belgian and Dutch irritation, and to prevent the collision which, we cannot but foresee, is imminent between these two parties.

These are the considerations that have guided me, since the Conference was informed of the obstinate refusal of the Belgians to agree to the bases of the separation, a refusal which has so greatly excited the Dutch and their government. I believe that the replies given to their plenipotentiaries here, have had the desired effect at the Hague, and, consequently, the causes for anxiety and hostility have thereby been for a short time removed.

The difficulties that we meet with here, in Belgium, and in Holland, proceed on one side, from the Cabinet of the Hague, which is anxious to involve the Powers in a war, and on the other, from the Russian Cabinet, whose object is to distract the attention of the Powers by turning it forcibly on the affairs of Western Europe. My language at the Conference has always been : "We do not wish for war, but we are ready for it and are not afraid of it."

Yet I do not think that the Belgian government has any decided design, but is only trying to create fresh embarrassments for us, in order thereby to obtain something favourable for itself.

Under these circumstances, I see Prince Leopold every day, and likewise the English ministers, as I am convinced, that with them alone shall we find the same views and interests.

In conclusion, my opinion, is that there will be no necessity to have recourse to the military measures for which I asked you to be prepared. We ought to be ready, but I think that we shall get out of the difficulty by quiet and conciliatory means, and without having to fire a shot. This is my firm opinion. . . .

LONDON, *June 14th,* 1831.

General Belliard, before his departure from Brussels, informed me that a proposal would be submitted to the Congress, suggesting that a Belgian and a Dutch commissioner should be sent to London to deal with the boundary question. He seemed to think this proposal would be entertained.

It might answer very well, if the commissioners had full powers, and if the arrangements they made did not require to be submitted to the Congress; but if this is not the case, you will quite see, they could only be provisional arrangements, against which the Congress could protest.

Prince Leopold saw the Belgian Deputies yesterday; they make some slight progress every day.

The English Ministry, while intimating their desire to return at an early period to the affairs of Greece, gave me to understand, that it might be advisable to place Prince Frederick of Nassau, the second son of the King of the Netherlands, on the Greek throne, instead of offering it to Prince Otto of Bavaria. I was obliged to decline this proposal, observing, that in my opinion it would be nominating a Russian prince, and that my authority for so thinking, was the great interest taken in the House of Nassau for the last six months, by the Court of St. Petersburg. . . .

LONDON, *June 15th,* 1831.

. . . . You will have seen by my letters of yesterday and the day before, that Belgian matters have made some progress, although no definite arrangement has yet been arrived at. The King of the Netherlands' plenipotentiaries offer resistance, and increase the difficulties with which we have to contend. In this position, M. le Comte, and despite the hope I still entertain of arriving at a successful issue, I think that the king's government must hold itself in readiness, but *my opinion* is, that there will be no necessity for action.

I had the honour to inform you, that the feeling here was quite in favour of the Poles, and that their treatment in Galicia has been universally condemned. The English government, relying on the opinion of the Crown lawyers, who declare that the law of nations has been violated by the Austrian Court, has made, and will continue to make, representations to Vienna. But they will act independently, and there is no need to form a compact on this subject, since England is the only Power with whom we could act in concert. Everyone here will learn with satisfaction, that the king's government was the first to employ its good offices in favour of General Dwernicki and the Poles under his command,[1] but we must not look for any great efforts, because the English government never takes up more than one subject earnestly at a time, and is at this moment rather over-burdened, as it has got two—the Reform Bill and Belgium !

For this reason, the arrival in Europe of the Emperor Dom Pedro and his family, has produced but a very slight sensation, and I can assure you, that this event is not causing any political combination at present ; but we shall come back to it, and have to attend to it later on. . . .

LONDON, *June* 16*th*, 1831.

We are continuing our negotiations with the Belgian Deputies and commissioners. Prince Leopold sees them ; they also come continually to me, as well as to the other members of the Conference, upon whose goodwill they have reason to count. Our relations are at last becoming more intimate, and we may hope for some result from these conciliatory interviews ; but the news received this morning, through commercial sources, from Belgium, again increases our difficulties. There is a report that the Belgians have attacked the Dutch at Antwerp, and that having got possession of Fort St. Laurent, they opened a heavy fire on the vessels in the harbour. General Chassé[2] had fortun-

---

[1] Joseph Dwernicki, a Polish general, born in 1779, took part in most of the campaigns of the Empire with the French army, and was made colonel in 1814. He returned to Poland in 1815. Made a general in 1830, he obtained the command of an insurrectionary army corps. Successful at first, he was intrusted to direct the rising in Volhynia, and ended by being surrounded and overpowered by numbers, when he retired into Galicia. The Austrian government arrested and tried him as a prisoner of war, together with the men who were under his command. He was released at the end of the war, when he retired to France, and settled down at Lemberg, where he died in 1859. The conduct of the government on this occasion, provoked the intervention of France and England.

[2] Baron Chassé, a Dutch general, born in 1765, had served in the French army till 1814. He returned to Holland in 1815, was Governor of Antwerp under King William in 1830, and defended this town in 1832 against the French. He died in 1849.

L. 2

ately been sufficiently firm not to allow a return fire from the
citadel; the inhabitants of Antwerp, however, justly alarmed,
sent a deputation with all haste to Brussels. The Regent at
once issued orders; the War Minister went to Antwerp; but
their authority was ignored; they were powerless to stop the
Belgians, and everything tended to prove that the anarchist or
war party have got the upper hand.

You will perceive to how many well-founded observations
on the part of the Dutch plenipotentiaries, this incident will give
rise. They assured me last night, in the most positive manner,
that there was no attack on their side. In fact, if all accounts
are true, it is clearly the Belgians who were the aggressors.

This occurrence will, no doubt, render the arrangements for
which we have been striving for some days, more difficult; and
objections will be raised, and with truth, that while the Belgians
have a deputation in London, charged with an entirely pacific
mission, they make an unprovoked attack, and entirely ignore
an armistice, which nevertheless is strictly insisted on by the
Powers, who are engaged in securing their independence. This
conduct is evidently the result of all those disturbances, which
are initiated by the enemies of peace and good order, who,
being unable to set France alight, endeavour to raise a conflagration in Belgium. . . .

LONDON, *June* 18*th*, 1831.

I have received the despatches you did me the honour to
write on the 13th and 16th of June, as well as a telegraphic
despatch of the evening of the 14th.

When I thought that some arrangement could be come to
between England and ourselves, relative to Belgium, it was, as
it were, only as a last resource, and in case the arrangements we
were endeavouring to effect, could not be carried out—in fact,
to try and do together with England, what we could not do with
the other Powers; but owing to the course the negotiations are
now taking, we need not fall back upon this combination, and
there is no reason to give any further consideration to the idea
suggested in my letter of the 12th inst.

The members of the Conference are discussing with Prince
Leopold and the two Belgian commissioners, the removal of
the obstacles which still present themselves to the arrangement
of Belgian affairs—obstacles always connected with the possession of Maëstricht, and the enclosed land belonging to Holland.
If the commissioners and the Belgian Deputies (as I had the
honour of telling you before), were men better versed in nego-

tiations, and more familiar with the manner in which these are carried on amongst old dynasties, these difficulties would be more easily overcome; nevertheless, I hope we shall arrive at a fairly satisfactory result.

I have told Lord Palmerston, after what you did me the honour to notify on the 13th, that on his arrival at Lisbon, Rear-Admiral Roussin[1] will put himself in communication with the English Consul, in order to arrange for the protection of the persons and interests of his Britannic Majesty's subjects. Lord Palmerston seemed much satisfied with this arrangement on the part of our government, which answers, in anticipation, the remarks I addressed to you on the 16th, as to the anxiety felt here in English commercial circles.

LONDON, *June* 21*st*, 1831.[2]

Lord Palmerston invited me to the Foreign Office yesterday, in order to have a conference with the Russian plenipotentiary, as to the affairs of Greece; I was prepared for this interview, by the despatch you did me the honour to write on the 1st of this month.

Lord Palmerston spoke to us of the troubles that have lately disturbed Greece, and the anxiety they had caused to Comte Capo d'Istria's government; he stated, that he thought all the Powers ought to feel desirous to see order re-established in that unhappy country, and particularly insisted, as did also Comte Capo d'Istria in his letter to Prince Soutzo,[3] on the necessity, of either guaranteeing a loan in favour of Greece, or of giving her prompt monetary assistance. I declined the former of these proposals, making use of the views indicated in your letter of 10th June, and recalling the fact, that the guarantee had only been agreed to by the Powers, when it was a question of Prince Leopold's acceptance, as it was with him alone that the Powers had had any engagements.

As to the question of monetary assistance, I pointed out to them, that it equally applied to the refusal of Prince Leopold, and I evaded a direct reply, although the case is not the same; as similar assistance has been given since this refusal.

---

[1] Baron Roussin, born 1781 at Dijon, entered the navy at twelve years of age; obtained the command of a vessel in 1815; rear-admiral in 1822; commanded the expedition against Rio in 1828, and was placed in command of the fleet sent to the Tagus in 1831. Promoted to vice-admiral, he went as ambassador to Constantinople. Became admiral in 1840, and Minister of Marine from 1840–1843. He died in 1854.

[2] This letter is not found in M. Pallain's collection.

[3] Agent to the Greek government in France. He was officially accredited to Paris the following year.

The Conference however came to no resolution at this sitting ; but Lord Palmerston did not fail to give me to understand, that the guarantee of a loan, being subordinate to the choice of a sovereign for Greece, and this choice, to a fresh delimitation, it was to be feared, that the departure of the French Ambassador from Constantinople, might indefinitely postpone the negotiations he was instructed to carry out on this subject, jointly with the Russian and English plenipotentiaries. I therefore beg you will let me know, what steps you think most advisable, in order to arrive at a definite solution of the Greek affairs. . . .

LONDON, *June* 21*st*, 1831.[1]

I have the honour to send you, herewith, the speech, made by the King of England, at the opening of Parliament this morning.[2]

This speech, as you will perceive, is very moderate and perfectly pacific. Referring to Belgian affairs, he said that they had not yet been definitely settled, but that the best understanding continued to exist between the Powers, whose plenipotentiaries were assembled in conference in London ; that these conferences were conducted on the principle of non-intervention in the home affairs of Belgium, but on the condition that, in the exercise of their rights by the Belgian people, the security of the neighbouring States should not be compromised.

This speech was thoroughly approved of by all right-minded men. . . .

The conferences between Prince Leopold, the two plenipotentiaries of the Powers and the Belgian Deputies, still go on. There are no longer any real difficulties but merely quibbles, which, without having any actual foundation, nevertheless prolong the discussions, which ought to have been ended days ago. I am doing all in my power to bring about a conclusion. . . .

And in truth, I did all I possibly could ; so much so, that I fell seriously ill, due partly to the fatigue and the late sittings, necessitated by this troublesome matter, and perhaps also to the impatience, which the shuffling of the Belgian Deputies caused me. I was confined to my bed for several days ; but, nevertheless, I continued to take part in the deliberations of the Conference, which assembled at my bedside. I also in the same

---

[1] Official despatch already published.
[2] This speech is copied in the *Journal des Débats*, June 23rd.

way, interviewed the Belgian commissioners, from whom, I must confess, I did not conceal my dissatisfaction. I even went so far as to threaten them, that if they persisted in their obstinate resistance, I should advise the partition of their kingdom, which could be effected without the war, which their foolish conduct would most certainly bring about.

As I never, even for a single day, interrupted my correspondence with Paris, the reflex of these various impressions will be found in the following letters:

THE PRINCE DE TALLEYRAND TO GENERAL SEBASTIANI.

LONDON, *June* 22*nd*, 1831.

MONSIEUR LE COMTE,

I have received the despatch you did me the honour to write on the 20th, in which you observe, that you have had no news from London for two days. This reproach has no foundation, for I have never allowed forty-eight hours to elapse, without having the honour of writing to you; and if there has been a day on which I did not send you a despatch, it was because it was one on which the Conference sat so very late, that I had not the necessary time.

You will, no doubt, have received a letter from me, very shortly after the departure of your courier.

The Belgians do not bring such a conciliatory spirit into the negotiations in which we are engaged, as one would expect if they really wished to complete them. Of this you may judge from the following fact. A few days ago they sent another note as to their demands. The two members of the Conference who more specially deal with the details of this negotiation, made their remarks on these demands, expecting that they would be discussed. The Belgian commissioners, however, did not take that line, and instead of replying, they have sent a second note, renewing all their demands without the least alteration, or making the slightest concession.

If the Belgians persevere in this course, if they will not yield a single point, if, on the contrary, they continue in their obstinate resistance, it will be impossible to negotiate with them, or to arrive at an arrangement.

After having exhausted every means of persuasion and condescension, and after having gathered so little fruit for all the labour expended, I believe it would really be better to carry out the idea[1] of dividing Belgium, in which division France would, no doubt, be able to obtain the share that would best suit her. You may be quite sure that this measure would not produce war sooner than any other, if we cannot come to some definite arrangement ; but of this latter I have not yet given up all hope.

I believe the Belgians would have shown themselves much more conciliatory, if they were less confident of the support which the agitators in every country have led them to expect, and if they were not encouraged to believe, that tenacity alone will gain the end they have in view. They find encouragement also in the general condition of Europe, the repulses the Russians have experienced,[2] and the peculiar position of France and England.

I believe it would be well to inform M. Lehon, in rather stern language, that France had been led to hope that the affairs of Belgium would be decided by the negotiations in London, but that she thought these negotiations would be of a frank and conciliatory nature, and that the king's government is greatly and justly dissatisfied to learn that, instead of negotiating, the Belgian Deputies do not even reply to the negotiations addressed to them, but ensconce themselves within a circle of demands, from which they do not seem disposed to emerge. Time is passing, and it seems as if the Belgians had some special motive for not turning it to better account.

I thank you for having sent me the information you have received from St. Petersburg, dated the 4th of this month. The particulars contained in M. de Mortemart's letter, which you have been good enough to send me, furnish another proof of some of the difficulties we have to contend with here on the part of Russia.

P.S.—Last night Prince Leopold and Lord Melbourne thought all was completed ; this morning fresh difficulties have arisen, but I had to think about them lying in bed, for I am very unwell. . . .

LONDON, *June 24th*, 1831.[3]

Although unwell for the last six days, I have never omitted seeing Prince Leopold and the members of the Conference, and likewise the Belgian Deputies. We have been in conference for the last forty hours, but the Deputies are so little accustomed

---

[1] Var. : qui est mon idée favorite = which is my favourite idea.
[2] In the war with Poland.
[3] Official despatch already published.

to such matters as they have now to deal with, and raise so
many difficulties, that there is no getting on ; nothing is finished ;
and I confess to you I am completely worn out.

A conference took place to-day at Prince Leopold's, which
lasted till eight o'clock ; it will be continued at my house this
evening, and will probably last far into the night. I will have
the honour to write to you as soon as anything is decided.

LONDON, *June* 26th, 1831.[1]

I believe that Belgian affairs are at last in a fair way of
being settled as we desire.

I have the honour to send you, herewith, the articles that
have been agreed upon between the Conference and the
Belgian Deputies.[2] All the points that must be arranged, con-
sequent on the separation of Belgium from Holland, are so
dealt with in these articles, as to remove the difficulties
which will be raised, without interfering with the rights of
the King of Holland to such an extent as would make it impossible for him to give his adhesion to them. Belgium is
undoubtedly favoured in these arrangements, and this she owes
to the influence of France. You will see how her interests have
been looked after and protected, by the manner in which the
articles connected with Maëstricht and the Grand Duchy of
Luxemburg have been drawn up.

Prince Leopold received the Belgian deputation at 10
o'clock this evening. I send you a copy of his reply to the
President's address. The prince handed him the articles which
had previously been drawn up.

The Deputies leave for Brussels this evening, in order to
submit these articles to the Congress. Representing as they
do, the views and all shades of opinion which exist in the
Congress, the Deputies seem persuaded they will gain the assent
of that assembly. As soon as it has been given, the Deputies
will return to London, and offer the crown to Prince Leopold,
who will accept it and proceed to Brussels without delay.

I think that when the Congress has approved the articles,
France can at once recognize Prince Leopold as King of
Belgium. The other Powers will do so a little later, but this
delay will not cause any difficulty.

M. le Baron de Wessenberg, one of the Austrian plenipoten-

---

[1] Official despatch already published.
[2] This is the draft of the treaty adopted by the Congress on the 9th of July, and
known under the name of the Eighteen Articles. See text of this treaty in Appendix.

tiaries at the Conference, and who has for a long time resided at the Court of the Netherlands, starts for the Hague on Tuesday, in order to exert all the influence he possesses with King William, to prevail upon him to accede to our articles. M. de Wessenberg has a better chance than anyone else of carrying out this mission successfully. If, notwithstanding some further concessions which are sought from the King of the Netherlands, his consent is gained, the affairs of Belgium will then be in a position to allow *the Powers*[1] to recognize her independence, and this independence will have been established without a war, or even any military preparations.

You perhaps will deem it advisable, to instruct M. Lehon to write to Brussels, or even to go there, so that he may use his influence to procure the adoption of the articles by the Congress.

Two o'clock in the morning. I attach hereto Prince Leopold's speech ; it is not what I could have wished, nor what I suggested to him. All that has passed between the prince and myself on this subject, will be fully explained to you by the letter I have just written to the prince, of which I have the honour to send you herewith a copy. . . .

SPEECH OF PRINCE LEOPOLD TO THE BELGIAN DEPUTIES

June 26th, 1831.

" GENTLEMEN,

" I am profoundly sensible of the earnest desire, of which the Belgian Congress has constituted you the exponents.

" This mark of confidence is all the more flattering to me, as I have not sought for it.

" Human destiny offers no nobler or more useful task, than that of being called to uphold the independence of a nation and to consolidate its liberties.

" A mission of such high importance could alone induce me to relinquish an independent position, and to sever myself from a country to which I am attached by the most sacred ties and recollections, and which has given me so many proofs of its goodwill and sympathy.

" I therefore, gentlemen, accept the offer you make me, on the understanding, that the Congress of the representatives of the nation will adopt those measures which alone can constitute the new State, and thereby secure for it the recognition of the States of Europe.

---

[1] Suppressed in the text of the Archives.

" It is only by so doing, that the Congress will enable me to devote myself entirely to Belgium, to consecrate to her welfare and prosperity the relations which I have formed with those countries whose friendship is essential to her, and to ensure to her as far as lies in my power, a happy and independent existence."

THE PRINCE DE TALLEYRAND TO PRINCE LEOPOLD.

HANOVER SQUARE, LONDON, *June 27th*, 1831,
One o'clock in the Morning.

MONSEIGNEUR,

I have just read your Royal Highness's reply, addressed this evening to the Belgian Deputies. I am sending it to Paris. My government will, I do not doubt, be well pleased that this difficult and complicated business is at last ended ; but I regret exceedingly that our Ministry will not find in your speech that which is needed to lessen French prejudices. I intreated your Royal Highness, in your reply to the Belgians, not to dwell on your attachment to England only, and I notice with much pain, even in your own interest, Monseigneur, that at the last moment you have omitted the conciliatory, advantageous, and prudent phrase, which you permitted the French Ambassador to send you in writing, which I reminded you of last night, and which you promised me you would insert. When it is a question of furthering the present and securing the future, it is necessary, carefully to avoid wounding the vanity or prejudices of others.

I am. . . .

THE PRINCE DE TALLEYRAND TO GENERAL SEBASTIANI.

LONDON, *June 27th*, 1831.

MONSIEUR LE COMTE,

I sent Prince Leopold two or three phrases which ought to have been inserted in his reply to the Belgian Deputies, and which, I think, would have produced a good effect. He promised me to insert them, and yet I have not found them there. I was exceedingly annoyed at this, and at once wrote a letter to Prince Leopold, a copy of which I have the honour to enclose. This morning I received a reply, which I send herewith, as it contains explanations which may prove of use at some time or other.

The Belgian question appears to me to be now arranged as well as could be hoped for, and I think the king's government will be able to repel any attacks that may be made on that subject. If any party writers were now to come forward, and compare the London Conference with the Holy Alliance, they would not be dealing honestly ; for the peace of Europe and the independence of Belgium have resulted from this Conference, and there is nothing in common with these results and those obtained by the Holy Alliance.

The Belgian Deputies leave to-night. M. de Wessenberg, who, as I informed you yesterday, returns to the Hague, quits London this evening. I have the honour to send you a copy of protocol No. 26,[1] of which he is the bearer, and also of the instructions which have been given to him. They are confidential, and should be secret. I thought I ought to write and request the French Chargé d'Affaires at the Hague, to do all in his power to further the success of M. de Wessenberg's mission, and work in concert with him, so that France should not appear a stranger to what was being done there. You will, no doubt, think it right to send him some instructions on this subject.

The objects of the Emperor Dom Pedro's journey to London, are not yet known ; he is living in a furnished house, under the title of Duc de Braganza.

I think I must again ask the king's government to keep the arrangements, that have been made with regard to Belgium, strictly secret. The enemies of peace must not be given the chance of influencing the Belgian population and the members of the Congress, and thus preventing the adoption of the articles, which the Deputies are taking to Brussels.[2] . . .

PRINCE LEOPOLD'S REPLY TO THE PRINCE DE TALLEYRAND.

MARLBOROUGH HOUSE, *June 27th*, 1831.

MON CHER PRINCE,

What I said with regard to England, is simply the relation of a *past* historical fact. I greatly wished to say something more positive about France, but I used the words which your colleagues said were yours in the draft of the Conference.

---

[1] This protocol of June 26th, contained the eighteen articles proposed by the Conference as preliminaries of peace between Holland and Belgium.

[2] This letter concludes the first volume of M. Pallain's work, *Talleyrand's Embassy in London*, the only one which has yet been published. Our comparison of the two must necessarily therefore end.

However, feeling the necessity of doing something, *after my speech, I invited the whole deputation to express themselves strongly and officially in my name* to the Congress on one point, which I considered very important : "that I was aware that some newspapers had pointed to the present arrangement as being hostile to France ; that nothing could *be more false ;* that intimate relations had existed for many years with the present reigning family of France ; that there were few countries I knew so well as France, having lived there a great deal in my youth, and that so far from being hostile to her, I looked upon her as an ally, as important as she was useful to Belgium."

This cannot fail to be widely known as soon as they arrive in Brussels, and to be *at once printed.* I think you should communicate what I now tell you, to your government, to which I am most grateful for all the marks of confidence and goodwill with which it has honoured me.

I may add that the Deputies asked me to send a few explanatory words to the Regent, as it was indispensable to tell the Congress that its acceptance of the articles would be sufficient for me, and thus prevent its thinking that my actual acceptance would be subject to the adhesion of Holland.

Pray accept. . . . .

LEOPOLD.

THE PRINCE DE TALLEYRAND TO GENERAL SEBASTIANI.

LONDON, *June* 29*th*, 1831.

MONSIEUR LE COMTE,

The Dutch plenipotentiaries went last night to Lord Grey with great complaints against the Conference, but they did not bring any written protests as had been reported. Difficulties can now, however, no longer come from them ; they will proceed from the Hague ; for this reason we may congratulate ourselves, that the articles which accompany protocol No. 26, will arrive there signed by the plenipotentiaries of the five Powers ; this fact will make the King of Holland see, that he will not be openly supported in his resistance by a single Cabinet having any influence in Europe.

If the king's government decides to recognize Prince Leopold as King of the Belgians as soon as the articles have been adopted by the Congress in Brussels, I believe that this recognition will be most helpful in the establishment of that country, and I also think it will be advantageous for France to be able to place Belgian affairs, with the exception of a few questions of detail, among matters that are settled. . . .

Belgian affairs were, however, less *settled* than I stated in this despatch, as will only be too plainly seen by what follows ; but I wished that the French government should be less occupied with them, and rather employ its skill in detracting public attention from this quarter. I ventured to convey this insinuation in my despatch, though I must own that it came very *mal à propos*, for at the very time we thought we had reached the end of this tedious negotiation, fresh and still graver complications suddenly arose, and almost made us think we should fail altogether. Perhaps the extracts I have hitherto given from my despatches have been too long, but I have had a double motive : to clear up thoroughly the various points relating to the affairs with which I had to deal, and also to teach those young diplomatists into whose hands these memoirs may one day fall, that patience is one of the first rules in the art of negotiation. The extracts from my despatches will be briefer in future, and the letters I received, will doubtless afford greater interest and better support my narrative. I had sent my last despatches to Paris by young M. Casimir Périer, one of the secretaries of the Embassy, who immediately after his arrival wrote to me as follows :

MONSIEUR CASIMIR PÉRIER, FILS., TO THE PRINCE DE TALLEYRAND.

PARIS, *July 5th*, 1831.

MON PRINCE,

The bearer of good news, and anxious according to your Highness's wishes, to be the first to announce them, I made all possible haste, and nothing was known until my arrival here. The Minister for Foreign Affairs and my father, whom I saw a few minutes later, received me with marked satisfaction, and appeared to me to be very glad to find, that just on the eve of the elections, the Belgian question, if not actually settled, was at least greatly simplified. Whatever the papers may say of the *mouvement*, the opinion of the majority here, has declared itself in favour of the results of this long and tiring negotiation. Reasonable people (and there are some still, notwithstanding all one sees every day) acknowledge most fully what France owes to her ambassador.

As for home affairs, I found the minister less uneasy than I had expected, respecting the result of this month's events. Measures have been taken to prevent any unpleasant scenes. Fêtes, no doubt intended to occupy the people, will be organized to celebrate the anniversary of a revolution, which some people would like to see begin again. Nothing, however, has as yet been arranged about this matter.

On the other hand, it is the eve of the elections, and both parties are in evidence, without either side daring to count on victory. In Paris, I think my father stands a good chance in the first arrondissement; but I fear that the other constituencies will prove themselves less moderate. ·

However, the Ministry seems determined, no matter what the result of the electoral struggle, to present itself to the Chambers. It knows that men when assembled together, are often not the same as when you take them separately, and it feels too deeply, how very serious matters are, to resign until every chance of success has disappeared. . . .

GENERAL SEBASTIANI TO THE PRINCE DE TALLEYRAND.

PARIS, *July 5th*, 1831.

MON PRINCE,

You have obtained a success on which I congratulate you, and thank you in the name of the king, who feels its full importance. If, as I hope, you can add thereto the dismantling of the fortresses that have been reared against us since 1815, the whole of France will applaud an arrangement which assures her a long and honourable peace. Prince Leopold must feel, that it is only on those terms that he can count on the friendship of so powerful a neighbour, sincerely desirous to unite herself with him by indissoluble ties. It is essential, to allay the natural irritation of a country unable to support any longer the insults of the Holy Alliance (your personal enemy) which, on your withdrawal from affairs, began that system of abasement of our country which it has pursued ever since that fatal period. The new King of Belgium will be popular in France, as soon as it becomes known that he does not share the hateful passions of our enemies, and that we inspire him with well-merited confidence. It is necessary, moreover, that we should be assisted in overcoming the enemies of social order in Europe, and this victory can only be gained, when unjust suspicion gives place to those sentiments which are our due. It is for your own fame's sake, mon Prince, that I commend this matter, the most delicate, the most important of all, to your care. Our peace at home depends thereon.

The king is delighted with his journey, which has produced an excellent effect.

We hope that our elections will be satisfactory ; we shall however have many new Deputies but little accustomed to business. Some disturbance is expected on the 14th July, but it will probably not take place, or will be easily put down.

The Chamber being in session, and the precautions that the government has taken, reassure us as to the 27th, 28th, and 29th.

It appears that the Russian general intends trying to cross the Vistula, close to the Prussian frontier. The Polish general has scattered his troops too much. The insurrection in Lithuania is taking a serious turn. Volhynia and Podolia, both require the presence of a considerable force, and even the Ukraine itself, shows but little affection for Russia. Your letter has given me much pleasure, which you can easily understand. . . .

General Sebastiani's letter is so far curious, inasmuch as beneath the flatteries, with which he clumsily tries to overwhelm me, one can plainly detect the views which the Buonapartist and Republican factions then strove to make prevalent in France, in order to inflame public opinion and rouse slumbering passions, instead of trying to soothe them. The question of the Belgian fortresses, which he so specially commended to my care, had already been settled by a secret protocol of the Conference in the preceding month,[1] a protocol in which, be it understood, I took no part whatever except to provoke it.

[1] Protocol of April 17th :

"The plenipotentiaries of the four Courts are unanimously of opinion, that the new position of Belgium, her neutrality being recognized by France, must alter her system of military defence ; that the fortresses are too numerous to be properly defended ; that the inviolability of Belgian territory offers a security which did not exist before, and that, lastly, a portion of those fortresses, that were erected under different circumstances, may now be demolished.

"Consequently, the plenipotentiaries have decided, that negotiations shall be entered into between Belgium and the four Great Powers, to decide the number and importance of the fortresses that are to be dismantled.

"ESTERHAZY, WESSENBERG, PALMERSTON,
"DULORD, LIEVEN, MATUSIEWICZ."

Following this protocol, a Convention was signed on December 16th, 1831, between the representatives of the four Courts and Belgium, which directed the

The plenipotentiaries of the four Courts, Austria, Great Britain, Prussia, and Russia, had recognized, that in consequence of the declaration of the independence and neutrality of Belgium, a certain number of Belgian fortresses ought to be dismantled. This had to suffice us for the present; the carrying out of the admitted fact could not fail to be accomplished later on. But in Paris they insisted on its being done at once, so that they might pompously announce the fact to the Chambers, and thereby gain a certain amount of popularity. It was necessary, therefore, to find some means of satisfying this requirement, and I obtained the consent of the Conference to the mention of its decision respecting the demolition of the fortresses, by the king in his speech.

In general, and herein lay my greatest difficulty, matters were only looked at from one point of view in Paris, and that view was exclusively a French one, without a thought of what was due to others. If it was a question of the affairs of Belgium, they only considered the Belgians, and gave no thought to the King of the Netherlands, whose interests therefore the other Cabinets had to protect. They forgot, or pretended to forget, that there was an English Parliament, to whom the English Cabinet was responsible for the measures they adopted, and they only troubled themselves about what they should say to the Chamber of Deputies in France.[1] In the very complicated position of Europe, such a disposition caused me infinite embarrassment; my duty was to get out of it as well as I could, and this was not easy. Under these circumstances, I urged Prince Leopold to give the French government such assurances as would tranquillize it, and I drew the following letter from him:

---

demolition of the fortresses of Ménin, Ath, Mons, Philippeville, and Marienburg. The other fortresses were to be kept in good repair by Belgium.

[1] ". . . . The French government constantly tells us that we ought, or ought not, to do certain things, in order to satisfy public opinion in France; but it ought to remember, that public opinion exists in England as well as in France, and that, although this feeling is not so easily roused by small matters as it is in France, there are nevertheless some topics (and Belgium is one of them) respecting which this feeling is extremely susceptible, and when once roused, it is not easily appeased."—[*Lord Palmerston to Lord Granville, August* 11*th*, 1831.] (Private Correspondence of Lord Palmerston.)

MARLBOROUGH HOUSE, *July 11th,* 1831.

MON CHER PRINCE,

I lose no time in replying to the remarks you have communicated to me, relative to the ultimate fate of the fortresses which were constructed in consequence of the treaties of 1815.

My opinion is, that the relations between France and Belgium ought to be based on *confidence and friendship.*

Seeing no reason, whatever, why the Belgian nation should not approve the conciliatory views of the five Powers, you may count on my sincere co-operation in the furtherance of any measure, the object of which is the adoption of these bases.

Pray accept. . . .

LEOPOLD.

When Prince Leopold wrote me this letter, cautious and reserved like himself, he was already King of the Belgians. He had been elected the evening before by the Congress of Brussels,[1] which had previously accepted the eighteen articles proposed by the Conference, by a majority of fifty-six votes (126 against 70). This was a great victory gained, but I was not long permitted to enjoy it. The following very remarkable letter from M. Casimir Périer, quickly called my attention to another quarter, where, unfortunately, there was but little reason to hope for success.

THE PRESIDENT OF THE COUNCIL TO THE PRINCE DE TALLEYRAND.

PARIS, *July 7th,* 1831.

MON PRINCE,

I am taking the opportunity of my son's departure, to say a few words to you. He bears you an important despatch, resolved upon by mutual agreement in the Cabinet Council, on the affairs of Poland. Very likely, mon Prince, you will consider this step too hasty, but the situation of the Poles, our correspondence from St. Petersburg, the tendency of public opinion in France, always more or less in sympathy with the Polish cause, and last of all, the attitude taken in relation to France by our article in the *Messager,* as well as the near approach of the session, do not permit our not following up our first overtures to the Russian government. Under all circumstances, therefore, the Council has deemed it good policy to make an overture to the London Cabinet, whatever

---

[1] Prince Leopold obtained 152 votes out of 196.

the result of it may be. Moreover, we set great value on receiving a prompt reply, and we can only confide ourselves as regards this, to your care and prudence.[1]

A telegraphic despatch from M. de Sainte-Aulaire, just come in, informs us that by mutual consent, and under a pledge given in presence of all the ambassadors, the Austrian troops will have entirely evacuated the Papal States before July 15th.[2]

There now only remain the affairs of Belgium. The news we have received to-day is better; a favourable resolution is promised us either to-morrow, or the day after, by a majority of one hundred and twenty out of one hundred and eighty. I hope it will be so, and still more earnestly wish it, but I shall not believe it, till it is an actual fact. At the same time, if matters do develop themselves in this way, it would be imperative on Prince Leopold to go at once to Belgium. A revolutionary spirit is stirring up the agitators, and those who wish to support law and order need a leader and a rallying-point.

General Sebastiani is writing to you about the fortresses ; we are longing, mon Prince, to have this matter settled.

Our elections are nearly over : my son takes you the list of Deputies elected up to six o'clock this evening. So far as results are known, the public feeling is favourable ; we have not yet got the Convention promised us by M. Odilon Barrot, nor shall we, I hope, find it in the legislative assembly either. Moderate men, up to the present, are far the most numerous ; we hope that the elections yet to come will retain the same character. If these men add a courageous patriotism to their spirit of moderation in politics, we shall perhaps be able to make a stand ; but the cause of all the evils we have to fear, lies specially in the audacity of our adversaries, strengthened by the feeble, one might almost say timorous attitude of our side. All will depend on the first majority. I am very much afraid, that the country does not realize the seriousness of the evil under which she is suffering, and that she will keep her eyes closed to the light, until she is awakened by the noise of a catastrophe. No doubt it is still distant ; but I

---

[1] An entirely platonic effort in favour of the Poles, had already been made by France to the Czar, during the month of June. It had no result. Under pressure, therefore, of public opinion, which grew more and more violent, the Cabinet proposed to England and Prussia to unite their efforts with France to bring about a joint mediation. Both Berlin and London refused to intervene.

[2] It will be remembered that after the insurrection which had arisen in the Papal States, the Austrians had entered Bologna (March 21st). The Cabinet of the Tuileries demanded the withdrawal of the troops. Austria answered by requiring the Powers to guarantee the temporal power of the Pope. France, on her side, declared that she would not subscribe to such a guarantee, unless the Pope accorded the liberal reforms demanded by the insurgents. Austria ended by yielding, and withdrew her troops on July 15th.

look upon it as inevitable, if from the opening of the session about to commence, the government is not supported by the Chamber in the vigorous and firm attitude which it must assume.

You see, mon Prince, with what frankness I am giving my opinion as to the position of our affairs. Do not however imagine that I despair of the success of our efforts ; far from it ; I should even say that the remedy was easy if home affairs were not incessantly overshadowed by foreign ones, and *vice versâ*. The reaction of these two vital questions upon one another, and the support that the question of foreign affairs finds in the military party, as well as the somewhat vainglorious tendency of our nation, plainly render the gravity of the situation more difficult to surmount. We seem under the impression, that we still have at our disposal, the armies of the emperor and the *finances of the Restoration*, and that we are able to pay both interest and capital at once, by making war ourselves ; no doubt we should not want for armies, but no one seems to remember, that the first shot may bring about a general war. Let us hope that the good sense of the country, aided by the remembrance of past misfortunes, will prevail, and save it from the spirit of infatuation, which has already carried away too many people.

Pray accept. . . .

I quite understood the interest taken by the king's government in the cause of Poland, which M. Périer recommended so strongly to me in this letter. There was no need to urge me with regard to it. The efforts I had made in favour of Poland, with the Emperor Napoleon in 1807, and at the Congress of Vienna in 1815, I was quite ready to make again with the English government, but I was met by coldness and opposition. The Tories were plainly unfavourable to Poland, and Lord Grey, influenced by Madame de Lieven, sought for pretexts to avoid all intervention on the part of England in a cause that was looked upon as lost. Motives of humanity have but little weight in English politics ; and no one would then have dared to maintain openly, that war against Russia ought to have been undertaken to save Poland. To my great regret, I did not succeed in extracting any effectual measures from the English Cabinet for this noble cause. After having informed M. Périer and the government of this, I wrote a letter to Madame Adelaide d'Orléans, which plainly depicts the situation of affairs at that time.

THE PRINCE DE TALLEYRAND TO MADAME ADELAIDE D'ORLÉANS.

LONDON, *July 20th*, 1831.

Mademoiselle will have, ere this, received a letter from Prince Leopold himself, written on French ground, which he desired to pass through, in order to have one more opportunity of showing his respect and attachment to the king. His last words, the night before he left for Brussels, expressed his desire to be allied to the king by the closest ties. I made no response to his observations, but I must repeat them to Mademoiselle.

Dom Pedro had the greatest wish to go to Paris. But he finds in his wife's name a drawback to doing so, and he does not want to cause any trouble.[1] He dines with me to-morrow ; his inclination is entirely towards France.

People here are still very indifferent to the Polish cause. Russians abound everywhere, since the arrival of the Grand Duchess Helena[2] and Madame de Nesselrode; they go on a twenty-four hours' journey to Sidmouth, where the Grand Duchess is taking the baths, and come back to London to use their influence against Poland.

Prince Paul of Wurtemburg has been to see his daughter, and is now here, where he is endeavouring to prove that no one is more suitable than himself to be King of Greece. I do not think that a single member of the diplomatic body is of his opinion.

I am impatiently awaiting the king's speech ; I believe that the Belgian fortresses will be spoken of in a manner that will be acceptable to Mademoiselle. The King of Holland is difficult to deal with ; I was very vexed, that, while M. de Wessenberg was at the Hague, there was no French minister there. M. de Wessenberg much regretted it. A Frenchman could have made use of different inducements to bring about an acceptance. We shall still have some difficulty with Holland. Real losses and a naturally bad temper render the acceptance of good advice somewhat slow. . . .

The news from the Hague was, in truth, sufficiently annoying to the Conference. M. de Wessenberg had not succeeded in over-

---

[1] The Emperor Dom Pedro had married, as his second wife, in 1829, the Princess Amélie-Auguste-Eugénie de Beauharnais, daughter of Prince Eugene.

[2] Frédérique-Charlotte-Marie (Hélène Paulowna), born in 1807, daughter of Prince Paul of Wurtemburg, married in 1824 to Michael Paulowitch, brother of the Emperor Nicholas.

coming the ill humour of the king, who after all the concessions
he had already made, would not add any more, and flatly refused
to consent to those contained in the eighteen preliminary articles
sent to the Belgian Congress and accepted by it.   Some expedient was therefore necessary to extricate ourselves from the dead-
lock to which we were brought ; the most feasible seemed to be,
to propose a definite treaty, although the preliminaries had not
yet been accepted ; this was rather unusual, it is true, but the
circumstances were sufficiently exceptional to warrant the adoption of unusual methods.   Only we could hardly hope that
Austria, Russia, and Prussia would follow us in this step, which, it
must be confessed, was not precisely one of equity ; and it is probable that we should not have succeeded in maintaining harmoni-
ous relations in the Conference on this point, if King William
himself had not aided us by committing a fault, as will presently
be seen, which could not fail to injure his position.   One fact at
any rate, resulted from the King of Holland's refusal, which was,
that the Conference did not sacrifice the interests of Belgium, as
the French papers and the opposition in the Chamber of Deputies
declared.   Meanwhile, Madame Adelaide sent the following
reply to my letter, quoted above :

MADAME ADELAIDE D'ORLÉANS TO THE PRINCE DE
TALLEYRAND.

PARIS, *July* 30*th*, 1831.

This same day a year ago, mon cher Prince, we were in a
state of great excitement, and truly we can but congratulate
ourselves on the generous and courageous resolution taken by
my brother at that time, and on the result of his loyal and noble
conduct.   He has just now received a most gratifying recompense, in the frank and sincere expression of affection manifested
by the whole populace during the three fête days which have
just passed.   I have never seen anything like the real enthusiasm, the affection, and the confidence which has been
shown him and expressed in every face ; it is a genuine triumph !
It is very remarkable, and most reassuring for the future, that at
the end of a year, in spite of real grievances and the machinations that have been at work to lead these good, honest people
into error, we should find greater enthusiasm than ever amongst

them, and a wish to keep the man they have chosen and in
whom they have confidence. Indeed, it speaks well for his good
sense and good judgment, which truly merit all confidence. I
am delighted with the past three days, which have been splendid. I am quite sure you will share my satisfaction with all
your heart ; I have therefore hastened to tell you of it, and at
the same time to thank you for both your charming letters of
July 20th and 25th, which, to my great regret, I have been unable
to do until to-day. I am delighted that you are satisfied with
the speech of our dearly loved king ; it has produced an excellent effect in the Chamber ; especially the announcement of
the destruction of the Belgian fortresses, which was very necessary for our country. I am vexed at the wrong way in which
the Belgians took it at first ; it was quite a mistaken irritability, which they will surely on reflection think better of, for
certainly it is quite as much in their interests as in ours, and
this they will soon feel. I confess I am not very uneasy, for I
am persuaded that they must soon agree with us about it.

Prince Leopold wrote me a nice kind letter from Calais, in
answer to that in which I reproached him with not having
mentioned France in his first speech to the Belgian deputation. This time he has said a word for France ; but why, when
responding to the fine, straightforward speech of M. Surlet de
Chokier, did he not speak of our king, whom the Belgian
Regent had so truly and so justly eulogized ? I confess I am
very much astonished at such a terrible blunder, and I shall
say something about it to Prince Leopold when I answer the
very amiable little letter which he has just written to me. I
have known for some time of his wish to be allied to the king
by the closest ties ; but you will understand that I can say nothing on that point.

Dom Pedro arrived here on the 26th, just as we were going
to dinner. We had a large dinner party on that day, which was
somewhat postponed on his account, and music in the evening,
when he was also present, and as well as on the three following
fête days. These were a good and very opportune spectacle
for him ; he ought to be very pleased with the reception the
king gave him. I should have liked him to leave his wife, and
his little daughter, the Queen, here with us ; and if he consulted his real interests, after paying his visit to England, he
would return here with her ; but I fear that he has no settled
plans.

You ask me what I think of the Chamber. The reception it
gave the king on the occasion of his speech gives me hopes of
its being satisfactory. I am all impatience for news of those

brave, interesting Poles. Everyone is just now greatly interested
in them, and I am grieved to see England so indifferent about
them.

Adieu, mon cher Prince. . . .

I have given this letter in full, as it shows so plainly the
various illusions, in which even so sensible a person as Madame
Adelaide could share. But we had no time to indulge in illusions ;
facts came only too soon to recall us to reality. The King of
the Netherlands, irritated at seeing the independence of Belgium
confirmed by the election and the acceptance of Prince Leopold,
hurt at not being supported in his resistance by a single Power,
and no doubt flattering himself with the hope of bringing about
a general war in Europe, suddenly took the desperate resolution
of attacking Belgium with the army under the command of his
son, the Prince of Orange.

On August 4th, he announced the rupture of the armistice
to the Conference, and on the 5th his troops entered Belgian
territory. On the other side, King Leopold, hardly in possession
of the crown, found himself surrounded by inextricable difficulties. It had been arranged before his departure from London,
that as soon as he was installed at Brussels, he should send two
Belgian commissioners, charged with the necessary powers, to
negotiate under the mediation of the Conference, a definite
treaty for the separation of Holland and Belgium, based on the
twenty-eight articles. The Cabinet which he had summoned,
flatly refused to send the commissioners, and maintained that the
Belgians could treat with the Dutch without meeting in person.
King Leopold had immediately informed the Conference of this
difficulty, telling them of the hostility of the Dutch, and that he
had begged for aid from France. It was necessary at once to
provide against the effect of these new and troublesome complications. Strange to say, just then I had been for twelve
days without any communication from my government. There
was, however, no time to lose in taking action. The Conference
drew up a protocol, in which, while severely blaming the rupture
of the armistice by the Dutch, it approved the employment for
a limited time, of the French army whose entry into Belgium

King Leopold had solicited, and decided that an English squadron should proceed to the defence of the Belgian coasts, and
repulse the attacks of Holland in that quarter.[1]

This protocol was essential to prevent a general conflagration resulting from the intervention of a French force in Belgium.
I can give no better idea of the incidents of this affair, than by
citing the correspondence to which it gave rise between Madame
Adelaide and myself.

MADAME ADELAIDE D'ORLÉANS TO THE PRINCE DE
TALLEYRAND.

PARIS, *August 7th,* 1831.

I am sure, mon cher Prince, that you were no less surprised than we were, at the incomprehensible declaration of war
by the King of Holland, which certainly fully justifies and makes
us feel the immense advantage we gain by the wise and noble
conduct of our well-beloved king and his government towards
Belgium, and how fortunate it is that you have conducted and
finished this important and difficult negotiation, with so much
prudence, zeal, and ability. By the agreement of the five Powers,
we are now enabled to hasten to the aid of this unhappy country,
at the entreaty of her king, against the infamous aggression of
the King of Holland, who ignores the treaties agreed upon and
just concluded between the five Powers, and does not even consult them as to this inconceivably culpable step, which I can only
explain by looking upon him as mad.

It seems to me incredible that when the King of the Belgians
asks for help and assistance from England, she should not at once
send her fleet to the Scheldt, in like manner as our king has

[1] Protocol No. 31 (August 6th, 1831).
The Conference further decided, that the French troops should confine themselves
to expelling the Dutch from Belgian territory, without entering Holland. Neither
were they to invest Maëstricht or Venloo, so as not to approach the German frontier.
Finally, the French government was to undertake to recall its troops as soon as
hostilities ceased.
It was difficult to obtain this protocol from the Conference, for the entry of
French troops into Belgium caused an indescribable feeling in the English cabinet.
Lord Palmerston even went so far as to accuse France of having a secret understanding with Holland. "This is a nice performance of the King of the Netherlands,"
he wrote to Lord Granville. "I cannot imagine who has set him on; we rather
suspect France. . . . If you remember, Talleyrand proposed to me some time ago
to excite the Dutch to break the armistice, in order to raise an outcry against them,
then overrun Belgium with troops and arrange everything to our own satisfaction.
Can this be the realization of the first act of the plot?" (Lord Palmerston's private
correspondence.)

sent his two sons and his army into Belgium;[1] but you can well imagine, with what impatience we wait to hear from you that this has been done! I am convinced, that the best way to end this incomprehensible and unexpected struggle by a durable peace, is for England to ally herself openly with us, which I confess I have every confidence she will do. It also appears to me utterly impossible, that Prussia, however closely allied by relationship and affection to the House of Nassau, should support her in an attempt, undertaken in defiance of the treaties which she herself has just signed, and against all the laws of nations.[2] It is a pity, that in the first instance, the Powers did not use such candid and firm language as would have convinced the king; but, on the contrary, he saw there was a wish to bring him back and keep him in Belgium, and this has given him confidence to attempt this incomprehensible enterprise; hoping by it to bring about a general war.

The king particularly wishes to know from you, and he begs me to ask you at once and privately, what you think should be done in order to put an end to this by a definite arrangement, which would no longer leave peace or war an uncertainty, and would allow us to withdraw our troops from Belgium as soon as possible. This is what my brother wishes, but of course it must be done in such a way as not to compromise our interests, or those of the King of the Belgians, and the independence of that country. You would have been pleased with the admirable letter which our dear king has written to the King of the Belgians. Please write to me as soon as possible.

PARIS, *August 9th*, 1831.

"When I wrote to you yesterday, mon cher Prince, I was very far from expecting such inconceivable conduct on the part of King Leopold towards the king, France, and the army! How is it, that for all response to the admirable letter the king wrote to him on the 4th, in answer to his of the 3rd asking for help, we have only the poor pretence, I can call it nothing else, of an article of the Belgian Constitution, which no reason whatever could support, put forward and upheld by some absurd and foolish articles in the Belgian papers; and up to the present, not a line

---

[1] The Duc d'Orléans and the Duc de Nemours. The former commanded a brigade of cavalry, the latter a regiment of lancers. The force was under the command of Marshal Gérard.

[2] Madame Adelaide is mistaken here. The King of the Netherlands had not signed any treaty in person; his fault was having broken an armistice which he had concluded eight months before, under the mediation of the five Powers.—(*Note of M. de Bacourt.*)

from him to the king? I cannot understand it.[1] Meanwhile I hope that at this moment our army is entering Belgium, avoiding the fortresses, and marching straight against the Dutch, who are devastating and desolating that unhappy country. The king's orders are to fly to her help, and to drive out the Dutch; and I am proud, I confess, of the greatness and generosity of our king and his conduct. I am sure that you too will be so, and that you will turn it to account, and make use of it to bring about an honourable, sound, and advantageous peace, for humanity and for Europe.

I am very indignant at Lord Aberdeen's speech in the House of Lords, which you, knowing me so well, will understand and feel more than anyone. But I am delighted with Lord Grey's reply; the king is quite touched by it; it would be well to tell him of this.[2] It seems from the English papers, that the fleet has orders to enter the Scheldt, and that the English government and the Conference look upon the rash deed of the King of Holland as it deserves, which pleases me greatly; but I shall not be satisfied, until I know all this from you, and until you have given me your ideas and opinions on the subject. I therefore await your first letter with indescribable impatience. I am vexed that poor King Leopold did not freely follow out his first idea, and that he had no good adviser near him to show him the blunder he made by following his second, a blunder into which he was drawn, I believe, by evil counsels. I fear that the delay in the arrival of our troops in

[1] There was a party in Belgium which viewed with impatience the idea of owing its deliverance to France, and desired to preserve to itself the honour of repulsing the Dutch. M. de Muelnaere, Foreign Minister, who shared these ideas, declared that the Constitution interdicted any foreign army occupying Belgian territory, unless by Act of Parliament, and he begged the king not to allow the French army to cross the frontier. The king yielded, and wrote to this effect to Paris. But after the dispersion of the army of the Meuse, he changed his mind, and begged Marshal Gérard to hasten his advance.

[2] House of Lords, sitting of August 6th.
LORD ABERDEEN protested violently against French intervention at Lisbon and the inaction of England. He called upon the Cabinet to protect the independence of Dom Miguel. "The government," he said, "has nothing to do with the character of the King of Portugal, but to see who is really the sovereign of that country. Our position with regard to Dom Miguel is the same as it was with the King of the French, after he had seized the inheritance of his young nephew, in favour of whom Charles X. abdicated. I say more : if, instead of the real Duc d'Orléans, that monster *d'Egalité* had been chosen, would not our policy have been still the same? . . .
LORD GREY. . . . "I will not speak of the expressions of the noble lord when he said that the King of France *seized* the inheritance of his nephew." . . .
LORD ABERDEEN. . . . "I did not say *seized*, but *occupied*." . . .
LORD GREY. . . . "That requires no answer. I would rather congratulate Lord Aberdeen himself and his old colleagues, on the promptitude they have shown in recognizing the true sovereign of France. The conduct of France in the affairs of Portugal has been entirely candid and loyal." . . .

Belgium will have placed his army in danger, for they say that in spite of the advice of our king he intends to commit himself to a battle, the consequences of which, if he lost it, would be terrible for him. This is very probable, according to what is said of the state of his troops. Adieu, mon cher Prince. . . ."

The Prince de Talleyrand to Madame Adelaide d'Orléans.

LONDON, August 10th, 1831.

I received Mademoiselle's letter of the 7th, and now hasten to answer it.

Mademoiselle asks me a question, to which the protocol sent by Neukomm is for the most part an answer. For it shows the path that must be pursued in order to arrive at a definite arrangement. This protocol was lengthily and hotly discussed. The Russian plenipotentiaries, particularly, were very difficult to bring round to our way of thinking ; we spent eight hours one day and six the next over it ; I think that I have obtained all that was possible, at a moment when the minds of all parties were very much disturbed. If the King of Holland yields, we shall only have some minor details, which will, I hope, prove much less difficult than those we have had to contend with over this very thorny business. Our troops can then retire, and perhaps in returning to France, put an end themselves to the question of the fortresses. My own opinion is that this will cause displeasure, but will not go beyond irritation. I only refer, of course, to the fortresses erected by the Holy Alliance. The march of our troops has startled most people, but it was the advance to the front that made everyone uneasy. What they might do at Maëstricht may lead to serious complications ; but their retreat will be upheld, because all sides will approve of this measure. They can thus pay themselves for the expenses of the war, and surely it must suit the King of the Belgians better, that an operation of this kind, which must sooner or later be done, should be performed by us, from whom he is obliged to ask for troops, the military force at his disposition being so weak. It also seems to me, that the destruction of the fortresses by a French army itself, would please the French people, and satisfy the most exacting requirements.

LONDON, August 11th, 1831.

" I executed Mademoiselle's commission to Lord Grey this morning. He was extremely touched by it, and said feelingly

" You cannot too strongly express to the king how much I feel the message he was graciously pleased to send me." After a few moments' silence, Lord Grey asked me if I was acquainted with the contents of the despatches that Lord Palmerston had just received from Holland. I told him that I had come to him first, and was going on to Lord Palmerston afterwards, as he had appointed two o'clock for a Conference. " You will see a letter there," he said, " from the Hague, which announces that orders have been given for the Dutch troops to withdraw into Holland at once. You know what trouble we are having over all this; you must have seen the agitation produced by the entry of your troops into Belgium. I implore you to get the king to recall them, directly he has official knowledge of the orders given by the King of Holland. We need this proof of moderation on your part. It is essential both for us and for you. Tell the king so from me. Two governments desirous to be quite in accord, must pay some regard to each other under all circumstances, and I repeat that we shall be much embarrassed here if you do not withdraw your troops."

I went on to Lord Palmerston, who read me M. Verstolk's letter ;[1] it is explicit as to the recall of the Dutch troops. It would, I think, be very serious if we refused to comply with England's present request, for the last twenty-four hours have altered the state of affairs. The retreat of the Dutch troops, on the one hand, and King Leopold's request, which he has made known here, on the other, are two very important incidents. It is certain that the English Ministry would not be able to face the general outcry that would be raised against it, if, when the Dutch retire, we were to remain in Belgium. The Tories are not alone in blaming the conduct of the English Cabinet in the Dutch question ; and the *leading article* in to-day's *Times* (the ministerial organ) is a very marked sign of this. But as our military manœuvre ought not to remain without some result for France, we must, it seems to me, obtain or extract from Belgium and her king, their pure and simple, but official consent to the demolition of the fortresses. Marshal Gérard could easily make this treaty when he leaves.

King Leopold, before quitting London, wrote me a letter on this subject, which I sent on to the government. When he arrived at Brussels, he changed his language, but now he must utter something definite.

[1] Jean Gilbert Verstolk van Soelen, a Dutch statesman, born in 1777, was judge at Rotterdam in 1801, then Governor of Guelderland. Under the French rule he was appointed préfet of Friesland. In 1815, he became administrator of the Grand Duchy of Luxemburg, and then minister at St. Petersburg. In 1825, he entered the Foreign Office, and remained there until 1840. He died in 1845.

' When once we have only the question of the fortresses to discuss with the four Powers, matters will have advanced greatly, because they have all been fully dealt with in the protocol of the 17th April.

In all that has taken place in Belgium, England might well have found reasons for thinking that it was not possible for Belgium to exist any longer, and that Europe could only obtain a positive guarantee of general peace in the scheme of partition. But England is very far from entertaining such an idea, and everywhere else also there are different views ; ambition has ramified somewhat. What is the opinion of France on this matter ?

This is a long letter ; old servants, however, are never brief, but they are warmly and truly attached. . . . ."

What other advice could I give to the French government, under circumstances which revealed such complications ? King Leopold did not want to-day what he wanted yesterday, and the blustering of the Belgians culminated in a disgraceful flight before the Dutch troops.[1] One might really be tempted to believe that neither Belgium nor a King of the Belgians existed ! But all this was most inconvenient when no one had desired a partition of the country. In England they feared increasing the power of France ; in France they wanted M. le Duc de Nemours ; the Russians and Prussians wanted the Prince of Orange, and Austria would have preferred a continuance of the present disorder, so as to annoy France in that quarter. All these causes had brought about the present situation. It had been my business to avoid war, and so far it had not arisen. At any rate we had had time given us to raise an army. The one essential was that M. Périer should remain in power, because opinion abroad was entirely with him. National tranquillity and French commerce were due to him ; it would not therefore do, to allow a handful of seditious men to lay down the law. I was resolved, while making as much as possible out of this critical moment, to finish up this tedious matter. As usual, I was not in any way assisted by France, where new demands were put forward as fast

---

[1] The Belgians had been beaten at Hasselt on August 8th, and at Louvain on the 12th.

as I obtained concessions in London, as the following letters
will show:

MADAME ADELAIDE D'ORLÉANS TO THE PRINCE DE TALLEYRAND.

PARIS, August 13*th*, 1831.

MON CHER PRINCE,

Up to now you have performed wonders. But the
king has acquainted Marshal Gérard, in a letter sent the day
before yesterday, that he must wait till you have done still
more, and that your ability would succeed in obtaining all
that was necessary for a lasting peace. The demolition of the
Belgian fortresses will no longer be considered a sufficient satisfaction, nor a sufficient security, after the attempt which the King
of Holland has just made, and which, but for the prompt action
of our king, and the arrival of our army in Belgium, would
assuredly have been successful, at least momentarily so, and then
King Leopold would have been dethroned. We wish to support
him as far as it depends on us; but to make this possible for the
king and his government, you must obtain such compensation as
will satify the national *amour propre* and the general opinion in our
country, which is quite unanimous on this point. I am perfectly
convinced, and I repeat to you in all friendship and confidence,
that *this is of the greatest importance* both for our beloved king,
his government, and your own existence as his ambassador. We
learn this morning by telegraph, that my nephews Chartres and
Nemours entered Brussels yesterday at two o'clock, amid the
acclamations and delight of the whole population, who were awaiting them with great impatience. The inhabitants had been in
such a state of terror at the prospect of the arrival of the Dutch,
that, the night before, M. d'Arschot could find no other way of
pacifying them, than by causing a dinner to be prepared for my
nephews at the Hotel d'Arenberg, and stating that they were
coming. Here, the discussion on the address in the Chamber of
Deputies still continues; we hope for a good majority. There
is no doubt that these late events have been very useful to the
government, and have strengthened it considerably. But we
must not ignore the fact that all these advantages will be lost,
and we shall even fall lower than we were before, if, in the end,
there is no record, no compensation given, which will satisfy our
nation. This matter cannot be in better hands than in yours,
mon Prince; I feel that the task is a difficult one, but you will
overcome it, I am sure, especially when might and right are on
your side. . . . .

PARIS, *August* 14*th*, 1831.

MON PRINCE,

My official despatch of to-day explains our position. The debates in the Chamber of Deputies will show you our perplexities. Belgium is a very delicate question, which needs careful handling of every description, and at all times. Our policy is neither changed nor modified ; we want to keep peace, without making any unreasonable demands, which might offend the Powers ; but the feelings of the country, which believes itself injured by the fortresses which have been raised against us, must be judiciously dealt with. The treaty of 1815, which you rejected, is still our great difficulty. We do not want to destroy it. But the Powers must prove to France that the systematic ill-will which imposed it on us, is no longer the sentiment by which they are animated ; you alone can make them clearly understand this. Your high position in Europe and in London, the confidence which you inspire, will create a real union between the governments, whose good understanding and concord will preserve social order from the dangers which threaten it. As soon as the Belgian territory is evacuated by the Dutch army, twenty thousand of the French army will withdraw into France. Marshal Gérard will only retain thirty thousand, who will fall back upon this side of Nivelles. This diminution of our forces is a guarantee, that we are anxious to prove the loyalty of our intentions to our allies. You see that your observations have exercised a great influence over our decisions. We desire to give the English Cabinet every proof of our wish to act with them ; but our position is even more embarrassing than theirs. Your presence in London reassures us as to the preservation of peace, which is the object of all our endeavours, and which you, like us, wish to be both honourable and dignified. The Chamber begins to work more with the Ministry, and if our foreign affairs were easier, we should be sure of a large majority. It is not the French Cabinet that we wish to preserve, but peace. . . .

These were indeed fine words, but it was easier to write them, than to satisfy the claims that they concealed. I had obtained from the Conference the sanction of the entry of the French troops into Belgium to aid King Leopold against the Dutch invasion ; it was felt that this decision of the Conference had greatly strengthened the position of the French Cabinet with

regard to the Chambers. Now the Cabinet asked for the demolition of the fortresses, which had already been accorded in
principle by the Powers represented at the London Conference,
in the month of April ; and it also wished to prolong the French
occupation of Belgium, until the entire demolition of the fortresses was carried out by order of the Powers. This it was
plainly impossible to obtain, just at the time when the Dutch
troops had retired within their own borders by order of the
Conference. The security of the Belgians and their king being
assured by this step, the continuance of the French troops in
Belgium could only excite the distrust of all the Powers, and
provoke attacks without reply in the English Parliament, under
which the Ministry would succumb.[1] The Tories, who would
succeed it, pledged by their policy to oppose the occupation of
Belgium by any French army, would be intractable on this
point, and war would be inevitable. It was necessary, therefore,
to assist the English Cabinet to keep in office, and not to put
forward unreasonable demands on the part of France, some
portion of whose government was a prey to evil influences.
One can judge of this by what the Duc de Dalberg wrote to
me on the subject.

THE DUC DE DALBERG TO THE PRINCE DE TALLEYRAND.

PARIS, *August* 13*th*, 1831.

MON CHER PRINCE,

I have only time to tell you, that Providence is more
watchful over France than those are who govern her. We are
employed in educating 200 new Deputies, who are more suited

---

[1] The attitude which the English Cabinet wished to preserve, on the question of
the retreat of the French troops and the demolition of the fortresses, is clearly shown
in the following letter from Lord Palmerston to Lord Granville :

"(*Private.*)   "FOREIGN OFFICE,
                                                  "*August* 17th, 1831.

"MY DEAR GRANVILLE,

"I have just been speaking to Talleyrand, who gave me a private letter to
read, which Sebastiani wrote to him on the 14th. In this letter Sebastiani announced the
return to France of 20,000 French troops and the withdrawal of the rest on Nivelles ;
but there is an ugly passage relating to the fortresses, inferring that some arrangement
must be made about them before the French evacuate Belgium entirely.

"Talleyrand asked me what I thought of this letter. I said that his government
was mistaken, if it thought that we should ever mix up the question of the fortresses
with that of the evacuation of Belgium ; that the French government had promised to

to regulating the affairs of a commune, than to deciding those of an empire. The last two days have, I think, shown an improvement in things. The Dutch invasion is of great moment ; it subdues the cackling of the Belgian and French revolutionists, furnishes the government with an opportunity of showing a little energy, and proves that England does not separate herself from the interests created by the revolution of July. I advise the hastening of a final arrangement between Holland and Belgium, and keeping a just and equitable balance in favour of *the former.* You must have the consent of the King of Holland, or you can settle nothing.

The folly which emanates from the French Tribune becomes truly insipid. On the other hand, it is high time that the *camaraderie* of the *Palais Royal* with the scum of the revolution should cease. Europe is asking how those in power can strengthen themselves by such means ! Messieurs Appony and Pozzo complain of the language used by the French agents in Italy and Germany. You may *be sure* that directly there is any insurrectionary movement in Italy the Austrians will invade it. In my opinion, they will be doing right.

Good Casimir Périer, to whom we have been holding on like grim death lest he should escape us, talks of nothing but retirement. The lowest intrigues are therefore now being hatched for the composition of the Ministry which is to succeed him. The heads of it are Odilon Barrot, Salverte, and Clausel,[1] who has been given the marshal's bâton to augment his importance. All this puts anything reasonable out of the question ; and you may think yourself lucky to be away from such follies. . . . . . .

The Duc de Dalberg touched in his letter, on the plan to which I was resolved to adhere, as soon as we should have passed the present crisis in Belgian affairs ; this was to

quit Belgium, and that we must wait for the fulfilment of that promise ; that as to the fortresses, we could not even take the question of their demolition into consideration before the French troops were out of Belgium. We have quite decided to dismantle several of these Belgian fortresses, but we will never suffer France to lay down the law to us on this matter, at the point of the bayonet." (Private correspondence of Lord Palmerston.)

[1] Bertrand Clausel, born in 1772, captain of the Pyrenean Legion in 1792, was made brigadier-general in 1799, and took part in all the campaigns of the Empire, notably in Spain. Condemned to death for contumacy in 1815, by his conduct during the Hundred Days, he fled to America, returned to France after the amnesty (1820), and was elected deputy in 1827. In 1830, he received the command of the army in Algiers, was recalled in 1831, and appointed marshal of France (July 30th). Appointed governor-general in 1835, he returned to France the year after the failure of the expedition of Constantine. He died in 1842.

pursue without intermission the conclusion of a definite treaty which would settle matters. Only I was quite determined that, if the King of Holland persisted in his system of opposition to a final settlement, I would content myself with a solemn treaty between the five Great Powers and Belgium, as I felt convinced, that such a treaty would protect the Belgians from a fresh invasion and insure the maintenance of peace. But before arriving at this point, the excitement in Paris must be quieted and the requirements of the really embarrassing position of the English Cabinet met ; to this end I wrote to Madame Adelaide.

THE PRINCE DE TALLEYRAND TO MADAME ADELAIDE
D'ORLÉANS.

LONDON, *August* 17*th*, 1831.

I have but one thought ever before me, the service of the king and the real welfare of France, which so many conflicting passions greatly compromise. Accidents also, it must be admitted, often cause our efforts and plans to miscarry ; and the present complication seems to me, without exception, the most annoying of any during this long and painful negotiation. For instance, the entry of our troops into Belgium was forced upon us, and their withdrawal presents difficulties, which, from their nature it appears, may compromise the existence of the wise, firm, peaceful, and enlightened Ministry which surrounds the king. The excitable French mind, roused by military demonstrations, must have victories and conquests. The retreat of the Dutch renders victories impossible ; and the interests of the Powers, whether rightly or wrongly, are opposed to con-quests. While this dilemma occupies the king's Council, events of importance are also taking place here.

On the very day our troops passed the frontier, a reaction commenced in the minds of the English public, of which the *Times*, which you should certainly read, gives some striking proofs.[1] This reaction has extended visibly ; it menaces the

---

[1] "You will have seen the violent language of the *Times* against France : we cannot prevent it. The *Times* breaks out now and then, and goes its own road, but the tone it has adopted lately cannot have done much harm, for it may serve to convince the French, that the language of the English government on the Belgian question might have been still more forcible, without going beyond the general feeling on the subject."—*Lord Palmerston to Lord Granville, August* 26*th*. (Private correspondence of Lord Palmerston.)

N 2

present Cabinet; it is becoming national; it is even putting *reform* in the background. Old jealousies are aroused, and irritability is displayed on all sides, for there is an English sentiment, which has for 200 years been so completely in unison with the Dutch question and that of the Netherlands, that one cannot touch it with impunity. Lord Grey and the entire Cabinet do not conceal this, and do not hide from me that it concerns, not only their continuing in office, but the preservation of peace. If they were to consent to the prolonged presence of our troops in Belgium, the Tories, who know that war alone can put off reform, will urge it with all their might, and will find, in the national *amour propre*, an echo which up to now has failed them in the country. If Lord Grey's Ministry goes out, it will be replaced by one, hostile to all that concerns peace. If Lord Grey is to stay in, he must be able to say that our troops will return to France, or that he has decided to act against us, as his country thinks best.

In this situation, what is the best way to conciliate everybody? No plan presents itself to me; I see difficulties everywhere. That which seems to me to offer the fewest would be this: it was at King Leopold's request that the king's troops entered Belgium; it was to his aid that we hastened with a speed and an expenditure for which he ought to be grateful. It is no less certain that we have rendered signal service, both to him and to his country, which, in a few hours, would have become a prey to war. Some mark of gratitude is due to us, we have certainly earned some compensation. To ask for this from the Conference would be a false measure; the English would say, We shall not ask for it; and the other members of the Conference would become uneasy. It seems to me that we must apply to King Leopold. A direct agreement between one independent sovereign and another, seems to me the most likely to extricate us from the difficulty we are in. If therefore General Gérard and General Belliard went straight to Prince Leopold, with the energy and promptitude that is used in military treaties, and if they said to him, " The retreat of our troops depends on such and such a thing; take advice of your Council and swear it to secrecy; we will do the same with Paris, and sign in two hours," what was agreed to then, would be a settled fact; the Powers would have to agree to it without war, for the treaty would have been made between recognized Powers, who have the right to do what they please, so long as they observe the regular forms of their own countries. Prince Leopold did not consult the Powers when he called the forces of

France to his aid ; he has no need to call upon them to make the troops retire. The necessity for urgency should regulate the whole of this question.

No one here appreciates the withdrawal of 20,000 of our troops, because 30,000 are sufficient to conquer the whole of Belgium when there are only Belgians in it.

In my despatch of to-day, I did not speak of the idea contained in this letter, because, with the king my duty is to hazard everything, but with the Cabinet one must keep within the bounds of prudence. The king will see if what I have suggested to-day is worth anything. My time is spent in searching for expedients,·but if this is worth nothing, it might be better, perhaps, to follow out Lord Grey's views. He again this morning pledged himself to the demolition of the fortresses when the time for this arrives. He wants it to be done, but not by us.

I have given the king's letter to Dom Pedro's *Charge d'Affaires;* he is to send it to him to-day. Dom Pedro left here yesterday, with all his family ; he is not very pleased with his late stay in England. . . .

LONDON, *August* 19*th,* 1831.

At the end of my last letter, I spoke to Mademoiselle of my idea of treating with Prince Leopold, but what I proposed must be kept a *profound secret.* The moment it is patent that we want to do something, we shall fail, and shall displease all the Powers. At the point where matters are now, one can no longer, without danger, do anything but make known officially the letter Prince Leopold wrote to me at the time of his departure ; the copy of it is at Paris. You may be sure that the fortresses will be demolished. Lord Granville will repeat the assurance of it to the king ; I, personally, have no doubt of it. Indeed, I think there is only one thing that would prevent it, viz., the desire to do it ourselves. This would make it a question of *amour propre,* and between great nations no one could foresee what that might lead to.

The king will have some good news to tell Dom Pedro : the Comte de Villaflor has landed at St. Michael[1] with 1500 men.

---

[1] The island of St. Michel is the most important of the archipelago of the Azores. Comte de Villaflor took possession of it on the 1st of August, in the name of the Regency of Terceira.

The Comte de Villaflor, general-in chief of Dom Pedro's troops, was born in 1790. He enlisted at eighteen, and became general of brigade in 1826, on the outbreak of the civil war. He sided with Dom Pedro. In 1829 he went to Ter·

He is master of the island, in which there was a large force of artillery and 2000 regular troops. There are now therefore 5000 men, including those which were at Terceira, at the disposal of the young queen, whose adventurous life would demand that she should be prettier.

The English Ministry has just had a parliamentary defeat ; it is to be hoped that it will recover itself, for it is very necessary to us. . . .[1]

After long discussions in the Conference, during which I energetically maintained that the prolonged stay of the French troops was necessary to the safety of Belgium, we at last agreed to impose on the King of Holland a new armistice of six weeks, during which a definite treaty should be concluded between Holland and Belgium, under the guarantee of the five Powers. Protocol No. 34, which contained these stipulations, declared at the same time that in consideration of such guarantees, the presence of French troops in Belgium ceased to be indispensable, and that they ought to retire, without however fixing any precise term for their withdrawal.   The English Ministry had insisted on obtaining this declaration, as vital to the existence of the Cabinet.   It will be seen that in Paris they considered themselves equally lost, if the French troops had to leave Belgium without having obtained either the immediate demolition of the fortresses, or new guarantees for their future demolition. King Louis Philippe himself, usually calmer and more capable than those who surrounded him, gave way to suspicions and uneasiness, which are plainly visible in the letters I am about to quote, and which, in my opinion, do more honour to his patriotism and loyalty, than to his political foresight.   He sent General Baudrand, his son's aide-de-camp, to me in great haste, bringing the following letters with him to London :

ceira, whence he departed in 1831, at the head of the expedition which accomplished the fall of Dom Miguel and the accession of Dona Maria.   In 1836, he was Prime Minister for several months.   During the whole period of the troubles which agitated Portugal for so long, he remained constant to Queen Dona Maria and the liberal charter.   He died in 1860.   Comte de Villaflor was created Duc de Terceira in 1833.

[1] In the House of Commons, August 19th, the Marquis of Chandos had presented an amendment, which proposed to accord the right of suffrage to all agriculturists, who had had, for one year, a lease of land of the value of £50 sterling.   This amendment, although opposed by the Ministry, was carried by a majority of 232 to 148.

King Louis Philippe to the Prince de Talleyrand.

Paris, *Saturday*, *August* 27*th*, 1831.

I feel, mon cher Prince, that I must open my mind to you about the protocol that you have just signed. If such acts are required, as I can very well believe, to maintain the English Cabinet, I cannot conceal from you that they are of a nature to ruin my government, and upset everything again here. The honour of France, which has been confided to me, and which is as my own ; her safety, for which I am responsible, and which constitutes mine, all forbid me to look upon myself as being bound by this protocol, unless other measures are taken to modify it and render it acceptable to my ministers. I wish to warn you of this myself, and ask you to use all your efforts to have them adopted. You would be rendering me a very great service, and I think the construction of the second paragraph gives you an opening for it.

I confess, mon cher Prince, that there is something strange to my eyes in this step taken by the Conference. I sent an army into Belgium to uphold its work ; without the presence of that army, Belgium would have been conquered, and Leopold dethroned. I promised to withdraw my troops, as soon as there was no longer any danger of leaving the Belgians and their new sovereign at the mercy of the Dutch, and the matter was so understood. But what may, nay, what must happen, were I to decide to recall the whole army into France in consequence of your last protocol? We should find ourselves again in the same position, as when it was necessary to come to an instantaneous decision, and take action with miraculous rapidity in order to save Belgium and Leopold's throne. We ought not to expose ourselves afresh to such great dangers. Holland has, at this moment, more than a hundred thousand men at the gates of Belgium, and the Belgians have nothing, absolutely nothing, to oppose to them. Thus, if scorning afresh the good faith of the armistice, Holland invaded Belgian territory a second time, or even if the suspension of arms expired without any treaty having been concluded, it is clear that the overthrow of the Belgian throne would be still easier and more certain than it was before. One might then well ask, if the Conference really wishes to destroy that which it has almost brought to an issue with so much care and trouble, or whether it desires that Leopold, left to himself and denuded of power, should fall, dethroned, and without defence, and that

Belgium, a prey to anarchy and desolation, ruined by the double scourge of war and inundations, should find her only salvation in reverting to the House of Nassau ?

Really, mon cher Prince, I must say with all the frankness of the friendship which binds me to you, that I cannot understand how the position of Belgium, of my government, and of myself has so far escaped you, that you should have made no difficulty about signing this strange protocol. You must absolutely find some way of getting us out of this crisis, which menaces the peace of Europe in the highest degree. My Ministry points out a way to you, which seems to me easy of adoption ; for to reject it, would be to justify the suspicions from which, as I told you, I with difficulty defend myself.[1]

Finally, mon cher Prince, believe me, and endeavour also to convince your colleagues at the Conference, that all it was possible to do, humanly speaking, I have done ; that, after having given very strong guarantees to my allies of the purity of my intentions, I owe my country others still more efficacious than such as would result from your last protocol, and this under pain of seeing myself powerless to restrain the fury and impetuosity of the nation. It is my thorough knowledge of this, mon cher Prince, which makes me so strongly urge the demolition of the fortresses ; for looked upon as they are on all sides as objects of temptation, which must not be allowed to stand within reach or sight of the players ; they cause all the perplexities and are the source of all the alarms.

Weigh well what I have said, and you will see that my eagerness to have this business ended, is the most positive proof of the loyalty of my intentions towards Belgium, and the straightforward policy of my government towards England and the other Powers. Be assured also, that it is this same loyalty and straightforwardness, which induce us not to wish to withdraw all our troops from Belgium, until efficacious measures have been taken to insure the preservation of Leopold on his throne. You know the prince ; and my friendship for him need not prevent us from acknowledging, that his disposition is a sure guarantee that he would not have asked to be allowed to keep

---

[1] The expedient demanded by the Cabinet was, that the French troops should not leave Belgium until they had obtained from the Belgian government a formal engagement to proceed with the demolition of the fortresses. It was to this end, that M. de Talleyrand obtained assurances from the English government that they would not insist further on the withdrawal of the French troops, and that, at the same time, the Cabinet of the Tuileries should send M. de Latour Maubourg to Brussels, charged with negotiating a secret arrangement with King Leopold as to the question of the fortresses.

our troops, had he not been convinced that he could not do without them.

Another very strong consideration is, that the King of Holland has had great trouble to assemble, keep, and pay his 110,000 men ; but he cannot afford to pay this *artificial* force much longer, and it is therefore evident that he only keeps it together to invade Belgium, where the distances are so short, that it is quite possible for whoever enters first to outstrip his adversary at every point. Far from diminishing this overwhelming army, the King of Holland continues to augment and re- cruit it at any cost all over Germany. Now, I ask, what con- fidence can one place in any armistice with him, in which the disbanding of this army is not insisted upon ?

But I see, mon cher Prince, that my letter is already longer than I could have wished. You must attribute it to my desire to speak openly to you, and I hope you will only see in my frankness, one more proof of my friendship and regard for you.

Yours affectionately,

LOUIS PHILIPPE.

The King added the following note on the same day, August 27th, 4 P.M. :

After I had written this long letter, mon cher Prince, I de- cided to send it to you by Lieut.-General Baudrand, my eldest son's aide-de-camp, who returned yesterday from Brussels with him. He fully understands the state of that country, and the painful and even precarious position of king Leopold, who has neither troops nor a government. It would be condemning him to annihilation if he was refused the real and moral sup- port that the presence of our troops can alone insure him, after the violent shock he has just experienced.

I have every confidence in General Baudrand, and I know that the terms he was on with the English army in 1816, have made him favourably known in England, and while there he can, if you think well, give a true picture of the state of things both in France and in Belgium. . . .

General Baudrand also brought me letters from Mademoiselle and from General Sebastiani, written in the same strain as that of the king. I will only give General Sebastiani's letter, who was even still more alarmed than the king.

GENERAL SEBASTIANI TO THE PRINCE DE TALLEYRAND.

PARIS, *August* 27*th*, 1831.

MON PRINCE,

Protocol No. 34, places us in a position of which it is impossible to foresee the results. The most probable and most imminent is, undoubtedly, the dissolution of the Ministry. It is impossible for us to agree to the immediate evacuation of Belgium, without any other guarantee than the suspension of arms for six weeks, when Holland is still keeping and increasing her army of a hundred thousand men, and has just shown so little regard for the pledges she gave to the Powers. It is not enough for us to be convinced, that the proposed suspension of arms will bring about a near and lasting peace, without any fresh danger to King Leopold. This conviction must be shared by the nation and the Chambers, and this we cannot hope for. Belgium is in a state of anarchy, her army is dissolved; King Leopold cannot organize either his army or the administration of the government, if he is not protected by a force of some kind.

The matter of the fortresses gives rise to suspicions that have their origin in only too many circumstances.

The indulgent and kind disapprobation expressed towards the King of Holland does not reassure us at all. All the ministers of the Powers at the Hague, including Sir Charles Bagot,[1] the English Ambassador, went to the Princess of Orange to congratulate her on the victories of the prince, as soon as the news of the battle of Louvain reached them. We send General Baudrand to explain to you the real state of affairs ; send him back as soon as you can spare him ; he is at your service. Settle this business for us, if you would prevent the formation of a warlike Cabinet. We hope everything from your ability and your love of peace. This is indeed a crisis. . . .

At the same time that General Baudrand brought me these cries of alarm, M. de Latour Maubourg had been sent to Brussels, to induce King Leopold and his government to sign a treaty by which they engaged themselves to demolish certain fortresses. I was informed of this (though not by the government) in time to warn M. de Latour Maubourg of the difficulties he would meet with, and the traps that would be set for him. He wrote to me on the 28th of August from Brussels.

---

[1] Sir Charles Bagot, born in 1781, member of the Privy Council, Minister Pleni-potentiary at the Hague, later on Governor-General of Canada. He died in 1843.

THE COMTE DE LATOUR MAUBOURG TO THE PRINCE DE
TALLEYRAND.

BRUSSELS, *August* 28*th*, 1831.

MON PRINCE,

The letter you were so good as to write to me here has
just arrived. The special object for which I came to Brussels
is not yet carried out; the people here are timid, distrustful,
anxious to obtain rather than to give, and taken up with the
care of insuring their responsibility against any future attacks.
I was assured when I left Paris that it would be quite a simple
matter. On my arrival I soon found that it was a very complicated one. I foresaw the rock ahead pointed out to me by
your remarks transmitted to Paris; thanks to your directions, I
have tried carefully to avoid it, and I think I have succeeded.
The English minister, Sir Robert Adair,[1] is displeased with the
alarm shown by the Belgian Cabinet on receiving the last protocol, No. 34. If, say the Ministers, the six weeks' armistice
passes without the negotiation being finished, we shall then be
without arms or any guarantee against the attacks of our
enemy. France could no longer aid us as she has now done,
with the approval of the Powers, and without compromising the
general peace. We tell them, that in such a case a new pro-
tective armistice, like the former ones, will shelter them from all
attempts from Holland. We do not, however, succeed in convincing them. They say that King William continues to recruit
his army; that the Rhine is covered with boats bringing men
into Holland, without uniform, but completely equipped, and
coming, according to them, from regiments by permission of
Prussia. It is certain that until the Conference succeeds in
bringing about the reduction of the Dutch army, we shall
have great difficulty in inspiring the Belgians with a sense of
security. . . .

I had taken steps, even before receiving the letters from the
king and General Sebastiani of August 27th, to satisfy, as far as it
was possible to do so, the demands made in them, and owing to
my urgent importunity, the Conference consented to shut its
eyes to the prolonged sojourn of the French troops in Belgium,

---

[1] Sir Robert Adair, English diplomat, born in 1763, entered Parliament at a very
early age, and sat on the Whig side. He was charged with a special mission to
Vienna in 1806; then to Constantinople. From 1831-1851 he was accredited to
Brussels; on his return he was made a member of the Privy Council. He died in
1855.

without however expressing their consent in writing ; this was all that was necessary. After having obtained this new concession from the Conference, I waited several days to allow General Baudrand time to judge of the state of opinion in London, and then sent by him the following letter to King Louis Philippe :

The Prince de Talleyrand to King Louis Philippe.

LONDON, *September* 2nd, 1831.

SIRE,

Your Majesty has written to me yourself, which is treating me with a graciousness of which I am fully sensible, and which, if there was any need, would still further increase my attachment to your person, and my zeal for your service. Both have urged me towards that honourable preservation of peace, which the king gave me as my watchword when I left France. The numerous events that have since then succeeded each other in every part of the globe, have not rendered this peace any the less necessary, but have rather tended to make it more difficult.

The latest events, especially, in bringing into question the interests of France and England, have opened up the most delicate point of the whole. I trust indeed that it will be determined peaceably, and that by avoiding any rivalry we shall arrive at last at a definite position, which will insure for some time at least the tranquillity of Europe. This definite position can only be so comparatively however, for we must not conceal from ourselves that we can only act provisionally ; but if this provisional arrangement lasts long enough to enable France to quietly regain her level, its final solution will naturally turn to her profit. This is the spirit in which I have conducted everything here, with which I have had to do. I must say, I thought that matters had been advanced a good deal in our favour by protocol 34, which it seems has excited such discontent in Paris, as I find it difficult to comprehend. It contained nothing but an armistice, and I thought that the less we said, the better we should carry it through. To make any official stipulation respecting the stay of our troops in Belgium, seemed impossible.

General Baudrand, whom I took to visit all the members of the Cabinet, and whom I subsequently asked to call upon them alone, will tell you his views with regard to this, and you can perfectly trust to his clear understanding in the matter. The retreat of our troops will not be ostensibly pressed. The eyes of the plenipotentiaries will be closed, as much as possible, to the slowness more or less of their retreat ; but the English Cabinet cannot possibly grant anything in writing, as to their prolonged sojourn ; and all King Leopold's attempts, as well as mine, will result in nothing, in face of the question *to be* or *not to be*, which Parliament places each day before the ministers.

I must beg the king to allow me to make an observation, which I think may be of much service to him. It is, that the greatest danger in all critical moments comes from the zeal of those who are new to their work. This zeal prevents them distinguishing matters of importance, from those which are only of secondary interest ; I am sorry to see that your Majesty has no minister at the Hague. Here I confine myself to turning aside and smoothing over difficulties. If I had attached any importance to the officious narratives and the benevolent anxiety of petty newsmongers, we might have believed ourselves menaced by the whole of Europe, and perpetually on the eve of a general war, of which happily there has been no question except in the newspapers. If your Majesty will, with that attention which you give to everything, read to-day's despatch from me to the Foreign Office, you will see the true state of matters and of opinions. I beg your Majesty to trust to what is said in it. I have always said, that the question of the fortresses could not be fairly treated by any but the four Powers whose representatives are now together here, and that so apparent a mission as that of M. de Latour de Maubourg would find itself impeded by the irritation to which it would give rise with the ministers of Russia, Prussia, and Austria. I fear my conjecture was right, but that does not make me doubt, for a moment, that the Powers will keep to their engagements of the protocol of April, which they have several times renewed to me since then.

I thank the king for having sent me General Baudrand. I was anxious that a man in his Majesty's special confidence should see England just now. . . .

I also wrote to M. Casimir Périer.

THE PRINCE DE TALLYRAND TO M. CASIMIR PÉRIER.

LONDON, *September* 3*rd,* 1831.

It is a long time, monsieur, since I have had the honour of writing to you, but knowing how occupied you are with all our

great political questions, I did not wish to give you another
letter to read, and I have left it to your son to inform you of all
that is going on here ; I am sure that he does it well, and I have
every confidence in what he writes to you; I place him in a
position to be able to judge of things, and I am quite content
with the work that he does for me. I sometimes put a stop to
his zeal, because in our career zeal is fraught with danger. The
reserve that I prescribe is not very popular, but I believe it to be
useful.

At such an important and delicate crisis, I cannot sufficiently draw your attention to the species of directions I
ought to receive from Paris. It is certain, that, if everyone keeps
cool, and we are allowed time to carry it out, in six weeks from
now (and after all, that is not very long) we shall arrive at the
signature of a definite treaty, which will assure to us the peace
which we desire, without having wounded either French or
English vanity, which are equally susceptible. If they were not
so ignorant in France, as they are, of what goes on outside their
own country, they could not fail to understand that we have
obtained in one year, a position that could never have been
hoped for in the first year after a revolution. But do not let us
be too hasty. We shall be refused, if we ask officially for things
which it has been already decided to grant us. The fortresses are
to be done away with, that is quite settled ; a formal agreement
to this effect would prejudice the English government sufficiently
to menace its existence. What I ask for is that we do not give
offence by too much agitation. Your presence in the Ministry
is above everything most useful to me, in calming the uneasiness which for a whole year has been caused and kept up
in every way by blunders. So long as you are in the Ministry,
no one will believe that Europe can be disturbed. Let me say
again, that you are essential not only to the destinies of France,
but to the preservation of law and order in Europe ; you give
strength to the government ; I hear this on all sides. Adieu,
monsieur. Again assuring you. . . .

After having thus appeased, at least for a time, the perpetual
agitation always going on in Paris with regard to foreign
affairs, I gave all my attention to the negotiation of a definite
treaty between Holland and Belgium under the mediation of
the five Powers. Circumstances were favourable to this. The
great Cabinets were displeased with the rash attack of the Dutch
on Belgium, which for a moment had threatened to bring about

a general war. They were therefore the better disposed to impose a decision on the King of Holland. Belgium, a little ashamed of her defeat, and the necessity she was under of having recourse to the protection of France, felt compelled to bring matters to an end, and emerge from her painful state of uncertainty. It was therefore decided in Brussels to nominate an envoy, charged with full powers to conclude a definite treaty : this was M. Van de Weyer, who arrived in London the beginning of September. The work this month had been a little too harassing for my age and strength, for while we had to continue our wearisome negotiation, the coronation of the English king took place on September 8th. The ceremony, though very grand, was very fatiguing. We had to be at Westminster at 8.30 in the morning, and to remain there until 4.30 in the afternoon ; then, in the evening, to be present at a grand dinner at the Foreign Office. Towards the end of the same month, the Reform Bill was to be brought before the House of Lords, a circumstance which did not tend to make the English ministers more easy to deal with.

In this last respect, an incident, apparently trivial, but for me very serious in its results, occurred to complicate my relations with Lord Palmerston, and make them for the time being most difficult. I am obliged to mention it, however ridiculous it may seem, because it had some very disagreeable consequences for me.

There exists in England a collection of political caricatures, dating back, I am told, to the Ministry of Lord Chatham. A clever draughtsman of that period made some caricatures of the principal personages of the day, on the occasions of the different events that brought them into prominence. These caricatures were signed H. B., by which name the collection has been known. One caricature, which formed part of it, was published during the year 1831. It was entitled " *The Lame Leading the Blind*," and was a perfect representation of Lord Palmerston and myself. There was nothing in it that at all exceeded the ordinary limits of lampoon and caricature, but it seems that Lord Palmerston resented it deeply, and I was not long in seeing that he was disposed, whether willingly or not, to show me that he did so. From that time until I left England in 1834, I very often came across traces of this resentment. I could do nothing ; there was no other course than to ignore it, if I did not wish to compromise the success of the matters that I had to carry through with him, and this I did most scrupulously, but I must confess it was now and then very awkward. Happily, Lord Palmerston's humour did not impede my efforts to arrive at the conclusion of the treaty, which I considered to be the only means of solidly assuring the maintenance of peace. The Cabinet, of which he formed part, was no less interested than we were in settling the Belgian business. The following letters will show, that just then it was principally from Paris, that the difficulties arose which threatened to compromise my work.

KING LOUIS PHILIPPE TO THE PRINCE DE TALLEYRAND.

PARIS, *Saturday*, *September 3rd*, 1831.

I have been at work, mon cher Prince, on a map which General Sebastiani is sending you, and although he is sure to give you all necessary explanations, I am very glad to furnish you with my views as to the proposed division.

One of the points I consider most important, is that our propositions should not only obtain the cordial assent of the English government, but that they should help to repulse the home attacks to which it is exposed, because no one desires more than I do, that Lord Grey and his colleagues should remain in office. I trust that the new demarkation will reconcile the interests of England with the natural and just demands of Belgium. Thus I quite see, on the one hand, that Belgium had a right to demand that the sluices of her canals, and the dykes which protect her against inundations, should not be in the power of the Dutch, because she could have no safety or independence, as long as it rested with her enemies to inundate her land, ruin her for years, and place Bruges and Ghent under the sea. On the other hand, Holland was right to preserve on her side a well-defended frontier. I think too that one of the best means of satisfying England, and protecting the responsibility of the English ministers from any settled attack, is, that Holland should continue to possess the whole length of the Houdt, or Western Scheldt, and that she should retain, even on the left bank, a sufficient barrier to guarantee her the possession of it.

I believe, mon cher Prince, that on examining our map, you will find these different advantages included in the new demarkation ; for if it is true that, in order to make Belgium independent, Holland must renounce the right or power given to her by the demarkation of 1790, to inundate the country when she pleased, she must first of all abandon : 1°, the Sluys (which is really the sluice of Bruges and the key of all the waters of West Flanders) ; 2°, the Sas de Gand (that is to say the sluice), which is at once the sluice of Ghent and the key to the waters of East Flanders. Therefore the Belgian frontier must be carried outside these sluices, namely, to the boundary of the first canal beyond the dykes, through which cuttings could always be made (as has already been done in so deplorable a manner), if they did not belong to Belgium.

I am sure that the safety and independence of Belgium cannot be guaranteed, if her frontier is not extended to the lines I suggest ; and I also believe, that by fixing it there, Holland is deprived of a means of attacking Belgium, and yet still preserves all means of defence for herself that she can possibly require. She loses the sluices of Ghent, Philippine, Ardenburg, and Sluys, with a territory of twelve to thirteen square leagues, but retains intact the course of the Scheldt as she now possesses it. She keeps the whole of the island of Cadsand, on which is the fortress of Breskens, which guards the mouth of the Scheldt on the south, as Flushing does on the north ; she keeps *Ter-Neuzen* and the fortresses of Ysendyke, Axel, and Hulst, which suffice to constitute a barrier behind a line of canals of separation, which of themselves already form an excellent one.

I believe that by adopting this division, subject to such slight modifications as the localities may require, which are better settled on the spot, a perfect neutrality would be established between the two States, from Antwerp to the sea ; for as both would be removed from reciprocal aggressions, all collisions between them would be rendered impossible.

But I cannot, mon cher Prince, impress upon you too strongly, that it is the present situation of the two countries which dis-quiets me more than the future. I cannot conceive how, in the last protocol, the Powers who all wish for and have need of peace, did not insist upon the reduction of the Dutch army. A Dutch army of more than a hundred thousand combatants, seems to me a monstrosity in the political order of Europe, which can no longer be allowed to exist without great danger.

It alone was the cause of our invading Belgium, and it alone retards our complete evacuation.   When once this army is reduced to a reasonable size, in accordance with the safety and the resources of Holland, there will be no more difficulties about anything, because there will be security for everyone ; and it is the most efficacious measure for achieving that general disarmament, which I desire for many reasons, but most of all, because I consider it the best means of assuring peace to Europe.   Pray tell Lord Grey and Lord Palmerston, that the reduction of this army is also the best way of reassuring France and Belgium, and that it will quiet all demands and fears, as well as quench *all hopes of war* among those who are deluded enough to wish for it.   Unfortunately, mon cher Prince, I feel bound to tell you, that all the reports we receive indicate an opposite course, and it seems that the King of Holland continues to recruit his army from all the vagabonds he can collect in Europe, so that the last report of his effective forces gives a total of 114,000 men.

Such facts, mon cher Prince, are to my mind more striking, than all the arguments that I could put forward, to show that it is not with a view to peace and defence that the King of Holland is taking upon himself such a burden, and that there is not a moment to lose in forcing him to free his neighbours and his kingdom from it.   I am convinced that the interests of England are one with ours on this point, and that it is equally so with all the other Powers.

I am adding an explanatory note to the scheme of delimitation which General Sebastiani sends you.

I must also tell you, that I have been persuading Dom Pedro to take a journey to London, in order to assist at the coronation of the English king ; believing, from what you said, that he would thereby be doing what is agreeable to the king and his Ministry.   I do not yet know what he will do.

Let me again assure you, mon cher Prince, of my friendship and regard for you.

Yours affectionately,
Louis Philippe

General Sebastiani to the Prince de Talleyrand.

Paris, *September 7th*, 1831.

Mon Prince,

I have this instant received your despatches of the 5th, numbered 215 and 216.   It seems that the Conference and the London Cabinet have no idea of the situation of France.

Heaven grant that the fruit of so much toil may not be lost! The Whig Ministry might easily have sacrificed the peace of the world to their convenience. I am going to communicate your letters to the king; the Council meets again to-morrow. In a few moments I shall have an interview with M. Périer. I am sorry your voice has been powerless to bring reason into the Councils. Are we the only ones who have been moderate and sincere? God only knows whither the affairs of Belgium will lead us.

Ever yours. . . .

PARIS, *September* 10*th*, 1831.

Mon Prince,

Among the reasons that make us defer the complete evacuation of Belgium, until the 30th of this month, is one which could not be included in my official despatch, but of which, nevertheless, I would not have you ignorant. We are now on the eve of the opening of the legislative debates on the peerage question. Necessarily these debates will rouse the feelings of the people afresh. We thought it would give them another pretext, and inflame them still more, if the return of our entire army into France coincided with this discussion ; and therefore we wished to avoid it. You can, mon Prince, use this consideration, in confidence with your colleagues, wherever you may judge it necessary, to prevent a protest on their part against the period assigned by us for the evacuation.

I have just left the Chamber. Some members of the opposition brought the affairs of Belgium and the Polish question on the *tapis*, also the conduct of Prussia with regard to Poland. We avoided being drawn into a discussion on these points, and considered it still more useless to answer our adversaries, as the majority of the Chambers showed weariness at the eternal reproduction of opinions and assertions, to which we have done full and ample justice. . . .

THE PRINCE DE TALLEYRAND TO THE PRINCESS DE VAUDÉMONT.

LONDON, *September* 15*th*, 1831.

You seem surprised that the convenience of the French Cabinet is not sufficiently considered here. Those who say so, deceive you. The French Ministry is liked and supported here by all men of any weight, no matter to which party they belong ; that is a positive fact. But they think that we

are too energetic, and that we are too excitable ; and a new
government which is excitable, disturbs everyone.   We have
need to become more staid, and constant action produces the
contrary effect.   With a conqueror, perpetual action explains
itself ; but when the throne is reached by the choice of the
people, tranquillity is looked for in the sovereign.   He
cannot calm the universal excitement, except by means of
peace.   He must only speak of peace ; and it must be the
theme of all his speeches and all his actions.   This, and this
alone, will establish him firmly ; we cannot too energetically
dispel all the military dreams of those who surround our Royal
family.   Such people know and wish for nothing else ; it is not
to our interest ever to listen to them.   It may be all very well
for them, but will never do them any credit ; we must establish
ourselves.   The king and his family are and will be, beloved by
France, for it has need of them.   If we have peace, it will be
through them that this happiness comes to us ; if we have war,
it will be through the military element, which wishes to pander
to the vanities of the country, and these vanities only last for a
time.   The king is a founder, and peace is his only measure.
Adieu.

THE PRINCE DE TALLEYRAND TO THE PRINCESS DE·
VAUDÉMONT.

LONDON, *September 17th*, 1831.

. . . . They ought to recollect at the Palais Royal that *all*,
absolutely all, that has been undertaken by Paris, has been
unsuccessful.   They have even been obliged to retract what they
had asked for, and that has never happened here to a single
thing with which I have had to do.   All this comes from a desire
to be doing something, which must be excused in persons quite
new to the work.   As regards the fortresses, it has been
necessary to refer the matter again to us here, where all had
been done, as I wrote to you, three months ago, since when
there has been no change.   Action, when it is of no use,
only impedes.   The disarming of Holland will take place ;
but a treaty must be made, and this will be done in the month
of October.   Put no faith in a rupture of the armistice ; I can
state positively that, as far as Holland is concerned, it will not
take place.   The Powers do not wish it, and the king has been
warned of this.   You may depend on this.   We shall draw up
the treaty, and it will be done in such a way that the King of
Holland can sign it ; without his signature, the Belgian business
will remain undecided.   This is carrying out the principles, and

when five Powers take matters into their hands, they must act
according to principles. Holland will revert to what she was in
1790, with part of Luxemburg in addition. It might be better
to create her anew, but that would be to enter on a sea of
intrigues and pretensions. What I write is only for your
conversations.[1] Adieu.

KING LOUIS PHILIPPE TO THE PRINCE DE TALLEYRAND.

NEUILLY, *September* 15*th,* 1831.

A few days ago, mon cher Prince, General Sebastiani
sent on to me, with some despatches for my perusal, a letter
from you, but it slipped into the pile of papers for signature,
with which my desk is too often encumbered, and in spite of my
impatience to read it and learn your opinion, which I always
prize so highly, it was only yesterday that I succeeded in finding
it, and now I do not lose a moment in thanking you for it.

The aspect of things has already changed. We have, as you
see, arrived at the most critical point of this great Belgian
business, from the necessity we are under of compromising ourselves one way or the other, either by leaving our troops in
Belgium as an advanced guard, or by withdrawing them altogether; and never, as you say, was there a more delicate question
to handle. I may perhaps be permitted to say, that it required
more loyalty and more resolution, to decide that our troops should
evacuate Belgium on the 30th of September, than it did to send
them into the country on the 4th of August ; and what is still
more strange and no less true, is that the same motives, and the
same object, determined both these measures, which the pre-
sumptuous superficiality of our time will probably represent as
contradictory. The former step obtained general assent, and its
success confirmed it ; if the latter does not at first obtain equal
approbation, I am still confident that its results in one or the
other hypothesis, of the renewal or non-renewal of hostilities by
the Dutch, will eventually insure it that unanimity of agreement,
which was perhaps wanting at first.

> . . . . et pour être approuvés,
> De semblables desseins veulent être achevés.[2]

I write therefore, mon cher Prince, to ask you to give me
all the assistance of which you are so capable, in order to
compass this happy consummation.

[1] The conversations with Madame Adelaide, who communicated them to the
king.—(*Note by Prince de Talleyrand.*)

[2] . . . . and to be approved,
Such schemes need to be completed.

It seems to me that there are three principal points to negotiate and to ask for, in the definite treaty between Holland and Belgium ; for I do not now speak of the question of the debts, the basis of which, badly arranged, in my opinion, in the month of January, seems now to have been suitably and justly set right by the eighteen articles;[1] these three points are :

1. The conferring of the country of Luxemburg on Belgium, in consideration of an equivalent price, and the preservation of the fortress of Luxemburg and its surrounding district, to the Germanic Confederation.

2. The preservation of Maëstricht to Holland, compensating Belgium for this by the rights of the Bishop of Liège, and giving her some contiguous territory between Maëstricht and Holland, which did not exist in 1790.

3. A guarantee against the inundation of Belgian Flanders, by giving Belgium the possession of the sluices of the canals and the dykes which protect her from the sea, without which her independence would be a chimera, as the possession of the sluices and dykes are its key and rampart.

I foresee no serious difficulty respecting the first point, and I do not think there will be any on the part of the King of the Belgians regarding the second if the third is given to him ; but he strongly objects to consent to the second, until he has some certainty that the third will be conceded. I must confess I think this quite reasonable, for I agree with him, that he cannot maintain his position in Belgium, unless he obtains it.

The possession of the fortress of Maëstricht is, without doubt, a great inconvenience, and even a great danger to Belgium, but treaties can efficiently protect her on that point ; and provided that the frontier is properly established, and the passage past the fortress assured to Belgian vessels, descending and ascending the Meuse, I think the matter could easily be arranged. As for the Flanders side, there can be no safety or independence as regards Belgium there, unless her frontier is carried beyond the neap tides, thus giving her the possession of the sluices and dykes, which preserve her present territory from danger and

---

[1] The Conference had to choose between two schemes respecting the question of the division of the debt between Holland and Belgium : either "to allow the joint expenditure to stand, to amalgamate the liabilities and make both countries jointly and severally responsible," or "to apportion the debt in accordance with its origin, relieving Belgium of what she had not herself contracted, and dividing between the two countries, in fair proportion, the expenses contracted in common since 1815." The protocol of January 27th had adopted the first scheme, based on the protocol of July 21st, 1814, which established community of expenses. The Treaty of the Eighteen Articles adopted the second scheme, which the Belgian Congress had always supported. A protocol of the 6th October following, regulated the division of the debt in conformity with this principle.

inundation. The map with the red and yellow lines was intended to show what was imperatively needed to achieve this end, and to prove that such cession only deprived Holland of a means of attack, but did not in any way lessen her means of defence. It would only cost her four small towns, fortified it is true ; some villages ; less than six thousand inhabitants ; and twelve and a half square leagues of a country devastated by fever, which the recollection of Walcheren will cause to be well remembered in England.[1]

I know, mon cher Prince, that the first objection to this arrangement will be, that in 1790 Holland possessed this territory ; but it is also right to consider, that at that time Belgian Flanders was part of the great Austrian monarchy, whose policy was always similar to that of Holland, and in whose support Holland found that valuable protection which she could not do without ; neither must it be forgotten that on her side, Austria sacrificed the commerce and riches of Belgium to those of Holland, by consenting to the closure of the Scheldt, and by allowing Antwerp, Ghent, and Bruges to be ruined, in order to benefit Amsterdam and Rotterdam. As such a state of things no longer exists, or can possibly exist, the reciprocal relations which resulted therefrom cannot exist either, and Belgium, now independent and neutral, can no longer exist under the same conditions and restrictions as when she formed only one or more Austrian provinces.

I desired to communicate these reflections to you, mon cher Prince, as they suggest themselves to me, to convince you that it is not from dislike to Holland—a sentiment that is far from me, for I desire her preservation as much as any one—nor owing to a predilection for Belgium, that we insist upon this cession to her of twelve square miles of Zealand 'Flanders, but with the view to establish the division of the two countries on the only practicable basis, namely, the separation of the interests and the independence of each, thus putting an end to all cause for collision between them. I cannot understand how a sound and definite treaty can be carried out except on this basis, and it is this which induces us not to acknowledge any arrrangement in which it is not adopted. But my paper, which is finished, warns me to end my letter by assuring you of my constant friendship for you.

P.S.—Pray, my dear Prince, do not lose sight, even from a commercial point of view, of the fact that the cession of twelve

---

[1] An expedition undertaken against Antwerp. The English troops were almost entirely decimated by fever in the isle of Walcheren, situated at the mouth of the Scheldt. The remainder, attacked by Bernadotte, had to re-embark.

square leagues will not materially injure Holland, since she has necessarily lost the closing of the Scheldt, and that the opening of this great water-way restores to the town of Antwerp the commerce which it had lost. Do not forget, also, the state of desolation and ruin into which Belgian Flanders has been plunged for many years, and that it is only fair to give her compensation, as much for those inundations, which nothing could justify, as for the expenses and other evils occasioned by the invasion of Belgium without justification by the Dutch army.[1]

It appears to me neither equitable in itself, nor consistent with the dignity of the Powers, that there should be no expiation for the violation of the armistice at three days' notice, instead of a month, and in contempt of the guarantee given by the Conference. Without doubt nothing must be required of Holland which could compromise her future existence, but it is equally necessary not to compromise that of Belgium, and I am persuaded that not only will this equilibrium be maintained by the arrangement which we propose, but that it is the only means of establishing it.

MADAME ADELAIDE D'ORLÉANS TO THE PRINCE DE TALLEYRAND.

PARIS, *Monday, September 19th*, 1831.

I have for some time past, mon cher Prince, so overwhelmed you with my letters and my writing that I wanted to leave you in peace, knowing also how very busy you were and all the writing that you have to do. But to-day I feel I shall be giving you pleasure, by telling you our news and describing what is going on here, which is sure otherwise to reach you in a very exaggerated form. Unfortunately, since Saturday evening riots have commenced again.[2] Agitators of all kinds found that the sad news of the defeat of the Poles (for whom so much sympathy exists here) and the taking of Warsaw, afforded a favourable opportunity for creating fresh disturbances. They therefore let loose their pack of hounds (for one can call it nothing else) ; but in spite of all their efforts, the populace would take no part whatever. There are plenty of idlers, lookers-on, and small groups of agitators, who excite the people to anarchy and disorder ; the Carlists, Buonapartists, and so-called Republicans

---

[1] The Dutch had, at the opening of hostilities, destroyed several dykes round Antwerp to stop the operations of the Belgian army.

[2] The insurrection of the 16th to 19th of September.

are perfectly agreed on this point. Their language is the same, and their sole aim is the overthrow of Louis Philippe ; of this there can be no doubt. Happily they meet with no response ; the people and the country will have none of it. In the midst of the crowd you see at most a hundred men, children, and outcasts, who shout : " Long live Poland ! Down with the ministers !"

Yesterday evening a good many arrests took place ; among others two chiefs of the *Ami du Peuple*, who had already figured in former disturbances. Now all is quiet in this part of the town ; the crowd and the agitators have gone to the Chamber of Deputies, where they hope to make a disturbance, in order to frighten the Chambers ; but I hope that it will have the opposite effect on the majority, and that the explanations and speeches which the President of the Council and the Minister for Foreign Affairs intend making, will serve to show the sound portion of the Chamber, that they must rally round and support the king's government and the Ministry, strongly and openly, and thus repress all those factions and their hopes of upsetting everything. Carlism has had much to do with these last troubles. It is evident that the men were paid, and that the riot was mainly caused by foreigners, refugees, and released criminals. . . .

TUESDAY, *September 20th*, 1831.

I continue my letter, which I was not able to finish yesterday. What I foresaw was happily verified yesterday in the sitting of the Chamber, which was a very satisfactory one. General Sebastiani's speech was perfect ; he answered the attack made on him triumphantly, and completely refuted the absurd accusations of M. Mauguin. The General had the greatest possible success, and so also had the President of the Council and M. Barthe.[1] The Ministry gained a decided victory, and the Chamber seemed very favourably disposed during the whole sitting. Small knots of agitators were scattered in various parts of the town all day long, and in the evening the rioting began again near the Palais Royal, and there were cries of " Down with the ministers !"

The National Guard and the regular troops dispersed them, and the night passed off quietly. The National Guard is very well disposed, furious with the agitators, and eager to put an

[1] Felix Barthe, born in 1795, an advocate of Paris under the Restoration. Attorney-General at the Courts of Paris in 1830, Deputy, then Minister of Public Instruction. Lord Chancellor in 1831, peer of France and first President of the Court of Exchequer in 1834. Minister of Justice in the Molé Cabinet, 1837—1839. He was appointed a senator in 1852, and died in 1863.

end to the whole thing ; they only ask to be allowed to fall on them.   In this and in everything else, they are in perfect accord with the army.   The hostile papers this morning give a per-fectly false account of what took place yesterday.   They say the soldiers were intoxicated, whereas they had not had a drop of wine, only a little vinegar and water had been served out ; of course all this is done with the view to rouse the populace, but it will meet with no success.

Up to the present, nothing has occurred to-day ; but fresh groups keep on forming ; they are angry because they see they cannot influence the Chamber, and I think they will attempt further disturbances.   They see that their game is lost, notwithstanding all their efforts ; but all our measures have been well taken, and the movement will be put down.   The good feeling in the Chamber is a great thing.   Marshal Soult is to speak to-day ; and I hope to-morrow, or the day after, at latest, we shall hear no more of those odious cries ; I feel sure that if anything more is coming, it will only be a very slight affair.

Chartres (the Duc d'Orléans) returned yesterday morning from his little expedition to Belgium.   The King of the Belgians was most kind to him ; his army is being organized, a most necessary measure, for he is in a very difficult position.

I should like again to say, mon cher Prince, that the king is as anxious as you are to see a definite treaty concluded between Holland and Belgium, for that will be a pledge of peace.   He tells me that he is not uneasy, except with regard to Zealand Flanders, without which Belgium cannot exist.   He told me just now, to bring to your notice, what would be the effect if a line of Dutch custom-houses were established between Bruges and the Sluys, and above all between Ghent and the Sas de Gand, which for thirty years have had free communication ; but, he added, " Tell my ambassador that I depend upon him to induce the Conference to see, what no one else could perhaps succeed in doing, namely, that Leopold in Belgium is the pledge of peace, and that, consequently, the giving up by the King of Holland of twelve square leagues must be the *sine quâ non* of the treaty, for common sense tells us, and Leopold too is convinced of it, that he cannot hold his position without it."

Therefore you, mon cher Prince, who are so persuasive, must use all your eloquence, and if you succeed you will have rendered to the king, to France, and to Europe, the greatest service that has ever been achieved.

The King of the Belgians has the same fear for Maëstricht and the right bank of the Meuse ; he is told that he must submit to it, but if he does not get the other part, it is very probable that he will succumb, and not be able to hold his ground. If that were to happen, we should indeed have cause for alarm, for then would not war be inevitable ? I much want to know what you think of all this. Adieu.

Need I again repeat, after reading such letters, what my position was in the Conference, where all the members were as well informed as I was of everything that was taking place at Paris ? Representative of a government that was daily threatened with destruction, I had nevertheless to be so importunate, as to ask for concessions and wrest new territories from the king of the Netherlands, already despoiled of the greater part of his kingdom. Yet, notwithstanding this, they were astonished in Paris that I did not succeed immediately, and accused the governments who were represented in London, of being distrustful of France, and me of being their dupe! But to continue.

THE PRINCE DE TALLEYRAND TO THE PRINCESS DE VAUDÉMONT.

LONDON, *September* 23*rd*, 1831.

I have not written to you lately, because the whole of London and all the papers, were full of the alarming events that had taken place in Paris. To-day it seems, according to the letters, that things are quieter ; I therefore write. I send by courier to-day, a protocol signed on the 19th,[1] which in my opinion, reinstates the French government in the position which the recent days of feebleness had taken from her. The path opened up by this protocol is a path of safety. I hope the king feels the full value of it, and I believe he will do so. It is a protocol of principles in accordance with what we have done, which admits that in it we were influenced by peace and the love of order. In addition, it puts us in accord with all the

---

[1] Protocol No. 41, signed September 15th, and not 19th. It notices the declaration announced by Prince Talleyrand that the French government will withdraw the last body of troops from Belgium, which had only been left there by the express wish of the sovereign of that country, and that the retreat of this body will commence on September 25th, so as to be completed by the 30th.

In reply to this declaration, the plenipotentiaries of the four Courts " testified to the plenipotentiary of France, the satisfaction with which they received it. This fresh manifestation of the high principles that governed the policy of France, and her love for peace, was only what the allies expected, and the plenipotentiaries begged Prince Talleyrand to rest assured, that their Courts would know how to appreciate at its true value the determination taken by the French government."

existing treaties. The Belgians have their rights, but they must not attack those of others.

Since the events of July, nothing has caused so much uneasiness in London among all classes, as the state of things which has existed for the last three days, and is not yet quite over. Adieu. I am very tired. Pray tell Mademoiselle, that it is by adhering to principles that one gains a strong and honourable position. Without this, one is a prey to intrigues of every sort. I think the protocol of to-day will put the king at his ease, as to the affairs of Belgium. He can always say: "It is not I, it is the Conference." It would be still better, to say nothing at all. Lose no time in seeing Mademoiselle.

THE PRINCE DE TALLEYRAND TO M. CASIMIR PÉRIER.

LONDON, *September 24th*, 1831.

You have achieved a triumph for which all Europe will be grateful to you.[1]   As a Frenchman, I thank you in the name of our country ; through you she is enabled to appear once more untarnished and honoured.   Here we are doing all we can to forward the disarmament which you mentioned so opportunely. If we succeed in effecting it, it will be due, principally, to the laborious week which you have brought to so happy a termination.

I leave it to your son to tell you of our past alarms and our present satisfactions.   All the intelligent men of England, and there are plenty of them, have shared our anxiety.

Adieu, monsieur.   I will only add my wishes for your welfare and that of France. . . .

THE PRINCE DE TALLEYRAND TO MADAME ADELAIDE
D'ORLÉANS.

LONDON, *September 24th*, 1831.

Mademoiselle is right : I quite believe in Sebastiani's friendliness ; he has just given me a fresh proof of this by apprising

---

[1] The Ministry had to submit, in the sittings of September 19th, 21st and 22nd, to a series of questions from several deputies of the opposition.   The question of foreign policy was the special subject of debate, for the events at Warsaw had greatly excited the public mind.   Home policy was also violently attacked.   After long speeches from MM. Mauguin, Lamarque, and Thiers, and answers from MM. Casimir Périer and Sebastiani, the Chamber, on September the 22nd, by 221 votes to 136, passed an order of the day, in which "it declared itself satisfied with the explanations given by the ministers, and trusted in their solicitude for the dignity of France abroad.

me by telegraph of the happy result of the sitting of the 22nd, which is so important to us, and which I awaited with an anxiety that made me quite feverish yesterday—I venture to say, that it is not the first time this has happened under like circumstances. At my age the nerves are easily shaken, but I hope I shall not have to give this trying proof of my devotion to the interests of the king any more. Those interests have indeed been most nobly and ably defended in the Chamber of Deputies. It produced a most favourable impression here, and I have made as much of it as I possibly could.

Concerning the treaty we have in hand, everyone seems equally animated with goodwill ; all are anxious to make a good piece of work of it. We have communicated to each party the propositions of the other. They will present their ideas to us on Monday the 26th, and in the discussion which will follow, I shall make use of the arguments with which the king has been so good as to furnish me. There is a general disposition to be fair and equitable to everyone, and conclude this matter.

The vessels that arrived from Lisbon yesterday, apprised us of fresh cruelties perpetrated by Dom Miguel ; this will facilitate the efforts of M. de Palmella,[1] whom I met again yesterday with great pleasure, and who leaves in a few days for Paris.

The English Ministry is entirely occupied with *reform ;* petitions are coming in from all parts ; the great debate will begin on the 3rd of October. . . .

THE PRINCE DE TALLEYRAND TO THE PRINCESS DE VAUDÉMONT.

LONDON, *September* 27*th*, 1831.

The business of the fortresses is causing great trouble, and I am very sorry for it ; but the fact is, that it has been complicated by M. Latour Maubourg's embassy to Brussels. For the past year, I have made a point of showing that we only acted jointly with the other Powers, particularly with England. All the confidence that I have gained respecting this, has been destroyed by the separate action taken through M. Latour Maubourg at Brussels. You will remember, that I told you all this at the

---

[1] The Marquis de Palmella was at that time Dom Pedro's ambassador in London. He was shortly afterwards placed at the head of the Regency of Terceira, then became Minister for Foreign Affairs and President of the Council. M. de Palmella had formerly known M. de Talleyrand at Vienna, where he represented Portugal at the Congress.

time. Now we must extricate ourselves from the position in which it has placed us, and endeavour not to forfeit the confidence that we have enjoyed. This is difficult, and such a termination of the question is most unpleasant for me.

We have had fogs here for the last eight days, which have not improved my head, already greatly confused by this fortress question, which ought to have been settled, if they had not interfered with it in Paris. I wished above all things to show that I was not intriguing ; that was my strong point. In Paris they did not like such a simple process, and they made a little side intrigue, which now has forced the others to take precautionary measures against us. All this wearies me to death. Adieu. . . .

The following letter from a friend of General Sebastiani's (a favourite adviser at the Palais Royal, and whose wish to replace me in London was even stronger than to keep his post in Berlin, where he only remained three months) is a sufficiently curious proof of the influence which change of residence exercises over certain minds :

THE COMTE DE FLAHAUT TO THE PRINCE DE TALLEYRAND.

BERLIN, *September 25th*, 1831.

I received protocol No 41, which you were so good as to send me yesterday ; had it not been for that, I should not have known a word of what was going on, for the Ministry gives no information whatever to its minister at Berlin. I think that the terms (of the protocol) are excellent, and repair the ridiculous and embarrassing position in which the speech of Marshal Soult [1] placed us.

To act in conformity with his words, it would have been necessary to break the most solemn and distinct engagements.

I hope to leave Berlin this evening, and profit by the holiday which the king has given me. For three weeks now, I have not been at all well, and besides, I want to go to Paris on private business. Shall I see you there ? It seems to me that you, more than anyone, have the right to take a rest, if your task is finished by the 10th. You are quite right in saying that our welfare

---

[1] Marshal Soult had declared, that the French army would remain in Belgium until the independence of that country should be solemnly recognized and proclaimed.

depends entirely on peace. · War will either hand us over to foreigners, or to our own blunders. The Poles serve to further these last, and I am beginning to keep aloof from them. They will alienate their best friends by such behaviour. They now turn our kindness to them into a crime. Meanwhile, their armies hope to obtain good terms by resistance ; and I believe they will only further injure their interests, for the soldiers are gradually leaving their regiments and returning home. They would have done better to profit by the favourable terms offered them by Paskiewicz,[1] but if courage is an attribute of this warlike nation, they are certainly not distinguished for common sense. They say that Romarino has entered Galicia with ten thousand men, and that the army at Modlin appears to wish to fly into Prussia.[2] You know. . . .

THE PRINCE DE TALLEYRAND TO THE PRINCESS DE VAUDÉMONT.

LONDON, *September 30th,* 1831.

Read the *Times* of to-day, the 30th. You must read it in the original, because the French papers, either intentionally or unintentionally, will misinterpret it. Lord Londonderry[3] attacked me, with regard to the influence I was exercising over the

---

[1] Ivan Feodorowitch Paskiewicz, Russian field marshal, born 1777, went through the campaigns of 1805, 1806, 1812, and 1813. In 1826, he received the command of the army of the Caucasus. In 1831, he replaced Marshal Dielbitsch at the head of the army of Poland, and after the peace, received the rank of field marshal and the title of Prince of Warsaw. He was then appointed Viceroy of Poland. In 1849, he commanded the Russian troops sent into Hungary. Finally, in 1854, when at the head of the army of the Danube, he was seriously wounded before Silistria. He died in 1856.

[2] After the peace of Warsaw, the remains of the Polish army, under Generals Romarino and Rybinski, retreated on Modlin. After a desperate resistance, it was dispersed and took refuge in Prussia and Austria. General Romarino passed into Galicia on September 16th.

[3] Charles William Stewart, Marquis of Londonderry, brother of Lord Castlereagh, who was often mentioned at the Congress of Vienna under the name of Lord Stewart. This is a portion of his speech which relates to M. de Talleyrand.—"HOUSE OF LORDS, *September* 29th.—THE MARQUIS OF LONDONDERRY. . . . France seeks every means of diminishing the influence of England and of forcing her to give way to her ascendency. The crafty diplomatist who represents her here, is no sooner beaten on one point than he turns to another. I made use of rather a strong expression, in speaking of the personage who at present directs the affairs of France in this country. I do not think you could find another such character in the whole world. He was, successively, the minister of Napoleon, of Louis XVIII., and of Charles X. When one sees the English ministers going one after the other to consult such a person, one is naturally filled with disgust. If your lordships want to know on what grounds my opinion of Prince Talleyrand are based, I ask them to read the memorandum he addressed to the First Consul, on the 15th Brumaire, in the year XI.

Conference and the English Ministry; and all this coupled with ingenious and subtle epithets, which were rather malevolent. The Duke of Wellington rose, and energetically repulsed the attack made on me, and insisted above all that I had always defended the interests of France, without anyone being able to attack my loyalty and straightforwardness. (This will prove to you that the man who loves you is both loyal and sincere.) Lord Holland spoke after the Duke of Wellington to the same effect, and very forcibly. Thus all parties united in a manner most flattering to me.[1]

[1] This is the extract from the *Times*, to which reference is made in this letter :—

"HOUSE OF LORDS, *Thursday, September 29th*, 1831

After Lord Londonderry's attack on M. de Talleyrand,

LORD GODERICH said in the course of his speech :

"Another part of his noble friend's speech to which he desired to advert, was that which related to Prince de Talleyrand, whom his noble friend had supposed to have great influence upon the councils of this country, and whom, proceeding on that supposition and upon certain parts of that illustrious person's past life, this noble friend has thought he was justified in pursuing with the most acrimonious animadversion, although an ambassador from a friendly Power. (*Loud cries of "Hear."*) His noble friend, to do him justice, had not dipped his arrows so deeply in gall on this as on a former occasion ; but still he must say, that he had, even on this occasion, indulged in language the most imprudent and the most indiscreet that any public man could be betrayed into with regard to an ambassador of a friendly Power. (*Cheers.*) He would not willingly have touched upon this part of his noble friend's speech, because he thought the sooner it was forgotten the better; but then, if he were silent with regard to it, it might be supposed that the government were of opinion that those animadversions were not misplaced : and, if that were the case, the plain inference was that Prince de Talleyrand ought not to be allowed to remain here. If the government entertained the same opinion as his noble friend of Prince de Talleyrand, it would be their duty to represent to his Majesty, the King of the French, that they could not transact business with such a person. He felt it necessary, therefore, to speak as he had spoken respecting these aspersions of the character of an individual, whose station ought to have shielded him from such an assault. (*Cheers.*) He knew that his noble friend would say, that because he protested against this indiscreet, imprudent, and unjustifiable language, the government was truckling to France. Let him, however, remind his noble friend that Prince de Talleyrand had been the minister of the last two kings of France ; that Prince de Talleyrand had also had a large and important share in the deliberations of the Congress of Vienna, the result of which deliberations the noble marquis thought so wise and so good. (*Cheers.*) Surely, the noble marquis might have thought of these facts ; but if he had, he would never have entered upon the unjust, as well as the invidious, occupation of ransacking every portion of Prince de Talleyrand's life, and bringing up in judgment against him, as present deeds and acts of this day, transactions which had taken place when the circumstances of France were so different, and when no man could act as his reason or his inclination dictated, but as the strong and uncontrollable tide of affairs compelled him to fashion his course.

"THE DUKE OF WELLINGTON.—Before he stated what his view of the subject was (*l'emploi d'officiers Français dans l'armée Belge*), he must be allowed to say a few words respecting an illustrious individual (Prince de Talleyrand), who had been so strongly animadverted upon by his noble friend near him. True it was, that that illustrious individual had enjoyed, in a very high degree, the confidence of his noble friend's deceased relative ; and true it also was, that none of the great measures which had been resolved upon at Vienna and at Paris, had been concerted or carried on

In Paris, for which I am working myself to death, no one would think of doing so much. They think enough has been done when you have written me a few kind words, and I am induced to believe that they are right.

The fate of the Reform Bill is still uncertain ; but it is certain that, whether the Bill is rejected or adopted, the ministers will remain in.

Just now we have conferences of from five to six hours a day ; we wish to finish and we intend to finish these matters. The King of Holland will not attack, whatever the papers and Messrs. Celles and Co. may say. Even if it was necessary to prolong the armistice for a few days, I believe he would agree to it. If we are only left alone, we shall finish all right. Adieu.

without the intervention of that illustrious person. He had no hesitation in saying, that both at that time, in every one of the great transactions that took place then, and in every transaction in which he had been engaged with Prince de Talleyrand since, the latest of which had occurred during the short period in which he (the Duke of Wellington) had been in his Majesty's councils after the late revolution in France, —he had no hesitation in declaring that in all those transactions, from the first to the last of them, no man could have conducted himself with more firmness and ability with regard to his own country, or with more uprightness and honour in all his communications with the ministers of other countries, than Prince de Talleyrand. (*Cheers.*) They had heard a good deal of Prince de Talleyrand from many quarters, but he felt himself bound to declare it to be his sincere and conscientious belief, that no man's public and private character had ever been so much belied, as both the public and the private character of that illustrious individual had been. (*Much cheering.*) He had thought it necessary, in common justice, to say this much of an individual respecting whose conduct and character he had had no small means of forming a judgment.

"LORD HOLLAND.—There was one part of the noble duke's speech which had given him the greatest pleasure, and which reflected the highest credit upon the noble duke. He need hardly say that he alluded to the temper, the manliness and the generosity with which the noble duke animadverted upon what had fallen from the noble marquis with regard to Prince de Talleyrand. On public as well as on private grounds, he thanked the noble duke for that part of his speech. There could be little difference of opinion, as to the injustice and the want of generosity of speaking in harsh and insulting terms respecting the ambassador of a friendly Power, resident amongst us. On the other hand, he felt that there could be no good taste in dwelling upon the virtue and the merit of a man's own acquaintance, in an assembly like that of their lordships ; yet he trusted that he might be allowed to observe, that forty years' acquaintance with the noble individual who had been alluded to, enabled him to bear his testimony to the fact, that although those forty years had been passed during a time peculiarly fraught with calumnies of every description, there had been no man's private character more shamefully traduced, and no man's public character more mistaken and misrepresented, than the private and public character of Prince de Talleyrand."

If one takes into consideration the well-known uprightness and truthfulness of the Duke of Wellington, and the friendship that existed for forty years between Lord Holland and the Prince de Talleyrand, the most prejudiced mind cannot fail to see, that what took place at this sitting of the English House of Lords was specially flattering to M. de Talleyrand. We must not lose sight of the fact, that the Duke o Wellington was the head of the opposition, of which Lord Londonderry, the attacking party, was a member, while Lords Gooderich and Holland were members of the Ministry.—(*M. de Bacourt.*)

M. CASIMIR PÉRIER TO THE PRINCE DE TALLEYRAND.

PARIS, *October 1st,* 1831.

I have received the two letters, mon Prince, which you addressed to me; you know what a pleasure it is to me to receive news direct from you.

I was very sensible of the kind remarks you were good enough to make to me, respecting the events of the past week. I only did, not perhaps without some peril, what, under the circumstances, was required by the gravity of the disorders and the necessity of thwarting evil designs, the pretext for which was furnished by an incident abroad.

Having succeeded in establishing order, and surmounting an evil which had found an echo in annoying parliamentary debates, we shall not neglect any effort to rescue France from the perils with which she is threatened by this trouble, and with her, the civilization of the whole of Europe. As you, mon Prince, on your side, apply yourself so nobly to this end, so will I also use all my endeavours, as long as it is given to me to be at the head of affairs, in the difficult task of restoring social order, disturbed as it has been by party attacks, and but little upheld by men of worth in general.

We have received your last despatch, mon Prince, to which was added protocol No. 44. The Conference, feeling the necessity of putting an end to the Belgian business, has decided to take the initiative. It has resolved to draw up a project for a definite treaty between the two countries.[1] We cannot fail to recognize the benefit of this measure.

We are equally desirous, of course, to see the question finally settled, and to deprive agitators of the pretexts for which they are ever on the watch ; but above all, we hold that the basis established by General Sebastiani in his different despatches, must be perpetuated in the projected treaty. Should the period till October 10th, be too short to obtain this result completely and securely, we ought then to beg for an extension of another fortnight.

It is of essential consequence in the position we now hold, that the solution of Belgian affairs should satisfy the views as well

---

[1] In the execution of the preliminary Treaty of the Eighteen Articles, the Conference proposed on September 24th, a scheme for a definite treaty which they addressed to the Dutch and Belgian plenipotentiaries. They replied on the 26th, by two counter-projects, entirely dissimilar. The Conference decided that these two parties would never agree if they were left to themselves ; it therefore drew up a protocol (No. 44 of September 26th), in which it decided to settle the articles of the projected treaty on its own authority. It was in consequence of this protocol, that the Treaty of the Twenty-four Articles was drawn up.

as the requirements of the government. This solution includes, up to a certain point, the question of our possibly remaining in power.

For this, mon Prince, a separation of the two countries, which removes from both any motive or pretext for quarrel, the possibility for both to enjoy in peace the independence which is necessary to them, and the advantages attached to their respective positions ; in fact, the adoption of such conditions as France has a right to insist upon, are necessities with which your wise prudence must be fully impressed.

Some overtures have been made to the government with the idea of placing a prince of the House of Nassau on the throne of Greece. Without prejudging the result of these overtures, they might be looked upon as a possible means of facilitating arrangements as far as Holland is concerned. The government would not be averse to entertaining them in that light. . . .

In this last paragraph of his letter, M Casimir Périer alludes to the idea that had been put forward by Russia—compensating the King of the Netherlands by giving the throne of Greece to Prince Frederick, the youngest and favourite son of that sovereign. But the king himself rejected the proposal, and the matter went no further.

THE DUC DE DALBERG TO THE PRINCE DE TALLEYRAND.

PARIS, *October 3rd*, 1831.

Your letter dated 29th inst, mon cher Prince, was a real comfort to me. You had maintained so prolonged a silence, that I could not account for it. In spite of the multiplicity of your engagements, I always hoped that you would find a moment to tell me of your health and welfare. You may feel assured that no one is more earnest in his wishes for your happiness than I am. I shall congratulate Europe, and especially France, if the Dutch question is settled by an *equitable arbitration.* So long as there is an impending question of war, it is not possible to hope for a return of confidence.

It is impossible to deceive oneself as to the consequences of war. It will lead to upheavals of every kind, and France cannot flatter herself that they will be to her advantage. All my information from Italy and Germany confirms me in the idea, that if the nations applauded the July revolution, they all see and calculate the consequences of the faults which are being

P 2

committed here now. A friend holding a high position in Germany writes to me :

"Your France and your Paris are really beginning to disgust us all. Take care! Some fine day you may easily, in a general war with us, share the fate of Belgium in the last squabble with Holland. It is not written in the book of fate, that victory will be everywhere and always faithful to the French army. Remember the last years of Louis XIV. and of Napoleon. This so-called sympathy of the nations is growing less and less. Everyone is wearied by your insurrections, and the aggressive boastings of your various factions."

Travellers returning from Cologne confirm these observations. At Cologne, the Prussians have a park of artillery of 200 guns, horsed. Comte Nostitz,[1] who commands part of the army there, said to a person whose name I cannot give, "We shall defend our treaty against France. She may do what she likes at home, but she must refrain from interfering with the position of her neighbours. Our army wishes for war ; we can enter the field with 200,000 men. Our organization and our numbers assure us of success. Prince Metternich has promised to support us. The Austrians and the German contingents will put the same number of men on the Rhine, and they will have as many more with the Piedmontese in Italy. If the King of France does not wish to become a mere King of Jacobinism, let him seek another theatre than Europe for his operations ; we shall certainly defend ourselves."

At Munich, the king has given himself over entirely to the Prince of Wrède. Sixty thousand Bavarians are at the disposal of the Cabinet of Vienna. For six months, Pfeffel[2] has not received a single word in reply to all the nonsense with which they credit him here at the Foreign Office. There is a M. Mortier at Munich,[3] who is very high flown and weak ; he ·is disliked by the king and everyone, and receives the cold

---

[1] Comte de Nostitz-Rieneck, general of cavalry, went through the campaigns of 1806, 1813, 1814, and 1815 ; after the peace, he commanded the cavalry of the guards. In 1830, Prince William, the king's brother, having been sent into the Rhenish provinces as civil and military governor, Count Nostitz accompanied him as chief of his staff. He left the army in 1848, was appointed minister to Hanover in 1850, retired in 1859, and died in 1866.

[2] Chrétien Hubert, Baron Pfeffel de Kriegelstein, son of the historian and diplomatist of that name, who had formerly served in the office of M. de Vergennes. Born in 1765, he entered the diplomatic service of Bavaria, and died as minister plenipotentiary of that country in 1835, at Paris.

[3] Comte Hector Mortier, nephew of Marshal Duc de Trévise, born in 1797. Was first secretary at Berlin under the Restoration. After the Revolution of July, he was appointed minister plenipotentiary to Munich, then to Lisbon, 1833 ; to the Hague, 1835 ; to Berne, 1839 ; and to Parma, 1844. He was created peer of France in 1845. In 1851, he became first chamberlain to Prince Jerome Napoleon, and died in 1864.

shoulder from all. Runigny is much regretted there, as although he was rather a gossip, he never made mischief.

Louis de Rohan has returned to Vienna. He says they are furious there against everything French, and that they are prepared to make a most vigorous defence. One of my friends, head of one of the Cantons of Switzerland, wrote to me on September 20th :

"The troubles that are agitating us all originate in your clubs. Mauguin, who took a journey to Switzerland this summer, has regularly stirred up the people. Several of our leaders, who have been in Paris, boast of having been encouraged by La Fayette and Lamarque and urge on our demagogues. All this is odious, and is preparing great trouble for you. Europe cannot continue in this state."

Regarding Poland, mon cher Prince, you ought to have more reliable news than I can give you. However, this is what I think and what I know. The Polish revolution was confined to the army ; the war to the Vistula. The Cabinets have the names of twenty-seven individuals who left Paris to stir up discontent in Warsaw. The first successes were due to a splendid Polish army, completely equipped, ready for the field, and possessed of from twenty to thirty millions of ready money. Some most respected names were involved, and help was expected from here. It had been promised !!! Marshal Diebitsch attacked them with an insufficient force, and winter fought on the side of the Poles. When, however, the Prussians at last got their army together and crossed the Vistula, victory did what she generally does, sided with the strongest. The Poles were shamefully treated ; Warsaw surrendered ; the Polish army, which the Emperor Nicholas did not intend should exist any longer, retreated, and opened negotiations ; but while awaiting an answer from St. Petersburg, it gradually dwindled away. Only about six thousand men remained under arms. In one day, six hundred officers tendered their submission. Defection is universal. This revolution began with assassination and crime, and finishes in the same manner.

The following, I believe, is the course the Russian Cabinet intends to pursue. It will not permit the intervention of any other Cabinet. It will allow the *boundary* and the *name* of the kingdom of. Poland to remain, but it will no longer consent to the existence either of a Diet, or a Polish army. And in my opinion it will be right. At the present time, the only ability needed, is to organize a strong authority and then maintain it.

The Palais Royal has so broken up all the bonds of political society, that it is time to look into this carefully. I advise our

Ministry thoroughly to realise this truth. It is to this end that I approve of all the arrangements favourable to the Dutch. Further, let me submit to you an observation founded on historical facts. Holland, strong and powerful as a State, and possessing a navy, is of more consequence to France than Belgium, boastful and turbulent as she is and will continue to be, for some time to come. Several days ago I remarked to M. Casimir Périer, that all this solicitude for the Belgian revolution seemed to me absurd, whereas whatever is done for Holland will be of real use. At least that is my opinion.

I had got so far, mon Prince, when the English papers giving an account of the idiotic behaviour of Lord Londonderry, were brought to me. He is what he has always been ; but I must congratulate you on the result of this parliamentary debate, so highly complimentary to your position. I rejoice at it for your sake.

Try and put an end to the Dutch business. If the King of Holland insists on having territory instead of money, you must give it to him. Luxemburg possesses 240,000 inhabitants. The fortress with its surroundings may be taken at 40,000 inhabitants. Well ! let the remaining 200,000 be given around Venloo and Maëstricht. What does it matter whether the Belgians have a few villages more or less ? The essential thing is to preserve peace. The day before yesterday there was a very lively discussion on this subject between M. Sebastiani, Werther (the Prussian minister) and Pozzo. The account of it was given me by one who was present. The former argued against the result of the *arbitration.* He declared that he could not defend it from the tribune ; he even said, that rather than adhere to it, France would withdraw her representatives, and would witness the end of the Conference without regret. M. de Werther[1] opposed him ; Pozzo said little, but as they left the room he said to Werther, "Why do you argue with him ? You know quite well that it is not with him that we do business." I therefore think, mon Prince, that M. Périer will not leave you in the lurch. Matters must come to an end, as you truly say. Later on, the infinite service that you have rendered to France will be recognized.

I have little to tell you of our Chambers. That of the Deputies is excessively dull ; and the Ministry and the king have abandoned that of the Peers. This is one of the greatest of the many indiscretions that are being committed every day.

Pray accept .'. . .'.

---

[1] Prussian Minister at Paris. His son was Prussian Ambassador at Paris in 1870, at the time war was declared.

I did not accept *everything* that M. de Dalberg's letter contained, as entirely exact ; but I had to admit that there was a great deal of truth in it.

THE PRINCE DE TALLEYRAND TO THE PRINCESS DE VAUDÉMONT.

LONDON, *October 3rd*, 1831.

I find that in Paris, Belgian affairs are very badly understood just now. They are trying to make a Belgium, by taking one part from here and another from there ; that is easy enough, anyone knows how to do that ; but that is not the point. We have to replace Holland and Belgium, in the respective positions which they occupied with regard to one another in 1790. Before that time Holland did not inundate Belgium ; there was a treaty of 1785, which prevented any devastation of that kind.[1] This might be renewed, and the proximity of France will have much more influence over Holland than Austria who is so far off could have. In truth, all the difficulties that are made at Paris, and which originate in the brains and are the result of the machinations of M. de Celles, are very feeble ; they could all be settled by a child. It is singular however, that we allow ourselves to be the dupes of such a worthless individual as M. de Celles, who dares not return to Belgium, and who fears matters will never be settled. This Belgian question is a question on which peace or war depends ; it can be satisfactorily ended ; when I say *satisfactorily*, I mean to the advantage of Belgium, without putting the King of Holland in a position to refuse his adherence. Why rob anyone ? Would that be a just treaty ? What is wished in France will not be consented to here. It is really seeking for hindrances. My common sense shows me nothing but misfortunes if we hold to the foolish ideas that the wire-pullers have started amongst us.

Adieu ; I would willingly only be annoyed, but I am more than that,—I am grieved. . . . .

LONDON, *October 4th*, 1831.

The first debate on the *Reform* Bill took place yesterday in the House of Lords ; it continues to-day, and perhaps will not end till to-morrow. The same uncertainty still exists about it ; but it is thought that several bishops were favourably inclined to the Ministry yesterday evening.

[1] Article VI. of the treaty of November 8th, 1785, between the Netherlands and the Emperor.

In the House and around it, there was an enormous crowd. I am now going to the Conference. We are ready to wind up matters, if they would refrain from trying to create a chimerical Belgium in Paris ; but they can, if they will, have a genuine Belgium. Stipulations will be made to 'prevent inundations ; there will be both Dutch and Belgian overseers at the sluices ; so there will be no more danger in that quarter. Belgium will have two more routes for introducing her products and merchandise into Germany. She will receive an increase of population of 50,000 souls, and France will see the destruction of the fortresses, which were designated by M. Latour-Maubourg, and with regard to which, General Goblet [1] is now here with us.

It seems to me that this is enough to content us. Therefore let us end, and seek fresh strength in peace. It is in this, that the government will find support and security of every kind . . . .

KING LEOPOLD TO THE PRINCE DE TALLEYRAND.

BRUSSELS, *October 4th*, 1831.

MON CHER PRINCE,

I had charged Baron Stockmar [2] with a letter for you ; as he has been ill, it is possible that he has not yet been able to deliver it to you.

We are awaiting the arrival of the courier here from the Hague. As time presses, I have had to make my military arrangements just as if war was certain ; but what else could I do ? I cannot wait until the last moment. Urge the Conference to some *energetic* measure ; it is plain that the King

[1] Albert-Joseph Goblet, Comte d'Alviella, a Belgian general, born in 1790, left the Polytechnic school in 1811, and served till 1815 in the French army. At that date he passed into the service of the King of the Netherlands. In 1830, he took part with the provisional Belgian government, which appointed him General of Brigade and War Minister. In 1831, he was sent to London as commissioner to the Conference. In 1832, he became Minister for Foreign Affairs. In 1836, he was elected deputy, and the following year sent to Lisbon as minister plenipotentiary. On returning to Belgium (1843) he again took up foreign affairs. He retired 1845. He was elected deputy over and over again, and always sat on the Liberal side. He died in 1873.

[2] Christian-Frederic, Baron Stockmar, born at Coburg in 1787, was physician in that town. In 1815, he made the acquaintance of Prince Leopold, who attached him to his person and took him to London. He lived with him during his whole residence in England, was made physician to the Royal family, and was specially intimate with the Duke of Kent, father of Queen Victoria. His position soon became a very important one. He was the influential counsellor and confidant of Queen Victoria. Thus the souvenirs and historical notes that he has left are a very precious source of information concerning the history of this period. M. S. René-Taillendier took from them matter for a series of articles which came out in the *Revue des Deux Mondes* of 1876 to 1878. After having remained many years in London, M. de Stockmar retired to Coburg, where he died in 1863.

of Holland will try and complicate matters, so as to profit by them. However, it is very desirable for everyone that war should not break out. You may count upon me ; you know my opinions ; I can flatter myself that I have contributed towards the maintenance of peace, and I shall not cease to uphold it. My object has always been to preserve good feeling between France and England ; I have succeeded up to now ; help me on your side. I look upon it as the *real welfare* of the whole of Europe. But in the present crisis, the Conference must display *energy ;* without that, matters will fall *into the utmost* confusion. Present my compliments to Madame de Dino ; still retain a little affection for me, and accept the assurances of my warmest regard.

LEOPOLD.

THE DUC DE DALBERG TO THE PRINCE DE TALLEYRAND.

PARIS, *October* 4*th,* 1831.

MON CHER PRINCE,

M. de Mortemart has arrived (from St. Petersburg). It is reported that he was very well treated by the Emperor Nicholas on his departure. Do not believe a word of it : the Emperor was polite, that was all. You may also believe that Pozzo no longer possesses his master's confidence. The emperor wanted to recall him. Nesselrode upheld him, by begging the emperor to consent to his likewise retiring from his post of Minister for Foreign Affairs. The emperor thereupon suspended his decision.

If they do not use the utmost caution here in their relations with the coalition, we shall have war in the spring. It is my opinion that the Dutch business must be concluded, or the Hague will remain a Pandora's box.

At Berlin, the king alone refuses to go to war. Flahaut has made a poor show there.

Here the Peerage question inclines towards the adoption of M. Teste's project,[1] an invention of Sémonville's ; they hoped to carry it yesterday, but I think they are sure of nothing.

[1] M. Teste had proposed an amendment, in terms of which the peerage should be transmitted to the eldest son of a peer, on condition that he was declared *worthy* by an electoral college. This amendment was rejected.

Jean Baptiste Teste, born in 1780, was advocate at Paris, then at Nimes, and Commissioner of Police at Lyons during the Hundred Days. Proscribed under the second Restoration, he took refuge at Liége, where he remained till 1830. He then returned to Paris, was elected deputy in 1831. Then he became Vice-President of the Chamber ; Lord Chancellor in 1839, Minister of Public Works in 1840, peer of France, and First President of the Court of Appeal in 1843. Implicated in 1847 in the action entered against General Cubières, he was arraigned before the Court of Peers, and condemned to three years' imprisonment. He died in 1850.

MADAME ADELAIDE D'ORLÉANS TO THE PRINCE DE
TALLEYRAND.

PARIS, *October 7th*, 1831.

I have been longer than I liked, mon cher Prince,
without writing to you ; but we have been in such a state of
confusion getting into the Tuileries, and I am still so unsettled
and so uncomfortable, that until I can get into the rooms of
the Captain of the Guard, which are being got ready as far as
possible, I am literally camping out. But putting all other
matters on one side, I must tell you how much I rejoice over
the triumph you have just had in the English Parliament, and
I congratulate you with all my heart.

Now what we must have as a result from this, is a really good
treaty for Belgium, which will give security and the assurance
that the King of Holland can no longer with ease, inundate
that unfortunate country, or invade it if the fancy takes him.
He must be made to disarm, and then you will be able to rest a
little from all your fatigues, which I have observed with much
pain, after what you have told me as to the state of your health,
which is of such importance to us. I trust you have not experienced another attack of that fever you spoke of in your last
letter ; I am longing to be assured of this by yourself. We are
also impatiently awaiting the result of the second reading of the
Reform Bill.

Our establishment in these melancholy, detestable Tuileries,
is said to have produced a most favourable impression. We
certainly need that to console us, for it was a great sacrifice for
the king to leave his beautiful, charming Palais Royal, our child-
hood's home, which we loved so dearly, and come to this dreary
palace, the most uncomfortable place in the world, in which it is
impossible to settle down conveniently or pleasantly, without
making great changes and causing much trouble. But patience !
We must keep the end solely in view, and move on towards it
without stopping to think of what we like or dislike, making
every sacrifice to arrive thereat. This is what our beloved king
does with the best grace in the world, and in the most touching
and admirable manner ; I always feel assured that he will be
amply rewarded, and I have need of this faith when I see how
his life, ever since he became king, has been one succession of
sacrifices and privations. Happily, in the midst of all this, his
health continues good. He charges me with a thousand remem-
brances to you, as also does the queen, who finds, with only too

much reason, an immense difference between her apartments at the Palais Royal and those she has here. It is going from good to bad. Chartres and Nemours left us on Sunday night for Maubeuge ; we have news of their safe arrival there . . . .

THE PRINCE DE TALLEYRAND TO THE PRINCESS DE VAUDÉMONT.

LONDON, *October* 8*th*, 1831.

. . . . The Reform Bill has been rejected by the House of Lords ; the majority against it was forty-one ; it is much larger than was expected. This number will probably prevent the creation of any peers ; all judgment is suspended, and everyone asks what line the king and the Ministry will take. A Cabinet Council has been sitting ever since the morning. No one knows what the result will be. . . .

LONDON, *October* 12*th*, 1831.

. . . . Every day I receive apologies for the foolish act committed at Brussels, in posting up a letter of Sebastiani's, which stated that the decisions of the Conference would not be recognized. Here it has had such a bad effect, that it has been found necessary to abandon this step and to attribute it to local causes, which necessitated such a communication being made, in order to prevent some folly. All this does not increase the respect for the course the government is pursuing ; they do everything much too hurriedly. England does not appreciate it. The Emperor Napoleon, who was a man of *action*, was always grateful to me for retarding the execution of his orders, as it gave him the opportunity of abandoning a resolution often made too hastily. I will adhere to my views of things to the end ; I intend to do all I can to secure peace ; that is my mission ; and everything that is necessary to that end I will do, without regard to whom I may or may not offend. . . .

THE PRINCE DE TALLEYRAND TO THE DUCHESS DE BAUFFREMONT.

LONDON, *October* 13*th* 1831.

. . . . Yesterday evening there was somewhat of an uproar in London. The windows of the Duke of Wellington's house, those of Lord Bristol[1] and Lord Londonderry, were broken. To-day all is quiet. In the country there have also been disturbances, but they have not been very numerous. I believe the conviction that the Ministry will remain in, will put an end to all these disturbances. But it is none the less a moment of great difficulty and fraught with danger, in the opinion of those who know what a political movement is when it is taken up by the people.

I have conferences here every day, and I think that our Belgian affairs will be ended, as far as the Conference is concerned, in eight days. But after that comes the adherence of the Kings of Belgium and Holland, and the ratifications of the great Cabinets of Europe. . . .

THE PRINCE DE TALLEYRAND TO MADAME ADELAIDE D'ORLÉANS.

LONDON, *October* 22*nd*, 1831.

I hope we are at last approaching the end, and that this difficult business of Belgium will soon be finished. The day on which I know it is decided, will be the happiest of my life, for I shall have been of service in performing something, which in all respects must please the king and Mademoiselle. It seems to me that this will make everything much easier for France ; a great weapon of attack will be taken away from the evil disposed, and the benefit of peace ought to unite all interests round the throne. I shall be very happy when I see you great and tranquil.

We must now turn the attention of active minds to home improvements, with which they can occupy themselves without fear in times of peace. The decentralization of the administration should, it seems to me, first claim the king's attention. It is necessary to give everyone something to do.

People are very clever in showing, as the King of England did in his speech,[2] how far the Conference has been of use, and also how far removed its work has been from that done by the Holy Alliance. I could write volumes about all this, and Mademoiselle knows it even better than I do. I beg her. . . .

---

[1] Frederick William Hervey, Marquis of Bristol, born in 1769, a member of the House of Commons from 1796 to 1803, when he succeeded his father in the House of Lords. He was Minister for Foreign Affairs from 1801–1803. Lord Bristol was one of the most zealous members of the Tory party, and an opponent of the Reform Bill. He died in 1859.

[2] Speech at the prorogation of Parliament, October 20th.

As this letter states, the Conference had somewhat advanced in the work of mediation between Holland and Belgium, which it had pursued so wearily for nearly a year. It had been necessarily obliged to retract some of its first resolutions, subsequent events having altered their bases. The reasons for this were explained in the protocols of October 15th. I will confine myself to quoting a few extracts here:

Unable any longer to leave uncertain those questions whose immediate solution has become a necessity for Europe; obliged to decide them, under pain of seeing the terrible evil of a general war resulting therefrom; enlightened, in addition, by the information that has been given to them by the Belgian plenipotentiary and the plenipotentiaries of the Netherlands, the undersigned have only carried out a duty, which their Courts owed to themselves as well as to the other States, and which all the efforts of direct mediation between Holland and Belgium have failed to accomplish. They have only caused the principal law, which guards the chief interests of Europe, to be respected; they have only yielded to a necessity, which has become more and more imperious, in fixing the conditions of a definite arrangement, which Europe, the friend of peace, and possessing the right to enforce its continuance, has for a whole year sought for in vain, in the proposals made by the two parties or agreed to by one and rejected by the other, in turn. . . .

. . . . The five Powers, reserving to themselves the task, and undertaking the responsibility of obtaining the adherence of Holland (and Belgium) to the articles in question, even if they are at first rejected, and also of guaranteeing their execution, and feeling convinced that these articles, founded on incontestable principles of justice, offer to Belgium (and to Holland) all the advantages which could be claimed as a right, can only here declare their firm determination to oppose, by all the means in their power, any renewal of a struggle which, having now no object, would be a fertile source of grave evils for both countries, and would menace Europe with a general war, which it is the first duty of the five Powers to prevent. But, in proportion as this determination is calculated to reassure Belgium (and Holland) as to its future, and also the circumstances which now cause such great anxiety, so it will authorize the five Powers to make use of all the means in their power, to bring about the assent of Belgium (and of Holland) to the articles mentioned below, in case, contrary to all expectation, it should be refused. . . . .

Following the protocols of October 15th, the Conference had drawn up the basis of separation between Belgium and Holland, in twenty-four articles, which it addressed to the Hague and to Brussels, requesting the agreement of the two governments to them. This step of the Conference was irrevocable, and put a stop to a renewal of hostilities between the two parties, since their differences would in future be settled by Europe. The correspondence which follows, will show that the matter was regarded in that light at Paris as well as everywhere else.

MADAME ADELAIDE D'ORLÉANS TO THE PRINCE DE TALLEYRAND.

October 19th, 1831.

I hasten with the greatest eagerness to congratulate you most heartily, mon cher Prince, on your great success in terminating in so fortunate a manner, this long and complicated Belgian business. Our beloved king charges me also to say how very pleased he is, and how satisfied *with his ambassador.* I know that these are the best thanks I can give you from him. I look upon it as insuring peace for us ; and that is everything ; for with peace, confidence will be restored, and with it the prosperity of our beautiful France. This great good news has created a wonderful effect, and caused general joy. I hope that now you will be able to rest and take care of your health, while enjoying your successes and the great results they will have. I do not for an instant doubt the acceptance of the King of the Belgians ; his people ought, indeed, to be only too delighted.

As for the King of Holland, he may well be content with what the Conference has done for him. I must confess I am not troubled on his account.

The fact that the English Ministry remains in office,[1] and that everything is settling down quietly and tranquilly from the real confidence it inspires, is another very good thing for us.

God grant that our great Peerage question may end happily ! We are in the same state of suspense over it, that you were in England over the Reform Bill. However, mon cher Prince, I am always very hopeful, and it seems to me that we are really making some progress. . . . .

---

[1] It had been feared that the English Cabinet would go out of office, in consequence of the vote in the House of Lords, rejecting the Reform Bill.

MONSIEUR CASIMIR PÉRIER TO THE PRINCE DE TALLEYRAND.

PARIS, *November 3rd,* 1831.

I need not tell you, mon Prince, what great pleasure I felt in receiving the last letters you did me the honour to write. The return of my son, bearer of the first of these letters, left me nothing to desire, since I at the same time received your news and the certainty that the important and difficult work confided to your great prudence has at last been accomplished.

That work, mon Prince, you have brought to an end, to our greatest possible satisfaction ; it is, and will remain, in spite of the attacks of the malevolent and the base interests that it thwarts, a fresh and immense service rendered to the country. Its effect has already made itself felt, though party spirit sought and still seeks to inspire fears, as to the reception this great determination will meet with from the parties directly interested.

A continuous peace, a peace reposing henceforth on a solid basis, is an event which can only have favourable results for France, both in respect to her home and her foreign policy ; and this event, which so thoroughly justifies your opinion as to the utility of the Conference, we owe, and so does France, mon Prince, to your noble efforts. But what causes me the most satisfaction is, that posterity will do you that full justice, which in times of social agitation, men charged with the public interests cannot expect to receive from their contemporaries.

Thus, mon Prince, it is with sincere pleasure I tell you, that our situation is without any doubt greatly improved by the maintenance of peace in Europe ; we must not, however, conceal from ourselves that we have still much to do, that the problem is not yet solved, and that we must find the real basis of support.

Among the home difficulties which we have still to surmount, that of the peerage is not the least perplexing. Various considerations, not without weight, which cannot have escaped your observation, made us desirous to avoid making any additions to the Chamber of Peers until after the adoption of the Bill, but we found that this was not possible, and that an immediate creation was indispensable.

Yesterday we received the news of the acceptance of the twenty-four articles by the Belgian Chamber of Representatives; it is stated that the Senate will follow their example at once.[1] Holland we must believe will accept. Thus the perilous difficulties abroad will be smoothed over; the great duty, which the present state of the nations of Europe has imposed on the men placed at their head, namely, that of preventing all collision between them, will have been accomplished. This is the happy result, mon Prince, of that confidence in the disinterested and loyal views of the King's government which you have been able to inspire.

The fatigue that you have undergone, mon Prince, has made me fear for your health. As your last letters do not refer to it, I hope that you no longer feel its effects. I cannot, however, refrain from entreating you to take care of a health so precious to the State and so dear to me. . . . .

THE DUC DE DALBERG TO THE PRINCE DE TALLEYRAND.

PARIS, *November 4th*, 1831.

MON CHER PRINCE,

. . . . The Ministry continues to negotiate with the Chamber of Peers, trying to persuade it to commit suicide. M. Périer has been to see me twice to discuss the question. I cannot but admit, that the king and the Ministry have themselves to blame for bringing this question up, but I have promised to assist in removing the too great dissidence between the two Chambers. To obtain the passing of the Bill, thirty or forty peers would have to be created, and to my knowledge ten or twelve creations have been refused. However, I believe an arrangement will be come to.

M. Sebastiani has given us another sample of his way of managing the affairs of his office. No one has any longer a doubt that the *duplicata* addressed to General Guilleminot [2] had no *primata*. . . .

---

[1] The treaty of the Twenty-four Articles was adopted on November 1st in the Chamber of Deputies, by a majority of 59 against 38, and on November 3rd in the Senate, by 35 votes against 8.

[2] The reasons which had provoked the recall of General Guilleminot, the Ambassador at Constantinople, will be remembered. On his return to Paris, the General spoke in the Chamber of Peers (sitting November 2nd), and in order to justify himself, declared that as he had never received any instructions from the French government, he could not be accused of having transgressed against them; that he had indeed received with his order of recall, the duplicate of a despatch which ought to have been sent to him before, but that he never had received this despatch. General Sebastiani declared that he had sent it, and the question was never cleared up.

PRINCE DE TALLEYRAND TO THE PRINCESS DE
VAUDÉMONT.

LONDON, *November 10th*, 1831.

.... The King of Holland will put off his acceptance,
until the return of the courier he has sent to St. Petersburg to
ascertain the opinion of the Russian Cabinet, which he believes
differs from that of its plenipotentiaries in London. The
answer will arrive in the beginning of December, and his reply
to the Conference through his plenipotentiaries will follow.
We shall therefore still have to wait for twenty days. This
gives the papers ample time to utter and write all sorts of
conjectures, one more senseless than the other. . . .

LONDON, *November 15th*, 1831.

Our articles are signed. The Belgians will cry out, but
they are wrong ; all has been done equitably, and I think
favours the Belgians, which is what I wanted, particularly as
regards the frontier adjoining France. Belgium pays a much
smaller share of the National Debt than she did before the
separation, so she cannot complain. Her population is increased,
and her home commerce will benefit greatly by the facilities
given her. Two routes for commerce between Belgium and
Germany, the right to use all the interior canals, the junction of
the Scheldt and the Rhine, and the benefit of all that has been
done at Mayence for the navigation of the rivers—all these
advantages Belgium will at once be able to enjoy.

I am terribly fatigued ; yesterday our conference lasted till
5 A.M., and the day before till 4. I believe I have obtained everything that it was possible to obtain. France must do all she can
in Brussels to support our articles, which are admirable. . . .

The result of which I spoke in my letter to Madame de
Vaudémont, was brought about by the Conference as follows.
The Belgian Chambers, after some very animated discussions,
accepted the twenty-four articles which we had addressed to the
Dutch and Belgian governments on October 15th, but the
Belgian Ministry had pledged itself not to give its definite
consent :

1st, until it had obtained, or attempted to obtain, some
modification of the articles ;

Q

2nd, until it had acquired the certainty, that the king chosen by the Belgians would be immediately recognized.

The Belgian plenipotentiary in London had sent us a memorandum on November 12th, insisting on these restrictions.[1] The Conference answered the same day, that the twenty-four articles could not be modified, and that it was no longer possible for the five Powers to alter any of them. By a second memorandum on November 14th, the Conference informed the Belgian plenipotentiary, that there was nothing to prevent the twenty-four articles receiving the sanction of a treaty between the five Powers and Belgium, which would satisfy the demand that the king elected by the Belgians should be recognized.

Meanwhile the Conference informed the Dutch plenipotentiaries on the 13th of November, of Belgium's acceptance, and offered them the initiative in signing the treaty. Their answer on November 15th having been in the negative, the treaty was signed between the plenipotentiaries of the five Courts and that of Belgium. This treaty first of all reproduced the Twenty-four Articles, to which the three following were added:

" Article 25.—The Courts of Austria, France, Great Britain, Prussia, and Russia, guarantee to his Majesty the King of the Belgians the execution of all the preceding articles.

" Article 26.—In consequence of the stipulations of the present treaty, peace and friendship will be established between their Majesties the Emperor of Austria, the King of the French, the King of the United Kingdom of Great Britain and Ireland, the King of Prussia, and the Emperor of Russia on the one part, and his Majesty the King of the Belgians on the other part, their heirs and successors, their States and subjects, respectively, in perpetuity.

" Article 27.—The present treaty shall be ratified, and the ratifications will be exchanged in London within the period of two months, or sooner if it can be done."

---

[1] In his memorandum of November 12th, M. Van de Weyer asked under the first head, 1st, a revision of the calculations which had served the Conference as a basis for the partition of the debt between Holland and Belgium ; 2nd, a rectification of the frontiers in favour of Belgium, at those points where the frontier line separated the metal factories from the ore necessary for carrying on their business ; 3rd, free access to and free navigation of the Moselle to the inhabitants of Luxemburg.

After the signing of this treaty, one might have imagined that the question of the fate of Belgium, which for nearly a year had kept Europe in a state of suspense, was definitely settled. if not as regards Holland, at least in all that concerned Belgium and the five Powers ; but it will be seen that the matter was not so simple, and that I was still a long way from the end of my labours. As hitherto, I shall let the correspondence describe (which it will do far better than I could myself) the new difficulties that cropped up.

THE PRINCE DE TALLEYRAND TO THE PRINCESS DE VAUDÉMONT.

LONDON, *November* 16*th*, 1831.

. . . . Yesterday we signed the treaty with Belgium, so now Prince Leopold is recognized, as well as his country. This is a great matter accomplished. The signature of the five Powers to the treaty necessarily involves the consent of the King of Holland. It is no use his being obstinate, he must give in. I think that at the Tuileries, they will welcome the courier whom I send with this treaty. It is the first the king has made, and it is important to France, whose frontier it protects, and to Belgium, whom it renders independent.

I am not thinking of returning to Paris ; I have not said so to anyone ; it is one of the tales invented by Madame de Flahaut, who is ever hoping she may come to England, where however she will not come, because she is detested, and because her husband is not a sufficiently important personage for the Embassy in London ; in other respects he might suit. He is amiable, knows plenty of people, and speaks English well ; but that is not all that is required here.

I am going to Brighton for a breath of fresh air and to pay my respects to the king. I have been working beyond all reason and require a rest. Tell me who is the so called " statesman," who has written the history of the Restoration. It is only true chronologically, and is full of falsehoods and inaccuracies [1] . . . .

MADAME ADELAIDE D'ORLÉANS TO THE PRINCE DE TALLEYRAND.

PARIS, *November* 18*th*, 1831.

The treaty arrived yesterday evening, mon cher Prince. I cannot express to you the pleasure, that the sight of the row of seals

[1] See page 294.

of the representatives of the five Powers, placed on our beloved
colours, gave me. You have accomplished a great work ; I
must congratulate you and compliment you, with all my heart.
Truly it has required all your zeal, all your talent, all your
ability, to achieve this fortunate result, so important to the
happiness of our beloved country, and indeed to that of all
Europe.

All that is now required to complete this great work, is to
compel the King of Holland to declare himself and to execute
the treaty. It is essential for *everyone* that this should be done
promptly, but specially so for the King of the Belgians, for if
this uncertainty is prolonged, it will place him in an awkward
position with his subjects, and one quite contrary to the dignity
and undertakings of the five Powers, who have just signed this
treaty. I am sure you will take the same view of this matter,
and that all your efforts will be directed to the speedy and
complete execution of the treaty, which, at least it seems so to
me, is quite as important as obtaining the King of Holland's
signature to it.

There is nothing fresh as yet with regard to our Peerage
Bill, which is also a momentous question. I am as ignorant and
expectant regarding this as I was when I last wrote to you.
Madame de Vaudémont communicated your last letter to me,
and I made its contents known to the right person . . . .

KING LOUIS PHILIPPE TO THE PRINCE DE TALLEYRAND.

PARIS, *November* 19*th*, 1831.
MON CHER PRINCE,

The treaty of London of November 15th, 1831, will be
a great epoch in history. The more its consequences develop
themselves, the more France will appreciate the great service
you have just rendered her, and I hasten to testify to you, how fully
I join in this appreciation, and in all the sentiments that this
great success ought to call forth towards you. It is indeed a
complete answer, to all the attacks which have vainly attempted
to upset the action of my government and your plans, during
these long and laborious negotiations.

It is to me the best recompense, for the constancy and
tenacity with which I and General Sebastiani have upheld you
in all the different phases of this long struggle. Now at last it
is terminated, in a manner both durable and honourable, for I
regard the treaty that you have just signed, as putting an end to

the hopes of those who think they can overthrow everything by war, and who only proclaim it as inevitable, in order to give themselves a greater chance of bringing it about. It is very remarkable that this has been the language both of the Absolutionists and of the Propagandists in all countries ; keep therefore in mind, that to succeed in paralyzing their efforts, we must obtain the King of Holland's signature and execution of the treaty, with the least possible delay. You give us an assurance that he will decide to do this, and I accept the omen with the greater pleasure, since I believe that, not only my own interests and even the interests of the whole of Europe require it, but that it is eminently his own interest and that of Holland which enjoins him to relinquish the system of procrastination, to which he seems to be inclined, and from which I think, only misfortunes for himself and his neighbours can be expected. It seems to me that the happy concord which is established between all the plenipotentiaries of the Conference, and which you have so efficaciously contributed to maintain, ought to suffice to make him feel that this is the best thing he can do now.

Assuring you, mon cher Prince. . . . .

THE COMTE DE FLAHAUT TO THE PRINCE DE TALLEY-RAND.

PARIS, *November* 19*th*, 1831.

At last you have reached the end, though not without anxiety. Your having succeeded in maintaining peace, in the midst of all these revolutions and distractions, is a great achievement. Who would have thought that the kingdom of the Netherlands, that work of the Holy Alliance, so hostile to France, could have been wiped out without a general war ? It has needed all your skill. You have been well supported by the present Ministry ; but at first you had to contend with some difficulties here. However, now you are at the goal ; for I do not believe in real opposition, either from Holland or Belgium. Yesterday Marshal Gérard was sent to Brussels, to tell them plainly that no assistance need be looked for from here in resisting the stipulated conditions. They thought of sending me ; but Gérard is much better fitted, and will have greater influence.

The Peerage Bill was passed by the deputies with a majority of 343 votes. There is no resisting so pronounced a manifestation. However, it is not yet known what the Peers will do. Something idiotic, I presume . . . .

THE DUC DE DALBERG TO THE PRINCE DE TALLEYRAND.

PARIS, *November 21st*, 1831.

Your short letter of the 15th, only reached me yesterday evening. I thank you most heartily for it. Each time you write to me you show me a light in the midst of the darkness, and I see that you are pursuing with energy, the task undertaken by the Conference. The separation of Belgium from Holland, destroys a powerful engine of war placed at the most vulnerable points on our frontier. *This is due to you;* and it is only the crass ignorance of our deputies and journalists, their bad faith, and their passionate language, which prevents this being openly stated and acknowledged.

The King of Holland has a right to resent vehemently the discourteous treatment of his allies. As Prussia and Russia have consented to sacrifice their family connections, and these two Cabinets seem to be sincere in their wish to maintain peace in Europe, I believe the King of Holland will accede to the agreements already drawn up, and even if his consent does not arrive in the beginning of December, it cannot be delayed long after that time. Besides you have allowed him two months, and I suppose you did this, so as to receive the answer from the north. He will therefore yield, but he will, like his ancestors William II. and William III., remain the most irreconcilable enemy of France, and will draw round him a perfect hotbed of intrigues, with the view to overthrow our government. There are powerful elements at his hand, and the alliance which has been formed with this object between the Carlists and Buonapartists, will second and foster his efforts.

Just now the attitude of the European Cabinets is calm. They are weighing their position and looking about them. But the feeling of distrust is still there, and how could it be otherwise? The speeches in our Chambers, the revolutionary intrigues that originate here without the government being able or willing to prevent them, and the wild and insulting language of our journals, are all so many incentives to them to confine themselves to the treaties of Chaumont, which were signed against the *French Revolution*. I am almost sure that the three Great Powers have come to a fresh understanding as to this. The language of their legations in Germany and Italy, though honeyed to our representatives, is very exciting towards the smaller States. They represent France as needing the strictest *surveillance*, and they try to strengthen and assure the bonds of a close alliance, in case the revolutionary and advanced party here should regain the upper hand. It is impossible that it should be otherwise. Until Europe is convinced, that the Revolution of July is consolidated, France will not be *welcomed anywhere*.

Nevertheless, believe me, as things are at present, they are already thinking of a marriage, both here and at St. Petersburg, if what has now been established, becomes permanent in two years; and Pozzo, who failed with that of the Duc de Berry, will try to achieve this one, which might perhaps be entertained. It is with this prospect, that the request of the King of Bavaria for his son has been declined at St. Petersburg. I do not doubt that if this project is ventilated in London and Vienna, those Courts will attempt to thwart it, as the latter has done all she can at Naples, to prevent a princess of Orleans going there. All this, mon cher Prince, proves to me that it will be difficult to establish confidence, and that everything that can injure it must be avoided.

You ask me who the statesman is, who published that indifferent history of the Restoration. He is a man named Capefigue,[1] a newspaper editor, and author of several other works. Connected with Mignet under M. Molé, he had access to the archives; he went to Molé and Pasquier, who read and corrected his publication. For several years, he tried to get together a number of anecdotes by conversing with this one and that one, and he hoped to make some money in this way. After the publication of the two first volumes, I was introduced to him by M. Buchon;[2] I wished to correct some facts put forward by him, but my efforts were useless. He writes for his bookseller; he intends to have ten volumes; and in order to fill them, he makes use of everything that comes to his hand. M. Decazes has now taken him up, and is furnishing him with materials for writing something about his ministry. M. Capefigue had, some time ago, a memorandum which he said had come from London, and from persons who were with you. It contained the suggestion of an alliance between France, England, and Austria, which was being negotiated. He wrote some articles on it for the papers; it made some talk; but the initiated at once said that it was a blind; that M. de Metternich perhaps

---

[1] Baptiste-Honoré, Raymond Capefigue, born at Marseilles in 1801, journalist and political writer. He contributed under the Restoration to a great number of newspapers, principally to the *Messager des Chambres*, which supported the Martignac Ministry. He is also equally known by a large number of historical works, which at first he always issued under the pseudonym, *Un Homme d'État*. He died in 1872.

[2] Jean Alexandre de Buchon, editor and political writer. Under the Restoration he wrote for the *Censeur Européen* and the *Constitutionnel*. He took up history as well, and published the *Chroniques Nationales Françaises*, a large work in forty-seven volumes.

might allow such a possibility to be supposed, but that, in reality, he would hold to the continental alliance with the Courts of Berlin and St. Petersburg.

At the present time there must be no division among the Powers. The world is sinking and dissolving beneath the blows of the mental anarchy, which has invaded society. We must always talk of reforming abuses, even do so a little, but we must re-establish authority.

The events at Bristol,[1] and those with which London seems threatened, reveal the deep sore which is eating into the heart of England. Lord Grey and his colleague Lord Brougham, have taken up reform on too vast a scale. It is like M. Necker with his *doublement du tiers.* When the masses rise, urged on by mischief makers and by La Fayettes, who can stop them ? It is from this point of view, that the success of the Belgian revolution produces an injurious effect, and it must be neutralized. Meanwhile, the Emperor Nicholas is doing this with Poland. Men's minds must be restored to calmness, or everything will go to the devil.

In Germany they are becoming quite foolish. The orators of Munich and Carlsruhe are in a state of frenzy. At Berlin and Vienna they are asking how this can be grappled with. I advise, that the Diet of Frankfort should decide that the debates shall not be published, and that the laws of the *general Confederation* are not subjects for discussion. That would put a stop to it.

Our Chamber of Peers has at last to-day received its finishing stroke.[2] M. Casimir Périer and the king have turned it into a corpse. The former thinks of dissolving the Chamber of Deputies, after the Budget for 1832 is voted. I do not advise this : they will probably get a worse one. We ought to let the present Chamber exhaust its stupidities.

Prince Paul of Wurtemberg begs me to remind you, of his wish and his ambition to undertake the risks of that unfortunate Capo d'Istria. I think the choice of him as King of Greece, would not be a bad one. . . . .

---

[1] A sanguinary riot had taken place at Bristol on October 29th, on the occasion of the arrival in that town of Sir Charles Wetherall, one of the members who had shown himself the most opposed to the Reform Bill. For two days, the town had been completely in the hands of the rioters, who had set fire to the greater part of the public buildings.

[2] An allusion to the order of November 20th, which had created thirty-six new peers. The object of this was to modify the majority of the Upper Chamber and make it more favourable to the Bill passed in the Chamber of Deputies, which abolished hereditary peerages. On the 29th December following, therefore, the Chamber of Peers pronounced against hereditary peerages by a majority of thirty-three.

THE PRINCE DE TALLEYRAND TO THE PRINCESS DE
VAUDÉMONT.

LONDON, *December 2nd,* 1831.

. . . . I know nothing of the affair at Lyons, except from
the papers ; it creates great uneasiness here.[1] The recollection
of Bristol, and fears for Manchester,[2] do not tend to free the
country from anxiety. It is earnestly hoped that an end will be
put to it, and that some arrangement will be made which,
without being too much of a concession, will satisfy those who
have no means of livelihood except the daily wage which is paid
them in the large manufactories. It is a problem difficult to
solve. In my opinion the population is not too numerous for
the country as a whole, but it is not properly distributed, and it
is with this distribution that the government ought to deal. To
this end, instead of giving help *en masse* in any place or
populous town, work should be given in some department
where large clearings have to be made and marshes drained.
Men from other departments who would come there, would be
paid for this work, for they will always flock where work and
wages are to be got. Thus, in Auvergne, Limousin, Nivernais
and Berry, there are not sufficient hands ; efforts should be made
to attract people there. This would ease those provinces that
had too many, and would enrich those that had too few. In
Berry, for example, we want about three hundred thousand men ;
in Nivernais there are also some needed. The advantages given
to those who go, will bring many others : that is what is meant
by good administration. . . . .

M. CASIMIR PÉRIER TO THE PRINCE DE TALLEYAND.

PARIS, *December 4th,* 1832.

MON PRINCE,

I have been wishing for a long time, to again express to
you the gratitude we owe you, for all your trouble in the difficult
course of these negotiations, in the midst of which you have
assured to the representative of France, that position and influence which are his by right.

[1] A terrible insurrection had broken out at Lyons on November 21st, provoked
by a fall in the price of silk. It was not a political movement. After two days'
fighting, the troops had to evacuate the town and await the arrival of an army of
32,000 men, under the command of Marshal Soult and the Duc d'Orléans, before
re-entering it.
[2] A repetition of the scenes at Bristol was feared at Manchester.

The government could expect nothing less from that great experience, that has so happily accomplished the treaty, which has just placed the relations of the great Powers on a footing of political equality and community of interests, henceforth incontestable to everyone.

I congratulate myself, mon Prince, in having to thank you, both as President of the king's Council, as deputy, and as a Frenchman, for the leading part that you have taken in the important transaction, which, as it were, commences the new era of another national law, the sole object of which will be to assure rest to the nations, and the peaceful development of the benefits of civilization.

But Europe, mon Prince, having entered on this path, can no longer allow anyone to strew it with obstacles. In this you will agree with me. Therefore I do not doubt that you will urge, and will continue to urge, with untiring perseverance, that the foolish obstructions which the King of Holland still seems desirous to oppose to the determinations of the Powers, should be removed. It is quite time it should end. The king wishes it as sincerely as his allies, who, with him, have undertaken to insure the execution of the twenty-four articles, and I venture to ask on your part, for the most active exertions to bring about this final guarantee for the work of pacification, the consolidation of which you will have all the more at heart, as you have had the most to do with it. It is the indispensable accompaniment to the general disarmament which is the desire and to the interest of all, and of which an isolated incident should not be permitted to postpone the execution.

I cannot, mon Prince, speak of the interests of the State to you, without seizing the opportunity of congratulating myself on the closer relations which have been established between us, and which my son's presence with you, makes so very valuable to me. I am glad to think that, by his diligence and zeal, he helps to bring his father to your remembrance, and my ardent wish is, that his future life should some day testify to all, under whose auspices he entered the service of his king and of his country.

THE PRINCE DE TALLEYRAND TO M. CASIMIR PÉRIER.

LONDON, *December* 10*th*, 1831.

MONSIEUR,

In the letter you did me the honour to write on the 4th instant, your friendship has caused you to say what I value very nighly. You forget that what I had to do, became far less difficult, from the moment that the administration of our country was directed by a strong will, and with that straightforwardness, which I hear highly praised every day, and which has become a guarantee of safety to Europe.

The obstinacy of the King of Holland prevents our saying that the affairs of Belgium are now ended ; but the fact remains, that sooner or later, that is in a few weeks, he must give in. The methodical course that we have pursued has succeeded with Belgium ; by not precipitating matters, we shall succeed equally with Holland. The friendly feeling which exists, and which must be carefully maintained, between the great Powers, will finally remove the difficulties which still remain. The answers from St. Petersburg ought, according to Prince de Lieven, to arrive in a few days, and dissipate the illusions with which King William is still possessed. Let us wait, if it is necessary. Deliberation in measures that have to be taken, has one great advantage, namely, that when we do not hurry it is a proof that all is well.

Permit me to persuade you, to allow the Assembly to make as many economies as it pleases ; it is not worth the trouble of breaking lances over it every day ; common sense will soon change all that the love of popularity has done this year. As the civil list is settled for the whole reign, it alone is worthy of your efforts.

I am very glad you will allow your son to remain with me for some time. In the course of his career, he will certainly find few circumstances under which he can learn so much—not only the political business that he goes through with me, but the parliamentary discussions of this year, will be of use to him all his life. I cannot give him too much praise for his diligence, the desire he has to be useful, and the manner in which his mind develops every day.

Assuring you, monsieur. . . .

P.S.—Do not be discouraged. That is all that Europe asks of you.

THE PRINCE DE TALLEYRAND TO THE PRINCESS DE VAUDÉMONT.

LONDON, *December* 15*th*, 1831.

An answer from Holland has just arrived. It is forty folio pages, and I have to read it.

I assure you I would rather read forty pages of your bad

writing. The result is, that the King of Holland accepts the boundaries; submits to the re-division of the debt; and asks that a treaty
which he wishes to negotiate, shall be made between him and
Belgium, in order to establish the navigation of the rivers
and the right to the canals.[1] That is to say, he adopts what
is good for himself, viz., the boundaries, and he refuses what
is beneficial for Belgium, viz., the free navigation of the rivers
and canals. All this will be settled, but not without some
trouble. King Leopold embarrasses us somewhat, by declin-
ing to carry out his promise as to the fortresses, a promise
that he gave to M. Latour-Maubourg, as well as in a letter he
wrote to King Louis Philippe.[2] We must settle it so as not to
offend him too much. The principle of demolition is established
and recognized; the injury done to France is repaired; and the
forty-four millions which the fortresses cost the allies, have been
wasted. That is the real result of this treaty, which would have
been a better one without the *separate negotiation* which was
attempted in Brussels, and which made everyone here very
distrustful. . . .

LONDON, December 17th, 1831.

. . . . I am going to hear the Note of forty pages read, which
was sent yesterday to the Foreign Office. When one has right on
one's side one does not write forty pages. In Paris there will be
some discontent about the fortresses in the treaty; but I have
nothing to do with this matter, in the Conference between the four

---

[1] This memorandum, dated December 14th, protests against the joint surveillance
of the pilotage, the buoys, and the police of the Scheldt; it claims the course of the
river in Dutch territory, as Dutch property, and also protests against the participation
of the Belgians in the navigation of the intermediary waters between the Scheldt and
the Rhine.

[2] The Belgian government had signed the following pledge on September 8th :
"His Majesty the King of the Belgians has authorized the undersigned Minister for
Foreign Affairs to communicate to the French government, by M. le Marquis de
Latour-Maubourg, that he consents and agrees (in conformity with the principle
enunciated in the protocol of April 17th, 1831) to join with the four Powers, at
whose expense the fortresses were partly erected, in prompt measures for the demolition of the fortresses of Charleroy, Mons, Tournay, Ath, and Ménin, erected since
1815 in the kingdom of the Netherlands."
    But during the negotiation in London as to this question of the fortresses, General
Goblet, the Belgian plenipotentiary, seeing the repugnance of the Conference to
agree to the dismantling of Tournay and Charleroy, had allowed those infinitely less
important fortresses of Philippeville and Marienbourg to be substituted for them. The
French Cabinet protested energetically, basing its protest on the formal promise
given by the Belgian government on September 8th. To this King Leopold replied,
that the arrangement was not a formal pledge, but a simple preliminary which promised nothing. France had to accept the matter as settled. The agreement of
December 14th, between Belgium on the one part, and the four Powers on the other,
sanctioned this substitution. The following pages will show the course of these
negotiations. See also on this serious question of the fortresses *Une Mission à Londres
en* 1831, by General Goblet.

Powers and the Belgian plenipotentiary. France may suggest, but must not answer or lead. Besides, Lord Grey is alarmed at Lord Aberdeen's motion,[1] which is supported by the Duke of Wellington, making it thus more difficult to defend the question of the fortresses. Since the negotiation of the matter has been transferred to Brussels, there is distrust arising here ; that business of a *separate treaty* has given great displeasure since it has become known. I advised that it should be kept secret, but this was not done. . . . .

To thoroughly understand this letter and those which follow, it is necessary to speak once more of the demolition of the Belgian fortresses. The affair at this period gave me the most trouble, because it had for some time retarded the despatch of the French ratification of the treaty of November 15th. By repeating the explanations already given, I shall go back to the beginning of the question. It is of sufficient importance, to gain me this indulgence from those who are condemned to read it.

I have already said that at my instigation, and by a protocol which I had not signed, the plenipotentiaries of the four Courts of Austria, Great Britain, Prussia, and Russia, had admitted the necessity for the demolition of a certain number of the Belgian fortresses. I think I ought here to give the protocol, which bears the date of April 17th, 1831 :

The plenipotentiaries of Great Britain, Austria, Prussia, and Russia, being assembled, have jointly taken into consideration the matter of the fortresses in the kingdom of the Netherlands (which were built after the year 1815 at the expense of the four Courts), and how they are to be dealt with, when the separation of Belgium from Holland shall have been finally settled.

After mature consideration of this question, the plenipotentiaries of the four Courts are unanimously of opinion, that the new position in which Belgium will be placed (her neutrality being recognized and guaranteed by France) ought to change the system of military defence adopted for the security of the

---

[1] Lord Aberdeen had then an idea of proposing a motion in the House of Lords, opposed to the Treaty of the Twenty-four Articles and the convention of December 14th ; but the illness of the Duke of Wellington, who had promised to support it, decided him to defer his motion until after the Christmas recess, December 26th ; it was therefore brought forward on January 26th. Lord Grey successfully defended the policy of the government, and the House approved it by 132 votes to 95.

Netherlands ; that the above fortresses are too numerous for the Belgians to keep in a proper state of defence ; that, moreover, the unanimously admitted inviolability of the Belgian territory now offers a security, which previously did not exist, and that, in fact, some of the fortresses, built under totally different circumstances, might for the future be demolished. The plenipotentiaries have consequently decided, that as soon as there shall be a government in Belgium, recognized by the Powers who are taking part in the Conferences in London, negotiations will be entered into between the four Courts and that government, in order to determine which of the said fortresses shall be demolished.

This protocol is as succinct and categoric as possible ; I knew of it as soon as it was signed. There existed therefore a positive undertaking on this point, on the part of the four Powers.

It will be remembered, that at the time of Prince Leopold's departure for Brussels, I had endeavoured to obtain from him a written declaration, which should confirm, on his part, the resolution adopted by the four Powers. The prince, it is true, gave me but a vague reply, but the terms in which it was couched, made it possible to deduce an undertaking therefrom. The French government was not satisfied either with this letter, or with the protocol of the 17th of April, which, it is true, had not been published. It desired, when the French Chambers opened, to proclaim a fact of such a nature, as would produce a certain effect on the new Chamber just assembled, and on men's minds in general throughout France. The plenipotentiaries of the four Courts at my request, therefore, consented, that the protocol of the 17th of April should be made public, and it was accordingly notified officially to me by them, on the 14th of July. They also addressed a notification to the Belgian government on the 29th of the same month. But before this last notification, King Louis Philippe, when opening the Chambers on the 23rd of July, had announced the demolition of the fortresses. This caused great excitement in Brussels and embarrassment to King Leopold, who in the face of the expostulations of the Belgians, showed at first some hesitation in complying with the conditions imposed upon him by the four Courts. In my opinion they were needlessly alarmed in Paris, and M. de Latour-Maubourg was sent at once to Brussels to obtain an acquiescence from the Belgian government, which just then was greatly compromised by the unfortunate expedition of the Dutch against Belgium. The King of the Belgians, impelled by these circumstances, ended by issuing a declaration on the 8th of September, which announced that, *in conformity with the principle laid down in the protocol of the 17th of April*, he was, conjointly with the four Powers, about to take steps for the demolition of a certain number of designated fortresses.

M. de Latour-Maubourg carried this declaration to Paris, and General Goblet arrived in London, intrusted with powers from the Belgian government to carry out the negotiation named in the protocol of the 17th of April, conjointly with the plenipotentiaries of the four Courts.

The publicity which King Louis Philippe's speech had given to this protocol, raised some questions in the English Parliament on this subject. Lord Grey had to lay the protocol of April 17th, before the House of Lords, Lord Palmerston doing the same in the Commons, stating that it was only a question of arrangement between the four Courts and Belgium, from which France was excluded. This silenced the clamours of the Opposition, but their disquietude was revived when it was known, that a separate negotiation was being carried on at Brussels between M. de Latour-Maubourg and the Belgian government, whilst French troops still occupied Belgium. This was a direct contradiction to the statements made in Parliament. Lord Granville expressed his anxiety to M. Sebastiani, who to appease it asked the four Powers to draw up another protocol confirming that of the 17th of April, which would still further bind the Belgian government to carry out the dismantling of a certain number of fortresses, and which would take the place of the convention made at Brussels. To this they agreed, but they forgot in this protocol, drawn up on the 29th of August, 1831, to name the fortresses which were to be dismantled, as had been done in the convention drawn up at Brussels between M. de Latour-Maubourg and the Belgian government.

Not only was I excluded from all these transactions, but

even the French government itself kept them secret from me. None the less, however, did I feel the effect of the distrust, that such a method of procedure could not fail to instil into the plenipotentiaries of the four Courts. I had great difficulty in removing it, as far as it concerned me personally. This distrust, made the most of by General Goblet, the Belgian plenipotentiary in London, brought about several modifications in the selection of fortresses to be demolished ; thus in the declaration given by the King of the Belgians to M. de Latour-Maubourg, the fortresses named for demolition were Charleroy, Mons, Tournay, Ath, and Ménin, while in a convention signed the 14th of December, between the plenipotentiaries of the four Courts and General Goblet, those of Ménin, Ath, Mons, Philippeville, and Marienbourg, were indicated for demolition. This last convention gave rise to the following correspondence, which we think we have now made clear :

KING LOUIS PHILIPPE TO THE PRINCE DE TALLEYRAND.

PARIS, *December 16th,* 1831.

MON CHER PRINCE,

From the despatches which General Sebastiani has just given me, I see that the negotiations relative to the dismantling of the fortresses, are taking a shape which causes me great anxiety, and which is doubly painful to me personally, owing to the solemn engagement I entered into on this subject with the Chambers and the nation, on the faith of the assurances given me. This has decided me to write to you myself, in addition to what General Sebastiani will send you officially, so that you may be the depositary of my personal views, and that you may be in a position, if necessary, to make them known to those with whom I like to think they might have some weight.[1]

---

[1] It will perhaps be as well to complete this account, by giving a *résumé* of the various phases of the negotiation respecting the fortresses since the convention of the 14th December, up to the final settlement of the question. In fact, this convention, so far from ending the discussion, only revived it. The following letter puts us *au fait* as to the opposite views taken in the debates, but it would be difficult to follow the thread, if we did not first know the principal lines.

The French Cabinet was dissatisfied with the convention of the 14th December, and for two reasons : first, that they wished to see Charleroy and Tournay substituted for Philippeville and Marienbourg ; the second, and more important, that, according to the text of the first article, the Powers seemed to arrogate to themselves "a kind of present and future patronage of the dismantled fortresses," and this all the more as

I must therefore begin by telling you, mon cher Prince, that I should not have signed the arrangements for Belgium, and that I should not, above all, have agreed to her perpetual neutrality, if I had not trusted to the undertaking that the fortresses which had been erected to threaten us, would be demolished, or if I could have believed that it was intended to allow armed arsenals to exist on neutral territory! Why, just think for a moment, mon Prince. In point of law, this preservation of the fortresses makes it no longer necessary for us to respect them, and after the promises given us, they would in my eyes be a legitimate object for war. I do not tell you that I therefore intend to make it in this instance, but merely that our right is incontestable, and that the question of making or not making war, would be optional. I do not think that it would suit England, or any other member of the Conference, to place France in a position in which she thinks she has this right; especially after the good faith and loyalty we evinced last summer, when we evacuated these fortresses after having occupied them.

Naturally, I shall be asked why I do not wish Philippeville and Marienbourg to be demolished like the other fortresses, and to this question I shall reply with the same frankness, that these two fortresses were not, like the others, built with the money of the Powers, but were ceded by France, and it is just because they were French, that the national pride would consider their demolition an insult.[1] We must not conceal from ourselves, mon cher Prince, that the cession of these two fortresses is an ever open wound to our national vanity; that the voice of the country would certainly be disposed to reproach me, as well as my government, for not having insisted at all hazards on their peremptory restitution ; and I think I may assert that there is no other way to appease it, than to preserve Philippeville and Marienbourg and destroy the other fortresses.

France had been excluded from this convention. It had, in fact, only been signed by the four Powers on the one side and Belgium on the other.

M. de Talleyrand received instructions to obtain some modifications from the Powers on these two points of the convention, and the Cabinet of the Tuileries added, that it would reserve its ratification of the treaty of the 15th November, until satisfaction had been given to France. M. de Talleyrand differed with the Ministry on this question. He dreaded seeing the whole of his work compromised for some detail which he declared was quite secondary. He therefore wanted to create a delay by proposing to adjourn the discussion about Philippeville and Marienbourg ; but this evasion was not appreciated in Paris, where they demanded a prompt and frank decision. It was not till the 23rd of January, and after many innumerable delays, that M. de Talleyrand obtained the declaration (p. 269) from the Powers which put an end to the discussion. Nevertheless, the French Cabinet was beaten on the question of Philippeville and Marienbourg.

[1] Philippeville and Marienbourg had been given to France by the Treaty of the Pyrenees, in 1659. The treaty of 1815, deprived her of them again.

If instead of this arrangement, on which I thought I might count, France sees Philippeville and Marienbourg destroyed, while Ypres, Tournay, and Charleroy are preserved, I believe a feeling will be roused, the consequences of which will be terrible ; in fact it is certain that Ypres at one end, and Charleroy and Namur at the other, connected by Tournay as the central point, present to France a line of operations which reduces the neutrality of Belgium to a mere farce. Moreover the preservation of these fortresses is ill judged, both as regards France and also the other Powers, in the present state of affairs ; for it must be admitted, without wishing, Heaven knows ! to raise suspicions against any one, that treachery or deceit could at any moment, so long as these fortresses exist, deliver them into the hands of either one or the other party ; and that consequently their existence is at once a cause of anxiety and an attraction, of which it is desirable for all parties to rid themselves.

It is besides very important in the interests of Belgium, as well as those of Europe, that she should not be weighed down by expenses, which she might find oppressive and probably could not in any way support. Such, however, would certainly be the maintenance of the fortresses it is wished to preserve, especially of their garrisons, without which I, more than any one else, may be permitted to say, they would be at our mercy, which I do not in any way desire. France could never consent that these fortresses should be looked upon as a depot of the Powers, left in the hands of the King of the Belgians, which, in default of Belgian troops, they might wish to confide to the care of strangers, for this would not only create a legitimate cause for war, but would force France to make war in order to oppose it. The exclusion of the King of the Belgians from the Germanic confederation is insufficient to remove all fear on this head, and therefore I can only say, that the greater the inability of Belgium to support these fortresses and place proper garrisons in them at her own cost, the greater becomes the need, in the interests of all, that they should be demolished.

I know, mon cher Prince, that your opinion and that of my ministers, is in accord with what I have just pointed out to you. But I am desirous that you should know my personal views for I always like to confide them to you, and to seize every opportunity of proving to you, how greatly I appreciate all you have done in the thorny mission in which you have just obtained a success as brilliant and important for you, as for France and myself. I hope you will succeed in consolidating it, by leading the negotiations respecting the fortresses in a better direction than they seem disposed to give them. M. Périer and M. Sebastiani will do their best to second you, as they have always done, and your united efforts will preserve France and Europe from the dangers to which this direction might give rise ; for, do not deceive yourself—this matter is very serious, and we have to deal with much friction and irritability.

Pray, mon cher Prince, accept the assurance of all those sentiments which you know I have so long felt for you, and which are thoroughly sincere. . . .

MADAME ADELAIDE D'ORLÉANS TO THE PRINCE DE TALLEYRAND.

PARIS, *December* 19*th*, 1831.

I thank you much, mon cher Prince, for your letter of the 15th of December, and I am charmed that you are satisfied with mine ; but I cannot tell you how surprised and grieved I am, at the way in which the Conference tries to conclude the affair of the fortresses, and at King Leopold's conduct in this business, which is entirely opposed to the engagements he undertook. All this is very wrong and scandalous, especially when our beloved King and his government have shown nothing but loyalty and frankness on their side; but it is *impossible* to allow ourselves to be made game of like this. I am very vexed that you were not present at the Conferences, when this detestable decision was taken, for I am very sure you would have prevented it. Now, it will be for you to bring it round again. I quite feel that this is a difficult task, but such suits you best, and you have good and strong weapons ready to your hand, by making use of the frankness and loyalty of our beloved King in this matter, and also by the withdrawal of our troops from these Belgian fortresses in the month of August, relying, as we did, on the honour of those who made the fine promises, which you, mon cher Prince, must now have carried out. This is a serious matter, and of the greatest possible importance both to our dearly loved King and to France. The task that, you have to perform is a grand and a noble one, and I am firmly persuaded, I can assure you, mon Prince, that when the Conference is once convinced that the King *will not* accede to this arrangement, it will do that which is alone compatible with the dignity of France.

It was because the King saw this tendency that he decided to send M. de Maubourg to Brussels, to deal direct with Prince

R 2

Leopold in this matter, and obtain an undertaking from him, which you could not do from London, and which you must acknowledge it is well now to have.

I am very vexed about this whole business, but nevertheless, mon cher Prince, I have every trust in our good right, and in your zeal and talent in seconding the efforts of our beloved King, which makes me feel thoroughly confident that he will come out of this horrid business advantageously. I am longing to hear from you, and what you think of all this ; but this time everything must be finished, and the King of Holland made to explain himself, and to adhere to what has been promised. . . .

THE PRINCE DE TALLEYRAND TO KING LOUIS PHILIPPE.

LONDON, *December 22nd*, 1831.

SIRE,

Your Majesty attaches great importance to the demolition of the Belgian fortresses, which were built in order to recall our defeats, and your Majesty feels that it is for you to efface these insulting witnesses of our misfortunes. But Sire, it would be taking too gloomy a view, to attribute what has just taken place, to a return to the Holy Alliance.

The pledges of wisdom and moderation which your government gives to Europe every day, have for ever destroyed this league, which was formed against the liberty of the nations.

I am intensely grieved that any trouble or anxiety should reach your Majesty, from a quarter where you are good enough to believe I have some influence. I should wish to have nothing to report to you but what your eyes could rest on with pleasure.

The Belgian intrigues, in which all the weakness of a new and uncertain government is plainly visible, have brought about the convention of which we have to complain. The grave circumstances in which the English Ministry now finds itself placed, and the exaggerated fears inspired by Lord Aberdeen's bitter attacks, have also assisted the Belgian intrigue. The evil has come from Brussels ; the remedy therefore can only come from the same quarter. In saying this, my object is not to spare myself any trouble, for I unhesitatingly discuss it with every one of influence, not merely with the members of the Conference, but with all those who have any weight in the English Cabinet. This evening, when thinking over the events of the day, my conviction grows stronger, and I feel fully persuaded that no effectual action can be taken except by Belgium. It is therefore your Majesty's influence on Prince Leopold that can alone effect the change you desire.

This question is full of difficulties, for the only solution that would suit us, is not one which the Belgian government would sanction, and yet this solution, which may be the only possible one, might compromise the fate of the treaty of November 15th, which forms ties between us and the Powers, which in the present state of Europe it would be very unfortunate to see weakened.

Your Majesty's strong and far-sighted observations gave me fresh material for discussion with Lord Grey and Lord Palmerston, and by adopting an injured, rather than an excited tone, I think I left nothing unsaid that could prove to them your just resentment. Lord Grey, who professes a sincere admiration for your Majesty, expressed himself greatly grieved at the manner in which this matter of the fortresses has been taken up in France. Lord Palmerston, also, regretted that the result of this negotiation should be displeasing to your Majesty's government. I believe that, so far, they are quite sincere in saying, that they neither of them can understand why the King's government should be so greatly hurt (as I said they were) about this matter.

I am deeply distressed, Sire, at the annoyance your Majesty is experiencing ; but I cannot help feeling that I am not to blame for it in any way. All this would have been avoided, if the Belgians when here had acted with less secrecy, not to say less intrigue, and also, probably, if the engagement at Brussels had been kept more secret.

I am . . . .

THE PRINCE DE TALLEYRAND TO MADAME ADELAIDE D'ORLEANS.

LONDON, *December 27th,* 1831.

From the way in which the Belgians have conducted this business of the fortresses, I fear it will now be impossible to carry out the King's wishes respecting them. Mademoiselle may feel assured that I have done my very best. But if we look at the matter fairly, we shall find that its importance is not so great after all. Ath and Mons, the fortresses nearest us, will be demolished : thus one reparation has been made to France. We must make the most of this, and remember for the future that new and weak governments must not be left to themselves. In the crisis which is still threatening, and will do so for some

time in Europe, it is of the greatest importance that those
governments, which have any affinity whatever, should hold
together. Interest in the Polish affair unites three of the
governments ; two alone have a separate interest ; it is important
that these two should remain united, and even, if necessary,
make some sacrifices to this end. I confide my opinions to
Mademoiselle that she may make what use of them she deems
best. . . .

KING LOUIS PHILIPPE TO THE PRINCE DE TALLEYRAND.

PARIS, *December* 26th, 1831.

MON CHER PRINCE,

Your letter of the 22nd seems to demand some explanations from me, and I am the more anxious to give them to
you myself, as General Sebastiani [1] is seriously ill, which grieves
me intensely. He is quite unable to write to you or attend
to any business, and I am most desirous that you should
thoroughly understand the view I take of this very important
Belgian matter.

We are blamed for several reasons, one of which seems to you
well founded—for although, with your usual thoughtful kindness
for me, you have not mentioned it in your letter, you have
several times spoken of it in your despatches—and that is M. de
Latour Maubourg's mission to Brussels. If this mission was in
a way characteristic of distrust, it could only, according to my
view, be with regard to King Leopold or the Belgian government,
but certainly not towards you, mon cher Prince, nor against the
four Powers. As for you, neither I nor my ministers have, nor
could possibly have, either suspicions or mistrust of any kind.
The protocol of April 17th, was, in a way, your own work, and it
is certainly due to you that France succeeded in obtaining it.
More than that, you conceived the happy idea of asking King
Leopold for a letter, which contained an undertaking respecting
the demolition of the fortresses, that is to say, an undertaking
almost similar to the object of M. de Latour Maubourg's mission ;
but the letter he wrote you was less an undertaking, than an
announcement that he would not pledge himself to anything.
It was therefore only natural, especially after the small service
we had rendered him meanwhile, that we should seek to obtain
from him in Brussels the promise which he had not given you
in London.

It was no more an act of distrust towards the Powers, than

---

[1] General Sebastiani had just had a stroke of apoplexy.

was your demand to Prince Leopold. It was solely a desire to obtain the same pledge from him, as the Powers had given us by the protocol of April 17th, so that the two parties who were to make a treaty between them and outside of us, on matters which were not foreign to us except in a pecuniary point of view, should be bound to us by a similar covenant. Surely, mon cher Prince, we have some right to insist that the Powers should not accuse us of distrust towards them, looking to the conduct of France during the whole course of these Belgian transactions, and more especially the manner in which we evacuated the Belgian fortresses, when it was in our power to blow them up at any moment. If my contemporaries do not do me the full justice in this matter which I consider I deserve, I have at any rate the firm belief that I shall obtain it from posterity.

I also see, in one of your despatches, that we are accused of having hampered this business by giving too great publicity to the protocol of April 17th.

Here, mon cher Prince, I must remind you, that before my council decided that it should be mentioned in the speech from the throne, General Sebastiani consulted you about it, and you agreed with us that it might be done ; and I can assure you, that if we considered this communication might be helpful in satis-fying our national pride, we also thought that it would serve to show that the Powers did not wish to wound it, or in any way injure the interests of France ; but, above all, we deemed such an announcement better suited than anything else, to reconcile public opinion to the choice of Prince Leopold, who, as you are aware, was not popular in France, being generally looked upon here only as a lieutenant of England or of the Holy Alliance. We desired to show France and also Belgium (where it would not have answered any better), that the policy of 1815 had been abandoned by the Powers, and that the dissolution of the kingdom of the Netherlands, which sufficed to render it impossible, as well as the demolition of the fortresses of 1815, and the exclu-sion of the King of the Belgians from the Germanic confedera-tion, was a pledge thereof. I have not the faintest doubt, mon cher Prince, that all this was eminently necessary, as much for. the maintenance of peace, as for the support of my government at home, and the establishment of King Leopold in Belgium.

It is not therefore the intrinsic value of these acts which has given the turn we now deplore to the negotiations of the fortresses ; but it is the simultaneous action, and perhaps united opposition, of the Tories and Belgian intriguers. You have done well to make this known to the English ministers, for it will prove to them that it is not to their interests, any more than ours, that M. Van de Weyer's or M. Goblet's treaty should be maintained in the terms in which it was signed.

King Leopold and his government ought to feel this even more, for what would become of them, if, in consequence of this unfortunate obstruction, the treaty which the Conference of the five Powers signed on the 15th of November, was annulled ? You say with truth, mon cher Prince, and all the more reason for fearing it, that this is just what the King of Holland wishes, and probably the Emperor of Russia also.   I think this is a point of which you can make very effective use with the English government, and no one is better able than you, to give full weight to these fears, which are only too well founded.

I have no hesitation, mon Prince, in asserting that the desire to go to war is as far removed from the English government as it is from that of France, and that on the contrary, both equally feel the necessity for peace and the wish to preserve it ; but peace really depends on the friendly solution of the Belgian question, and this solution cannot be effected except by the close union of France and England.   Nevertheless, in order that this union may continue, it is necessary that they should first understand one another, before making arrangements with others who might disturb it.   Such has been the result of the mystery shown to us, both in London and Brussels, with respect to the arrangements for the fortresses.   They did not wish us to interfere in this negotiation, as we had not co-operated in that which preceded it—this one could understand ; but if they had told us what they intended to arrange, they would not have placed us, nor would they have placed themselves, in the difficult position from which it will now take all your efforts and all your skill to extricate us.   But if the English government on the one side, will only be thoroughly convinced that we have *no arrière pensée* in what we now seek, and if we on the other, only ask that it should not renew or perpetuate an impossible system, (such as that on which the kingdom of the Netherlands was founded), it will then see the danger which threatens us from Holland and Russia, and will modify the treaty respecting the fortresses in such a manner, that King Leopold will not in future be placed in relations with four of the five Powers, other than those which have been established with all five.   This must be a *sine quâ non* for France, the rest is but a secondary matter.

Although this letter is already far too long, I wish still to draw your attention to what would be King Leopold's position, if he were to ratify a treaty with four Powers collectively, before the fourth had even ratified this particular treaty, much less the general treaty of the five Powers which establishes the independence of his kingdom and recognizes its king.

I think, therefore, that under the circumstances, the ratification of the treaty with the four Powers ought not to take place, as long as Russia does not adhere to that of the 15th November; all the more so, that as long as Russia does not adhere to it, neither of the five Powers can be called on to ratify it, and France less than either of them, so long as the treaty of the fortresses has not been modified. But if it were, and I can see no reason why this should not be possible, since there is no real difference of interests between the five Powers as regards the fortresses, then the united action of France and England would oblige the King of Holland to ratify it, and Russia would no longer oppose it. Without such agreement, believe me, mon cher Prince, not only will Holland refuse to ratify, but King Leopold will probably have much trouble in keeping his position in Belgium, where, in my opinion, he cannot maintain himself without the support and consent of France and England. This support and consent my government have always given him, and are anxious to continue to do so ; but it must be made possible to us, and nothing must be required from us that others would not themselves agree to.

This letter is a thousand times too long, but since it is written, it may go. I am sending it open to M. Périer, so that he may read it before forwarding it to you, and I again repeat with all my heart, the assurance of all those sentiments you know I have for you.

L. P.

P.S.—Are you aware that this place, Marienbourg, which is counted as one of the fortresses, is a miserable hole with five earthworks, and an area about as extensive as the *parterre* of the Tuileries ?

M. CASIMIR PÉRIER TO THE PRINCE DE TALLEYRAND.

PARIS, *December 27th*, 1831.

MON PRINCE,

I have the honour to inform you, that General Sebastiani is very seriously unwell, and that the King has entrusted the Portfolio of Foreign Affairs to me for the time being. Were it not for the sad circumstance which necessitated this step, I should congratulate myself greatly on being thus called upon to hold continuous official communications with you. But kindly excuse me if I make this a very brief letter, and do not here enter into particulars of our position. I must, however, tell you that the Chamber of Peers, in to-day's sitting, adopted Article I., on the law respecting the peerage, by a majority of 103 votes against 67. I shall have the honour of writing more fully to you to-morrow. . . .

M. DUC DE DALBERG TO THE PRINCE DE TALLEYRAND.

PARIS, *December* 28*th*, 1831.

MON CHER PRINCE,

I do not wish another year to commence, without adding my wishes for your happiness, to the many others that will be offered you ; pray believe that they are really sincere.

The Chamber of Peers, as might have been expected, has acted in a most suicidal manner. It is a monument of dastard-liness worthy the Senate of Napoleon. It has caused a very painful feeling here. All the peers declared that the King was alone to blame for having brought matters to such a state. If, some day, a fresh crisis arises, he who heads it will find that the principle of hereditary right will ensure him a hearty welcome at the Luxembourg. This was the remark made to me by M. de Bassano, who wished to be my neighbour.

I was not mistaken as to the replies received from St. Petersburg respecting Belgian affairs. Fresh indications, both from thence and Berlin, make one wish that the King of Holland would be satisfied with some other protocols. The position of the home navigation is inadmissible even for the Dutch ; it would be a perpetual source of bickering ; how is it that Wessenberg, who is up in all these details, did not perceive this ?

The illness of your chief, Sebastiani, is entirely due to his idiotic behaviour when he presented himself on the tribune of the Luxembourg. He puffed himself out like a toad, trying to look important, and the blood flew to his head. The public and the diplomatic body would like M. Périer to replace him. There was some idea of getting Mounier[1] to join d'Argout ; but the former has refused a place in the Ministry. All confidence in the future is growing less and less. The language held by the Russian agents contributes greatly to this. It is very

---

[1] Baron Claude Mounier, born in 1784, auditor to the *Conseil d'État* in 1806, then Intendant of Saxe Weimar and Silesia, Intendant of the Royal Palaces, *Conseiller d'État* (1815), and peer of France in 1817. He refused to join the Ministry in 1840, but was made Director-General of the Administrative Department. He sat in the Chamber of Peers till his death in 1843.

evident that General Pozzo has no longer the confidence of his government. The Austrians also declare that sooner or later Belgium will have to be restored to Holland.

People are asking themselves how the foreign affairs of France can be carried on, when there is no minister either at Berlin, Copenhagen, Madrid, or Constantinople. The complaints in the offices increase daily, respecting the total absence of protection in the different countries. It is only right that you should know this. . . .

M. BRESSON TO THE PRINCE DE TALLEYRAND.

BERLIN, *December* 29*th,* 1831.

MON PRINCE,

I yesterday received the letter you did me the honour to write on the 20th ult. I have not been able to see either M. de Bernstorff or M. Ancillon, but I have arranged that this letter should be long enough in their possession, to enable them to show it to the King if they thought fit. I have done more : the words it contains are so noble and so wise, that they cannot fail to do good wherever they are read, and the Emperor of Russia himself shall receive an extract, omitting the first paragraph. I hope, mon Prince, that you will condescend to approve of this. Unfortunately, there is no longer time for action by the King of Prussia, if he decides to take any, to produce so desirable a change in the Emperor of Russia's resolutions[1] before the 15th of January.

The Prussian Cabinet, whose intentions seem very frank and loyal, has neglected nothing to impress on St. Petersburg all the danger that would attend a disagreement on the important act of November 15th between the five Powers, whose Ministers signed it. We have but faint hope that these representations may produce some effect. The King of Prussia has not withdrawn his promise to ratify, but M. de Bernstorff and M. Ancillon think that the non-ratification of one of the five Powers annuls the treaty. Their argument is, that unanimity has been the basis of all the transactions of the Conference, and that the appeal of the King of the Netherlands was addressed to all the five Powers, as was laid down in the protocol of Aix-la-Chapelle. Nevertheless, I think it important that Prussia should give her ratification, such as it is, and I trust it will be sent to you within

---

[1] This was in reference to a direct application from the King of Prussia to the Russian Emperor, with the object of inducing him to ratify the treaty of November 15th.—(*Note by M. de Bacourt.*)

the time limited for the treaty. Should any unforeseen accident upset this act, which settled everything, we might then perhaps have recourse to the two measures proposed by M. Ancillon. But I think the second one, that is to say, *the unanimous declaration of the five Powers, that Holland and Belgium* SHALL NOT *recommence hostilities,* would be the true point of departure to take ; the first, or its equivalent, that is to say, *offers of mediation from the Conference for a treaty between Holland and Belgium on the basis of the twenty-four articles,* might then be tried.

When M. Ancillon, in October, did me the honour to communicate these twenty-four articles to me, I at once placed my finger on that which accorded home navigation to Belgium, and told him that all the difficulties would rise from that source. It has had the effect of bringing the King of Holland and his subjects together, who, before this clause, neither considered or viewed the Belgian question in the same light. . . .

THE PRINCE DE TALLEYRAND TO MADAME ADELAIDE.

LONDON, *December 30th,* 1831.

I am unceasingly occupied with the affairs of the fortresses, though I feel sure the importance of it is greatly exaggerated. This matter has assumed a false aspect in Brussels, the doubts and suspicions which spoil everything have induced every one to grow too cautious. Hence all the objections and secret protocols. However, we must get out of it as best we can, and I think the King cannot fail to be struck with the remarks and explanations that Lord Granville has given him ; but we must go further than that. I shall have the honour to write to the King as soon as I know more. . . .

THE PRINCE DE TALLEYRAND TO THE PRINCESS DE
VAUDÉMONT.

LONDON, *December 30th,* 1831.

I am truly sorry for Sebastiani's mishap ; he was sometimes a little troublesome, but he also had his good points. He had ability, he knew how to behave, and I am sure he was good hearted ; all that is something. He will be a loss to the King whom he served faithfully. So the affair of the peerages is finished at last, and finished without shaking the ministry. We must now finish the Belgian matters, and this we shall do whatever people may say. I could almost die of it, like Sebastiani, only that it is my battlefield. Please Heaven, it may prove a field of honour!

Your Belgians are weak and false, besides they have been fighting in Luxemburg;[1] all this is not honourable. I still hope to get the ratifications from Berlin before the 15th January ; and if we receive them, we shall not have to wait long for those from Vienna. St. Petersburg exhibits her grandeur, as the *beau monde* in Paris show their gentility, by arriving late. . . .

THE PRINCE DE TALLEYRAND TO M. CASIMIR PÉRIER.

LONDON, *January* 2nd, 1832.

MONSIEUR,

I have received the departmental despatch under date of 30th of last month, and I think that in addition to the official reply, contained in my despatch of to-day, it is my duty, in face of the sincere friendship I have expressed for you, to draw your attention to the want of exactness in the facts and arguments which have been sent to me from Paris. Moreover, rather too much zeal is being displayed, and I also think that the pen of the head of a department should never be made the medium of his own individual opinion. In affairs like those we have to deal with, it is very important not to set up any system, for a system in political matters is very apt to be based on suppositions, and then one is soon led astray. On the contrary, one must, not try to find anything in the acts, but what is actually there. If they were to make it a rule in the various Foreign Offices, to follow the steps taken by the Powers, by always crediting them with Holy Alliance schemes, a phantom would quickly be raised, that would end in misrepresenting and embroiling everything. Your clear judgment will enable you to direct the affairs over which you preside into a better channel.

I notice, with much regret that the affair of the fortresses (which, if the papers get hold of it, may give the government some trouble, but which in itself is only a secondary matter) has somewhat retarded the progress of a much more important matter, namely, that of the disarmament, to which you gave so happy an impulse. In that, you will find a ready answer for all those who only see the Holy Alliance in everything. Can there be the slightest sign of such a league, when all the Cabinets, even

---

[1] An Orangist insurrection had broken out on the 20th December, in Luxemburg, under the leadership of Baron Torcano. The insurgents, victorious at first, had proclaimed the restoration of King William. The civic guards and the Belgian troops soon, however, overcame this movement.

that of Russia, express the wish to reduce their armies, in order to relieve their people? Believe me, Monsieur, we must take care that in attaching too great importance to this affair of the fortresses, we do not appear to rather flatter or humour the extreme party—a party which the Powers have looked upon as vanquished, since your acceptance of office. The banner of the Holy Alliance has been lowered before that of France by the protocol of April 17th; we might wish, but we should do wrong to ask for more. The principle of demolition has been admitted; demolition once commenced, we must on the whole be satisfied.

I pray you, Monsieur, take up again quickly the disarmament question, which will add so pure a glory to all your successes, and will so happily lighten the French Budget. We were obliged to increase our taxes when we deemed ourselves threatened; but I do not think we ought to continue them on account of combinations, the result of which can be of no real importance; for the fortresses that are left to Belgium will either fall in ruins, or become our property at some time or other. All that is really necessary for the firm establishment of France will consolidate itself, if we keep our present relations with England. All the efforts of the Powers are directed to prevent this: I hope and I believe, that they will fail. . . .

THE PRINCE DE TALLEYRAND TO THE PRINCESS DE VAUDÉMONT.

LONDON, *January 2nd*, 1832.

I would really like to know how Sebastiani is; on one side I hear that he is very ill, others say that after a few days' rest he will be able to return to his work again. Pray tell me what is true of all this, for I always believe what you say. When I like a person, I believe them; sometimes I have been mistaken; nevertheless such is my nature. This business of the fortresses, which is exciting every one so greatly in Paris, more especially our chiefs, is really only of secondary importance. What is really essential to us, is to secure the ratification of Prussia and Austria, and keep united with England; the rest are but cavillings which must arise sooner or later. The principle of the fortresses had to be obtained: this we have got; therefore let the King be satisfied. I have done all in my power to secure the ratifications of the treaty of November 15th, and hope I have succeeded. I only really care for those of Vienna and Berlin; having got them, the others will follow, even your dearly beloved King of Holland.

I am working too hard; I write all day, and will end with some mishap, like Sebastiani.

M. CASIMIR PÉRIER TO THE PRINCE DE TALLEYRAND.

PARIS, *January* 1*st*, 1832.

MON PRINCE,

I am taking advantage of Messrs. Rothschild's courier, to send you the King's speech in answer to the ambassadors. This speech is much more pacific than our diplomatic reports. Nevertheless, we trust that you will still succeed in changing the views of the English Cabinet with regard to the Belgian fortresses. I believe we shall end in procuring the ratification of Prussia and Austria without any conditions. I am just expecting the English ambassador, who is to inform me of the communication made by his Cabinet to the Courts of Berlin and Vienna, relative to the delays interposed by Russia, to the ratification of the treaty of the 15th November. If this communication is firm, and peremptorily insists on the fulfilment of the promises given, I have no doubt whatever that it will decide Prussia, and especially Austria, whose political views on this question seem to be more nearly allied to those of England.

The despatches I have to-day received from M. Bresson, inform me that Prussia, in the midst of all her hesitations, has, nevertheless, not dared to promise definitely to follow the line Russia seems inclined to adopt. I therefore think that if we remain firm, as we have every right to do, we shall succeed in conquering this difficulty.

There then still remains the treaty of the fortresses, which will have to be modified, and I earnestly hope, both for our peace as well as that of Europe, that you will succeed (as I had the honour of telling you in my confidential letter) in obtaining those modifications which we deem indispensable. I must add that the position we have taken here towards the ambassadors, showing our dissatisfaction in a guarded, though in a decided way, seems to us to have made a great impression.

We have no wish to abuse our position, but considering the frankness and loyalty we have shown in all our relations, we have the right to count upon their being respected.

Accept, mon Prince. . . . .

M. DE FLAHAUT TO THE PRINCE DE TALLEYRAND.

PARIS, *January* 2*nd*, 1832.

I think I can announce to you Sebastiani's restoration to health. To-day he is so much better, that I trust his convalescence will be more rapid than I at first dared to hope. His illness occurred at a most inopportune moment, but I do not think it will cause any change in the Ministry. He will be able to return to his work before his temporary substitute, d'Argout, will have had time to grasp the details.

People here are disquieted, by the report which has got abroad that the ratifications will not reach us by the 15th. That would be very unfortunate, and would greatly increase the strength of the war party ; and if war once broke out, instead of a few million florins, and the navigation of some canals, it will be a question of the destruction of France, or the overthrow of all the thrones of Europe ; for even sane people here will arm themselves with a stick surmounted by the red cap of Liberty. If, after all the efforts that have been made to preserve peace, the foreign governments make game of us and ignore their ambassadors, there is nothing left but to draw the sword.

THE PRINCE DE TALLEYRAND TO THE PRINCESS DE VAUDÉMONT.

LONDON, *January 5th*, 1832.

I am sending you to-day a huge bundle of papers, which will probably weary you more in reading, than they did me in writing them. I have found a solution of this question of the fortresses, which occupies the King far too much.[1] By it I have secured all that it was possible to obtain under extremely difficult circumstances, owing to the action taken in Brussels. We need now no longer dread the phantom called the Holy Alliance, which can never exist as long as we keep friends with England. That is the real support of our new dynasty. Everything in Europe can be settled without war, if we and England remain united. France has never before adopted this policy ; it was reserved for the King to demonstrate its importance. I shall end my career with brilliancy, by attaching my name to this grand union. . . . .

The following note was sent by Baron Pasquier, President of the Chamber of Peers, to the Princess de Vaudémont for communication to M. de Talleyrand.

---

[1] M. de Talleyrand, seeing the hostility that the Convention of the 14th December, met with in Paris, and in the face of the refusal of the Powers to substitute Tournay and Charleroy for Philippeville and Marienbourg, had proposed the following wording : " The plenipotentiaries of the four Courts have begun by decreeing the demolition of Mons, Ath, and Ménin, reserving to themselves to decide later on the fate of the other fortresses." The French Cabinet did not admit this solution, for it always allowed it to be supposed that France did not recognize the sovereign right of the Powers to dispose ultimately of the Belgian fortresses.

PARIS, *Tuesday, January 4th,* 1832.

It is important that M. de Talleyrand should know this: I have just returned from seeing the President of the Council, and have had a long talk with him about our present foreign relations. His position with respect to these affairs is really very difficult, and as every one both at home and abroad is interested in his retention, it is as well this should be known, in order to act accordingly. I found him full of confidence in M. de Talleyrand, and quite sensible that he alone was able to guide the vessel of these negotiations, in the handling of which he has shown so much ability, safely into port. This ability was never more needed than it is at present. There are two points in dispute—the ratifications, and the treaty signed between the four Powers relative to the Belgian fortresses. In themselves these points are not perhaps so important as is supposed, but what matter, if the result is the same? I have no doubt that sooner or later the ratifications will arrive. The affair of the fortresses affects our self-esteem more than our actual interests, but it is just on this account that it acquires a real importance. If the treaty was accepted as it stands, I do not believe that the present or any other Ministry, could carry out the agreement. It would be considered too great a humiliation, and there is no good reason or explanation that could efface or even palliate this view.

If England therefore wishes to see the present order of things in France consolidated, and it seems to me that this would be to her interest, her Cabinet must come to some arrangement on this point. I have no doubt that both countries have the same difficulties to contend with, and that the English Cabinet has to humour the Tory opposition, as the French Ministry has equally to humour the Liberal and Republican opposition ; but the cases are not quite the same, for the position here is much more threatening.

M. de Talleyrand has already rendered enormous services, but in my opinion he cannot perform a greater one for futurity than that in which he is engaged, for this act will consolidate all the others. It would result in bringing about a fresh arrangement and, above all, a fresh form of arrangement, with respect to the fortresses. It is, in my opinion, indispensable that whatever arrangement is made, must be agreed to and *signed* by the five Powers, else it will always be looked upon here as an affront, and there will be an explosion. Though, in reality, if they liked, they could easily see in France's request for the demolition of the fortresses a proof of her good faith, for it is perfectly evident that, at the very first signs of a rupture, these fortresses would fall into her hands, and that it would suit her better to have them fortified than dismantled.

Let them therefore think twice before they turn a question, so trifling in itself, into a cause for rupture. If, on the contrary, this question is once arranged, I do not see how any opposition could make a stand against the close union of France and England —a union of which both countries would soon feel the benefit.

M. de Talleyrand has already done much to further this work! Let us hope that he will accomplish it, otherwise one cannot help foreseeing great difficulties, if not something worse.

THE PRINCE DE TALLEYRAND TO THE PRINCESS DE VAUDÉMONT.

LONDON, *January 7th*, 1832.

I have received your letter of the 5th, inclosing one from M. Pasquier. M. de Maubourg's mission, which is constantly thrown at my head in all the conferences here, annoys me greatly. The *refrain* is always: " You make use of us when it suits you, but you manage your affairs independently when you think it is more to your advantage." No confidence can be established in that way. I am sending M. Tellier to Paris, to explain what they do not seem able to understand.

I have written, dictated, and conferred so long, that I am fairly exhausted. The fortresses (the principle of their de-molition having once been accepted) are a very minor matter if rightly understood. The fact is, no one considers it of any importance. It is only our self-love that is affected by it, and very foolishly so. If there is no war, they will fall to ruin, for no one will repair them ; if there is a war, we shall take them ; that is how it stands.

Return my best thanks to him who sent you the note.

M. BRESSON TO THE PRINCE DE TALLEYRAND.

BERLIN, *January 7th*, 1832.

I have just sent you the following telegraphic despatch, viâ Metz :

" Prussia will not exchange the ratifications which she is sending to London to-morrow, unless all the other Powers, without exception, ratify."

The Prussian Cabinet is greatly exercised. It would certainly have wished the Emperor of Russia to ratify purely and simply. Now it will not commit itself either with him or with us, and takes shelter behind its interpretation of the acts of the Conference. It never from the first approved the treaty of November 15th. Nevertheless, it ratified it from love of peace, which is a distinctive trait of its policy and the inclinations of its king. It only made two reservations: the first was, *the rights of the Confederation over Luxemburg;* the second, *that Prussia would never join in any active coercive measures against the King of the Netherlands.* The refusal of St. Petersburg has supervened, accompanied by pressing solicitations to Prussia and Austria to follow her example. They were probably not disinclined to accede ; but I at once declared, that, in that case, there remained no other alternative for our government, than to take Belgium, as constituted by the twenty-four articles, under her protection, and boldly announce that neither Holland nor any of the other Powers, should touch her. Thereupon, after some mature reflection and much hesitation, the somewhat equivocal line was adopted, an account of which I sent to Paris and communicated to you briefly by my telegraphic despatch.

The Emperor of Russia will not succeed in inducing the Prussian Cabinet to adopt, either violent views or hostile measures. Here, all the advantages derived from the *statu quo* are fully appreciated and will not be forfeited. I am convinced, that M. de Bülow will receive instructions to favour any measures and any arrangements which would prevent a rupture of the negotiations, or the secession of one or more of the Powers.

M. Ancillon has announced to me in due form, *that the King of Prussia considers himself the guardian of the peace of Europe ; but his policy is an entirely impartial and non-aggressive one, and that he will always respect the rights of those who will respect his.*

You have received the ratifications ; they have been signed by the king, but their interchange will be suspended, until all the other Powers have given in theirs. This is not what you would have wished, mon Prince ; nevertheless, it is a good deal. The Emperor of Russia remains isolated in his refusal, whereas he expected greater compliance. . . .

LORD PALMERSTON TO THE PRINCE DE TALLEYRAND.

STANHOPE STREET, *January* 3*rd*, 1832.

MON CHER PRINCE,

The report that Esterhazy and Wessenberg have just brought me, of the communication they have received from their Courts, is not nearly so bad as that which your government seems to have received from Count Appony. It appears the

S 2

Court of Vienna admits, that the Conference found itself obliged to arbitrate between Holland and Belgium ; that this same Court approves the Act of Arbitration laid down in the twenty-four articles ; that it considers these articles, accepted as they are by Belgium, as constituting a solemn convention between the Belgian government and the five Powers, and as the treaty is in effect the articles, the Court of Vienna has decided to ratify it ; but, nevertheless, it will for the present postpone the ratification, in the hope of inducing the Court of Russia (*sic*).

You will see that all this does not look like an official declaration made by Austria in the name of Russia and Prussia.

I am very sorry that your Court thinks of refusing its ratification to the treaty of November 15th, because it is displeased with the convention of the 14th of December. But how can it find any valid reasons for connecting two entirely different and separate transactions ? How can it refuse its ratification, without disowning you and recalling you ? And what a triumph this would be, for all those who have perpetually tried to inspire us with distrust of France ! Is this method of treating thus lightly the solemn transactions between governments, conducive to inspiring confidence in those who will in future have to do with France ? But I am sure that it is quite needless for me to suggest to you, all the grave considerations which cannot fail to have already presented themselves to your mind, with regard to this unpleasant subject. . . .

This letter from Lord Palmerston will show the nature of the opposition which I encountered in London, in trying to satisfy the requirements of the French government concerning the convention of the 14th December, relative to the demolition of certain fortresses. I had, nevertheless, succeeded in obtaining some concessions, under the form of an explanatory protocol, from the convention. I sent it to Paris by M. Tellier, the first secretary of my embassy, whom I also intrusted with full explanations. The following letters will show the result of this fresh line of negotiation :

THE PRINCE DE TALLEYRAND TO THE PRINCESS DE VAUDÉMONT.

LONDON, *January 10th*, 1832.

I hope that all the explanations I have given, besides those which M. Tellier bears, will induce our Cabinet to come to some decision which will preserve our friendly relations with England, for it is to this end I have worked for the last eighteen months, and it will prove our salvation. My belief is, that there will be delays, but no refusals with regard to the ratifications. When once they have arrived and been interchanged, matters will be arranged without much difficulty. There will then only be a King of Greece to be decided on. Have you got anyone in view? They say that Greece, in her present state, will need a sovereign who has both good and bad qualities. This, probably, has made some people think of Prince Paul of Würtemberg. He has a few good qualities— ability and intelligence, these are very fair—and faults in abundance. . . .

LONDON, *January* 12*th*, 1832.

I received your letter of the 10th, about an hour ago. I have read the information it contained with close attention. This is how matters stand at present. On the 31st, positively, we shall have the ratifications from Austria and Prussia, those from Russia will come later on. We shall not wait for them to effect the interchange. This once done, Holland will enter into some explanations, and we will do our very best ; the fact is, we want to arrange and finish everything. No difficulties can come from Belgium. They can only come from France, which by twofold intrigues always embarrasses its affairs. It is a fact, that but for M. de Latour-Maubourg's mission to Brussels and M. Sebastiani's conferences with Lord Granville, which brought about the protocol of the 29th of August, of which I was not even informed from Paris, matters would never have been plunged into a series of complications from which it is very difficult to get clear.

The protocol to which I refer was not my work, but that of the four Powers, who sent it to Lord Granville, who in turn passed it on to Sebastiani. I first heard of it by a letter from General Belliard, written to me in the end of December. Is that the way to conduct and carry on business ?

They mismanage everything, and then turn round on me. I am beginning to get very tired of all this. Nevertheless, I will go on to the end. I should like to finish the business I have taken in hand. After that they may spoil it if they like. . . .

Whilst I was sending letters and despatches in this spirit from London, I received the following from Paris :

M. CASIMIR PÉRIER TO THE PRINCE DE TALLEYRAND.

PARIS, *January 9th*, 1832.

PRINCE,

My official despatch, which will reach you at the same time as this letter, will make known to you the various solutions of the serious difficulty that has arisen from the treaty of the 14th December, and the inadequacy of the modifications contained in the diplomatic Note which you have received from the ambassadors of the four Powers. As a despatch does not permit of a detailed explanation of the reasons which prevent the consent of the king's government to the interchange of ratifications,— as doing away with his adhesion to the principles sanctioned by the treaty of the 14th December, if it was not first modified—I have asked my brother Camille[1] to go to you. My conversations with him have made him acquainted with the question. He will corroborate all I have had the honour to tell you, as to the annoying effect of the serious fault committed by the Powers, in leaving their intentions respecting the interchange of the ratifications so long uncertain, and also the necessity of giving such a form to the acts which will terminate this delicate negotiation, as will make them unobjectionable in the eyes of a people so justly jealous of whatever touches the national honour.

In an interview I had this morning with Lord Granville, I renewed the assurance of the desire of the king's government to strengthen the ties which unite both nations, and to continue the same policy which has reconciled their interests since the revolution of July ; but I also entered into the reasons which would not allow us to accept the treaty of December 14th. My communications went so far as to discuss confidentially the measures for solving the fresh difficulties raised by it. He did not in any way disapprove these measures, which induces me to hope that you will find sufficient support in the co-operation of the British Cabinet, to obtain the adoption of some of them. . . .

M. CASIMIR PÉRIER TO THE PRINCE DE TALLEYRAND.

PARIS, *January 11th*, 1832.

PRINCE,

I have read the despatches you sent me by M. Tellier with great interest. You will have seen by those I intrusted my

---

[1] Camille Périer (1781–1844) formerly auditor to the *Conseil d'Etat* and *préfet* under the Empire and the Restoration. He had been a deputy since 1828. He was made a Peer of France in 1837.

brother to give you, and which you will by this time have
received and read, that we have in a manner met half way, as to
the means of getting out of the difficulty which the treaty of the
14th December, relative to the fortresses, has caused, both to the
London Cabinet and our own. I wish most earnestly that you
could finish this important affair.

You will see, Prince, by my official despatch of to-day,
that we give you greater latitude than in those my brother
brought you ; in a word, if you cannot end the matter in the
way pointed out by the protocol I have sent you, we shall content ourselves with the expedient suggested to us in your
despatch No. 291. But it is indispensable, Prince, that the
declaration should be clear and distinct throughout, like the
protocol we have sent you. The Kingdom of Belgium, and its
king, must be entirely absolved from all engagements, anterior
or posterior to the acts of the five Powers who recognize the
independence and the neutrality of Belgium ; this is what the
country demands, rightly or wrongly, this is what it wants ; and
friends or enemies, all would abandon us, if we gave in on this
point. As for the root of the question, we do not lay greater
stress on it than it deserves ; with the exception of Philippeville
and Marienburg, which are not included among the fortresses,
in the list of the protocol of April 17th, it does not matter
much to us whether this or that fortress is demolished ; but
when the four Powers have once decided which fortresses are to
be so dealt with, they must have no further rights over these
fortresses, except such as would be common to the five signatory
Powers of the 15th of November.

I shall await the result of this affair, both for our country
and our Cabinet, with great impatience ; but even if the three
Powers do not accord their ratifications at once, it will suffice if
France and England are agreed by the respective interchange
of their ratifications, for the moral effect of this decision would
prevent all serious thoughts of a collision that might lead
to war. It would be evident to everyone, that France and
England once united, would make it difficult, not to say impossible, for the other governments not to yield to the decision
of these two great Powers.

I need not repeat, Prince, what I have already had the
honour to tell you, that our policy with regard to England is
entirely in conformity with yours. I have directed M. Tellier,
with whom I have entered into full explanations, to reiterate
this particularly, and to tell you how urgent it is for Europe and
for us, that we should frankly enter upon the system of disarmament, which we have announced so decidedly on the

strength of the promises of all the ambassadors, who assured us in the most explicit manner, that the ratifications of their Cabinets to the treaty of November 15th, would only be a matter of form.

I wish still to believe that there is no wrong intent on the part of the different Powers, above all those of Austria and Prussia ; but they have committed a serious fault (if they sincerely wish for peace, as they have so often assured us) in not ratifying at the appointed time, and thereby shaking the power and moral strength of our Cabinet, in its system of peace and disarmament. If the difficulty respecting the fortresses disappears between us and England, and our ratifications are interchanged, we can once more ward off this danger. The fall in the public funds, the general anxiety in everyone's mind, will all show you the imminence of the danger far better than I could describe it.

Our fate, Prince, lies in your hands. I trust entirely and unreservedly to your great wisdom and your patriotism to wind up this negotiation, on which the peace of our country and the civilization of the world may depend. I have given Lord Palmerston's letter to M. Tellier ; it has only been read by the king and myself.

Accept . . . .

CASIMIR PERIER.

P.S.—I recommend my brother to your kindness if he is still with you.

KING LOUIS PHILIPPE TO THE PRINCE DE TALLEYRAND.

PARIS, *January 11th,* 1832.

I have this moment, mon cher Prince, received your letter of the 8th, brought by M. Tellier, and also, two days ago, that of the 5th. Much as I should have liked to have seen and spoken to you, I am nevertheless very glad you did not come, for in addition to the fatigue and inconvenience of such a journey during this weather, I should have looked upon your absence from London, when the despatches M. Périer sent you by his brother arrived, as a real misfortune.

I think they will have allayed your anxieties, and that you will find the proposals they contain well calculated to overcome all the difficulties, and to enable the *five Powers* to escape from the false position, in which the deplorable treaty of December 14th, has placed them with regard to one another. I sincerely wish that it may prove so, and I hope that the English government

will see therein a fresh proof, of the great value both I and my
government place on the continuance of those cordial relations
between us, which are the best guarantee for the peace of
Europe, and the stability of social order. This treaty must be
so arranged, that the former engagements of the King of the
Netherlands are not curtailed by the King of the Belgians, and
that in future, his position, his relations and his engagements, are
identically the same with all the five Powers, so that no single
one of these Powers retains a special suzerainty over the fortresses
in his territory, and then nothing can further disturb either our
union with England, or consequently the general peace.

You may give the assurance, mon cher Prince, for I know that
M. Périer has also given you the same with fuller details, that
this is all that France wants, but that it is what she *does* want,
and that it is really extraordinary that people should see anything but what it really is, in a demand so just, so simple, and so
moderate, and that they should desire pretexts to arouse suspicion
and accuse us of having mental reservations, which our own
proposal denies in so plain a manner, and which, I venture to say,
the whole of my conduct and that of my Cabinet, should suffice
to refute.

Besides, it is rather singular, that it should be the very people
who made a mystery to us of this treaty, while insisting as a *sine
quâ non* on the signature of that of November 15th, which was
a joint one, who imagine they have a right to suspect
us, and that a *want of sincerity*, which is certainly not on
our side, would injure the confidence we ask for, and of which, it
seems to me, England has had ample proofs.

Moreover, it is because we had the firm conviction that the
views of the present government, relative to Belgium, were in
entire conformity with ours, that we were lulled into such
complete security respecting the negotiations of the fortresses.
It is precisely because we had no anxiety to fear from that
quarter, that we did not seek to obtain from it any other engagement than the protocol of April 17th, but it is also because,
after what had happened, we could not have the same confidence
in the Belgian government, that we wished to have a special
undertaking from it, and sent M. de Latour-Maubourg there on
a mission, to which we gave all possible publicity, communicating
all these particulars to Lord Granville and Sir Robert Adair,
who were fully cognizant of what we intended to ask. The forms
and terms of the engagement demanded of the King of the
Belgians, had been arranged with them, it having been contracted with their full cognizance and even approbation, without
which King Leopold would not have signed it.

I must confess, mon' cher Prince, that I cannot even now understand, notwithstanding all the explanations we have received respecting the suspicions that this mission has excited, how such could ever have arisen. But let us put the past on one side, and occupy ourselves exclusively with the present and the future.

We are fully persuaded that the fear of the attacks of the Tories, seconded by the Belgian intrigues, decided the form and the terms of the treaty of the 14th December. We believe that the present English government has entirely renounced the policy of the Holy Alliance, neither does it favour that which seeks to make Belgium a *tête-de-pont* against France, and that it has substituted the wiser policy, which we also have adopted, of the permanent neutrality and independence of that new State.

All we now wish, all we now ask for, is the frank, full, and entire execution of this policy of Belgian neutrality and independence. We have no mental reservations either with regard to Philippeville, Marienbourg, or anything else. We do not attach the slightest importance to these two fortresses, which are valueless to France, except as regards the memories attached to them—memories which ought to have been kindly dealt with, instead of being made a subject of irritation. My government has never had any other wish than to allay this feeling, and only spoke of these fortresses with that intent, and in order to be able to say that it had done so; but when it was found that this demand might prove an impediment to the grand object of a universal peace, it desisted; and, as a fact, you are aware that there has been no question about these fortresses since, either in London or Brussels, at least by us; for I believe that many others have busied themselves about this matter in a contrary spirit, and of this the treaty of December 14th, is sufficient proof.

We were so anxious to avoid everything that might recall the memories of Philippeville and Marienbourg, that when the French army entered Belgium, Marshal Gérard was instructed not to occupy those two fortresses.

I pray you, mon cher Prince, to have the goodness to tell Lord Palmerston, with my compliments, that this is my personal policy, quite as much as it is that of my government, and you may also add—if you can do so without offending him, which I particularly wish you to avoid—that it was only from your despatch that I learnt the assertions of the *National*, which I do not read any more than the other papers, and which is the bitterest enemy both to me and my government. If he still desires to learn more about it, I should like him to hear the *opposite side* to the extracts from the *National, La Tribune,* and Co.

I again renew, most sincerely, mon cher Prince, the assurances of my old friendship for you.

LOUIS PHILIPPE.

THE PRINCE DE TALLEYRAND TO THE PRINCESS DE VAUDÉMONT

LONDON, *January* 14*th*, 1832.

The Prussian ratification has arrived ! A courier from Berlin brought it this morning. The Belgian question has thus been powerfully strengthened. It is believed that Austria's ratification will arrive next week, but certainly before the end of the month. This is a great point settled, and we may now hope that this thorny Belgian business will end without a war. Peace must now do her part in allaying the excitement. The agitators will lose their greatest levers for creating disturbances, by peace. . . .

LONDON, *January* 17*th*, 1832.

. . . . I am trying to obtain the explanations demanded from me in Paris, respecting the demolition of the fortresses. I hope I shall obtain satisfactory ones, but this is not easy. You know what it is when a matter has been badly started, and people are trying to pull it both ways. I have had more trouble here in undoing, than in making. The word " jobber," which was used formerly, often recurs to me now ; but we must make the best of it, for there are some natures that one cannot change, and poor Sebastiani was bon so, though it does not prevent his having a fair share of intelligence.

Is it true that a violent attack on the budget is expected ? I hope and think, that everyone ought to wish the Ministry to come triumphantly out of it, for it will require all M. Périer's strength of character and ability to bring matters into order again. The king needs him specially. That is the opinion of everyone here. If M. Périer leaves the Ministry, all the Powers would at once expect a new order of things.

Parliament reassembles to-day, but there will be nothing of importance till next week. . . .

LONDON, *January* 19*th*, 1832.

I think all the Cabinets are becoming more friendly, and that the ratifications will now soon arrive. If some of them are slightly delayed, that will not affect the decision. Consideration for the King of Holland, more than anything else, has occasioned these delays. I believe I shall arrive at what our government wishes with regard to the fortresses ; we shall receive such explanations as even the most sensitive could not cavil at. . . .

LONDON, *January 23rd*, 1832.

M. Camille Périer returns to Paris this evening. He takes documents back with him, which I think will be thoroughly satisfactory. I have had to be, what I am not fond of being, most tenaciously importunate; but I have succeeded; there was no possible chance of obtaining anything more. I can assure you I am working far too hard, but I shall come out of it with honour. . . .

In order to make plain what M. Camille Périer took back to Paris, I must here give an extract from the convention of the 14th December, 1831, between the four Powers and Belgium, relative to the fortresses. I will confine myself to giving the text of Article I. of the convention, which is the most important :

" Article I.—In consequence of the changes that the in-dependence and the neutrality of Belgium have wrought in the military position of that country, as well as in the measures which might be required for her defence, the high contracting parties consent to the demolition of such of the fortresses as were raised, repaired, or enlarged in Belgium after the year 1815, either in whole or in part, at the cost of the Courts of Austria, Great Britain, Prussia, and Russia, as the maintenance of these would in future be a needless expense.

" In accordance with this principle, therefore, all the fortifica-tions of the fortresses of Ménin, Ath, Mons, Philippeville, and Marienbourg, will be demolished within the time specified in the articles below."

The articles that followed, regulated the manner of the demolitions.

The French government, fancying they saw in the drawing up of these articles, a desire on the part of the four Powers to claim a sort of special patronage, both present and to come, over the fortresses to be demolished—a patronage from which France was excluded—I had to insist on obtaining a distinct declaration from the plenipotentiaries of these Powers, which should put an end to any uncertainty on this point. After innumerable efforts, I at last succeeded in inducing them to adopt the following declaration, dated January 23rd, 1832 :

" The plenipotentiaries of the Courts of Austria, Great Britain, Prussia, and Russia, in proceeding to exchange the ratifications of the convention of the 14th December last, now declare :

" 1st. That the stipulations of the convention of 14th December last, caused by the change that has taken place in the political position of Belgium, cannot and must not be understood except with the reservation of the full and entire sovereignty of H. M. the King of the Belgians over the fortresses mentioned in the said convention, and also of the neutrality and independence of Belgium—an independence and neutrality which, guaranteed under the same titles and the same rights by the Powers, establishes in this respect an identical bond between them and Belgium.

" 2nd. That the sums mentioned in Article V. shall not be reckoned except for deduction, it being the intention of the Courts that if the deduction shows a balance, this balance should go to assist Belgium with the expenses she will be put to, in demolishing the fortresses mentioned in Article I.

" 3rd. Finally, the reservation made by the four Courts to Article VI., having no reference to Articles II. and III., applies consequently only to the fortresses that are to be demolished.

" By this declaration on the above three points, the plenipotentiaries of the Courts of Austria, Great Britain, Prussia, and Russia, place beyond a doubt, that all the clauses of the convention of December 14th, are in complete accordance with the character of the independent and neutral power, assigned to Belgium by the five Courts."

This was the declaration that M. Camille Périer took back to Paris, and which was at last deemed sufficiently explicit :

M. CASIMIR PÉRIER TO THE PRINCE DE TALLEYRAND.

PARIS, *January* 23*rd*, 1832.
PRINCE,
I have seen with great satisfaction from your official despatch, and more especially from your private letter, that you expect to obtain the modifications we have asked for relative to the convention of December 14th, which was so opposed to our rights and, I venture to say, to our dignity.

M. Van de Weyer ought by this time to have received the most positive instructions from his government, directing him to arrange with you the modification of the articles which have so justly offended us.

We therefore hope, Prince, that you will be enabled to over-come the obstacles which prevented the exchange of the rati-fications of the treaty of November 15th, to which we called your attention by the model protocol which we drew up, while explaining to you in the most explicit manner, how impossible it would be for us to ratify, if we did not obtain entire satisfac-tion on all these points.

Now that you know all our difficulties, Prince, (if, as you give me reason to hope, they have been settled in a manner con-formably to our wishes and instructions,) we cannot see any objections to your signing the ratifications on the 31st of this month. This will be an immense service you will have rendered, and one more obligation for which Europe will be indebted to you.

If we and England ratify alone, before the other Powers, we must, I think, reserve to ourselves the means of not excluding entirely all ways of reconciliation between Holland and Belgium, as regards navigation ; above all, it is necessary, that England should not be able some day to hold up our signature of the treaty of November 15th to us, as a *sine quâ non* that would present an invincible obstacle to these modifications, which are the only reasonable pretext for opposition that the King of Holland can bring forward, in the position in which he is placed.

I quite approve of what you say, Prince, that it is best not to make these ratifications a matter of too great importance with the other Cabinets ; but such a step would give them something to think about, and while we do not wish to separate ourselves from them, it is as well that they should see we can do without them, and it will not escape them, as you so truly remarked, that such an understanding between England and ourselves is, in fact, an offensive and defensive treaty. . . .

THE PRINCE DE TALLEYRAND TO THE PRINCESS DE
VAUDÉMONT.

LONDON, *January 27th*, 1832.

The English Ministry has got very well out of the attack made on it by Lord Aberdeen.[1] Lord Grey, in his reply,

---

[1] Lord Aberdeen had interrogated the English Cabinet on the affairs of Belgium, and had violently opposed the French intervention.

brought forward some very strong points in favour of France. The Duke of Wellington supported Lord Aberdeen, but he respected all the usages of the House, which had been completely violated by Lord Aberdeen.

But enough, we will not waste time over this political gossip. The real point is, that our union with England, and that alone, will establish us securely. All my policy is confined to this.

I await impatiently your opinion of all I have sent by M. Camille Périer. I believe that my demands will be granted. I must receive the ratifications before the 31st. . . .

MADAME ADELAIDE D'ORLÉANS TO THE PRINCE DE TALLEYRAND.

PARIS, *January* 29*th*, 1832.

It is with great eagerness, mon cher Prince, that I hasten to thank you for your letter of the 23rd, and to tell you what sincere pleasure it gave me to hear, that the greatest difficulty in this long and painful negotiation about Belgium, has been overcome. I congratulate myself as well as you, most heartily, and it is surely only fair to give you the full credit of it. Truly it is a grand and noble thing, that this Belgian question has ended in this way, more especially as we must unfortunately admit, that it was very badly seconded by the Belgians themselves, for this last difficulty was certainly their work, and I can quite understand what all this must have been for you. However, we must console ourselves, for all that somewhat wounds our small conceits, or our national glory, if you prefer it, by constantly repeating what you wrote to me, "There was nothing further to be obtained." And, truly, Philippeville and Marienbourg are not worth a war. The chief point has been gained ; of that there can be no doubt, thanks to your zeal and your ability. I hope and very earnestly wish, that as you say, next month will see the end of your labours. I know, mon cher Prince, that you have great need to take care of yourself and get some rest, and we can but be thankful that your health has so far borne up under all this great moral and physical fatigue. I trust, from the bottom of my heart, that now you will only have to enjoy your successes, and the happy results arising therefrom, for our dear France and our beloved king, who also stands in need of some repose.

Sebastiani is much better, in fact almost well. The difficulty now is, to get him to take a sufficiently long rest, and not resume work too soon, which I think is most important to thoroughly re-establish his health. . . .

THE PRINCE DE TALLEYRAND TO THE PRINCESS DE
VAUDÉMONT.

LONDON, *January* 31*st*, 1832.

I have exchanged the ratifications of France with Belgium
this evening, and am very pleased to think that England has
also in the same way, exchanged her ratifications with Belgium ;
this business is therefore happily ended.

That France and England should co-operate in anything,
is more than I dared to hope for. Now we must patiently bide
our time ; the rest will follow. We must be neither exacting
nor triumphant, nor embarrass England by what she has done,
or the whole Tory party will censure her. We must not let her
think, that by her alliance with us, she has been forced to
go further than she would otherwise have done. This is a
matter that requires prudence and discretion. The English
Cabinet must be treated with the utmost consideration, for
their position here is a very delicate one. In my opinion, we
shall not have very long to wait for the ratifications of Prussia
and Austria ; those of Russia will follow shortly. Having
obtained these, we may safely wait for Holland—for whatever
she says, will not affect anyone much. Spain once took eighty
years to assent to a similar recognition, and Europe was quite
undisturbed thereby, and settled her own affairs independently.

Of the internal state of France I know little. I fear however
it is not very satisfactory ; but as to her foreign affairs, the
policy we have just followed, has placed her in the position the
king desired, but hardly dared to hope for.

This must rather astonish the croakers against the policy of
non-intervention, who made a noise and believed in war. We
have adopted an excellent system, namely, leaving the protocol
open, as to the proposals of Russia, Prussia, and Austria.

The way in which this protocol has been drawn up ought to
give great satisfaction at the Tuileries. . . .

KING LOUIS PHILIPPE TO THE PRINCE DE TALLEYRAND.

PARIS, *February* 4*th*, 1832.

MON CHER PRINCE,

I heard a great deal in my youth about the talents of
the Comte d'Avaux, and the length and the difficulties of the
treaty of Westphalia. That was the infancy of diplomacy, and
I think the five months of the London Conference, the fifty-five

protocols, all signed unanimously by the plenipotentiaries of the five Great Powers, present a far more imposing spectacle of talent, and difficulties overcome, than anything that has ever preceded it. It will be a grand thing for you, for my ministers, and I venture to say also, for me, that following the revolution of July, this great crisis has been conducted in such a manner, as to produce the results ultimately arrived at, without the internal peace of France being disturbed, or Europe becoming a prey to the conflagration with which it was threatened.

You see, mon cher Prince, that I agree with your opinion that the ratifications of France and England, mutually exchanged, insure the exchange of the other three, for it has almost become a matter of course to say, that when France and England are agreed there is no longer any fear of war in Europe.

I have always thought our two countries might understand each other and work together, without either one or the other losing any share of their national honour or their political interests ; but I have also felt that for both nations to approve such an undertaking, it must be made evident to them that their governments had not sacrificed anything for it, and for this reason, therefore, mon cher Prince, was I so often persistent about some points of the negotiations, which my government had real cause for wishing to rectify. Now success has crowned both its efforts and yours ; and this is perhaps the best answer to the abuse of which we are all the object.

I earnestly wish, mon cher Prince, that the ratifications of the other Powers should not be long delayed. It is to their interest as well as ours, for nothing but a complete interchange will prove to the unbelievers, that they must relinquish all hopes of war and disturbances. By that alone, will they be convinced of the stability of the actual state of affairs, and the impotency of their efforts to upset it.

It is always with my whole heart, mon cher Prince, that I renew the assurances of my sincere friendship for you. . . .

THE PRINCE DE TALLEYRAND TO MADAME ADELAIDE D'ORLÉANS.

LONDON, *February 6th*, 1832.

I entreat *Mademoiselle* to let me hear from her. The night of the 2nd of February, must have been a night of agony,[1] and

---

[1] M. de Talleyrand here alludes to the so-called plot of the " Rue des Prouvaires." Two or three thousand men had been hired by the legitimist agent Poncelet to attempt a *coup de main* on the royal family. The police arrested the heads of the

although the danger was not known until it was virtually over, you must have passed some anxious hours. It is very hard when, as you all do, one only thinks of doing good, to meet with difficulties and intrigues of all kinds at every step. I am uneasy at not hearing; no one writes to me. I conjure you, *Mademoiselle*, not to leave me any longer in such complete ignorance, on a matter which is of such great interest to you. . . .

MADAME ADELAIDE D'ORLÉANS TO THE PRINCE DE TALLEYRAND.

PARIS, *Monday, February 7th*, 1832.

MON CHER PRINCE,

It is truly amiable and good of you to have written to me at once, at two in the morning, as soon as the ratifications between Belgium, France, and England, had been effected. I cannot tell you how greatly I appreciate it, and I thank you with all my heart. This good and important piece of news arrived most opportunely, to compensate our beloved King somewhat for all he has suffered from the infamous plots of the Carlists and republicans, who for the present seem of one mind in their intrigues, and their very culpable aim. You will learn by the papers, of the foolish but shameful conspiracy which, thanks to God, was discovered just as it was about to be carried out. The police on this occasion behaved splendidly, for the whole affair was ended without causing the slightest disturbance in Paris. It all took place during our grand ball of the 2nd, which, notwithstanding, lasted till five in the morning. It was whispered in the ball-room that some attempts at a riot were expected during the night, but we were far from imagining that it was so serious a matter. It was only at three o'clock, when the Queen and I retired from the ball, that we heard of the arrest that had been made of that armed band. They cannot raise any more riots in the streets; the people will not have them; they resort to conspiracies, and horrors like the infernal machine of Napoleon's time. A hundred and ten people all bearing arms were arrested. This time therefore there can be no doubt as to their good intentions. I trust this will lead to some satisfactory result, and I feel sure it will be advantageous to the government. The King is admirably calm and self-possessed. I confess to you that I think he is always too confident; it is a subject we often discuss. . . .

plot on the night of the 1st of February, in a house in the Rue Prouvaires, and the movement was quelled.

THE PRINCE DE TALLEYRAND TO MADAME ADELAIDE D'ORLÉANS.

LONDON, *February 13th*, 1832.

. . . . The Emperor of Russia has sent Comte Orloff[1] to the Hague, to inform the King that if he will not decide to adhere to the articles of the Conference, he must not in any way, or under any circumstances, count on his assistance. This will probably delay the despatch of the Russian ratifications for eight or ten days, but it is quite certain that they have decided to send them. . . .

LONDON, *February 14th*, 1832.

. . . . I only heard of the despatch of troops to Italy when it was a fact : as a project, I knew nothing of it. But I suppose that[2] some understanding has been come to with Austria, respecting this matter ; for otherwise, complications will arise which will cause more trouble than profit. However, I know nothing, and can only reason about all this in a blind fashion ; I will not therefore speak of it to any one but you. It is quite enough to trouble ourselves about what is entrusted to us ; only a fool would meddle with other people's business, especially when he knows but little about it.

I wrote to you yesterday respecting the arrival of Comte

[1] Alexis Feodorowitch, Comte, afterwards Prince, Orloff, was born in 1786, and served in the Russian army during the wars of the Empire. He was made general in 1828. In 1829, he signed the treaty of Adrianople with the Porte, and was sent to Constantinople as ambassador in 1830. In 1832, he was entrusted with an important mission to the Hague and London ; on his return to Russia, he obtained command of the army sent into Turkey against Ibrahim Pasha, and signed the treaty of Unkiar-Skelessi (1833). Soon after he was made State Councillor, Director of the Secret Police, took part in the Conferences of Berlin and Olmütz (1853) and represented Russia at the Congress of Paris (1856). Shortly after he received the title of Prince, was made President of the Council of the Empire, and of the Council of the Ministers. He died in 1861.

[2] This was in reference to the expedition to Ancona. This town was occupied on the 22nd February, 1832. It will be remembered that in July, 1831, M. Casimir Périer had succeeded in getting the Austrian troops to evacuate the pontifical territory. A few months after, however, fresh disturbances arose in the Papal States. The Pope appealed to the Austrians, who hastened thither in January, 1832. M. Casimir Périer saw injury to the dignity of France in this act, and wished her to participate in the honour of defending the Holy See. This was the cause of the expedition which left Toulon for Ancona, taking that town by surprise during the night of the 21st of February. Austria's anger was very great, though impotent, and the other Cabinets were much excited. The Russian ambassador received orders to quit Paris, if the Austrian ambassador demanded his passports. In London, the Tory Opposition, led by the Duke of Wellington, were loud in their recriminations. But it all ended in words.

T 2

Orloff at the Hague. This mission will probably delay the ratifications for ten or twelve days, but it insures them. . . .

M. CASIMIR PÉRIER TO THE PRINCE DE TALLEYRAND.

PARIS, *February* 13*th*, 1832.

PRINCE,

I delayed longer than I wished before answering the two private letters you did me the honour to write, but the opening discussions on the Budget have been very troublesome and laborious for me. So far we have carried all the important questions. We had, more especially, to oppose the Chamber on retrenchments and economies which might greatly embarrass the government. However, we were determined to fight to the end, and not to allow purely financial questions to be made party ones, and we shall continue to use all our endeavours to consolidate that system of policy at home, the recognition of which you, Prince, have so powerfully contributed to abroad.

I received yesterday the Belgian ratifications which you sent me, together with your despatch of the. . . . I noticed therein with great satisfaction, what you say about Lord Palmerston's speech, which I have seen this morning. The King's government congratulates itself warmly on this conformity of views and feelings, from which the two countries may expect such happy results.

This frank and sincere manifestation may apply to many things, and be of real use to us. In it, we shall find a confirmation of our foreign policy, justified by so happy a result in its most important aim.

My first official despatch, Prince, will give you full details respecting Italian affairs, but in answer to your wish, I hasten to inform you at once, that we have reason to hope his Holiness will accede to the urgent entreaties we have addressed to him, and will be decided by them, to withdraw his refusal to permit us to occupy Ancona, the news of which M. de Saint-Aulaire junior has brought us.[1]

Our troops have received provisional orders to enter Ancona, unless the Austrians are there before them. In that case they will go to *Civita Vecchia*, and will occupy that place.

We do not intend turning aside from the object we have in

---

[1] General Cubières had sent to Rome to advise the Pope of the occupation of Ancona by the French troops. The Pope was at first very angry at this act of violence, and protested loudly against it to M. de Saint-Aulaire. It was not till the 16th of April, that a convention was made between the Cabinet of the Tuileries and the Court of Rome, in accordance with which the Pope authorized the French occupation.

view, namely, to show Austria that we only permit the occupation of the Romagna if it is for a short period, and to show
the Holy See that we wish to obtain from it the concession
solemnly promised by it to the Powers.[1]

However, without in any way departing from this constant
desire, we do not intend to give up our policy, which we wish
to be both moderate and just, and at the same time firm and
worthy of France ; and we shall, as long as we can, avoid a
collision, against which our efforts have always been directed....

THE PRINCE DE TALLEYRAND TO THE PRINCESS DE VAUDÉMONT.

LONDON, *February 17th*, 1832.

. . . . In England, up to now, the Portuguese question has
only been glanced at. I am surprised at the small amount of
interest shown in this matter, either in one way or the other.
When the climax arrives, perhaps this will be changed. The
Reform Bill and Belgium have engrossed all the anxieties of
the nation. I begin to think I must have gained some credit in
Paris, as I see I am being libelled in the newspapers and
pamphlets. One must submit to that if one wishes to serve
one's country, and if one tries to find means to stem the popular
torrent. Moreover this will pass over like everything else.

February 24th, 1832.

There will be no Congress just now. Comte Orloff keeps
all in suspense ; he has not been entirely open with any one in
Berlin. If Pozzo says so, he is inventing ; he knows no more
than M. de Lieven, who knows nothing. Comte Orloff ought to
have arrived at the Hague on the 20th, he will remain there
five or six days, perhaps eight, and then he comes on
here. If Lamb[2] and Esterhazy have succeeded in despatching
Austria's ratifications, as they ought to have done ; if
Metternich has the good sense not to let Austria be taken in
tow by Russia, then we shall have no further trouble whatever.
It is time that Russia's pride should give way. . . .

February 25th, 1832.

I am told that Maubreuil is again going to appear on the
scene, and bring forward some very injurious complaints against

---

[1] The Austrian occupation only ended in July, 1831, on the promise by the Pope,
made to France (as mediatrix), and to Austria, of an amnesty and liberal reforms.

[2] English ambassador at Vienna.

me in my capacity as President of the Provisional Government
in 1814.[1] This will cause a day or two's scandal, and will end
in not being proved. However, this wearies me, but does not
greatly trouble me. It is one of the peculiarities of the age,
that I can be attacked by a man whom I have never seen, and
who in 1814, tied the Cross of the Legion of Honour to his
horse's tail, and that such a man should now have as his partisans
the Liberals of the present day.

February 27th, 1832.

. . . . I know nothing of Comte Orloff except by hearsay,
but I know that, whatever demands he may make, I shall not
give in to the alteration by France of a single comma in a
treaty that I have signed. The other Powers must ratify; that
done, I shall become complaisant, and will consent to the modifications between Belgium and Holland being made according
to agreement ; I will facilitate them and encourage them as
much as I can. I even go further, for I am ready to guarantee
the treaty (if England will consent to do the same) which will
be made between Holland and Belgium. That is my pro-
gramme ; it will not be changed. I am of opinion that I shall
succeed in what I want to do, and that before very long. . . .

February 28th, 1832.

. . . . We have obtained all the concessions from the Pope
that the Liberals could reasonably ask. Though this has been
done, the Liberals are rebelling once more ; we cannot again
interfere. It is now a question of police, in which the Pope
must do as seems best to him. But we have done all that we
owe to those principles which we profess, by inviting the Pope
to take that course which the ideas of the age in which he lives
force him to adopt. This therefore does not concern us at
present. It is by keeping this line that we shall inspire Europe
with confidence, and be safe from disturbance by any one.
Besides, it is well to make our policy known, it is a convenience
to all. This is my way of reasoning in the midst of all my
turmoils.

Do you know that Dom Pedro's expedition, with my idea of
neutrality, will probably succeed, if we can depend on the accounts from Lisbon, which are more reliable than those from

---

[1] We do not know to what incident M. de Talleyrand here alludes. At this
period M. de Maubreuil, entirely forgotten and stripped of all resources, was travelling
abroad. He was for some time in England.

Pozzo.[1] If we keep united with England, we are in a position to settle our home affairs without being disturbed by foreign matters, which makes Metternich furious. Spain, which is held up as a bugbear to every one, has not a penny, and is in a very critical position; hers may certainly be called the army of barefooted friars, of whom there are dozens in the so-called peninsula.

Here party spirit is getting more bitter; each side thinks it will be victorious when the discussion comes on in the House of Lords. I believe that the Ministry will have a majority at the second reading, but in Committee, where they no longer vote by proxy, the matter is not so sure.[2] Lord Grey's answer in Parliament ought to please the French Government. He showered contempt on Lord Aberdeen, who was very bitter, and whose language respecting France was in the worst possible taste. Let us keep as we are; let us say it and maintain it, and we shall soon be clear of all difficulties.

I will not, in these or the following letters, pause longer over Italian affairs and the occupation of Ancona than to state, that I differed with the French Government on both these points. I thought it had thereby involved itself in fresh difficulties before solving those which had deferred peace for the last eighteen months, and I did not consider this sound policy. I was perfectly aware that in Paris, the Opposition made a great outcry with reference to the entry of the Austrian troops into the Legations, but I thought that by using a little firmness one might have silenced these outcries, and awaited the time when the treaty of Nov. 15th, ratified by all the Powers, would place the French Cabinet in a better position to insist upon the withdrawal of the Austrian troops from the Papal States, by threatening to send a French expedition to free them. I feel assured, that we should have received the assent of the English Government to such an action, founded as it would be on the treaties

---

[1] Dom Pedro had started on his expedition to Portugal. He left Belle Isle on February 13th, and landed at Terceira on March 3rd. He appeared before Oporto on July 8th.

[2] According to English procedure in Parliament, every public Bill must first be discussed by the Commons, and then by the *whole House in committee*. The word "committee" does not in this instance mean a commission, selected by the members for the purpose of discussing the Bill, it means the whole House. When the assembly of the committee is announced, the Speaker leaves his seat, and from that moment, by a fiction consecrated by usage, the sitting of the House is suspended, and that of the committee begins.

and the principle of non-intervention, in this instance prudently applied. Whatever may be said on this point, there would have been greater dignity and real vigour in such a policy, than in the furtive capture of Ancona, from whence we should have far greater difficulty in withdrawing than we had in entering. Every one will appreciate my opinion, which I wish to express very plainly here, and which will besides be found throughout my correspondence on Belgian affairs. This matter, which was my real occupation, continued to pass through such varied phases as might have tired out the most patient individual. Thus M. Bresson wrote to me from Berlin on the 23rd February, that he had just sent a courier to Paris, announcing that the Emperor Nicholas had decided to disavow his plenipotentiaries in London, that he would not ratify the treaty of Nov. 15th, and that he had notified this to the Prussian Cabinet ; then a few days later I received the following letter from him, stating quite the opposite.

M. BRESSON TO THE PRINCE DE TALLEYRAND.

BERLIN, *March 1st*, 1832.

MON PRINCE,

I have only a moment before the courier starts, to inform you that a Russian courier, who passed through here at four o'clock this morning, brought an order to Comte Orloff to declare to the King of the Netherlands, that the Emperor has been very grieved to see the project of the treaty which the Dutch plenipotentiaries have communicated to the Conference ;[1] that he considers that the King, by refusing to admit the political separation of Belgium as a settled fact, calls into question all the negotiations carried on by the Powers during the last eighteen months ; that to act thus is, to desire war and not peace ; and that if the King does not abandon this *inadmissible* proposal, the Emperor *might* consider himself freed from the engagements which bind him, and modify on various points Comte Orloff's instructions, especially with regard to the very important one concerning the non-recognition of King Leopold, until this has been done by the King of the Netherlands himself.

---

[1] Project of a treaty communicated confidentially to the Conference by the plenipotentiaries of the Netherlands, dated January 30th, 1832. Martens vol. xxiii, p. 349.

The Russian *Chargé d'Affaires* at the Hague will make this communication, if Comte Orloff has already left that city for London. . . .

THE PRINCE DE TALLEYRAND TO THE PRINCESS DE VAUDÉMONT.

LONDON, *March 1st*, 1832.

There is no news whatever. The Dutch mail is five days behind time. I do not know what day Comte Orloff will arrive, but he is expected at the Lievens, who are giving entertainments to show that they are pleased at his coming to London. The truth is they are greatly put out by it. I persist in the opinion that all will be satisfactorily settled, and within a few days of the time I said.

The King of Bavaria has accepted the Greek crown for his son Otto ; [1] this is a choice which shows the *disinterestedness* of the Powers, as it was necessary it should do, besides which, the King of Bavaria was the only prince in Europe who appeared at all favourably disposed towards the Greeks. I did not suggest this choice, but I consented to it for want of a better. The choice of Prince Paul of Würtemburg would not have inspired anyone with confidence ; the Prince of Saxony [2] and the Margrave William of Baden [3] had both refused. Bolivar [4] was dead. Who else was there ?

March 6th, 1832.

This capture of Ancona places me in a very awkward position. Why enter the place by force ? Had no arrangement been made with Austria as to what would be done ? In order to get out of this, the Pope will have to fulfil his promise, the action of the officer who commanded the squadron must be disowned, and Vienna must be informed by England, that we are ready to retire, as soon as the Pope has carried out the engagement he has entered into with the Austrian, English, and

---

[1] The crown of Greece had been offered by the Conference to Prince Otto, in January. His father accepted in his name, and on the 7th May following, a definite convention was signed to this effect, between Bavaria on the one part, and France, Russia, and England on the other.

[2] Prince John of Saxony, born in 1801. He had married Amelia, daughter of King Maximilian of Bavaria. He succeeded to the throne in 1854, and died in 1873. France favoured his selection for the Greek throne.

[3] Guillaume-Louis-Auguste, Margrave of Baden, born 1792, married to Elizabeth Princess of Würtemburg. He died in 1859.

[4] Simon Bolivar, the famous liberator of South America (1783 to 1830). He had been made dictator of Columbia and Venezuela in 1819. He retired from power a few months before his death.

French plenipotentiaries. And all this must be done at once. Delays do not help to repair foolish actions ; they must be made good before other people become embittered, and proceed to measures that might prove troublesome. That is what I should do if I was M. Périer, and what I should advise him to do were I near him. But as I had the good fortune not to be mixed up in this matter, and had not to give my opinion thereon, I do not wish you to quote me. If anyone asks you what M. de Talleyrand says about it, you can say : " He has nothing whatever to do with it ; he has enough on his hands with Comte Orloff, and I do not think that what has just taken place in Italy, will make this any easier for him."

Our friends in England are in despair ; they will be attacked in Parliament, and will not know what answer to make about this infernal expedition. The ministers will be closely pressed by Lord Aberdeen's bitter arguments. The Austrians will cause mischief—this business of Ancona will serve them as a pretext. . . .

LONDON, *March 7th*, 1832.

. . . . Comte Orloff is expected to arrive here by the steamer of the 9th. If you see the king, tell him that England considers it necessary, that the action of the officer (who I am told went beyond his instructions by entering Ancona) must be disowned. When a matter is important, one must never complicate it with interests that may prejudice it, even if they are foreign to it. . . .

M. PÉRIER TO THE PRINCE DE TALLEYRAND.

PARIS, *March 7th*, 1832, 8 P.M.

MON PRINCE,

Having just quitted the Chamber, I hasten to send you the speech I made, in the general discussion on the budget of foreign affairs. You will be pleased to hear, mon Prince, that the policy adopted by the government has been fully approved.

This morning I received very satisfactory news from Vienna, both with regard to Italian affairs and the ratifications. As, however, they wrote to me, while still under the first impression, I do not know what view may perhaps be taken of our somewhat irregular entry into Ancona, especially as the consent of the Holy See had not been given in a sufficiently explicit manner.

I am not sending you a long letter to-day, mon Prince, as I think you will like to receive the earliest accounts of to-day's sitting. . . .

THE PRINCE DE TALLEYRAND TO THE PRINCESS DE VAUDÉMONT.

LONDON, *March* 13*th*, 1832.

The King of the Netherlands is now making use of this Ancona business, and the hope that the Reform Bill will not be passed, to retard the departure of Comte Orloff; this is insupportable. M. Ouvrand, and also M. de la Rochejacquelin, mix themselves in all the King of Holland's affairs, and every means of intrigue they furnish to the king is welcomed by him. I will not lose courage, but this business will end by killing me. This fresh difficulty, which keeps Comte Orloff at the Hague, is very unpleasant for me. It must now be admitted, that if we had not obtained the ratification from England, and if we had not allied ourselves with her, we should at present be utterly powerless. By remaining as we are, joined together with England, we shall pull through ; that is the solid basis of our dynasty. I attach the greatest possible importance to this.

The Reform Bill will pass the second reading as it is ; there will probably be some amendments when it goes into committee. As to this, they are not quite agreed. I do not think that the alterations will affect the principles of the Bill. . . .

March 15*th*, 1832.

Vexatious as it is, we must not imagine that Comte Orloff's procrastination will cause more than a fortnight's delay, for I am certain the ratifications will arrive, and but for this business about Ancona, they would have been here already. As, however, so much has been said at the Hague, that this affair would alter all the resolutions of the St. Petersburg Cabinet, and that it was necessary to await the effect it would produce, before coming to London, as it might possibly change the instructions that Comte Orloff had received, he has consented to stay on. But we shall be so stiff with him here that he must come. I expect all this will take about a fortnight. Except for the buccaneering expedition to Ancona, all would have been finished by the 10th, as I had said. If no fresh incident occurs, this will be the case by the 30th. Of this I am quite sure. I do not care about your speaking of the bad effect of Ancona, because that would harm the Ministry, and they must be supported in every way. . . .

M. Casimer Périer to the Prince de Talleyrand.

Paris, *March* 14*th*, 1832.

Prince,

My son, who is returning to his post, will take this letter to you. He will tell you that General Sebastiani, who is much better, has taken up work again to-day. I think it is best to leave foreign affairs in his hands, at a time when France has taken a suitable place in all her relations with the other Powers, and when we have better hopes than ever of securing peace and disarmament, a result towards which all our wishes and all our efforts have been directed. To arrive at this end, we always count, Prince, on your kind and powerful co-operation. I must confess to you, that the ardent wish to succeed in securing this peace, so necessary to our country, can alone make me endure the painful task with which I find myself charged. The session which is almost ended has been a very trying one for me. We found a spirit and a tendency in the Chamber, which are the natural consequence, foreseen by us, of a change, such as that resulting from its last electoral laws. We have in great part to do with men who are not able to think, and whose hands are more fitted to pull down than build up. With such materials, it is easy to revolutionize, but not to consolidate. We have therefore had to contend with many obstacles in our Parliamentary procedure. Lastly, we have been worried by economies very embarrassing to us, and without any advantage to France. Nevertheless, I must say, that the truth (which we have not hesitated often to utter distinctly) has not been quite thrown away. The country is returning to ideas of order and government. Without fear of being accused of self-praise, we may affirm, that at no period has our home policy been more solid or better able to withstand attacks than now.

I will not enlarge, Prince, on our relations with the Powers; my two last despatches will have told you of our system of home policy. After the exchange of the ratifications, which we are impatiently expecting, we shall have nothing further at heart, but to see the speedy termination of Italian affairs. I think we shall arrive at this, with the help of the representatives of the Powers at the Court of Rome. I had a meeting this morning with the ministers of the five Powers on this subject. Two schemes were discussed. The first was, to continue the simultaneous occupation by the Austrian and French troops, while soliciting the prompt settlement of the differences of the the Holy See with the Legations ; the second was, to replace the present occupation by Swiss regiments from the kingdom of

Naples. But as this last measure would entail long delays, we are very anxious that matters should be settled before the time required to put this scheme into execution. All this, however, has been nothing more than a simple conversation between the Ministers of the five Courts and myself.

THE PRINCE DE TALLEYRAND TO THE PRINCESS DE VAUDÉMONT.

LONDON, *March 17th*, 1832.

Notwithstanding all the dilatory measures adopted by the King of the Netherlands, I believe now that Comte Orloff's ratifications will arrive at the same time as himself, and that he will be here in a fortnight at latest. The Dutch ministers' courier has arrived with a memorandum ; but I fancy they will have some difficulty in making a fresh communication to us, before we have sent Comte Orloff an answer to the Note, added to the draft of the treaty which he transmitted to us a month ago. But as I am quite determined, and as England is also, to listen to nothing, before the ratifications have arrived, they are greatly exercised to find some way of entering into relations with us. This determination will compel the dispatch of the ratifications. But this business about Ancona must be settled in Paris, as it serves as a pretext for everything that is said against the French government at the Hague. Ill-disposed persons always connect Holland's system of delay, with the hope that the English or French Ministry will be forced to go out of office. . . .

March 22nd, 1832.

The effect produced by this affair of Ancona increases every day. People are terrified, and one constantly hears : " Revolutionary times are come back again." Italian affairs caused the despatch of the last courier by Comte Orloff. The Pope has sent Captain Gallois'[1] proclamation everywhere ; it has greatly exercised both friends and enemies. If we are in this position when the Reform Bill comes up for decision, I do not know what will happen. I must tell you candidly, that it would seem very hard to me to founder within sight of the haven, after eighteen months of difficulties successfully overcome, all for the sake of a foolish expedition devoid of every grain of common sense. Of what good are two or three thousand men at Ancona when the Austrians have sixty thousand in Milan ? It is enough to drive one mad. . . .

[1] Captain Gallois commanded the squadron sent to Ancona. He became rear-admiral in 1835.

THE PRINCE DE TALLEYRAND TO M. CASIMIR PÉRIER.

LONDON, *March 22nd*, 1832.

The confidence, nay, I may say the friendship, you have shown me, monsieur, make it my duty to draw your attention to the extreme importance of present circumstances. The expedition to Ancona has greatly complicated them, our friends have become alarmed, and a very lively satisfaction is evident among the enemies of our government, who seek means therein for attacking the loyalty of our Cabinet, which they have not had the opportunity of doing, since you have been at the head of affairs. Your thorough uprightness has given a strength to our Cabinet, which we must on no account lose; you would have less power to contend against home follies, if Europe ceased to look upon you as the preserver of good laws and good order.

I therefore beseech you to bring this affair of Ancona to a speedy termination, and lay the blame of it on some juniors who have not yet quite forgotten the days of the Revolution. The opinion of all parties here is very strong on this matter; the English Cabinet does not know how to explain or to justify it. You will see by my despatch of to-day, though I toned down the words, how the King of England spoke about it to me this morning. If this tiresome business is not settled before the Reform question comes on, and if the latter turns out badly for Lord Grey's Ministry, I really do not know what will happen. Truly, three thousand men at Ancona is too trifling a matter to satisfy the *amour-propre* of France; and yet our sojourn there threatens to involve the whole of the south, and increase the difficulties and prolong the delays in northern affairs.

From this letter, monsieur, which I write with regret, you will see how greatly the interests of our government and your glory, in especial, occupy me.

Accept. . . .

THE PRINCE DE TALLEYRAND TO THE PRINCESS DE VAUDÉMONT.

LONDON, *March 27th*, 1832.

Comte Orloff is to arrive in London to-morrow. He gained nothing at the Hague. The king would not agree to anything. There is no doubt that we shall receive the ratifications of Prussia and Austria in a few days. The declaration made by Comte Orloff before leaving, expresses itself very forcibly as to what the Emperor Nicholas wished pointed out to the king. He says that as the king has refused to follow his advee, he can no longer count on any support from him.

Matters are progressing as I desire. We shall triumph, but the Belgians must not commit any follies. Who is to be sent as our minister to Brussels? They cannot be too careful in selecting a discreet man. The debate yesterday on the Reform Bill was favourable to the Ministry; the Bill will pass the second reading, which is fixed for April 3rd, after which some amendments will be proposed in committee. . . .

March 28*th*, 1832.

Comte Orloff arrived last night, as I informed you yesterday. He came to see me this morning. During this first visit, I confined myself entirely to the reserve of a visit of ceremony. He spoke to me of his journey to Holland; he praised M. de Mareuil (I have mentioned this in my despatch), and appeared to infer, so it seemed to me, that he had plainly asked the king whether he would—*yes* or *no*, adopt the twenty-four articles. The king having said *no*, he had delivered a declaration, of which M. de Fagel has a copy, and left for London. That is all that is known so far. . . .[1]

March 30*th*, 1832.

" They had promised to send French troops into Italy, if the Austrians entered the Papal States." That is what they said to you. Well, it is utter foolishness. To whom were they promised?

[1] This is the declaration, which is sufficiently decisive : " After having exhausted all means of persuasion and every method of conciliation, to assist His Majesty the King of the Netherlands, to establish by a friendly arrangement, and at the same time one compatible with the dignity of his crown and the interests of his subjects who have remained faithful to him, the separation of the two great divisions of the kingdom of the Netherlands, the emperor does not see the possibility in future of lending him any aid or support.

" However dangerous may be the position in which the king has placed himself, or whatever may be the consequences of this isolation, His Majesty, while silencing the feelings of his heart with inexpressible regret, feels it his duty to leave Holland to take the sole responsibility of the consequences that may result from this state of affairs. Faithful to his principles, His Majesty will not join in any coercive measures, the object of which is to constrain the King of the Netherlands, by force of arms, to subscribe to the twenty-four articles.

" But seeing that they contain the only bases on which the separation of Belgium and Holland can be effected, ... His Imperial Majesty recognizes it as just and necessary, that Belgium should remain in the present enjoyment of the advantages resulting to her from the said articles, notably that, which declares her neutrality to be already recognized in principle by the King of the Netherlands himself. As a natural sequence of this principle, His Imperial Majesty could not oppose the repressive measures that the Conference may take to guarantee and defend this neutrality, if it should be violated by a resumption of hostilities on the part of Holland. . . . ."

To the Pope? He never asked anything from France. Was it to Austria? The very idea is ridiculous. It was therefore either to M. Mauguin, or to M. Lamarque : a fine promise truly! Is it possible to compare the position of Austria, *vis-à-vis* to Rome, with that of France? When there is any popular demonstration in the Legations, Austria, being next door, is threatened; is that the case with France?

I tell you again, that Lord Holland, Sir Francis Burdett,[1] and Lord Grey, all declare, that there is no possible excuse for this expedition ; they put it in a very friendly way, but this is their opinion. Anything that needs constant excuses, is pretty sure to be wrong. I stand up in its defence as far as I can, only because it is my duty to support whatever my government does ; but nothing but trouble can come of it, for it changes the anti-propagandist position we have wished to take up. Truly at a time when there are disturbances in Vendée, and the south is ready to rise in many quarters, it is madness to introduce questions and differences with Rome, which possesses such influence in Vendée and in several of the southern towns. Finish this affair of Ancona, and everything else will go right. I will take care of that. Only this morning, Comte Orloff said to me, " This expedition is a matter for which we can see no plausible reason ; not that it really is any concern of mine. I only mention it to you, as being a mere outsider I can touch on every topic. . . .

April 4th, 1832.

Russia keeps us waiting some time. The order for the exchanges has not yet arrived ; probably we shall get it to-morrow ; this however pleases the Russians, who like to think that other people have to wait for them, which is not quite the case, though on the whole it suits us very well. The affair ends there, for we may consider the matter as settled. . . .

In the interval of our negotiations, cholera, which had been in London for several months, broke out in Paris, and M. Casimir Périer, President of the Council, was attacked,[2] which produced the following letter from General Sebastiani :

---

[1] Sir Francis Burdett (1770–1844). He entered the House of Commons in 1796, where he became one of the principal leaders of the Whig party. He represented the borough of Westminster in 1831, and energetically supported the Reform Bill.

[2] The cholera had overrun Europe towards the end of 1831. In January, 1832, it reached London. On the 29th March, it was noted in Paris, where it immediately assumed formidable intensity. On the 3rd April, M. Casimir Périer was attacked on his return from a visit he had paid to the Hôtel Dieu, together with the Duc d'Orléans. He struggled for six weeks against this scourge, but succumbed on the 16th of May.

GENERAL SEBASTIANI TO THE PRINCE DE TALLEYRAND.

PARIS, *April* 12*th*, 1832.

MON PRINCE,

I can to-day speak with entire confidence and certainty as to the state of the President of the Council. Not only is he out of danger, but there seems to be no longer any doubt that he will before long be able to resume his work. For my part, I had quite decided to leave the office, if his health had necessitated his retiring into private life. Fortunately, however, for France and for Europe, we shall be able to keep him at the head of the Ministry, and all the interests of primary importance, which are so closely allied to the policy we have adopted, will find in the assured continuance of this system, the guarantees they need.

However, as you may imagine, mon Prince, the adversaries of the government have not failed to make the most of the uncertainties to which the President's serious illness at first gave rise, to prepare men's minds for fresh ministerial combinations. But their powerlessness in this respect was too notorious to make much impression ; and discovering very soon, from the sustained character of public anxiety, how small their influence was, they have thought it best to change their tactics, and now express the earnest desire that M. Périer may remain at the head of affairs so that, as they say, they may see him succumb later on to the strain of his own system.

All this, mon Prince, is only very foolish but not at all alarming. The Ministry will continue to pursue the same course with firm steps, and if the President's health requires that for some time he should use great care, circumstances now, fortunately, no longer oblige him to wear himself out with arduous labour, as he has been compelled to do during the past year.

The session is drawing to an end. To-morrow, or the day after, the Chamber of Deputies will be closed ; they are all anxious to finish and return to their homes. You will have noticed this, from the rapidity with which they voted the last legislative proposals.

The king's government will therefore find itself less hampered and more at liberty to act : it will no longer have to waste the time which the actual interests of the country claim almost entirely, in useless and often inopportune discussions. The cause of peace cannot but gain thereby, and it will not be our fault, mon Prince, if the Powers do not profit by this interval, to strengthen and draw closer those ties, the maintenance of which is equally important to all.

Accept. . . .

THE PRINCE DE TALLEYRAND TO THE PRINCESS DE
VAUDÉMONT.

LONDON, *April 16th*, 1832.

The Austrian and Prussian ratifications have arrived ; the
power of exchange has also come ; but a strong wish is expressed
at Berlin to await, if possible, the return of the Russian courier.
The object of all this is to place the responsibility on M. de
Bülow and M. de Wessenburg, who are not liked in Berlin and
Vienna, as they signed the treaty of November 15th. I am urging
them, though not too strongly, for the truth is, that at the time
when the treaty was signed they were very good, very courageous,
and very decided, believing they were doing what was best for
their governments. All will be settled to-morrow evening. Will
three or four more days be granted, or will matters be completed
to-morrow ? I cannot yet give an opinion on that. . . .

Evening of the 16th.

I wrote to you this morning when half asleep. The sitting
in the House of Lords was not over till seven in the morning,
and I wished before going to bed, to inform you by telegraph
of the success of the English Ministry. There was a majority
of 19 votes ; that is a good thing finished. I had therefore
told the government exactly, what the result of this important
affair would be. The committee for arranging the details
of the Reform Bill will not meet until after Easter, for
everyone is tired and wants to get away to the country.
Nothing fresh from Russia. We are waiting, for we can
do nothing else ; but everyone is getting impatient. I will hold
out to the end. I will not consider my age until the ratifications have arrived ; after that, I will think a little about it, and
talk about it seriously. I am pleased to think that I shall end
my career with a great work and a great act of devotion ; the
great work is, peace and our union with England ; the act of devotion is, having given up two years of time, while undergoing
strong mental fatigue, with a complete change of life, in order to
establish our dynasty abroad, this required a solid basis at any
price, and it is in England that this will be found. I can assure
you it will not be at Ancona, whatever they may say, that
troubles will spring up. There has been too much desire to
please the Opposition ; all that has been misunderstood, It is
no use trying to please them ; nothing ever will do so. You must
restrain them, and you can. I can reason thus dispassionately, for
I am not, and would not on any account, be in office again. . . .

Evening, April 17*th,* 1832.

The reply to the despatch of March 14th, sent by Comte Orloff when at the Hague, has arrived at the Russian Embassy here ; but as it is not decisive, we shall proceed independently of it to-morrow, and induce the Austrian and Prussian pleni-potentiaries to exchange their ratifications with the Belgian plenipotentiary. To-morrow therefore, the 18th, at four o'clock, this matter will be completed. Then there will remain only Russia, and she will certainly acquiesce by the end of this month. To have waited any longer for her, would have been too great a deference to Russia. Consideration, I can under-stand and admit, but a deference which would seem to recognize her superiority, we neither could or would agree to. To-morrow, therefore, we shall quietly put Russia on one side, and get the other two ratifications exchanged. One must not be unbending, unless it is necessary, but when it is necessary, one must be immovable.

April 23*rd,* 1832.

I do not understand a word of what our Foreign Office in Paris writes to me, respecting the ratifications of Prussia and Austria. The fact is, the Austrian and Prussian ministers were not authorized to make their exchanges except with the con-sent of Russia (or at least at the same time as Russia), and this consent they have not got—that is to say, not just yet, as the Russian ratifications have not yet arrived. I fancy it is in order to deprive me of the small amount of credit this affair deserves, that they have taken the trouble to declare that M. de Bülow had received positive instructions to make the exchanges at once. However, it really matters very little to me, for here, they know the rights of the case. . . .

THE PRINCESS ADELAIDE D'ORLÉANS TO THE PRINCE DE TALLEYRAND.

PARIS, *April,* 20*th,* 1832.

I thank you heartily, mon cher Prince, for having told Madame de Vaudémont to communicate to me the letter you wrote to her on the 17th. This she did yesterday with friendly anxiety for me, and by six o'clock, the king received by telegraphic despatch the confirmation of the important and good news of the exchange of the Austrian and Prussian rati-fications, which had taken place on the 18th, as you had in-

U 2

formed us the night before.[1]   I must express to you at once my
satisfaction thereat, and offer you my congratulations, for it is
certainly due to your long labours, your ability, and your
firmness, especially in this last business, that we are indebted for
this happy result, which insures us the great and incalculable
advantages of peace, in which I have always believed.   But the
prolonged delay of the ratifications by Austria and Prussia,
placed a powerful weapon in our enemies' hands to throw doubt
on it and spread anxiety respecting it, which did great harm.
Thanks to you, it is at last finished, and without waiting for
the ratification of Russia, which is a great victory for us, and I
feel convinced that no one but you could have gained it.

This piece of good news came just in time, to somewhat
comfort and console our good king for all his trouble and
anxiety.   This terrible cholera has attacked us here in a very
sharp and cruel manner, and plunged us into the deepest
distress ; it is a frightful calamity.   M. Périer had it very
severely, he is now convalescent, but it seems that the convalescence after this illness is a very tedious matter.   M.
d'Argout has also had a severe attack.   You can imagine how
very anxious all this makes the king. . . .

Saturday, **April** 21st.

I take up my letter again, as I could not finish it yesterday.
All foreign difficulties seem to quiet down, for the king yesterday received the news, that the Pope consents to our troops
remaining at Ancona as long as the Austrians are in his States,
and this morning he heard of the recall of Cardinal Albani.[2]   I
am glad to be able to send you this good news, which I hope
will reconcile you somewhat to our expedition to Ancona, which,
if you think it did us no good (as some people of your acquaintance, and of *mine* maintain) you will at least agree has done no
harm, and that is something.

---

[1] The ratifications of Austria and Prussia contained a reservation respecting *the
rights of the Germanic Confederation as to the articles concerning the exchange of
part of Limburg for part of Luxemburg.* Moreover, by a declaration inserted in the
protocol, the Austrian plenipotentiary provided for the *necessity* of a future arrangement between Holland and Belgium for the conclusion of a treaty containing the
twenty-four articles, with such modifications as the five Powers might consider
admissible.

    The Prussian ratification was a perfectly plain and ordinary one. Nevertheless,
M. de Bülow verbally adhered to the Austrian reservation, and also inserted a declaration in the protocol, showing the *great sympathy* his government felt towards that of
the Hague, and his wish ultimately to make such additional articles to the treaty, as
might improve the position of Holland.

[2] Joseph Albani, of the illustrious Roman family of that name, was Apostolic
Commissioner in the Romagna, where he signalized himself by extremely rigorous
dealings. He died in 1834.

The *Courrier Anglais* contains a very good article, which I read this morning, on Louis Philippe's right to the throne, in answer to Sir Robert Peel's detestable speech in the discussion on Monday about the Brazilian captures.[1] But I should have liked it to have been shown that Dom Miguel had accepted the Regency, and that consequently he only held the crown of Donna Maria (which he appropriated to himself) in trust ; whereas Louis Philippe had undertaken no engagement whatever, he absolutely did not wish for the crown, and only decided to accept it, when he felt convinced that there was no other means of saving our beloved France from anarchy and the most serious disasters. It was only then that he gave in to the *universal and earnest wish ;* of this you were at that time witness, as well as I. . . .

THE PRINCE DE TALLEYRAND TO THE PRINCESS DE VAUDÉMONT.

LONDON, *April 24th,* 1832.

. . . . The letter I have received from Mademoiselle is full of Ancona. I am delighted that this business is taking a proper turn ; it was its revolutionary aspect that frightened all our friends. The Austrians had been called in ; we had not ; in this lay all the difference. When the Emperor Napoleon entered into Spain—a detestable enterprise, from which period dated the decline of his power—he got the King of Spain to summon him, and took care that this was carried out. We are just out of a revolution, and in such a case, if you want to establish a footing, you must show the other governments, who are naturally disquieted, that you have no revolutionary tendencies. This I have always kept in view since I have been here, and therefore I have succeeded. . . .

THE COMTE DE FLAHAUT TO THE PRINCE DE TALLEYRAND.

PARIS, *April 24th,* 1832.

. . . . Our home and foreign affairs would go all right, but for the vexatious complications caused by the illness of M.

---

[1] In the House of Commons on the 16th, a discussion arose respecting the claims of the English subjects, on account of the capture of English merchantmen made by the Brazilian government, then at war with the Argentine Republic. Brazil had promised an indemnity, which had never been paid. Sir Robert Peel rose, and at once took up the question on political grounds ; he protested against the support given by England to Dom Pedro. He compared Dom Miguel to Louis Philippe. "In what way," he said, "are his rights inferior to those of Louis Philippe to the crown of France ? Surely not on the grounds of legitimacy. . . . "

Périer and M. d'Argout, and the state of Sebastiani, although the latter has greatly recovered. M. Périer is no longer laid up with cholera, but a recovery like that of Broussais[1] is worse than a mortal illness. Meanwhile the ministerial intrigues go on as usual, and there are always traitors in the camp. . . .

THE PRINCE DE TALLEYRAND TO THE PRINCESS DE VAUDEMONT.

LONDON, *May 1st,* 1832.

How can I tell you about the Russian ratifications, before they are known in Paris? It is from Paris alone that I hear about them, and they only arrived here last night, whereas in Paris you knew of them three days ago. Lord Palmerston does not return from the country until Thursday, 3rd. Between this and then, we shall hear nothing reassuring. On the 3rd, we shall have a conference, and I will on that day write both to you and to the Office.

MADAME ADELAIDE D'ORLÉANS TO THE PRINCE DE TALLEYRAND.

PARIS, *April 29th,* 1832.

The ratification of Russia has arrived; it is a splendid triumph, mon cher Prince, and one which assures us the best of all things—peace.

Our king had need of this good piece of news to console and comfort him for the fresh embarrassments caused by the illness of M. Périer, which grieves him greatly. Unfortunately, his convalescence is far from being an established fact, and his present state leaves the greatest uncertainty as to what the result may be. But whether his illness is prolonged or not, the king intends following the same system of government, which I know is yours also. It is for this reason, even without saying a word to our beloved king, to whom just now especially I would not cause any additional worry, that I want to consult you about a fresh difficulty, which the state of poor General Sebastiani's health (about which I am not at all satisfied) makes me dread. If he should not be able to return to the Foreign Office, what would you advise respecting the very important choice of the person who is to replace him? I ask this in all confidence, and you can answer me in the same way, feeling

---

[1] Doctor Broussais, professor of medicine in Paris (1772-1838), head of the *école physiologique*, who after enjoying a wide popularity fell into great disrepute.

quite *sure* that this will remain *between you and me.* But I lay great stress before occasion arises, on getting your views on this matter, which I consider very important as your experience is so great. I will give this little note to Madame de Vaudémont, so that it may reach you through safe hands, but she is perfectly ignorant of its contents. You will see what value I place on this remaining entirely secret between you and me, so that no one should suspect the question I have asked you, the more so as it is only provision for the future, and any indiscretion would run the risk of disturbing and spoiling the present. . . .

This letter from Madame Adelaide, although she infers that the king was in utter ignorance of it, was probably dictated by him in order to sound me as to what my personal views were on the question which formed the subject of the letter. Other people had written to me from Paris to know whether I would not join the Ministry, either in M. Périer's place or that of General Sebastiani, if these two ministers retired. Several envoys were even sent, and instructed to make overtures to me from different quarters on the same subject. This decided me to write the following letter to Baron Louis, who had been employed as an intermediary, begging him to make what use of it he deemed best :

THE PRINCE DE TALLEYRAND TO BARON LOUIS.

LONDON, *May* 3*rd*, 1832.

It is a long time since I have seen your handwriting, mon cher Louis. Your letter has given me much pleasure. It will be treated confidentially, and thereby replaces me in the position I have always wished to hold with you.

My opinion is that one ought to devote oneself to what one can do, and never undertake what one is not sure of being able to perform better than anyone else. That is why you wished to undertake the control of the finances, and no one could be better there than you. For the same reason I came to London, believing that I was better able to secure the maintenance of peace than anyone else. We have both been right ; for our finances are in a satisfactory position, and peace has been secured. This will close my political life. I have served France for fifty years,

for she always had to be considered ; you have thought and
acted in the same manner. At every period, good has to be
effected, or evil prevented, and therefore, when one loves one's
country, one can, and in my opinion one must, serve it under
whatever government it may choose to adopt.

Now I must tell you, that I intend to remain here until I am
fully assured that the object of my journey has been reached,
or is about to be so. Then I shall ask for four months' leave to
drink the waters and look after my own affairs, about which,
for the last two years, I have known nothing ; for since I have
been in London, I have not given a thought to anything but
what would further the result we desired so much, as without
peace no one could tell where we might end.

Do not therefore think of me for any ministerial post, which
I should most certainly refuse. You speak of a Minister for
Foreign Affairs ; there are only two who could be chosen, M.
de Rigny, or M. de St. Aulaire. Anyone else under present circumstances would be a mistake, and would throw our foreign
relations back into that system of distrust, out of which M. Périer
and I have drawn it. M. de Bassano would be a *fatal* choice,
and such old servants of the emperor as you and I, ought to
know this better than anyone, for in truth it was he who caused
his master's fall. He is with reason considered both incapable
and hostile. Write to me what they think of doing. Adieu.

A thousand good wishes,

T. . . .

THE PRINCE DE TALLEYRAND TO THE PRINCESS DE
VAUDÉMONT.

LONDON, *May 5th*, 1832.

This morning at 3 A.M. the ratifications were exchanged
with Russia, and it has been a long and difficult business, because the ratification was not a pure and simple one.[1] It was
necessary to strengthen it, and this I think we succeeded in
doing. I have not attended to anything but this for the last
thirty-six hours. Now matters are satisfactorily arranged.
Comte Orloff leaves to-night. I am writing both officially and
privately to ask for four months' leave, with permission to

---

[1] The Russian ratification contained an important reservation. The Emperor
Nicholas only ratified " subject to the modifications and amendments to be brought
into a definitive arrangement between Holland and Belgium respecting Articles 9, 12,
and 13." Now the articles in question, relating to the navigation of the intermediary
waters and the division of the debt, were precisely those that the Hague refused to
recognize.

take it at whatever time I may find it most convenient. I absolutely need some rest ; for the last twenty months I only exist to-day, to maintain the ground that I attained yesterday I must spare my limbs and my eyes, and look after my affairs. I have asked that M. Durant de Marcuil[1] should replace me here, but without prejudice to his advancement, pointing him out as the only person fit to handle a difficult matter. . . .

LONDON, *May 8th*, 1832.

The first schedule of the Reform Bill names a certain number of boroughs which will lose their franchise ; the second schedule points out a certain number of large towns which will acquire the electoral privilege.

Lord Lyndhurst[2] proposed that the second schedule should be discussed first. This motion, opposed by Lord Holland and Lord Grey, was supported by Lord Harrowby and some others of that party, and carried by 151 votes against 116, that is to say, by a majority of 35 against the Ministry. Lord Ellenborough[3] in the form of suggestions, made several objections to the Bill, in more than a liberal spirit, with a view to making the government unpopular. In this he acted like our *Gazette de France*, with its universal suffrage. In their dread of being liberal, all these people, no matter of what party, become radical. Is it not curious that Lord Ellenborough should take his political views from M. Genonde ?[4] These are strange times!

Lord Grey and the Chancellor went to Windsor this morning to request the creation of sixty peers, or the acceptance of their resignation. They will not return till night.

This is how matters stand now. . . .

[1] At that time French ambassador at the Hague.
[2] John Singleton Copley, Baron Lyndhurst, born in 1772, had been first a member of the House of Commons. He was Lord Chancellor in the Wellington Cabinet. He retired in 1830, again took this office in 1834 and 1841. He died in 1863.
[3] Edward Law, Earl of Ellenborough, born in 1790. Member of the House of Commons, he succeeded his father in the Lords in 1818, where he sided with the Tory party. In 1834, he was made President of the India Board, and Governor-General of India 1841. First Lord of the Admiralty in 1846, and President of the Indian Board of Control in 1858.
[4] Antoine Eugène Genonde, born in 1792, was at first professor at the university. Later on he made a name for himself as an ultra royalist political writer and journalist under the Restoration. After 1830, he continued his fight in favour of legitimacy in the *Gazette de France*, of which he was the proprietor and chief editor. He was elected a deputy in 1846, and died in 1849. M. Genonde entered Holy Orders in 1834. Just when the electoral law was under discussion, the *Gazette de France* had asked for universal suffrage, with the sole object of opposing the Cabinet, which demanded a qualification of two hundred francs.

LONDON, *May 9th,* 1832, 10 A.M.

The king has accepted the resignation of the ministers. He has not yet called upon anyone to form a new government.[1] At home we must show great calmness, continue to follow the same course, retain the same ministers, await M. Périer's restoration to health, and congratulate ourselves on having come to some settlement in Italy, and that all the ratifications have been exchanged. . . .

May 10th, 1832.

. . . . Here, nothing is yet decided. *Pourparlers* are still going on, and probably the whole day will pass in this way. Pray let nothing but curiosity be shown with us regarding the change of Ministry in England. We must be quiet, and the advantage of being quiet is, that in the eyes of others, we appear to have no anxieties, because we are immovable.

This affair of Madame la Duchesse de Berry[2] proves how very weak the Carlist party is. The only really dangerous party is the Republican one, and it has every reason to believe that any disturbances, no matter from which side they come, are to its advantage. Our government, on the contrary, ought to wish for stability everywhere; that is the only way to become firmly established. I shall have much to say on that point, but it is too long for a letter. . . .

May 12th, 1832.

Nothing is yet completed. The only thing that is sure is, that the Duke of Wellington and Lord Lyndhurst have been nominated and have accepted.

If under such circumstances we were to seek for strength among the revolutionary party, everything would become difficult, and no difficulty can be removed with men who are involved in the movement. If we are quiet, Europe will accept

---

[1] The king had refused to create the sixty peers for which Lord Grey and Lord Brougham had asked. He preferred accepting the ministers' resignations. The Duke of Wellington was requested to form a new Ministry, but his efforts were unsuccessful, while at the same time a strong opposition was shown in the Cabinet against any change of Ministry. At last, after a crisis which lasted sixty days, Lord Grey withdrew his resignation, and the Cabinet was reconstructed.

[2] Madame la Duchesse de Berry had disembarked on the coast of Provence on the 29th of April; the next day there was an attempt at insurrection in Marseilles, which was speedily quelled. The Duchesse seeing that she had failed in the south, travelled secretly across France, reached Vendée, and arrived on the 15th of May at the Château Dampierre in Saintonge, whence she organized the rising which broke out in the west, during the night of the 3rd June.

us, and that completely. If we become propagandists, she will never accept us. That idea must be given up ; there is nothing to be gained by taking up that line. . . .

KING LOUIS PHILIPPE TO THE PRINCE DE TALLEYRAND.

PARIS, *May* 12*th*, 1832.

In truth, mon cher Prince, and I am delighted to tell you so, you have most happily achieved the principal aim of the grand mission with which I entrusted you. This success therefore, which has so often seemed to escape us, is a crushing answer to all the diatribes of our journalists, to whose foolish predictions it has given the lie. Nothing less than your perseverance, your ability, and your devotion, could have succeeded in solving one of the most difficult and most thorny questions that European diplomacy has ever had to deal with, and it is only fair that you should now give yourself a little rest, by taking the leave you have asked me to grant you. I grant it with all the greater pleasure, as it will give me the satisfaction of seeing you again, of conversing with you, and telling you of my old and constant friendship for you.

My ministers agree entirely with the wish you have expressed to me, that M. de Marcuil should take charge during your absence, which will only be short, and, as you wish, when most convenient to you. M. de Marcuil will join you as soon as we can replace him at the Hague, the importance of which post you will fully recognize, and from whence we receive only bad news and bad indications. That Cabinet still hopes to initiate a war, and they think that as long as the King of Holland refuses his consent, there is a chance of collision between the Powers. I therefore consider that the chances of a war will not be entirely removed, until the King of Holland has signed the treaty with the King of the Belgians, and more especially, until the citadel of Antwerp has been evacuated, and the treaty of November 15th has been fully executed ; this we may still have some difficulty in getting carried out, all the more so as the dissolution of Lord Grey's Cabinet will probably inspire the King of Holland with fresh hopes, though he ought to know, that England is not likely to change her foreign policy, and that the concord between the five Powers will not be disturbed.

Nevertheless, mon cher Prince, it seems to me that you must not dream of quitting London, until matters have resumed their former position, and I do not hesitate to ask you to make this fresh sacrifice. As soon as the Ministry is reorganized, the

Conference will take up the question of the King of Holland's reply, which will again be a refusal, judging from his answer on the subject of M. de Thorn.[1] I am convinced that this arrest and these arrogant replies, have been made in the hope of drawing the Belgians into hostilities, and thus bringing about a war. I trust we shall be able to thwart these fatal schemes ; but until they are upset, you will be greatly needed in London, and I repeat again that this business will not be finished, until the King of Holland has signed the treaty with the King of the Belgians, and until Antwerp is evacuated. Let us try and achieve this as soon as possible. Meanwhile, mon cher Prince, I again renew. . . .

THE PRINCE DE TALLEYRAND TO THE PRINCESS DE
VAUDÉMONT.

LONDON, *May 16th,* 1832.

The Grey Ministry remains in ; the details of this arrangement are being carried out while I am writing to you. The crisis is nearly over. We certainly have passed through the strangest three days that the history of any country could show. Every one returns to his place this evening. I am most anxious that all that has taken place here should be fully understood in Paris, and when fully understood, it certainly does not militate against the Duke of Wellington's character as a man.

I have got my leave, and Durant will start for London whenever I write to him ; he has been appointed officially. Lord Granville returns to Paris.

I will not take my leave until matters are fairly settled here, and have got back into their old groove.

The king's dinner party yesterday was a curious one, not a single minister or high official being present. The resignations were not withdrawn till ten o'clock in the evening. . . .

GENERAL SEBASTIANI TO THE PRINCE DE TALLEYRAND.

PARIS, *May 16th,* 1832.

MON PRINCE,

I have to announce a sad piece of news to you. M. Périer has ended his honourable and laborious career.

---

[1] M. de Thorn, a senator, and the King of Belgium's governor at Luxemburg, had been arrested by order of the Dutch government on the 17th of April, 1832. King William, in a note dated May 7th, made it a condition of his liberation, that those persons who had been arrested in Belgium during the Revolution should be set free, and all persecutions against the insurgents stopped. M. de Thorn was not liberated till November 23rd.

You will share with me, mon Prince, and with all those who appreciated the enlightened devotion of this noble citizen, the deep sorrow that his premature loss causes us—a loss which we now feel all the greater, as a crisis, which we trusted might terminate favourably, led us to hope up to the last few days, that he would be restored to his work and to his country.

In these first moments, given up to regrets at the sad ending of so noble a life, nothing has yet been arranged, mon Prince, that it is important you should know.

When the ranks of those whom one loves and esteems, are being thinned, it is necessary to cling still closer to those who are left to us. The sad news which forms the subject of my letter, affords me the opportunity, mon Prince, of renewing the expressions of my devotion and my confidence in your. . . .

THE PRINCE DE TALLEYRAND TO THE PRINCESS DE VAUDÉMONT.

May 23rd, 1832.

The sitting in the House of Lords yesterday passed off as I expected. Many of the Peers in the Opposition withdrew, many did not vote at all, the result being a majority for the Ministry of fifty-two votes, on the important question which has been decided.[1] The other clauses will probably share the same fate, and the question will, I believe, be settled on Wednesday, 30th.

The grief felt here at the death of M. Périer, has shown itself in all sorts of ways, and among all classes of people. It has been noticed with some surprise, that M. le Duc d'Orléans did not hold one of the cords of the canopy. Here on several occasions, this office has been performed by the most important persons, such as the Prince of Wales and the Duke of York.[2] Each country, it is true, has its customs, and our precedents are not in England. Moreover, it is a matter of small moment, and more a piece of society gossip where one side is always ready to find fault. Let me know when Sebastiani goes to drink the waters ; I should like to see him before he goes, and this I think is only natural. . . .

[1] The House had assented to the clause in the Bill which entrusted the electoral franchise to one of the London suburbs ; this clause, and likewise all those which gave additional members to the large populous centres, had been hotly contested by the Tory party.

[2] Frederick, Duke of York and Albany, second son of George III., born in 1763, married to the Princess Frederica, daughter of the Prince Royal of Prussia. He died in 1827.

LONDON, *May 24th*, 1832.

The Tories are not very numerous in the House of Lords. The Bill is passing very quietly, the discussions yesterday not being half so bitter as on the preceding days. This does not lessen the hatred, which is very strong between both parties, but it delays the action. The king has announced that he wished the Bill to pass, and it will pass. Those who are opposed to it, have absented themselves.

M. de Rémusat[1] has arrived here with his wife, and brought me some letters from Paris. . . . Nothing fresh about Holland ; the Dutch ministers, here, have received no answer to the last communication they were directed by the Conference to send to the Hague.

I have neither love nor the opposite for the Belgians ; I have undoubtedly been of greater service to them than any-one, but I do not want them to commit such follies as would perhaps involve us in a universal war, and they have so little sense, that they cannot understand this. . . .

May 25th, 1832.

Ever since M. Périer's death, the tone of the despatches of our department for Foreign Affairs does not please me ; there is a very perceptible change. I should not have noticed it, but that I must not let matters retard my departure. I am doubt-ful about this journey to Compiègne.[2] It will make the Belgians still more difficult to please, and nothing can be settled, unless they on their part facilitate matters. People think themselves very clever when they manage to raise difficulties ! A fine science truly ! Anyone can do that ! But to resist no further than is necessary and to know when to stop, is what very few people can accomplish. The King of Holland asks for nothing better than to initiate reasons for fresh delays, and yet he must not be pressed ; first, because it would not be easy to do so, but still more, because it would be neither fair nor profitable. This I will maintain as long as I am entrusted with the affairs of France. I hope that during my absence they will do the same, but I do not feel quite sure of this. However, Durant, if he is allowed to do so, will follow my line better than anyone else.

---

[1] François Marie Charles, Comte de Rémusat, born in 1797, nephew of Casimir Périer, was at that time deputy for Muret. He became Under-Secretary of State for the Interior in 1840. He lived in retirement under the Empire. In 1871, he was made Minister of Foreign Affairs. He died in 1875.

[2] King Louis Philippe went to Compiègne to meet the King of the Belgians, and arrange the preliminaries of the marriage of the latter with the Princess Louis-d'Orléans.—(Note by M. de Bacourt.)

We are living in strange times, and they are strange everywhere. What things have I not seen during the past fifteen
days! Enough to talk about for a year!

The English are sending a fleet to the Tagus ; I suppose we
shall do the same. When troubles threaten any place, it is
necessary to protect the people of our country who may be
exposed thereto. . . .

LONDON, *May 27th*, 1832.

In eight days, the third reading of the Reform Bill will come
on, and the Bill will be passed precisely as it was brought in.
Thus the temper shown by the Tories, will deprive them of
some ameliorations that would have occurred during the discussion. I have a talk every day with Madame de Rémusat,
who in the name of all M. Périer's friends, urges me to accept
the Presidency of the Council in Paris. I am greatly flattered
by their opinion, but I have quite decided not to accept anything. I say this quietly and temperately, as one does when
one is immovable. . . .

May 28th

There was a grand reception at Court to-day, in honour of
the king's birthday ; it was a very brilliant gathering ; both
parties were present, and all on the best terms with each other.

I know nothing of Holland. The king wishes to stir up
the Belgians, hoping that in that way some quarrel or some
steps taken on his territory, would give him an excuse for hostile action without any fear of reproach. . . .

KING LOUIS PHILIPPE TO THE PRINCE DE TALLEYRAND.

ST. CLOUD, *Sunday Evening, May 27th*, 1832.

MON PRINCE,

There was no need that you should tell me of all the
care and discretion with which you will arrange for everything,
during your absence from the important post where you have
done such great service both to France and me. I feel sure that
you would not leave, until your absence could not cause any
troublesome mishaps. I earnestly hope that that period may
not be too far distant, but I must confess that I do not think
that it has yet arrived.

General Sebastiani will have told you of the interview about
to take place between King Leopold and myself. You know
the reasons for it, and you can have some idea of the subjects
to be discussed. The ratifications of the Great Powers having

been exchanged, we deemed it best that the interview should no longer be deferred, and that it would even help to accelerate the King of Holland's compliance. I am not taking any of my daughters to Compiègne ; and you will understand that, as this interview may exercise a great influence on my eldest daughter's destiny, there is the more reason for my not taking any of them there. I am therefore only going with the queen and my second son. . . .

I had written very fully to King Leopold, but unfortunately without success, urging him to accede to the proposals of the Conference, by declaring his readiness to enter into negotiations with the King of Holland ; he has done, or at any rate his ministers have made him do just the contrary ; he has very foolishly taken on himself the chances of a refusal, which the King of Holland seemed determined to spare him.[1] Nevertheless, I hope this is not irrevocable, and that with the assistance of General Sebastiani, who accompanies me to Compiègne, we shall succeed in dissuading him from following the erroneous course he has pursued. But there is all the greater need, mon cher Prince, that the Conference should take such action towards the King of Holland, as will make him cease his resistance as soon as possible. Above all he must evacuate the citadel of Antwerp, for that is the crucial point of the matter. It is for England to strike the decisive blow, and this will in every way suit us best, and will also, it seems to me, conduce more to the general interest of Europe.

Completely absorbed, and with reason, in the stupendous affair of the Reform Bill, the English government cannot well trouble itself with continental matters, until that is passed ; but, this affair once ended, not a moment must be lost in dealing with the King of Holland in such a decisive manner, as can alone settle this affair. You may rest assured, that he is quite as well aware as we are, that the peace of Europe cannot be fully insured

---

[1] The Conference had signed a protocol on the 4th May, by which Belgium and Holland were invited to enter at once into the negotiations for signing a definite treaty. King Leopold replied to this invitation, by a note dated May 11th, which declared that he would not entertain any negotiations until the execution of the treaty of November 15th, had commenced. He insisted on the evacuation of Belgian territory, especially Antwerp, and the free navigation of the Meuse. Through some carelessness, this note was published in the papers before it was sent officially to the Conference. The Belgian government drew up another, which General Goblet brought to London in the beginning of June. It repeated in precise terms, the note of the 11th of May. The Dutch Government likewise replied to the Conference by a note dated 7th. In this note it declared "that it saw with deep regret, that the plenipotentiaries of the five powers looked upon the treaty of November 15th, as the unalterable basis of the separation, the independence, and the actual state of possession of Belgium, while for its part it must continue to consider this treaty as completely opposed to the protocol of January 27th, 1831."

until General Chassé has left Antwerp, and until he has entered into negotiations with King Leopold. It is to this point, therefore, that you must direct all your diplomatic energies, and it is only when this last success has been obtained (without doubt the most difficult of all) that you will have completed the great task which you undertook with so much devotion, and which you have carried out with so much talent and skill.

I will say no more, mon cher Prince, and will confine myself to renewing, with all my heart, the assurance of my sincere friendship for you.

LOUIS PHILIPPE.

P.S.—I have signed M. de Marcuil's credentials as you wished ; he will go to you as soon as the Marquis de Dalmatie[1] has arrived at the Hague.

GENERAL SEBASTIANI TO THE PRINCE DE TALLEYRAND.

PARIS, *May 28th*, 1832.

MON PRINCE,

I leave for Compiègne in a few hours, and expect to arrive there in the evening. To-morrow we shall see King Leopold, and will discuss the business with him, that takes him there. This meeting, the importance of which you will no doubt appreciate, will give me a valuable opportunity of working more directly and without any intermediaries, on the feelings of the head of the Belgian government, and proving to him that the welfare of his country (to which our sovereign consents to unite, by a fresh tie, the destiny of ours) depends as much upon his confidence, as upon the projects of our Cabinet and those of our allies. In this way, we shall continue the work at Compiègne which you have so ably conducted in London, and you will be punctually informed of all the results that may interest you.

Having spoken about State affairs, mon Prince. I must now say a few words about our own. My doctor has ordered me to take the waters of Bourbonne, and my intention is to go there about the 2nd of July. Among the many reasons which have decided me to put off till then, a journey which I believe is necessary for my health, you can certainly, mon Prince, count

[1] Napoleon Hector Soult, Marquis, then Duc de Dalmatic, son of the Marshal. Born in 1801, he entered the army, became Captain of Artillery, but retired in 1830, when he entered the Diplomatic Service. He was successively accredited to Stockholm in 1831, to the Hague, 1832, to Turin and to Berlin. He was elected deputy in 1843, and died in 1857.

my wish to await you in Paris and meet you there. After an absence which events have made long, though the time has been short, you will hardly credit how much value I attach to a few hours' conversation with you, and the pleasure I shall have in repeating by word of mouth, the expressions of affection I here beg you to accept. . . .

THE PRINCE DE TALLEYRAND TO THE PRINCESS DE VAUDÉMONT.

LONDON, *June 2nd*, 1832.

I am working hard, so that Durant may find our affairs with Holland in a fair way of being settled, and I really believe that the interests of Holland will oblige the king to give in. All the support he counted on has failed him. I shall remain here until after Durant's arrival, and will set him going fairly.

Everyone here is exceedingly gracious to me ; they insist on my giving my word of honour that I shall return. I have given my promise, but my movements will depend upon the state of France ; that must decide me. I have done what no one else was able to do, that is, keep all the five Powers united ; they are so now, and my mission, if I wish it, is ended, though it was considered more than a difficult one. The king will I hope, by some act, convince all Europe that he intends to follow M. Périer's system at home and mine abroad. . . .

MADAME ADELAIDE D'ORLÉANS TO THE PRINCE DE TALLEYRAND.

ST. CLOUD, *June 2nd*, 1832.

I have been in such a whirl of excitement for the last week, mon cher Prince, that notwithstanding my wish to do so, I have found it utterly impossible to write to you. But having re- turned yesterday evening from our trip to Compiègne, I hasten to give you an account of this little journey, which has been most satisfactory in every way. Our beloved king, as he well deserves, was received everywhere with the greatest tokens of affection, and his appearance and his speeches have, as they always do, produced the best possible effect at Compiègne. This makes me regret that he cannot go about more frequently, as nothing can equal the good effect of his words.

We are perfectly contented with King Leopold. It is

impossible for him to be more satisfactory than he is at present. He was perfect and good. The great business of the marriage has therefore been settled, and I am anxious to be the first to tell you of it. The date at which it is to take place, has not yet been decided, but it will be in August at latest. This marriage, so suitable from a political point of view, is also from King Leopold's character, his affection for us, and the proximity of our two countries, equally that which, according to our dear Louise's inclination, offers her the greatest chances of happiness. But the poor dear child is greatly affected at the thought of being separated from her father, her mother, and *all of us ;* that is only natural. What is now needed to insure the security and happiness of this union is, that you should succeed in getting the Dutch to evacuate Antwerp. This is of the utmost importance, not only for Belgium, which will always be disturbed as long as they are there, but also for us, for in France as well as Belgium, most people will not believe in peace, until the King of Holland is brought to reason, and submits to the treaties of November 15th. It will be for you to conclude this great and noble work, and it is very important for the general peace that it should be done quickly.

We have, fortunately, received very good accounts of the *chouans* [1] and La Vendée. Thanks to the measures that have been taken by the government, the good feeling of the people, and the National Guard in those parts, the scheme of a general rising has fallen through, and been found to be impossible. It is true there are some slight mishaps to deplore, and those who thus stir up and foment a civil war, are truly criminal. But in the end, I have no doubt that this evil will result in good. What appears to me incredible, though unfortunately a fact, is that no one seems to know for certain where Madame la Duchesse de Berry is, whether in France or in Spain. [2] This uncertainty is very trying, not on account of what she can do, but because of the anxiety and worry which all this causes us.

We have very good accounts from Chartres. His journey has been very successful, and I believe that just now his presence in the south is most useful. He will not return till the end of this month or the beginning of next ; and you, mon cher Prince, what are your plans ? I am longing to get a letter from you, and to learn your opinion of what is passing in England. I will leave off here, as I want this letter to go as early as possible.

Accept again, mon cher Prince. . . .

[1] Royalist insurgents.
[2] The Duchesse de Berry was then in Vendée.

THE PRINCE DE TALLEYRAND TO THE PRINCESS DE VAUDÉMONT.

LONDON, *June 7th*, 1832.

The courier has arrived, but has brought me no letters from you, when the whole town is filled with the deplorable news from Paris. I am terribly anxious. . . .[1]

KING LEOPOLD TO THE PRINCE DE TALLEYRAND.

BRUSSELS, *June 5th*, 1832.

MON TRÈS CHER PRINCE,

I received your kind letter by M. de Bacourt shortly before starting for Compiègne, and I have waited until my return, in order to write to you. You know the friendly ties that have so long bound me to the Royal Family ; you can therefore easily understand how pleased I was to spend a few days with them. The king, the queen, and Madame Adelaide, are all equally and truly attached to you, and we spoke a great deal about you.

The marriage of the Princess Louise is now settled to the satisfaction of all parties. This event seems to cause great pleasure in France, and the masses, who are not easily influenced, all testified their goodwill towards me. This affair of La Vendée has caused some little anxiety ; nevertheless, I fancy it may rather strengthen the government. I pray you in your wisdom, advise them so that they may act vigorously. The extreme kindness the king has hitherto shown to this party, now doubly entitles him to do this.

Notwithstanding my week's absence, and the great distance I was away, there has not been the very slightest disturbance in Belgium ; I think I have a *right to proclaim this aloud.* But it is time all this was ended ; the army and the zealous patriots are very eager for war, and it might so happen that I should not be able to restrain them.

England is determined to finish the matter. Nothing is easier. Let a fleet be stationed in the English Channel, and the Dutch be told, that after a certain date they will lose the arrears of the debt, and that a portion of the capital of the debt will be deducted each day. I believe these two measures would have great influence, without any danger whatever. The last reply from Holland renders the execution of the treaty imperative.

---

[1] After General Lamarque's funeral, there was a terrible outbreak in Paris. It began on the 5th of June, and continued until the middle of the next day, the 6th. These two days are known in history as "the days of June."—(Note by M. de Bacourt.)

As for me, they may rest assured that I will do my utmost to maintain peace, and I have on this point faithfully performed my duty ; but I wish it to be *clearly understood*, that I will not allow myself to be overthrown without defending myself to the last, and causing many others to fall with me. I have come to this decision with the greatest deliberation. It is absolutely necessary for the tranquillity of France, that the Belgian question should be definitely settled. Louis Philippe told me himself, and with great reason, that confidence would not be restored in France until this matter was ended. The kindness you have shown to M. Van de Weyer has given me great pleasure ; he merits it fully, and he has been very unfairly treated here.

Kindly recall me to the recollection of Madame de Dino, if she has not entirely forgotten me, and believe in the feelings of esteem and sincere friendship which I shall always have towards you.

LEOPOLD.

THE PRINCE DE TALLEYRAND TO THE PRINCESS DE
VAUDÉMONT.

LONDON, *June 8th*, 1832

I begin my letter before having received any news from Paris. I have heard nothing since nine o'clock on the morning of the 6th ; you can understand my anxiety. I trust all has ended favourably for the government, and that the government will take advantage of it to re-establish by strong and constitutional measures the order, which has been so seriously disturbed. It is in constitutionally established order that one must seek for popularity ; such policy alone is sound. Pampering the rabble only emboldens them, and does no good.

It is said that the king showed great calmness and firmness on the evening of the 5th, and during the whole night, which he spent on horseback ; his conduct is much approved of here. . . .

KING LOUIS PHILIPPE TO THE PRINCE DE TALLEYRAND.

PARIS, *Friday, June 7th*, 1832.

MON CHER PRINCE,

I know that General Sebastiani has written to you in detail, concerning the events that have taken place in Paris. You will share in my grief that French blood should have been spilt, but you will also share the true satisfaction I feel in being able to glory in the fact, that I have no more provoked this struggle, than I have omitted anything that could terminate it happily and honourably for France and for myself. Those who have both at home and abroad so constantly declared, that the throne of July would fall before the union of the Carlists and Republicans, like the walls of Jericho before the trumpets of Gideon, will now have to recognize that a frank and real nationality, a holy respect for the sworn faith and for the institutions, the laws and the liberties of one's country, are better bulwarks for the throne, than absolute power with its mob of courtiers and satellites.

But having gained this great victory, we must now consolidate it, and utilize the strength we have won thereby, to put an end to all the uncertainties and evasions from without, which might still endanger our safety abroad and disturb the general peace.

I congratulate you most sincerely, mon cher Prince, on the great success you have obtained, in procuring the ratification of the treaty of the 15th November by all the five Powers ; but it is as much due to their dignity, as it is absolutely necessary for France and England, that the *execution of the treaty* just ratified, should at once follow *the exchange of the five ratifications already effected.* I must tell you that the 63rd protocol seems to me on this point to be surprisingly weak and feeble.[1] But be that as it may, now that this mark of consideration has been shown to the King of Holland, the manner in which he has received it, is a still further reason for adopting a different tone, and insisting on his fixing a definite period for handing over the citadel of Antwerp to the Belgians. I believe that the English government, is like ourselves, ready to make this explicit declaration to the King of Holland, and that it realizes quite as strongly as we do, that it is only by compelling His Majesty of the Netherlands to evacuate that citadel, that we shall get him to recognize the independence of Belgium and sign the treaty with King Leopold.

I feel assured that the three Powers, Prussia, Austria, and even Russia, quite expect France and England will jointly make this declaration to the King of Holland, and that they

---

[1] This protocol had been drawn up on May 31st, in answer to a note addressed to the Conference by the Dutch plenipotentiaries containing some fresh proposals.
In this protocol the Conference declared "that the proposals in this note did not differ in any way from those which had been presented to Comte Orloff at the Hague, more than two months ago, and which occasioned his declaration of the 27th March last." That, consequently, there was no need for the Conference to take any notice of the said note, "and that it must now occupy itself with the resolutions, which the gravity of the circumstances demanded."

will not place any obstacles in the way, for they are quite as well aware as we are, that this declaration is the only measure that will oblige the King of Holland to relinquish his futile resistance, and quench the foolish hopes he still entertains, of becoming the general disturber of the peace of Europe. Besides, I think it will be perfectly easy to prove to those who do not wish us to attack the King of Holland, that the only way to prevent this, is to convince him that he will be attacked, if he does not evacuate the citadel of Antwerp on the day fixed by us. You may fully assure the English government and the Conference, that we on our side are most anxious not to be obliged to send our troops to besiege this citadel, but that we have decided on so doing, if we find there is no other way left of forcing him to carry out this evacuation on the day named. It would, I think, be well to fix this for the 1st of July prox.

If, as I do not doubt, the English government combines with mine in adopting this course, then I think it would be advisable for you to make a declaration jointly with Lord Palmerston to the Dutch plenipotentaries, stating, that you will not receive any communication from them, until their king has given an undertaking, that he will accede to the views of the five Powers by evacuating Antwerp, and that if this evacuation is not carried out by the 1st of July, the Dutch ports will be blockaded by our combined squadrons.

I fancy that I am right in thinking that this mode of procedure will suit England, and as for us, we shall infinitely prefer it to the more costly measure of sending troops into Belgium. This would expose us to various complications which we are doing our utmost to avoid, but which nevertheless we are determined to risk, if the shuffling, that we neither can nor will any longer tolerate, is persisted in.

You will perceive, mon cher Prince, that according to the popular saying, I wanted to *have my say out* with you, as I know well you will only make a good use of it, and because I like to be open with you in all confidence, according to the old habit, which I always wish to keep up with you. I was all the more induced to do this, as the matter, after the crisis we have just passed through so triumphantly, is a very serious one, and it is therefore desirable that you should make use of the short time you will still be in London, to give the right impetus to this affair, which you, more than anyone else, have the means of doing.

I have not time to tell you of my interview with King Leopold at Compiègne. I will only say, that we have settled his marriage with my eldest daughter, and that I also found him so well disposed, that I had no difficulty in obtaining from him all I told you I intended asking of him. He has also promised me to send M. Van de Weyer at once to London.

Good-night, mon cher Prince ; you know all my friendship for you.

LOUIS PHILIPPE.

MADAME ADELAIDE D'ORLÉANS TO THE PRINCE DE TALLEYRAND.

TUILERIES, *Friday, June 8th,* 1832.

I hasten, mon cher Prince, as soon as I have a spare moment, to give you news of us, feeling sure that you would be anxious to hear, after the very important events which have just taken place. It has been a most anxious and painful time, owing to the blood that has been shed. The whole affair had been prepared for some time by the two factions which now only form one—the Carlists and the Republicans ; and there is no doubt that this conspiracy is connected with those disturbances in the south and La Vendée. Our dearly loved king, as he always does, quickly decided and secured the victory by his presence here, his firmness, his courage, and his energy. No sooner did he hear at Saint Cloud, on Tuesday evening, what was taking place in Paris, than he ordered his horses, and the queen, Nemours, Marshal Gérard, and I got into the carriage with him, and along the whole route all the people we met, all the carts and all the public conveyances rang with the cry of *Vive le roi !*" It was the same when we reached Paris. You cannot have the slightest idea of the enthusiasm of the troops and the National Guard, who were in the *Place du Carrousel.* After he had reviewed them, and on leaving, the king said, " *To-morrow, dear comrades, I shall count on you.*" These words were rapturously repeated. " *Yes, yes ; to-morrow, to-morrow !* " and in truth they all behaved admirably, and our beloved king encouraged them afresh, by showing himself in every part of Paris, greatly against the advice of Marshal Lobau, who strove to prevent him from going to those parts of Paris where fighting was still going on ; but, thank heaven, the bullets spared him ! Marshal Gérard, who was with him, told me that he had never seen anything like the enthusiasm of the whole population. They followed his steps in crowds shouting, " *Vive le roi,* (Long live the king). *A bas les Carlistes !* (Down with the Carlists). *A bas les Républicains !* (Down with the Republicans)." There were also cries of, " *Prepare Paris for a state of siege !* " and numbers coming up to the king, as close as they could, called out, "*Above all, no mercy to the Carlists.*"

Never has our beloved king received greater proofs of affection and devotion, than at that moment. All the National Guard from the outskirts came pouring in, and did wonders ; they fought like lions. Yesterday, all those from the department of the Seine and Oise arrived, and when those at Havre heard what was taking place, they also wanted to come. Ah ! our dear Louis Philippe is very strong and thoroughly identified with our great and beloved nation. This is a satisfactory reply to all those who were in doubt as to whether he could remain on the throne, and whether he would have strength enough to contend against all the factions. I trust the European Powers will now feel *reassured* on this point, and believe that when the safety of his kingdom requires it, Louis Philippe knows how to be both strong and energetic.

This wicked and shameful conspiracy has occasioned much bloodshed ; it grieves us greatly, but the results are immense. I think it would be a good time to get the Conference to put an end to matters with the King of Holland, and show him plainly that he must carry out the treaty signed by the five Powers. In truth, it is not possible any longer to give either reason or excuse for prolonging this state of uncertainty, so hurtful and so contrary to the interests of France and Belgium. Your zeal and your ability will enable you to insure this decision, and I hope, mon cher Prince, that you will bring us this good piece of news.

Our beloved king wishes to write to you, and hopes to do so as soon as he can find a spare moment, as he is very anxious about the evacuation of Antwerp, and that the Conference with regard to this, should not delay in taking measures to force the King of Holland to comply, if he will not do so willingly.

We have very good accounts from Chartres ; he is very well satisfied with his journey. We know by telegraphic despatches that he arrived at Marseilles on the 7th of June, at three in the afternoon, amid a great concourse of people and loud acclamations. Here we are all in very good health, and I wish that you could say the same for yourself.

So the Reform Bill is passed ! Accept, mon cher Prince. . . .

THE PRINCE DE TALLEYRAND TO THE PRINCESS DE VAUDÉMONT.

LONDON, *June* 10*th*, 1832.

At present, everyone here is convinced that it was the people of Paris who commenced the insurrection ; everyone therefore approves the action of the government. It ought to gain sufficient strength from this circumstance, to prevent such a crisis ever occurring again. The king must remember that in all the crises in which the government has won, the elections have generally been satisfactory, and that in all those in which it has lost they have been the reverse. The refugees ought also to be sent away, without exception. They do no good in Paris. They should be scattered in small numbers through the various departments ; the refugees of the south, in the towns of the north, and the refugees of the north, in the towns of the south. The Loire should be the line of demarcation. Spaniards and Portuguese to Normandy and Picardy, Piedmontese to Flanders, and Poles to Algiers. They would then either fight or colonize there. . . .

June 11th, 1832.

If money, and a good deal of money, has been distributed among the rioters in Paris, it seems impossible to me that they cannot discover where the money comes from. Caution is not usual with the class of people who take five, ten, and twenty francs.

As far as Holland is concerned, I am quite disposed to press for a decision, but I do not think we must hurry anything. We must not, now more than ever, take any separate action from that of the other four Powers. In that lies the strength of the king and his dynasty. We must never for one moment lose sight of this. I think, and I believe, that England will at present act with us, but soon all the other Cabinets will try their best to separate her from us. Are we sure that she will resist ? or that she will resist for long ? If a change of Ministry takes place here, what would then happen ? You must not imagine that there is not a strong party against us here. All this gives grave matter for thought. A hasty decision may lead us all astray. Let us make yet one more attempt ; that done, all conciliatory measures will have been exhausted,[1] and then the Powers who do not act, must tell us that we are free to do so. That is my way of looking at it. Believe me, disturbances, no matter how well they are put down, give the impression abroad, that fresh troubles may at any moment arise again, and that is not conducive to confidence. Let us not therefore separate ourselves from the other four Powers, unless by their advice. . . .

[1] The Conference, in effect, had renewed the negotiations with the King of the Netherlands, by the protocol of June 11th. It contained the concessions which the Conference deemed they might grant to the Netherlands. On the 30th June, the Dutch plenipotentiaries replied, but their answer did not yet end the matter. All these documents are in vol. xxiii. of Marten's Collection, page 415, and following pages.

June 12th, 1832.

I am awaiting Durant ; I will leave a position in his hands which I consider excellent, namely, the confirmed union of the five Great Powers, based on the maintenance of property and principles. This alone can arrest the progress made by the spirit of the times, towards destroying actual civilization in order to arrive at a chimerical one. Tell me when the king expects me. I shall not leave here till I am no longer needed, that is certain ; but I should like to know when I am expected.

As I do not wish to fill any post in France I should prefer arriving there when everything has settled down again, and when all the places and situations have been filled. I am only of use here ; one must do the work to which one is called. I shall therefore return here, no matter what they say. I shall leave this on the 21st, at latest, and be in Paris on the 24th. . . .

LONDON, *June 15th, 1832.*

I expect Durant here on Sunday, the 17th. I will give him the 18th and 19th, for his introductions. That done, and a few directions given, I will proceed slowly towards Paris. I have arranged matters in such a way, that after we have exhausted all considerations, England and France will be at liberty to act as they think best, without fear of any coolness with the other Powers resulting therefrom. I have taken upon myself to prolong the delay till the 30th June, because I consider the union of the three Powers as the chief point, and because I feel sure that after having consented to this delay, which they themselves wished, they would look upon a combined maritime action by France and England as a matter of course. The French Cabinet would like more prompt action, but I think they have rather succumbed to the urgency of the Belgians, who hurry on our Ministry, through M. Lehon.

General Goblet, who is in London, and M. Van de Weyer, who is in Brussels, are of the same opinion. I therefore maintain my view ; and in truth, a delay of fifteen days is no very great matter, when one feels assured that this complaisance has gained the assent of the Great Powers, who are our colleagues in this affair. And then all will be done, and I am sure that it is well done.

I am writing to you during an interval in this morning's conference, at which we have to settle the fate of M. Thorn.[1]

---

[1] M. Thorn, a Belgian subject, had been arrested by the Dutch authorities in the fortress of Luxemburg, the territory of which belonged to the King of Holland, but the fortress belonged to the Germanic Confederation.—(Note by M. de Bacourt.)

We shall insist upon the Germanic Confederation ordering him to be set at liberty, and allowed to leave, despite any objections the King of Holland may raise. Durant will only have to follow my lead : union with England, accord between the five Powers, a joint armament with England to oblige the King of Holland to give Belgium back her territory, and above all to force him to evacuate Antwerp. I think I have placed and left the affairs of France, in this respect, in a very good position . . . .

As a fact, I did leave London on the 20th June, and a few hours before my departure, I received the following note from Lord Palmerston : .

LORD PALMERSTON TO THE PRINCE DE TALLEYRAND.

FOREIGN OFFICE, *June* 19*th*, 1832.

MY DEAR PRINCE,

I have just received the three memoranda,[1] which I have signed and will send off at once.

Good-bye once again ; give good advice where you are going ; take care of your health, get over the fatigues of our long conferences as quickly as you can, and come back here soon ; but above all—come back.

Ever yours,
PALMERSTON.

I reached Paris on the 22nd of June.

[1] Memorandum addressed to the Austrian, Prussian, and Russian plenipotentiaries by the French and English plenipotentiaries, dated June 19th.
 This memorandum declared that the French and English plenipotentiaries had consented to enter into fresh negotiations with the King of the Netherlands, solely because they did not wish to break through the united action of the five Powers ; that the object of this fresh negotiation was to suspend the execution of the treaty of the 15th November ; that it was greatly to be regretted that the plenipotentiaries of the three Powers could not, for want of instructions, assign a limit to this suspension, that, nevertheless, the undersigned thought they ought to warn the plenipotentiaries of the three Courts, that they could not consider this suspension as unlimited, and that if by the 31st of August, the King of the Belgians demanded the execution of the treaty of November 15th, their governments could not refuse to satisfy him.

END OF THE TENTH PART.

APPENDIX.

As in the preceding volume, this appendix is added, containing a certain number of private or confidential letters, which seem to us to offer a special interest. All these letters, selected from M. de Talleyrand's papers, have been copied from the original manuscripts which are among the Prince's documents.

MADAME ADELAIDE TO THE PRINCE DE TALLEYRAND.[1]

PARIS, *January 3rd*, 1831.

THIS wretched Belgian business is worrying our beloved king more than I can tell you, mon Prince, and places him in such a difficult position that he does not see his way out of it. You know how fond of, how attached we are to the Prince of Coburg, and the king would certainly in every way prefer him to any one else, but unfortunately here he is only looked upon as a tool of England, and, it must be admitted, is exceedingly unpopular. If he were to reach the Belgian throne by marriage with one of our dear girls, it would be regarded here, as a sale of that country to England ; and the king neither can nor will, expose himself to such a risk, which might deprive him of all his popularity here, and probably would not, for the same reason, be acceptable to Belgium. What she wants is, either the Duc de Nemours, or to be united to France ; this latter would inevitably bring on war, and must not therefore be thought of ; Nemours, the Powers would likewise not accept, and besides, even if they did consent, there are so many difficulties in the way, that the king is far from wishing it. A Regency would have to be appointed : how and of whom would it be composed ? Who is there to send with that child ? Such a future frightens both the father and king, who sees therein nothing but troubles, difficulties, and anxieties, without any assured advantages. Besides, the vexed question of Luxemburg adds still further to the perplexity ; the Belgians will not recognize the decision of the Diet in that matter, it excites them more and more, and makes them eager for war ; and then, add to all this, the bad faith of the King of Holland, who is always deceitful, and does all he can on his side to bring on a war, and who by his unworthy conduct towards them has exasperated the whole of that unhappy country.

As to Prince Charles of Naples, nobody wants him. The king really does not know which way to turn in this unfortunate business ; it makes him

---

[1] See pages 6, 10, and 12.

terribly anxious, for he cannot see what side he ought to take. . . . In pity, write and give me your advice, entirely in confidence, and tell me what you think is best to be done; but do not lose sight of the fact that the irritation which exists here on this Belgian question is very great, and the nation's desire to see her become French again is very strong, for it is only the king who hesitates about it; and it needs all the confidence and all the love every one has for him, to induce them to be patient over this matter. But if, when the arrangements are made, it is thought that any foreign Power has been specially favoured, it will be very dangerous both for the king and our peace at home.   Keep this well in view, for it is a fact. . . .

MADAME ADELAIDE TO THE PRINCE DE TALLEYRAND.[1]

PARIS, *January 5th*, 1831.

THE hot-headed party here would like to entangle us in these Belgian affairs, and force France into a war, by asking for the reunion of Belgium, and hoisting the French tricolor cockade; they flatter themselves that such an attraction would be irresistible; but they flatter themselves in vain.   My brother has declared that he will not encourage this vain hope, and that he will show them whether it is the king, or the students of Paris, who will decide the question of peace or war. . . .

He was much perplexed the day before yesterday, as he could not see what arrangement would really suit the Belgians, and wrote to ask your advice as to suggesting one; but a despatch from M. Bresson having informed him that the Belgians were disposed to ask for Prince Otto of Bavaria, he at once put aside any other idea, and accepted this suggestion, not that it might be said that he desired to impose this Prince or any other on Belgium, but in order to show that he had no objection to him, that he thought the matter ought to be finished quickly, and that, consequently, he was very pleased with the choice. . . .

M. BRESSON TO THE PRINCE DE TALLEYRAND.[2]

Private.

BRUSSELS, *January 13th*, 1831

MON PRINCE,

I received the night before last, the letter you did me the honour to write on the 9th ult., as well as the documents which accompanied it. I have taken it so much to heart that I should have displeased you, that I attach the greatest importance to making clear to you the circumstances, which led to the sudden combination, which I see plainly now, could not have suited the Conference.

The Republican and French parties had all their batteries ready; we were being hurried onwards; we dreaded either a popular demonstration, or a proclamation of the reunion with France, from Liége or Verviers. We thought that if there was the least complication, the Congress would declare itself in favour of M. le Duc de Nemours.   These dangers were imminent, and were those which our Government dreaded most.   It was necessary to make a diversion, and offer an object of some sort to the moderate and sensible people.

A Bavarian prince was therefore brought forward, and as I had been informed from Paris that anything would be better than M. le Duc de

---

[1] See page 7.   [2] See page 9.

Nemours or the reunion, and believing we had not forty-eight hours before us, I saw no objection to this idea, and I therefore allowed it to go on. But, mon Prince, I should wish the Conference fully to understand, that what has been done in this matter was done in opposition to the indefatigable efforts of the war party, and without any other idea or *arrière-pensée.* Lord Ponsonby, who was cognisant of all my actions, can, and I am sure will, confirm all this.

Moreover, mon Prince, immediately on receipt of your letters, I did my very utmost to enlighten the members who had adopted this arrangement, as to its very great disadvantages, which you had pointed out to me, and they at once abandoned it. We shall now have time to look around us. The Congress, it is true, has decided in to-day's sitting, that no special commissioners will be sent either to London or Paris to facilitate the choice of a head for the State ; but the negotiation remains in the hands of the agents who are with you now, and we need no longer dread any of those sudden and hurried decisions with which we have been threatened for the last ten days. . . .

GENERAL SEBASTIANI TO THE PRINCE DE TALLEYRAND.[1]

PARIS, *January 14th*, 1831.

MON PRINCE,

. . . The new direction that your despatches have given to him (M. Bresson) has been a matter of great surprise to the king ; and the despatch Lord Ponsonby has received from his Government, causes us serious anxiety as to the issue of the Belgian question.[2] The advice it gives will encourage the few partisans of the Prince of Orange, and will irritate the Catholic, the Republican, and the Constitutional parties. The revolutionary feeling will be prolonged, and will bear bitter fruits. The renewal of hostilities can no longer be prevented, and it is difficult to see where all this will end. Is it the Prince of Coburg whom they are keeping in the background, whom they are working for, and whom they hope to secure? That combination is no longer possible. We were quite in favour of the one for the Princes of the House of Nassau, as long as we thought it had any chance of success. We were also quite as sincere in our acceptance of the Prince of Coburg ; but time has revealed the truth to us : the Belgians must have a Catholic prince. Let him therefore be chosen from among the Houses of Saxony, Naples, or Bavaria ; we don't mind which, provided he puts down anarchy and establishes a proper government at once. The English Ministry has a great respect for public opinion, and they are right ; but they ought also to admit that we likewise must respect it ; and France has shown sufficient generosity, loyalty, and disinterestedness, to be allowed some voice in the selection of a sovereign who will reign at her very doors.

If Belgian affairs affect the policy of England and of the other Powers, they equally affect our policy, and even actual safety. The London Conference has counted too much on its influence in Belgium ; its slow and measured progress rather recalls the old policy of those wearisome negotiations of the Treaty of Westphalia. . . .

I am sure, mon Prince, you yourself must be tired of this easy-going part which they wish France to play, and that you would far rather take one suitable to a powerful king and a great nation. Europe will never clearly

1 See page 12.
2 Respecting the disagreement between M. de Talleyrand and the French Cabinet, of which M. Bresson suffered the consequences, see page 38. Lord Ponsonby on his side received instructions in favour of the Prince of Orange.

understand our policy until she realizes that it is not the fear of war that stops us, but rather the fear of seeing social order in Europe overthrown, of letting loose all the evil passions, and exposing nations and their Governments to endless dangers—such a fear is alone worthy of us, for it is a moral one, and is both politic and far-seeing. People are also apt to forget, that our power over the wishes of the country has its limits, and that it would be most imprudent for us, and fatal to Europe, to go beyond these. . . .

THE PRINCE DE TALLEYRAND TO MADAME ADELAIDE.[1]

LONDON, *January* 16*th*, 1831.

I herewith send Mademoiselle a document which will interest her, but which no one except herself and the king must know anything about. Written in the name of the Prince of Orange, it is Lord Grey who is the real author. He was so interested, and laid such great stress on it, that we could not refuse to allow him to make this fresh trial. If it succeeds, matters will be arranged according to the king's wishes; if it fails, it will leave us a freer hand, to propose what we deem best and most needful to secure. . , .

Document included in the above Letter.

LETTER OF THE PRINCE OF ORANGE TO . . . .[2]

THE late events in Belgium have drawn such misfortunes on me, on my family, and on the nation, as I can never cease to deplore.

Nevertheless, in the midst of these calamities, I have not renounced the fond hope, that a time might come when the purity of my motives will be recognized, and when I may personally co-operate in the happy work of reconciling all parties, and restoring peace and prosperity to a country, to which I am united by the ever-sacred ties of duty and the most tender affection.

The choice of a sovereign for Belgium, since its separation from Holland, has been accompanied by difficulties which it is needless to describe. May I without presumption believe, that my presence now offers the best and most satisfactory solution of these difficulties?

There is no doubt . . . that the five Powers, whose confidence it is so necessary to secure, would see in such an arrangement, the surest, the quickest, and easiest way, to restore tranquillity at home and insure universal peace abroad.

There is, too, no doubt that recent and detailed communications, received from the principal towns and from several provinces of Belgium, offer a striking proof of the confidence still accorded to me by a large portion of the nation. . . .

As far as I am concerned, the past will be completely shrouded in oblivion; I shall make no personal distinctions due to political actions, and my constant efforts will be directed to secure for the service of the State, those men, without exception and without regard to past conduct, whose talents and experience render them best fitted to properly carry out public duties.

[1] See page 17.
[2] This letter was written by the Prince of Orange to those whom he considered devoted to his cause in Belgium.

I shall devote the utmost care to assure to the Catholic Church and its ministers, the constant protection of the Government, and to surround them with the respect of the nation. . . .

One of my most earnest desires, as well as first duties, will be to join my efforts to those of the Legislature, in order to complete the arrangements which, founded on the basis of national independence, will give security to our relations abroad, while improving and extending our means of prosperity at home. . . .

I come thus, with all the frankness and sincerity that our mutual position demands, to offer myself to the Belgian nation. On the intelligence that guides her in appreciating the needs of the country, and on her attachment to its liberty, I rest my chief hope.

It only remains to assure her, that in my present action, I have consulted my own interests less, than my earnest and constant desire to see reparative, peaceful, and conciliatory measures put an end for ever to all those evils with which Belgium is still afflicted.

M. BRESSON TO THE PRINCE DE TALLEYRAND.[1]

Private.　　　　　　　BRUSSELS, *January* 20th, 1831.
　　　　　　　　　　　One o'clock in the morning.

MON PRINCE,

The partisans of the Duc de Leuchtenberg were quite prepared to make their *grand coup* during the last forty-eight hours. M. le Duc de Bassano and M. Mejéan [2] are the principal actors in this deplorable scheme. I have been forced, in order to parry these imminent dangers, to assume a responsibility which I can only justify by my earnest desire to prevent great misfortunes.

I declared that, if M. le Duc de Leuchtenberg was elected, I should at once break off all communication with the Belgian Government, and quit Brussels within twenty-four hours. This declaration did us good service.

It seems incredible to me, that you can have been left in ignorance as to our instructions with regard to the Prince of Naples and Prince Otto of Bavaria; I will not therefore enter into them here.

There were not sufficient reasons for opposing the Prince of Naples to the Duc de Leuchtenberg, but sufficient to create a diversion. We availed ourselves of it by opposing to these intrigues a medium proposal. The conclusions of the report of the central section, which were in favour of the immediate choice of a sovereign, did not obtain priority.

THE PRINCE DE TALLEYRAND TO MADAME ADELAIDE.[3]

January 24th, 1831.

THE arrival of M. de Flahaut, who was able to answer all my questions, and give me good reports of the Palais Royal and of Paris, has afforded me great pleasure. He found Belgian affairs far more advanced than he imagined, and he has already been able to assure himself that this neutrality, which has been gained with so much labour amid the present discussions,

---

[1] See page 21.
[2] Etienne Comte Mejéan, born 1766. Advocate, then journalist during the Revolution. On the 18th Brumaire he became Secretary-General to the Prefecture of the Seine. Subsequently he followed Prince Eugène to Italy, then became State Councillor, and in 1816 was elected by the Prince as governor to his children. He died in 1846.　　[3] See page 24.

appears to all right-thinking people the only solution of the great problem. I feel convinced that Mademoiselle's quick and sensitive mind will have fully appreciated all these advantages. I believe in truth, that this measure was the only one that could have resulted in peace for us, and the only one by which we can indemnify England without admitting her supremacy. To have given her an actual footing in Belgium, would have been like giving her a new Gibraltar in the north, and some day we should find ourselves *vis-à-vis* to her, and in the same position as the Peninsula is. Such an expedient would be making too dangerous a sacrifice of the future to the present, and at a price which one may safely put down, as equal to that of ten lost battles. The annexation of the remainder of Belgium, would be but a poor equivalent, compared to this first footing on the Continent.

If France had any need to extend her frontier, she should look towards the Rhine, it is there that her real interest lies, and where she will gain real power and acquire a useful frontier, but just now, peace is worth far more than all this to us. Belgium would bring us more trouble than profit, and this latter has been pretty well secured to us by her neutrality. . . .

MADAME ADELAIDE TO THE PRINCE DE TALLEYRAND.[1]

PARIS, *January* 28*th*, 1831.

MON CHER PRINCE,

. . . Certainly when M. de Flahaut left here he did not expect to find matters so far advanced with you. It is a great success[2]; nothing but your zeal and your talents could have achieved it, and we are greatly touched and fully convinced by the reasons which make you doubly rejoice. As you truly say, all those who think and reflect cannot fail to appreciate the immense advantages that this neutrality must give us. You will see that the discussion yesterday in the Chamber of Deputies was very satisfactory, and entirely favourable to the Government[3], which is supported by the Chamber, owing to dread of a ministry from the extreme left, which it is determined to keep out ; for we must not conceal from ourselves that the earnest desire of a large number, not to say the generality of people in France, is in favour of the annexation of Belgium, and that the tiresome dilatoriness England has shown, in not obliging the Belgian Congress to decide on the choice of a sovereign, places us, both as regards France and Belgium, in a very difficult position ; and all this, because of the *arrière-pensée* on the part of England, to try and bring back the Prince of Orange. The inadmissible question of the Duc de Leuchtenberg has arisen ; we could not but reject it. England is aware of this and admits it, but at the same time Lord Ponsonby says that he has no instructions with regard to it. So now this question has become freshly complicated, in a very unpleasant and tormenting manner. Whose fault is it ? Certainly not ours, for we have been thoroughly frank, loyal, and straightforward. . . .

Saturday Morning, January 29*th.*

P.S.—We have just learnt that there is no longer any alternative possible in Brussels, except either Nemours or Leuchtenberg. Could one believe that under these circumstances Lord Ponsonby gives a decided preference to Leuchtenberg? Truly it passes all comprehension ! Nevertheless it is the

---

1 See page 15.
2 The protocol of January 20th, which insured the neutrality of Belgium and had been very cordially welcomed by the Cabinet of the Tuileries.
3 At the sitting of the 27th January, M. Mauguin questioned General Sebastiani as to the attitude of the Government respecting the Polish question.

fact. What, however, is less certain, though it is reported, and to judge from Lord Ponsonby's language seems only too probable, is, that M. Van de Weyer has brought assurances from London, that England would recognize Leuchtenberg if he were elected.[1]

M. BRESSON TO THE PRINCE DE TALLEYRAND.[2]

BRUSSELS, *March 8th,* 1831.

MON PRINCE,

Not being able to obtain any decision from the Conference respecting myself, I have determined to forestall it. I have the honour, therefore, to send you my resignation of the post of its Commissioner in Belgium. I also transmit the same by Lord Ponsonby. Herewith inclosed you will find the letter I have written to the Conference, and which I beg you will lay before it, together with copies of my letters to Lord Ponsonby and M. Van de Weyer.

I expect to leave this for Paris on Friday or Saturday. I shall make but a short stay there ; my earnest wish is to find myself once again with you.[3]

GENERAL SEBASTIANI TO THE PRINCE DE TALLEYRAND.[4]

PARIS, *March 20th,* 1831.

I HAVE nothing fresh to tell you about the formation of the Ministry. You know the members of whom it is composed as well as I do ; the peace party is almost strong enough for unanimity. I think you would do well to write a line to M. Casimir Périer, who will be charmed to receive a letter from you. He gives unity to the action of the Government, and shows himself determined to fight vigorously against the anarchists. . . .

. . . M. Lafitte has most unwillingly retired from office, and shows some little irritation. The financial state of his affairs was the chief cause of his political overthrow. The *Bourse* made a stir, which found an echo in the Chambers.

The elections are just now the great business of the day. I believe the result will give us a Moderate Chamber, which will be a great support for the maintenance of order, and to the Government.

I believe we shall avoid a war. If the Austrians do not enter the Papal States, peace is assured ; I have devoted all my energies to its preservation.

DESPATCH OF SIR R. GORDON[5] TO LORD PALMERSTON.[6]

Confidential.

CONSTANTINOPLE, *March 31st,* 1831.

MY LORD,

Since my last confidential despatch of the 25th, Reis Effendi has assured me that the French Ambassador has presented a note to the Porte, which, although much more reserved than his verbal communications, contains the three following very important points.

1 , The principles of the French Government are so diametrically opposed

---

1 M. Van de Weyer was mistaken, for on the 7th February, eight days later, the London Conference signed a protocol which excluded the Duc de Leuchtenberg.   2 See page 48.
3 M. Bresson did not return to London. After a short stay in France, he was sent to Berlin, to which at the end of some months he was definitely accredited.   4 See page 67.
5 Sir R. Gordon, Lord Aberdeen's brother, was English Ambassador at Constantinople.
6 See page 103. It will be remembered that General Guilleminot, French Ambassador at Constantinople, was recalled in consequence of the incidents which caused this despatch.

to those professed by Russia and Austria, that a war between these two Powers and France is inevitable.

2°, In this war England will either remain neutral, or will become the ally of France.

3°, The French Ambassador, on the part of his Government, therefore, prays the Porte immediately to take the necessary measures to insure her independence, warning the Ottoman Government that if, on the contrary, she espouses the cause which is opposed to the principles and views of the French nation, the Porte will later on, seek in vain for exemption from those losses which, as a necessary consequence of the war, she will have to submit to.

I have the honour . . . .

(Signed)   R. Gordon.

The Prince de Talleyrand to Madame Adelaide d'Orléans.[1]

June 27th, 1831.

AFTER having overwhelmed Mademoiselle with copies of my last night's correspondence by the courier of to-day, I must still send her King Leopold's reply, which I have just received, although it does not satisfy all my French requirements, and though friendly letters are but a very poor substitute, for what would have been far better stated officially. However, we must perforce be satisfied ; it is no use being otherwise. It is as well, however, that my letter of yesterday has brought forth the Prince's written explanation, which contains some slight excuse. He tries to justify himself, by what some of the other members of the Conference may have said to him. It would have been much simpler, and more straightforward, if he had kept to the phrase I wrote to him and left with him. Let us now hope that the Belgians, ever ready to be carried beyond bounds, will not forget the assurances of devotion for France that the Prince has made them.

Mademoiselle will remember that the first accounts of whatever I have lately written, must come from Brussels.

Wessenberg is to try and make the King of the Netherlands more amenable. It is no easy task we have set him.

Lord Palmerston to the Prince de Talleyrand.[2]

Saturday, July 9th, 1831.

My dear Prince,

We have received letters from Brussels, dated the evening of the 6th. All was going on well, and they expected to have a large majority. It was thought that out of 174 who would vote, 125 would be in favour ; but I think the most incontestable proof that the proposals will be accepted is, that Van de Weyer has promised to speak in their favour, and our little friend, like Cato's gods, likes to find himself on the side of the victors, and he would not have shifted his ground, had he not felt a strong presentiment, that Victory would range herself on the side of the Prince's proposals.

Lebeau's speech has converted many, among others Rodenbach[3] and Coppens,[4] and they declared in Brussels, that this speech had made a stammerer speak and a blind man see. However, it was thought that the decision would not take place till to-day.

[1] See page 156.   [2] See page 162.

[3] Alexander Rodenbach, born in 1786, a Belgian politician and writer. He had made a name for himself under King William's Government as a Liberal journalist. He was elected Deputy in 1830. He sat in the Chamber till 1866, and died in 1869. M. Rodenbach had been blind since his eleventh year.

[4] Deputy of the Congress. and one of the most turbulent members of the Assembly.

THE PRINCE DE TALLEYRAND TO THE PRINCESS DE VAUDÉMONT.[1]

July 15th, 1831.

THE King of Holland has not yet replied, but Wessenberg's power went no further than according a few days' delay. His reply will not be given till Wednesday evening, and Wessenberg will start on Friday (that is to-day). My opinion is, that, notwithstanding some explanations that have been given, the king's reply will not be a favourable one. What result does he expect to gain by this attitude? I really can say nothing, for matters have come to such a point that it is no longer possible to give in. One may ameliorate matters by explanations, but it is impossible to go further. Prince Leopold will therefore leave here to-morrow as arranged. He is desirous of pleasing you all, and is going *via* Calais for this reason. He is most anxious to marry one of our Princesses; he said so again to me this morning. They are very foolish in France when they will insist on looking upon Prince Leopold as an English Prince; he is quite the opposite.

This last difficulty with the King of Holland is very unpleasant for us, and will also, I think, be perfectly useless for him. We must wait for his first letters, they will tell us his views exactly. . . .

ADMIRAL DE RIGNY TO THE PRINCE DE TALLEYRAND.[2]

PARIS, *December 28th,* 1831.

MON PRINCE,

You will have seen how we came out of the peerage question yesterday. In the other Chamber, there is a sort of revolutionary murmuring, which sufficiently indicates what would have been the result of the rejection of the law. Such is the country.

Sebastiani has had a slight attack of apoplexy; he is better, but it is thought that it will be some time ere he can resume his work. His anxiety on this point is very evident. Pozzo does not attempt to conceal his satisfaction, and promises us much greater facilities in all matters. To-morrow he is to interview the *Corps Diplomatique* on the subject of Belgian affairs, and he promised me yesterday evening that he would try and obtain the demolition of Tournay, instead of Philippeville and Marienburg. If this arrangement seems advisable to you, kindly send me word through Madame de Dino, and I will act here accordingly, for I can do things more easily now. . . .

Accept . . . .

DE RIGNY.

M. BRESSON TO THE PRINCE DE TALLEYRAND.[3]

BERLIN, *January 26th,* 1832.

MON PRINCE,

I was aware that your letter of December 20th, had been laid before H.M. the King of Prussia. He wrote to the Emperor, urging him too strongly rather than too gently (at least so M. de Bernstorff told me), to accede to the views of the allies. Thus, mon Prince, the effect you desired has been produced.

On learning that the exchange of the ratifications had been postponed until January 31st, great regret has been expressed here, that it was not fixed for March 1st. I made some fresh efforts yesterday, to get the ratification pure and simple of the treaty of November 15th; but they proved ineffectual. The English Minister, who was intrusted with a similar mission by his Government, was not more fortunate either. Prussia maintains the same position she has taken since the Emperor of Russia's refusal, and the postponement has not in any way altered her views. There is only one alteration in M. de Bülow's instructions, which I think rather important. He has been directed to point out to the Conference, that if on January 31st, one or several of the Powers, think it expedient to exchange their ratifications with the Belgian plenipotentiary, the *protocol* should be left *open* as regards the others, until some definite period, say March 15th, for instance ; always with the reservation, on the part of Prussia, that the treaty even then should not be valid, unless all the Powers in turn had fully ratified it. Such a postponement has its advantages as well as its disadvantages. M. Ancillon thinks that such an interval of time might be profitably employed, either in bringing Russia round to the decisions adopted by the Conference, or in convincing or satisfying the King of Holland. A rough draft of a definite treaty between Holland and Belgium might be drawn up and submitted to both of them ; or else some additional and explanatory arrangements might be added to the twenty-four articles, which would bring about the acceptance of the Cabinet of the Hague, or decide Russia to consider herself free from all engagements or undertakings towards her. These are the ideas of the Berlin Cabinet. I thought that it would interest you to know them, mon Prince. . . .

MADAME ADELAIDE TO THE PRINCE DE TALLEYRAND.[1]

TUILERIES, *March 4th*, 1832.

. . . So we are actually at Ancona, and openly and with all loyalty, for the Pope as well as the Austrians knew, that if they entered the Papal States a second time we should go to Ancona ; of this they had been informed long ago. I quite think, between you and me, that they flattered themselves we should not dare to do it, just as the King of Holland flattered himself that we should not enter Belgium ; therefore I must own to you, mon cher Prince, that, on this same account, I am very glad that we have kept our word in this as well as in everything else. All the ambassadors were simultaneously informed, when the order was given, of the departure of our expedition ; and as we most certainly do not want a revolution in Italy, but, on the contrary, promise to use all possible means to prevent it, as will be and has already been very clearly explained, I do not feel disposed to worry myself as to the result of this expedition, which proves to the Powers that what we say, we do— a very great advantage in my eyes.

LORD PALMERSTON TO THE PRINCE DE TALLEYRAND.[2]

STANHOPE STREET, *March 15th*, 1832.

MY DEAR PRINCE,

Our Cabinet took the question into consideration last night, as to what would be the best course to pursue respecting the proposals which Holland has announced she intends to make us, and the opinion of our

1 See page 275.   2 See page 285.

Government is, that I can neither say or do anything at the Conference, except to ask the plenipotentiaries of the three Courts : Will you, or will you not ratify ?

It appears to us, that as long as the five Courts are not agreed respecting the all-important question of the ratifications, it is impossible for the Conference to reply to the Dutch communication, or to make any communication whatever to Holland.

If we call upon the King of Holland to give a categorical answer, as to whether he will accept the twenty-four articles within a given time, that would naturally infer, that when the period had expired we should proceed to carry out the treaty, whether Holland were willing or not. But would the three Courts be ready to join us in arranging coercive measures ? Certainly not, at least as far as one can judge. The same, demand, therefore, would not mean the same thing for all the Courts. For us, the question would mean coercive measures ; for the other three Courts, relinquishment, but inaction. It therefore seems to us, that we should do well to hold the ground we now occupy, and not allow ourselves to be drawn into any joint discussion or action with the Conference, before knowing with certainty whether we are two or five.

If you can come to the Office to-morrow between three and four, you could then tell me what you think of this business.

Ever yours.

THE PRINCE DE TALLEYRAND TO LORD PALMERSTON.[1]

Private.

March 17*th*, 1832.

DEAR LORD PALMERSTON,

I agree with you, that after all these delays, we are decidedly bound to have a Conference, to ask the Austrian and Prussian plenipotentiaries what decision they have come to respecting the exchange of the ratifications. Every possible consideration has been granted them, and all the ordinary delays have been liberally extended. I think matters have now reached their limit, and that we should only be abusing the influence we have with Belgium, if we still further postponed the time of her deliverance from the anxiety which is distressing her.

To again prolong the delays, would be an excess of condescension that might be called by another name.

I will come to you after the *Levée* to-morrow, ready to do whatever you think best and most conducive to preserve intact the dignity which our two countries must maintain.

LORD PALMERSTON TO THE PRINCE DE TALLEYRAND.[2]

STANHOPE STREET, *April* 5*th*, 1832.

MY DEAR PRINCE,

I beg you to come to the Office at three. Bülow has not yet received his authority, and I think we shall have to put the question we spoke of, to the Conference. I wish to propose to you that we should say to the plenipotentiaries of the three Courts : Two months have now elapsed since the 31st of January ; the protocol of ratification is still open ; the season is advancing, and the roads are quite passable ; have you all received your ratifications

[1] See page 283.   [2] See page 285.

and are you ready to exchange them ? Those of you who are not, have the goodness to state on the protocol, the reasons that prevent your doing so.

I shall invite Comte Orloff to come, so that we may speak to him.

THE PRINCE DE TALLEYRAND TO THE PRINCESS DE VAUDÉMONT.[1]

Evening of May 1st, 1832.

THE ratifications have arrived ; they are conditional, but I will arrange all that and make them plain, by the declarations I shall obtain from the Russians ; but do not mention this to *any one*, for the orders I might receive, no matter from whom or whatever their nature might be, would hinder me, and I want to have all finished before Friday. For this reason I do not wish any one to write to me, therefore complete and total silence !

The hope of seeing you next month, has restored all the powers of my youth, and all my energy for the business I am intrusted with, the conclusion of which I am longing to see.

Adieu. I may die in the attempt, but I shall succeed. Would that all Government *employés* would do as much to insure peace.

Adieu, dear friend.

[1] See page 294.

END OF VOL. IV.

RICHARD CLAY AND SONS, LIMITED, LONDON AND BUNGAY.